Foreword

Preface

Cold, but together.

Astriea

The cold had been the worst part.

Astriea thought she'd known it well from her time in the mountains and thought that she could endure it. But now, crouched in a Telish cell, the only thing that pushed her survival was Seraphina.

A single barred window that just barely sat atop the ground's surface exposed the small stone cell to the elements. The only light was that of a lonely candle—lit at the guard's station down the corridor—and the dim, gray sunlight that leaked in through the window.

She'd floated in and out of consciousness in the weeks or months that passed since Vera had taken them and did gods knew what with the rest of the crew. Since she'd seen or heard from Thomas. Or Damian.

For all she knew, she could've thrown them all into space or some dark and empty world.

And now the only friend she had was the woman leaning against her in the cell's corner. The woman who still looked lovely even after these weeks of near starvation and the torture of being swept under again.

Her jaw was so sharp it could've cut glass and her nearly black eyes were the one thing she could always find in the cell's darkness.

Guards came every day to inject her with a disgusting substance. Seraphina told her it was a concoction of sedatives, iron, and an extra ingredient that swirled around like ensnared shadows. She didn't say if she knew what it was, but Astriea had an idea.

LEXA HARTWELL

Throne of Ice and Ash

No two souls have ever loved as we have loved.

— said every love-struck couple, ever, including these.
Enjoy.

She couldn't move, couldn't eat, and couldn't get to Zaniah. But worst of all, while she lay paralyzed in her own body and tumbling into the dark, she felt completely and utterly *useless*.

I

Dark and Lovely Flower

1

Seraphina

They'd been unconscious for a few days before Seraphina had woken in the cold cell. The Telans left Astriea on the floor next to her, her arms tied behind her and face pressed into the dirt.

She moved closer and removed her bindings before picking her up and resting her on the small wooden cot against the back wall.

She wished she'd had time to think, but guards came in suddenly and grabbed her.

Sera thrashed against them, wrapping her legs around one's throat and snapping his neck as she flung her body free from the other guard's grasp. She landed on her feet and pulled his dagger from its sheath around his waist.

A wicked grin broke from her lips.

"Oh, you're *finished.*"

That blade swiped through the air with unnerving efficiency, tearing through his throat. Blood splattered across her face before she took up a fallen sword and launched herself forward. Descending upon the guards lining down the dungeon corridor like death-given form.

Blood sprayed with every blow. Now that she was awake, she *remembered.* Remembered why they were here.

Her sword drove into a guard's chest and her dagger flew down the hall into another's eye.

She remembered Tristan. The sweet boy who she loved like a brother. Who'd been a lifelong friend.

She gripped the sword with both hands and swung its blade through a guard's shoulder.

She remembered a dagger in Tristan's chest and the light leaving his eyes.

His mother's eyes. How would she ever face his mother again? What could she say to Lady Ashin that could possibly remedy the anguish?

Another guard was coming for her. She slammed her foot into his midsection. Her bare, *freezing* foot. The shot of pain it sent through her did nothing to bring her out of this. Everything became a blur of shadow and red as she pressed on through the unending dark, moving against the sounds of clashing metal.

Of garbled pleas as she filled her ledger.

Hands were on her shoulders, her arms, and waist. Before she knew it, she was screaming. Guttural and hungry.

Vera. Vera had done this.

Vera had deceived her, betrayed her, betrayed them all. She had been the one to throw them in that cell; it was her blade that pierced Tristan's heart. And she would pay for it tenfold.

About thirty men were pressing forward and forcing her arms down. She screamed until the act seared and burned her throat.

Blood-red hair appeared for a moment. Only a moment before she felt a stinging sensation in her neck, and darkness clouded her vision. Her body relaxed—went limp completely—and she dropped her sword as she fell to the ground.

Vera looked at her now. Her expression was almost *upset.*

But Sera let the thought die as she drifted away into unconsciousness yet again.

* * *

When she woke, Astriea was still sleeping on the cot. And when she tried to move to her, something snagged at her wrists and ankles.

Shackles.

Seraphina yanked against them, only gaining unbelievable pain.

"Fuck."

What could she do now? Slowly wither and die in this cell? How would she get them out?

Uncertainty clouded her mind, and then her chest tightened. Worry and panic settled on top of her. The only sounds now were the whimpered cries that escaped her mouth while she fought for air.

And then all those thoughts cleared. Banished.

Instead, a creeping male voice echoed to her. *Such a shame for someone of your beauty to be wasted down here.*

Her head shot up. She glanced around.

"Who said that?" she asked the icy darkness. But there was no response or sounds bouncing back to her off the stone walls. No, that voice had been in her mind. So Sera thought back, *Who are you?*

It is not I who you have to fear. But these monsters who would keep you buried beneath the palace? I would never do such a thing.

Sera didn't answer the voice. Didn't trust it. Especially one that made her spine freeze solid. That made her blood jump and tingle beneath her skin. But the voice went on and asked, *What is your name, child?*

None of your business! Now leave me alone to die in peace. She shot back.

She waited for an answer, but one never came. So, Seraphina sat in the cold cell until her eyes closed and her mind drifted away.

2

Seraphina

The loneliness of the cell didn't have time to take root in her heart when a guard slowly made his way inside a few days later.

Tenderly—as though he didn't want to startle her.

If she hadn't felt so disoriented and nauseous from whatever they'd drugged her with, she would've thrashed out at him as he knelt.

Her breaths were wheezed and sickly sounding. She hated it. Hated feeling so weak and vulnerable.

The guard reached to her limp, bound wrists, and gently removed her shackles. Then he moved on to her feet. His hands were shaking a bit, though most of his features remained clouded, she could barely tell that he had long, dark hair falling from his helmet. Then she saw it, shining silver coming from the eye slits.

Curious.

He moved on to where Astriea lay unconscious, and she used all the strength she had to thrash her body towards him. She failed, falling over and scraping her elbows across the rough dirt floor. The guard unbound Astriea and made his way back out. It was then that he whispered, "Her Highness will be here at midnight to speak with you."

"Tell her to fuck off." Sera coughed. The guard simply lowered his head and quietly shut the cell door.

What could Vera possibly have to say? That she's sorry she murdered one of her closest and oldest friends? That she's sorry she lied to her, deceived her, went to bed with her, and pulled out every bit of information she could?

Gods.

This was all her fault.

Sera didn't move her body from the floor she still lay in—face first. This was the punishment she deserved for being such a fool. She'd gone out into the world for the first time and fell in love with the first woman who paid her any mind.

But was that what this was? Love?

It must have been.

What else could tear her heart to pieces, if not love?

Stupid, naïve, unbearable love.

She was just about to fall asleep when she heard the single guard at the end of the hall gather his things. He made quite a bit of noise trying to do so. Then the light was extinguished and darkness loomed everywhere.

At least she was alone now. Alone with Astriea.

Something dark and primal tingled across her skin. Something in the emptiness warning her she was not truly alone. That someone lingered in the shadows of these dungeons.

"Seraphina."

She knew that voice. Would never forget it.

It was the voice of the woman she'd loved. Reyna's voice, perverted by a Telish accent.

"Leave me to die, *Vera.*" Sera spat her name, and she could feel her flinch at it.

"Look, I just came to tell you that the Tzar will have you and Astriea brought to him at dawn. He wants answers. You need to give him what he asks for."

"I'll tell you what I told your guard. Fuck off. I'd rather die. Astriea can't even move because of what you did to her. So you and your entire family can burn in hell."

"Sera, please… I wish I could explain—" she pleaded.

Sera shot up and looked dead into near-glowing green eyes, illuminated by the small flicker of a single candle, and said, "Don't. I wish I could *erase* you. Wipe you away and be finished with this game. Wake tomorrow, far from your reach, to a bright and lovely mourning."

Vera's jaw snapped shut, and she didn't speak again. Sera laid back down on the floor and the presence that once lingered on the other side of the cell's barred doors dissipated.

She sat in the silent emptiness and fought back tears. Forced them to take form into something else.

Something hot and radiating.

Something that seared the cracks in her heart instead of healing them.

She would never be so vulnerable again. Sera would find a way to wake Astriea and Zaniah. She would free them from this place and if she couldn't, she would slaughter anyone who raised a hand to them.

"They're coming," Astriea whispered in her sleep. She twitched a little, and Sera hoped that was a good sign. That maybe the concoction they'd drugged her with was wearing off. Maybe she'd wake fully in a day or so.

She didn't hold on to any hope, though. Just moved over to Astriea and climbed into the small cot with her.

Her friend, her goddess, her sister.

Seraphina thought about all the ways she'd failed her only mission. How many times now had they been taken or nearly killed? How many more would she allow before she got her shit together? And... And how many times did Astriea love her anyway, no matter how often she'd failed?

Sera pushed the thoughts away and pulled Astriea's limp body against her own—doing her best to keep them both warm for yet another cold night.

* * *

Astriea tossed and twitched throughout the night, as much as the space would allow. Whatever those healers have been injecting her with seemed to take all the energy and power she had. Constantly draining her into

8

unconsciousness. And part of Sera worried if there would be long-lasting effects from that poison.

That's all she could assume it was; poison.

She slid out of the bed and dropped to her hands and knees on the floor. Before the motivation left her, she started push-ups. Sera pushed herself up and down from the cold floor over and over. Until sweat was dripping off her and her breaths became heavy pants of pain and suffering. When her arms finally caved in on her, she dragged herself to her feet. Before she could change her mind, she lifted her body on the bar hanging across the doorway and squeezed her calves in between the bar and the stone door-arch. She fell back and let the blood rush to her head while hanging upside down. The thoughts of Tristan's death flashed before her. How he jumped from below deck and tried to save them. How it sounded when Vera's blade pierced his flesh. The thought made her so angry she wanted to scream.

Needed to.

But Astriea still slept, and if she released it Sera was sure she would rattle this entire kingdom awake. She'd done it before. Unless she'd hallucinated that day on the beach after the Shadon witch-hunters left her for dead. Maybe she'd been so distraught that she imagined it. Maybe she'd never gone into the water at all and made up the vision, too.

Sera doubted everything now.

So instead, she bit her tongue and willed her core to lift her body before steadily falling back down. She did those sit-ups until she was sure was going to be sick. Unfortunately, when she fell to the ground and hurled over, there was nothing in her raging stomach to release.

She breathed out a sob while she leaned against the stone wall. Quiet, tearless, and unnoticeable.

And then that slithering male voice appeared in her broken mind again.

Why do you weep, Dark and Lovely Flower?

Sera didn't know what to think or how to rid herself of it, so she answered.

Because I keep failing. What if they realize that and leave me behind?

There was a pause. Only a moment, but the voice she could only explain as her mind cracking apart, whispered.

You've come here with The Child of Prophecy, the girl born of two worlds long since shifted apart. The child of the beautiful Atara and the noble Aaron. You weep for your failure to keep her safe. You weep for the lover who has wronged you, and yet cannot tear yourself apart from her.

Seraphina flinched at the truth only she could hear. But she said nothing as it went on.

Who are you? It asked.

I am Seraphina Ophelia Blackspear, child of no one. Orphaned by the sea.

You are very peculiar, 'child of no one'. The way will come to you. I hope to one day see your perfection in the light of day. And in Telas, a Blackspear is never a 'child of no one'.

What does that mean? Sera asked, shocked. She sat up off the wall and straightened her spine. *Hello? What do you mean 'a Blackspear is never a child of no one'?* She asked again, but that voice disappeared from her mind completely.

Hopefully, she'd just gone insane. That she was talking to a piece of her mind that had broken from betrayal.

All throughout the night, Sera hoped.

* * *

The guards yanked them both from the cell before the dawn had even broken and covered their heads as they walked along several sets of halls and staircases.

Left, right, right, left, right. It even felt as though they'd gone in circles a few times, too. As though they knew she was counting.

Eventually, the sacks were removed just outside the small halls that opened into a vast, towering corridor. Dark stone walls were accented with rounded archways—made of an ominous-looking dark wood—all leading to a massive matching one at the end. The beautiful doors were nearly black, but carved with silver painted symbols.

In the language of the old gods, she assumed.

It was stunning, but not nearly as gorgeous as the throne room the guards now led them into. Those towering doors opened with a loud creek, and then a staff pounded onto dark, blue, and gray stone floors—giving her an eerie feeling. As though it were the reflection of the open ocean as a storm approaches.

But the most marvelous part was that of the beaming sunlight on her skin. Ricocheting off the walls and smooth marble floor in pale shades of blue. Each ray shone through the tipped point of one of the silver towers—its peak made of near turquoise ice, but showing no signs of giving way under the burning sun the structure was so desperately reaching out for.

The guards dragged them inside, feet sliding along the marble. Astriea was still unconscious and limp. If she didn't eat soon, Sera was sure she would starve to death. She'd already grown thin. Every single urge of anger was barreling to her forefront now.

The guards dropped them both at the room's center and Sera's skin crawled at the sight of the Tzar and his seven lovely, terrifying children.

With a handsome guard standing rather close to him, the Tzar sat upon an icy blue throne made of blue-tinted ice. One that looked as if made of ice itself.

"So this is the Goddess and the Assassin?" The Tzar laughed. He was very handsome for his age. His sharply chiseled features shone brightly against his long white hair and beard. He looked like he could've had any woman he wanted when he was young, even without a crown. The five young men that stood at his side were even more handsome. Each of them adorned in Telish leathers and armor.

What looked like the eldest three brothers—a set of identical twins and a slightly younger boy wore the royal crest in the throne room's matching colors—a sword through the head of a white dragon; along with black pants, boots, and chain mail.

The younger two wore no crest, but dull brown fighting leathers. Like they'd been in training before coming here.

Each of them had short black hair—aside from the young man standing next to the twins—Vera, who stood at the Tzar's right side, and the young princess who sat on the Tzar's lap. They all had the same blood-red hair.

Vera's sister looked no older than nine, the other's ages seemed to range anywhere from fourteen to twenty-three. Each stunning in their own unique ways.

"I thought you said they were powerful?" The Tzar scoffed at Vera.

She bowed her head quickly and said, "Yes Father, they are. The drug the Science Guild provided us has indeed proven successful. The goddess is dormant in Astriea's body, although—"

"She's near dead. I can't get the answers I need if she's dead!" He yelled, and for the first time since the day they pulled Vera from below deck, Sera saw her flinch. A real flinch, because it was so different from the one she'd faked on the ship.

Because, today, she could tell how hard Vera tried not to do it. Because it was hidden so very well. If Seraphina hadn't been plotting ways to kill the Grand Duchess, she never would've noticed it.

The others didn't move. Not even the small girl sitting in his lap.

It was then that a servant scurried to the throne and escorted the little princess from the room, her pearl-colored dress swishing as she left. Vera backed away as the Tzar rose and walked forward to Sera and Astriea.

He glided over to them, his black and light blue robes dragging gently across the clean floor.

She didn't know what to do. Astriea lay on the ground, asleep still, and now the Tzar of Telas was staring down at her.

"What are the Goddess' plans? How does she plan to free magic? How did she do it in Shadon?"

Sera didn't answer, and in response, he backhanded her across the face. Clean and swift and stinging. The red mark already forming.

"Father—" Vera said.

"Silence, Vera!" He yelled back at her.

Sera only got a glimpse of the princess to see her grip tightening on the hilt of her sword sheathed at her side. An Heir ready to strike. Seraphina imagined it would only take one swing for Vera to take her head off. One swing and it would all be over.

"I'll ask you again, what are the Chosen's plans to release magic?"

"Go fuck yourself." Sera spat. Literally spat at his feet. The Tzar looked up at two guards. His dark eyes darted from them to her.

She saw something in his eyes, then. Like shadow flickering in and out. A dark wind brushing against a single candle flame in an empty room.

The guards approached, bound her hands and legs, and beat her.

The first hit to her face. Then her legs, gut, and chest. Sera thrashed and fought against them. The two of them pushed on, kicking her as hard as they could. All over.

"Enough!" Vera yelled, now suddenly above her and shoving one of the guards to the ground, only for four more to yank the princess back.

"You do not answer to her." The Tzar said.

So the guards obeyed him.

Their boots continued to collide with bones and organs alike. Then, once the smell of her blood leaking out filled her senses, she jerked her head around from the floor and buried her teeth into one of their calves.

Before they could break free, she bit down into muscle and ripped it free.

The guard screamed and blood gushed all over. Sera had torn through his muscles and pants and ripped it all out.

The other guard jumped back as she broke her ankles free and rose to her feet. Her hands still bound behind her back.

Crouched over Astriea, with blood dripping from her mouth, Seraphina snarled at the Tzar of Telas.

"Send that animal back to the dungeon! Take the other one to the healers and wake her up. Scythe will be here soon, I... I can feel it. If they are rabid, he'll kill us all."

That cloud of darkness in the Tzar's eyes seemed to fade just a bit. Like he was seeing her differently, if only for a moment.

Guards grabbed her and started dragging her back through the massive doors. The Tzar moved back to his throne and looked at Vera, who stood with the guards who'd dragged her away, her eyes looking anywhere but at him.

"Perhaps, father, they would not behave as animals if we did not treat them as such." Vera's tone was sharp. Irritated. *Angry.*

As she was lugged across the floor, Sera felt a rumble. Everyone in the room felt it, too. The guards even hesitated.

"All of you, leave. Except my heir. Go." He commanded.

The others left the room immediately. Sera only glimpsed Astriea being carried through another door in the throne room. Only glimpsed Vera's gaze catching her own, before those doors closed once again.

3

Astriea

The room was unfamiliar when she woke. She wasn't in the cell anymore but in something like a glass box. People were standing around her in sage green robes and masks that covered everything below their eyes.

They didn't hit her or try to hurt her.

As she regained consciousness, she saw a robed woman bring over a warm washcloth and gently lay it on her forehead. It felt nice. That's when realization dawned on her.

They were in Telas. She was a prisoner and Sera—*Where is Sera?*

Astriea sprung up in bed and hyperventilated. Gods, she was dizzy. Everything in the room was spinning now and soft hands were on her. Trying to guide her back down.

"Easy! Easy." Someone said. She turned her blurred eyes to the voice and couldn't make out the face, but she'd recognize that hair anywhere. *Vera.*

Astriea's expression turned feral with rage. She lunged off the bed towards the grand duchess, but her legs gave out the second she stood. She hit the floor and quickly started fighting against the people trying to get her back onto the bed.

"Where is Sera? What have you done to her?" She screamed and fought.

"Sera is fine," Vera said softly.

"Where is she? Where is my *sister?*"

Astriea kept screaming that.

Over and over, until she felt another sting on her neck and went limp once more. She didn't stop asking, though.

Those screams died into whispers until the concoction yanked her back into sleep, this one more peaceful than any she'd had before.

4

Seraphina

It had been a week since she'd met with the Tzar.

Since they took Astriea.

And every day had the same screams and questions:

Take me to her or I'll kill you all. If she's dead, I'll tear you all to pieces, etc.

Being parted from Astriea felt wrong. Like nothing was ever going to work if they weren't side by side. Everything became hollow and awful. The gears of a clock not shifting into place.

But Sera almost cried as Vera led a group of armed guards to her cell, with Astriea in their arms. Clean, healthier looking, and sleeping. They opened the door and sat her gently on the cot.

She rushed to Astriea's side the moment the guards passed back into the hall. She checked her, panic rattling her bones.

Her scar was healed and there was a mark left behind, but not nearly as bad as she'd expected. Her hair looked clean and beautiful, and this time she didn't sleep like she was drowning. She looked peaceful.

"What is it? Wanna be on her good side when she wakes?" She sneered at Vera.

"You're next." She replied.

Vera moved faster than anything she'd ever seen. A needle was already deep in Sera's neck by the time she'd reacted.

Her eyelids grew so heavy, then her head and the rest of her body.

She'd been lunging up to fight when Vera jabbed her with that needle. If there was one thing this place was good at, it was incapacitating people. Now she was falling, not to the floor, but into Vera's arms. Burning hate barreled through her senses. And her face was the last thing Sera saw as she drifted away.

Vera's stupid, beautiful face.

5

Astriea

Astriea flung up from the old cot with a deep gasp of breath.

"Sera!" she yelled.

"I'm here! I'm here." Sera said in the faded moonlight of the cell.

She noticed how clean she was, how clean they both were.

"They took you too?" Astriea asked.

"Yeah. Drugged me and made me more presentable, I guess. Who is *Scythe?*"

"I have no idea. And I'd rather not stick around to find out. Any plans on how we get out of here?"

"Nothing. We've been here for four weeks, though. I honestly can't think about anything other than how hungry I am." As soon as the words fell off Sera's lips, Astriea's stomach clenched in on itself, hard.

"Gods." she croaked, leaning over and clutching her stomach.

"Right? I can't remember the last time we ate something solid. The guards bring by old broth now and then. And by *now and then*, I mean once or twice a week."

Astriea tried to think about it as hard as she could, but honestly, she couldn't remember solid food since they were on the ship.

The light at the guard's post went out, and he took his leave.

It was quiet for a while in the dark. Sera sat on the cot with her and

19

cuddled in close to fight the cold. Then, there was a loud creak down the hallway and a small golden light bounced lightly towards them.

A small red-haired girl, dressed in beautiful Telish finery, stood outside their cell with a single candle sconce in her hand. Alone.

Not one guard or adult escorted her to the dungeons of all places.

"Hello. My name is Thea, Princess of Telas." She said and gave her best curtsies. She was so unreasonably cute that Astriea answered her with a bright smile.

"Hello, Thea, my name is Astriea Blake."

"I know. My sister told me about you. You're the Goddess of Magic!"

Astriea was confused but curious. She sounded happy about that fact. Was she happy the goddess of magic was being held prisoner in her dungeons? Surely a child wouldn't be so *morbid*.

"And you!" She pointed at Sera, who sat up then. "You're *Seraphina*." She said like a love-struck schoolgirl, with a little swoon to add dramatic effect. Astriea had to fight back the urge to laugh at the girl's acting. Her cute little button nose was splattered evenly with freckles, and she had the same emerald green eyes as her elder sister.

"Vera told me all about you. She loves you, you know."

"I think you are too young to know what love is," Sera responded as kindly as she could.

Astriea's heart sank at the sad tone she used.

"No, I'm not! Everyone says that children are too young for everything! I know she loves you because she protects you, like she protects us," Thea shot back, arms crossed.

Astriea was shocked by what the young princess had revealed, and Sera's expression reflected it.

"What do you mean?" Sera asked, standing and slowly inching closer to the door. She sat down in front of Thea with her legs crossed and waited for her answer. Astriea sat back on the cot and listened.

6

Seraphina

Seraphina waited as Thea tapped her foot for a moment, but sat down in the hallway and crossed her legs like she did.

"Father says there is a great darkness. That it makes him do bad things." Her small voice echoed through the stone halls. "Sometimes he can fight it, but sometimes..." The sweet-faced princess paused for a moment, looking both ways down the corridor, but went on. "Sometimes the darkness makes him forget all the good things. All the things he loves. *Us*. He came after us once, and Vera stopped him. She's like a fable hero in that way. But by the time the darkness went away, she was... I didn't see her for a few weeks. It's happened more than once actually..." Her head drooped down. She was sad. "Vera takes it all so we don't have to. It's why none of my brothers tries challenging her for the throne. We love her."

Sera could've cried. Could've cried and screamed and cursed whatever gods made her pity Vera.

"Thank you, Thea. I think you should head up to bed before they catch you down here." Sera said with a forced smile.

The princess stared at her for a few moments. Seraphina thought of what else she watched. What else she observed in this castle. But she bid Seraphina and Astriea goodnight and left. The only light dissipated as she went.

21

* * *

Before the dawn rose, the cell was cast in a shade of pale blue. Astriea still slept, but Sera stretched her sore muscles.

She started the morning with an excruciating pain in her stomach. She was starving but had to push through it. Had to do anything to keep her going, to keep her from breaking under the weight of the castle sitting above them.

She hooked her hands under the bar, ran across the cell doorway, and started doing pull-ups. Her arms and core screamed at her and her skin was freezing, but the heat in her blood as she pulled herself up and down again and again made sweat break through.

A creak sounded down the hall, sending her dropping onto her feet, before backing away and waiting for whatever was coming.

In the dim light, she could see the figure who stalked toward her. A hooded cloak doing its best to cover her face and hair.

Vera.

Sera sat down against the wall. She had nothing to say to her. Nothing.

"Sera," Vera whispered to her outside the cell. "Sera, please. I just want to talk to you. If only for a moment." She lit the sconce hanging on the cell's outer door. Golden light filled the space and Vera pulled back her hood.

Gods. *Her face.*

Her beautiful, broken face. Green bruises covered the Grand Duchess's cheeks. Her eyes were nearly purple and swollen a bit. Her perfect and sensuous lips, which Sera once worshiped, were now busted and scabbed over.

She hadn't meant to make a face, but she was shocked, and worst of all, she was furious. Every single part of her ached to rip the Tzar to shreds. She did her best to shove that feeling away. Did her best to keep her face neutral, but failed.

Vera saw her expression and immediately raised her hood again.

"I'm sorry. I'm not used to hiding my face around here."

22

Sera didn't respond. She looked at the cell wall across from her, arms on her knees.

"Please, Sera, I…"

"Just go, Vera." she finally said. How could she ask her to listen to whatever she had to say?

"Seraphina—" Vera started, but Sera cut her off. She needed her to leave. To walk away before she started crying. So she looked away from her and said, "You'd think starvation would've done it. Or the unforgiving cold. Maybe even the loneliness of this dungeon. It could've even been watching Tristan die at your hand." She could almost feel Vera wince at the words. "Any of those things could've broken me. But even in this dark place, the sun still rises." Sera pointed to where the sunlight finally began to beam in. "Still creeps in the window. And with every dawn, I thank Zaniah for my hatred of you. It's what keeps me sane in this cell." She sneered, while every fiber of her screamed it was a lie.

But she would tell herself that lie, over and over and over until it became the only truth she knew.

She took a breath and said over her shoulder, "The only thing you care about is yourself. So run back to your master and do not let me see your face again, or I will end you as you ended Tristan."

Vera rose from the floor and left without another word.

7

Astriea

Sunlight woke Astriea, making her stomach turn and roll as she rose from the cot and leaned against the cell wall. Sera was sitting in the corner with her legs crossed and eyes closed; meditating. Astriea nodded to herself and tried to remain quiet.

She'd woken for a moment last night while Vera and Seraphina were talking. Heard the heart-wrenching blow Sera had dealt her. She couldn't lie though, Vera deserved it. For all the things she did, she deserved it tenfold.

Rumbling came from down the hall and the guards were at their cell. The door unlocked and flew open. Then Vera herself appeared from behind them.

Oh gods. Her face.

Had Sera seen her face?

The woman looked like she'd been beaten within an inch of her life, but she stood tall and proud as she said, "Bind them, and cover their eyes."

Vera's gaze darted to Sera, still meditating in the corner and paying no mind to any of them. She turned back out of the cell, her caliginous cloak bellowing behind her. Her voice was so different from how she'd spoken to Seraphina last night. Astriea tried to fight against the guards as they bound her arms and ankles in shackles, and then placed a blindfold around her eyes.

She tried to count the turns on the journey through the castle, but couldn't focus past her unending hunger. When her footsteps stopped scraping across dirt and started tapping lightly on smooth floor, she assumed they were being taken to the throne room for more questioning. She heard a door creak open and bump against the wall. Before she knew it, glorious sunlight blinded her. Golden and warm.

Her heart broke at the empty hope that Thomas would be at the other end of that light. Her vision cleared, and she was standing in a large, beautiful room. There was a massive bed in the middle against the far left wall, adorned with at least a dozen pillows, shining silver sheets, and beautiful dark brown and black furs.

Similar furs lined the smooth black marble floor. A fire was going in the hearth next to them by the door and there was only one window, perched in the corner directly across from them by a lonely bookshelf. On the left side of the windows were tall, outward swinging, glass double doors. Towering over the room and opening to a large stone balcony. The entire perimeter of it caged. No way of escaping.

"What is this?" Astriea asked.

"Your new accommodations," Vera said abruptly. "The Tzar has decided that rotting in a cell won't make you inclined to tell us anything."

"So what? You think because you give us a nicer room we'll betray everything we've worked for? Everything we believe in?" Sera spat at her. Disgust wrenched in her voice.

Vera nodded at the guards and all but one left the room.

"According to the Tzar, there are actions that our parties can undertake for mutual benefit."

"Oh, there are, are there?" Astriea said, rolling her eyes. Then she jingled her shackles at Vera.

Vera nodded again, and the remaining guard quickly moved to Astriea and released her from her binds. His helmet covered his face, but Astriea noticed his eyes through the slits. *Silver.* The entirety of them was completely silver.

She'd seen nothing like it, save for the single slice across her own. She wondered if he could *see* at all, but he paused at her gaze. Locked it with hers. Then he went on to Sera, breaking the connection.

Astriea wondered if he'd been born that way. If he had spent all his life with such curious eyes. Though, to some, they would likely be terrifying.

"Lunch is already on the way up." Vera breathed and then left without another word.

The room was silent for a long moment after they left.

"Do they really think this is going to work?" Astriea asked as she flopped onto the bed. Gods, it was so soft she jokingly considered hearing them out for a moment.

"The Tzar couldn't possibly think we'd just give up the mission without a fight," Sera said.

"You saw Vera's face?" Astriea asked.

"Yeah." Sera set down the silver cup she was inspecting on the table in the living area by the hearth. "I saw."

"Do you think the Tzar did it?"

"I can't think of anyone else. I can't feel bad for her, though, Astriea. The moment I do, I'll start excusing everything she did. I can't do that."

"You don't have to. She betrayed us. She fucking killed Tristan. Fuck her." Astriea responded.

"Yeah. Fuck her." Sera mumbled.

"Come on," Astriea said, reaching a hand out for Sera's. "Let's get some fresh air in this bird cage."

That put a smile on her face. They walked onto the beautiful balcony and laid out on the soft green sofa.

Honestly, the view was stunning. There were walls of nearly crystallized mountains surrounding the palace. Shimmering in the sunlight and shining like beacons. All of them curving around a bustling city beneath them.

The castle and city resided in a fjord between two frozen mountains. Nothing about this place felt safe, though.

If anything, Astriea looked at those mountains and realized that her true captivity lay not in the dungeons, but in the city itself.

8

Thomas

It'd been five weeks since Astriea sent Thomas, Draes, and Damian through the rift and back to Triscillia. Back to the palace throne room where she'd broken Shadon's former king. Five weeks since he'd said words that tasted like ash on his tongue now. He should've known better. Should've thought before he spoke.

Careful how you speak, Thomas. It can take only moments to break someone, but decades to heal them.

Draes told him things like that all his life. Told him to *mind his fire*.

Thomas had been completely oblivious to what that actually meant until recently. Until he watched Astriea's heart break at his hands. Or his by hers. He wasn't sure anymore.

The dragons made themselves at home. Sixty others emerged from the earth in the weeks since the mountains cracked open, with more still coming in every day.

Now, Thomas found himself walking down the long hallways of the palace once more after leaving the nests. While approaching the throne room now he wasted no time waiting for the guards to open the beautiful, newly replaced, white oak doors that towered over him.

He shoved them open with little effort, only to see King James' golden throne sitting empty.

Thomas stormed through the room to the other side and only spoke to the servants that lingered.

"Where is he?" He asked. Irritably.

"The King is in the war room with his generals, Lord Hellion." A young male servant answered quickly as Thomas strode to the back of the throne room and through the back doors.

While it had only been a little over a month, he still wasn't used to having a title. Didn't care about it, really.

He didn't like being addressed as *Lord* anything, didn't care about the coin the title came with, or the politics of it. The only thing he held close to his heart was that James had granted him and Astriea the lands where Monolith had once been. *Lord and Lady of Monolith,* he'd said. All of it to do with as the two of them saw fit. The chance to go back home and make things right.

Thomas continued to barrel through winding halls until he finally came upon the war room. He swung the doors open without thought and saw James standing over the massive carved table, assessing where his ships might align for the coming war.

"Hello, Thomas. How has your day been?" James asked without looking up.

Others surrounded the King of Shadon, Damian and Mira stood at his right, Draes at his left, and the two generals he'd brought in from the capitol—Antony and Masoni, who talked quietly by the wall. Thomas didn't bother to look up as he walked past them to the balcony where Milly and Richy—Helena's eighteen-year-old twins and James and Mira's favorite servants—laid out wine, bread, and cheese along with baked boar and flame-roasted chicken. He poured himself a heavy glass before taking a swig and speaking.

"My day would be better if we were ready to set sail," he said with a bite.

"It's been five weeks, Thomas." James started.

"Exactly, it's been five weeks that Astriea and Sera have been wasting away in a Telish dungeon! That we have sat here and *prepared.*" Thomas mocked.

"It's been five weeks and I am doing everything I can to rally an army.

Would you like to go out there and convince these people to fight for you? Die for you? Do you have any idea what you are asking of *my* people?" James snapped, nostrils flaring.

The flame behind Thomas's blue eyes lit with gold and his brows knitted.

"She *is* your people! Her family was Shadonian, *she* is Shadonian. And you've left her there to suffer!" He fired back, moving forward two large steps.

Before he knew it, Draes came up, stepping in between them.

"That's enough." He said with a hand extended to both of them. "Your majesty, we understand these things take time. We cannot thank you enough for everything you are doing for us." Draes turned his gaze to Thomas. "It is a debt that will not be easily repaid." He said with a snarl at his younger brother.

"There is no debt owed from you. From any of you." The King said. He released a deep breath and rubbed his temples with a finger and thumb. His blonde hair was messy and his green eyes were bright, despite the dark circles underneath them. He looked exhausted.

They all were.

Sleep had been something Thomas dreaded more than anything. Every night, he had the same dream, the same nightmare. He would find himself in the vast emptiness Astriea had thrown them through. He would be stuck there, alone, until he'd hear her screaming. Every night Thomas found Astriea in the darkness with him and would see her over a great distance. He ran to her but each time, as he grew closer, hands of black oil and darkness wrapped themselves around her. They covered her mouth to silence her screams and yanked her away.

Thomas decided he'd just rather not sleep.

"Thomas, let's take a walk." Draes breathed.

He shoved the fire deep down and nodded as Draes led him out of the war room, through the halls, and into the gardens.

"I don't need a mediator, Draes. I can handle myself." Thomas said in an irritable tone.

"If that were true, your power wouldn't be rearing its ugly head at the

King of Shadon. You lost your temper in there and it could very well cost us this alliance. I understand that you're angry—"

"No. You don't understand."

"I don't?" Draes countered. "You think I don't see the anger boiling beneath your mask? That I don't see you haven't been sleeping? You think I don't see you sneaking away in the night to train? Gods, Tommy, you've nearly doubled in size in *five*—"

"That's because of the power—"

"I don't care! This…" Draes gestured to Thomas's entire body. "It isn't something I ever prepared for. None of our ancestors channeled the kind of power that you do. If you don't want to explode onto your loved ones, I suggest you let them take some weight off your shoulders."

Thomas didn't answer. Didn't look at Draes either. Just kept his eyes on the cliffs at the other side of the courtyard, kept his eyes on the sea. He couldn't worry them further by telling them about his nightmares.

He could bear it. The weight of it all.

He'd carry it until it crushed him into nothing. But his brother was wiser than that. Could see through Thomas even after all this time apart.

"Tell me about the dreams, Thomas," Draes said, crossing his arms like he was ready to stand there all day.

"No." He almost growled.

"Thomas, if you tell me what's happening in the dreams, I might be able to help you work through them."

"I am doing everything I can to stop seeing it. So leave me be." He shoved Draes out of his way with his shoulder and made his way to the cliffs.

Draes did not follow.

* * *

Forty-four dragons nestled in the open fields atop the cliffs, all different and beautiful. Some were deep green and brown, meant to nest in the mighty trees like the mother oak that once stood in Monolith. Sixteen others were already claimed and were now out bonding with their riders.

Some of them were colored like pale sand and horned all over. Mighty winged serpents ready to crawl beneath the dunes of the southern deserts and soar beneath the boiling heat of the sun. There were three that looked as if someone had dipped them in gold. They shimmered in the sunshine as they rolled lazily in the grass. Thomas often thought of them as the *godliest*, as they only cared for sunbathing and being admired. But they were so stunning that it honestly made sense. As though they were made to be worshiped.

The sea dragons were Damian's favorite, though. He lit up every time he saw them. Though, they stayed close to the water most of the time.

Thomas sat next to a great white dragon, an arm leaning against its massive scaled neck as his feet dangled off the cliff's edge. He'd grown very close to not only the white silver-eyed dragon but the one black as night as well. It spent most of its time in the sky—where it glided now—guarding the rest of the flight.

Something like a sense of claiming had happened when he'd approached the black dragon for the second time. So much so that he'd looked into its eyes and asked it—with his mind—if he could name him. Or her. Whatever it was, he wanted to make sure they had a name.

The dragon had looked at him curiously. Seeming to give it great thought. So Thomas said the one name he couldn't get out of his head since he'd laid his eyes upon the magnificent beast.

Night-cleaver.

He would never forget the feeling that washed over him when he spoke the name aloud to the dragon. *His* dragon. As if Night-cleaver had slept for centuries and waited for their rider all that time.

Of course, Thomas hadn't had the balls to jump on their back quite yet.

And this was the closest the white one would let him near. Thomas worked with it daily, but they snarled a bit when he tried to move closer.

Today, though, he was able to sit right up against it.

He looked at the shallow bay below to see Damian standing on one of the large stones on the beach. He came out here every day to watch the water dragons burst from the sea. The scales on them glittered in greens, blues,

31

and purples. Their long, slithering bodies resembled that of the desert dragons. Like serpents of the sea and sky, they erupted from the water and extended their wings from nothing. Letting the air catch in their nearly sheer webbing. Like large, serpentine dragonflies funnily enough.

They splashed and performed tricks like they'd never been so grateful to feel the tides once more. And Damian's eyes always shone so brightly when he watched them. Thomas watched him kneel on the rock as waves crashed against it. He couldn't blame him for spending all his time here. It's exactly what Thomas was doing. Trading the company of people for the company of the dragons.

Sera was basically Damian's sister, and he'd been very quiet since they came through the portal. He wondered if nightmares plagued him as well.

Eventually, Thomas made his way into the palace once more and into his and Astriea's room. The bed remained the same, but untouched since her departure. He walked past it and sat on the sofa that had been placed by the hearth at his request. His large body hung off the edges of it, but he didn't care. He just adjusted his pillow and covered himself with the soft green blanket Astriea had clutched to while she healed in that bed across from him. He didn't want to sleep, but his eyes were so heavy. His body was so tired, and if he didn't at least try, he'd lose his mind.

So, with fast, heavy heartbeats, Thomas fell away into the slippery darkness that held his love hostage.

9

Damian

Horns sounded from the palace, and Damian figured that meant it was time to leave the beach. He'd spent most of his time here. Meditating.

However, his thoughts never excluded Sera and Astriea. His anger at the woman who'd killed his friend always lingered in his chest. But coming here felt like a cooling mist of water on his soul.

He gave a half-smile, but it quickly withered.

"I will admit, it pains me to see how talented you've become at keeping hidden."

Then, as if she peeled herself from the rock of the nearest cliff, Mira stepped from the shadows. Clad in black. Her jewels and lovely colors were absent completely. Her hair pinned in a tight braid from the top of her head and falling down her back.

"We had little choice." She said sadly but went on, "We were separated when I was thirteen. I know you think they could still be alive, Damian, but they killed two slave owners trying to get me out." She stopped. She didn't need to go on, but she said, "I was underage for marking, so they never found me."

Damian broke the tension by throwing one of his massive arms around his sister's shoulders and giving her a little squeeze.

"How goes James' petition to the lords of the realm?" He asked.

"The release of all slaves in Shadon? Not well. He said they were very concerned about what the loss of labor would do to the market here. James doesn't think they will agree to release them. The lords said that while *they* can afford to pay their servants, smaller folk aren't so well accounted for." She rolled her eyes. "So, instead, James declared the buying and selling of slaves to be illegal. All he could do for now, I suppose."

"How did the lords take that news?"

"Not well." She laughed. "We've been receiving letters on the matter for days. They are furious, but we have responded to each one all the same: *Your King so kindly requests your obedience or your heads. Any person found guilty of slave trading, sale, or trafficking will face execution by means of beheading.*"

"Damn, didn't know he had it in him." Damian laughed.

"You forget who his father was." She cut her eyes to him and smiled widely.

"Well, come on then, let's go see what those horns are about."

* * *

They had prepared a feast in the great hall when Damian and Mira arrived back at the palace. Servants rushed in and out of the massive open doors, placing trays of food and pitchers of wine and ale down the four long tables that stretched from the entry to the dais end of the room, where a fifth table sat facing them. It being reserved for the royal family and important members of state.

"What's going on?" Mira asked as a servant made to rush past her with his arms full of cutlery.

"His Majesty has ordered a feast for his nobles. The new Lords and Ladies of Shadon and some of the old noble families will all be in attendance."

"And what of the *court*? Does the King mean to bring them here?" she asked nervously.

"Yes, my lady. We just received word that guests should arrive in a few hours."

Mira's face turned bright red. He nodded the servant away and gave him thanks. They stood there for a moment and Mira started pacing near the tables, looking for the King.

Finally, James Aurelius strode into the great hall, two people following behind him and taking notes of every word he spoke. Golden blonde hair fell past his shoulders, and he wore everyday sparring leathers. His green eyes shimmered in the sinking sun that peered through the stained-glass windows. But then he saw Mira, and the outrage clearly plastered on her face. Damian gritted his teeth and took a step back from her. James winced at the look she was giving.

Damian whispered to Mira, "Try thinking about how handsome he is before you kill him."

"James!" Mira shouted. The chatter and hustle in the room died.

"I'm sorry, love, I must get dressed," he said, backing away from her to the doors behind him. He pushed one of his scribes in front of him.

"Don't you dare run from me!" Mira responded and bolted towards him.

James was at the door when she caught him. His guards reached for their weapons. He smiled and waved a hand at them, then let Mira go on.

"You have made this haven into a den of snakes by bringing them all here."

"Some of them are good men, and some are my family."

"My statement remains." She said, not losing eye contact with him.

"Can we talk about this privately? We both need to get ready." James gave her a flirtatious smile, took her hand, and kissed it.

Damian watched as some of that fire died out and cooled. Mira then made her way back to him.

"We will be having quite an extravagant week. I'll have clothes sent up to all your rooms. This meeting is important. Please try your best to keep Thomas from roasting anyone." Mira made to leave.

"I can't make you any promises about that," Damian said with a laugh. Though, now he worried it would be *her* whose fire needed to be minded tonight.

Mira's laugh echoed back to him, reminding him of their mother's.

"I will do my best." He said.

"One more thing. Some of these nobles are vile and vindictive. Cruel beyond all measure. They will not take kindly to the matter of my relationship with the King, given my station they will likely have unpleasant things to say. I plead you to ignore them."

"Again, I will do my best, sister." Damian bowed his head to her before making his way out the doors and up to his room.

10

Thomas

The vast, unending void of darkness swirled and bent into steady ground beneath his feet. He stood there for a moment—trying like hell to tame his racing heart—and blinked before he sent a silent prayer to *Candra*, the goddess of truth and justice. Prayed that she would show him the path—the true path. Then he prayed there even *was* a Candra. Prayed that she was real and not some bit of flourish on a story told again and again throughout the ages. He fell to his knees and pulled a deep, burning breath into his nostrils.

"Take me to her." He pleaded to the goddess, to the void, to whatever would help him.

Then he heard the screams. Screams that he wished he didn't recognize. They were earth-shattering but muffled. As if something stood between them.

Thomas stood to his feet and tried to listen more closely. Tried to find her, even blinded by the dark.

He felt a thud against the bottom of his foot. When he looked down, fear and panic bounded through him.

There she was.

Trapped under the floor like she'd fallen through ice on a lake and it froze over again. She was screaming and beating against it.

Thomas threw his body down. Astriea appeared to be engulfed in a sea of despair. She scratched and clawed and screamed—

Then she stopped moving and thrashing altogether.

He didn't know if he was breathing as he beat against the floor again and again. All his strength seemed to pour out of him as he did, and there was not a single crack, regardless of how hard he hit it.

He stopped.

Thomas sat up, breath still heavy and broken, and commanded his heart to still, if only for a moment. Commanded his lungs to slow, and his mouth to part for steady, even breaths. In an instant, a fiery glow replaced the blue of his eyes. His raven hair blazed with golden fury, and his skin shimmered with a gilded sheen.

Thomas, once again glancing at the floor, fixed his gaze upon Astriea's lifeless face, and with a surge of sorrow, he clenched his fist and struck it at her feet.

The heat shattered a large hole into the floor in front of him.

Thomas wrapped his arms of gold and flame around her waist before jerking them both up.

Wherever up was.

The dark, spiraling fluid spilled out of Astriea and slithered away from the light as the floor solidified beneath them again. He looked at her, lying there—gasping for air—and a tear fell from his eye to have her in his arms again. If this were only a dream, then it'd been the best one he'd had in weeks.

"Thomas?" she whispered.

"I'm here. I'm right here." He said, bringing his shining forehead to hers.

Thomas's golden light became accompanied by Astriea's beams of silver.

The icy blue of her eyes was so bright he could feel every beat of his broken heart try to mend itself at the sight of them.

"I love you, *Starlight*, I'm sorry and I love you and I don't care if this is some twisted dream because I have to say it to you. Because I can't bear the thought of going a moment more, letting you think I hate you." He spat the words out as fast as he could say them.

"Thomas, this isn't a dream. I'm here, you're here. They've been injecting me with something. It knocks me out, sends me to drown in that..." she said, cutting her eyes to the floor, now barren. "Whatever *that* was... But I was wrong to keep Draes from you. I was wrong to be willing to let him die. That was wrong. Zaniah and I are on better terms and understandings now. I'm never going to let any of you die. I love you—"

He kissed her.

Thomas brushed a warm, flaming hand behind her head, his fingers lacing into her hair. Her lips were soft and warm, even in this place where everything was cold and dark. Astriea tilted her head back to allow him better access to her mouth, and the kiss deepened. It felt like every hope and dream had led to this. But he stopped and breathed onto her lips, "What I said to you was cruel. You didn't deserve that."

"I deserved it. I needed to hear it and I needed to hear it from you."

She pressed her nose against his, and for a moment, everything was fine. For a moment there was no impending war, no imprisonment, no seas separating them. For a moment, there were only the two of them. Desperate not to lose hold of one another.

"You're sure it's not a dream?" He breathed against her.

"If it is, I don't think I would ever like to wake up, Thomas..."

But Thomas began to fade. Astriea's touch falling away with the picture of him.

"What's happening?" he asked, shaking. She fell straight through his legs onto the floor.

"I think you're waking up. Thomas, listen to me. I think we're in the northern palace in Telas. Vera had us moved to the royal suites in some attempt to sway us. She's smart, Thomas, be smarter than her!"

"Astriea!" He yelled in response. "Wait, I have so much to tell you!" He was fading more quickly now.

"Tell me when you get to Telas, my love. Sera and I will make do on our own, until then... Until then, I need you to get some sleep, gather your strength, then *come get me.*"

The words came out so quickly, but there was something else in them. Suddenly, the hopeless ember in his heart ignited. Burning through the worry and doubt.

She tried to cup his cheek, but her hand passed through him like a ghost.

"Don't do anything to get yourself killed, *Starlight*."

Thomas said as he faded away completely. Leaving Astriea alone in the icy darkness she'd been drowning in.

11

Astriea

Astriea flung from the soft bed, beading in sweat and panting. Sera woke immediately, shooting up next to her, and instantly had a hand on her shoulder.

"Gods, I didn't know when you'd wake after that last injection. Breathe…" Sera coaxed.

Astriea struggled but managed to balance her breathing. Then she leapt out of bed.

She went to every painting and looked behind them on the walls. Checked the caged balcony for any lights in the neighboring rooms, and quietly listened through the door for guards in the hall. Sera tip-toed behind her, a curious look on her face.

Gods she was soaked. The breeze coming through the balcony doors felt ice cold against her skin.

"What are you doing?" Sera whispered from behind.

"I'm checking for any listening ears."

She rubbed her eyes and followed Astriea to the large couch by the hearth. They sat down and Astriea took a deep breath. Happy to know they weren't being spied on, at least at the moment.

"Every time I pass out after an injection, I fall into this *darkness*. This thick, drowning darkness. But I don't die, just drown again and again."

"Gods, Astriea…" Sera said, covering her mouth.

Without a second thought, Astriea took the terrors of her recent unconscious and neatly placed them in a box before tossing them to the back of her mind. When she won the war, she didn't really know if she would survive the fallout of that act alone. Because she was not meant for that darkness. And every time she entered, whatever entity it belonged to made sure to try and weed her out. As though she were a disease.

Her visits there were never pleasant.

But, once again, and like always, she trudged on.

"Until tonight. Thomas was there this time. He broke through the magic. He saved me and I spoke to him!" she said in a whispered shout.

Sera placed a sympathetic hand on her shoulder and said, "You're sure this wasn't just a dream?"

"I've never been more sure of anything. And my power! I could feel it again."

"And… Zaniah?"

Sadness sunk Astriea's heart like a ship's anchor cast into the sea.

"No. I didn't even feel her presence." She whispered.

"So, what do we do? Find a way to escape?"

"For now, we do our best not to get killed. Keep an eye out for any weaknesses in the fortification of this place."

Sera rubbed her forehead and said, "This castle is at least ten times that of the Shadon summer palace. Mapping a way out will be difficult."

"Yes, it will. So, any time we leave this room, we'll have to do whatever we can to remember the routes we're taking. We'll go over and sketch a map that reflects our outlook of the city from the balcony."

Sera nodded her agreement.

"Come on, back to bed. You need *proper rest*." Sera nudged her.

"That's not a bad idea." Astriea agreed before changing clothes and climbing back into bed to drift away atop the soft pillows.

Right now, that was something she could be thankful for. A warm bed with soft sheets and pillows. Although she'd never admit it to Vera.

Seraphina stroked her hair until a gentle, welcoming sleep washed over her.

12

Thomas

When Thomas awoke from the dream, that was not a dream, his flames still burned bright and hot. Damian and James burst through the door just as he woke, and cold buckets of water were being tossed onto him. The shock of it made his flames sputter, but that water evaporated into nothing quickly. He shot to his feet.

"Thomas, you're going to burn down my palace! I *really* need you to get your shit together!" James shouted over roaring flames.

In an instant, the fire went out. Even the small tendrils that burned away at the couch, curtains, and some blankets.

"Shit!" Thomas shouted as he started looking for that green velvet throw that still smelled like Astriea.

It was a little singed and there was a new ashy smell on it, but *there...*

He could smell her scent, gardenia, and citrus. Like she'd been meant for an entirely different world.

He sighed with relief and—like a child—clutched it to his chest before gently placing it on the bed.

James and Damian were there in an instant. Thomas was naked save for the towel he now covered himself with. And he was soaked in sweat.

"Gods, mate, you're not cooling off. Let's get you into some water." Damian said, throwing Thomas's left arm over his shoulder and leading him to the bathroom. Both hissing against the heat the whole way. Draes

43

came running into the room. He'd been gone the last few days. Here and then off again on various missions for James. Thomas couldn't blame *him* for it, though. He couldn't bear to keep Draes in one place for too long. Couldn't bear to make him feel like a prisoner again. And after their heated discussion right as he returned from his most recent assignment, he was sure Draes was going to give him an earful.

"What's happened? Are you alright?" Draes took Thomas's right arm over his shoulder in James's stead. Thomas didn't mean to, but the weight of his sweat-drenched head became too much and he dropped it against Draes' with a small thud. The heat didn't seem to bother him, though.

"Gods, Tommy, you're burning up. *What happened?*" This time, the question was more of a shout. This wasn't the first time this type of incident had occurred in the past few weeks. His nightmares would wake him in flames. Sometimes the heat died out quickly, but sometimes he had to find his way to a cold bath. Which had to be drawn and then dumped and then drawn again. It was a real task, and this time his lungs felt like they were burning. His breath became struggling wheezes and his vision clouded.

What was happening to him? Was Zaniah wrong to unlock this power before he was ready to unlock it himself? Would he ever have been able to with Zaniah imprisoned? The Dragon of Telas was known far and wide throughout her imprisonment, but they had only ever been capable of minor acts with it. Regardless, he couldn't *breathe*.

James ran out into the hall and spoke with a guard while Thomas gasped. Draes looked so worried.

Shit, maybe he *should* be worried. Thomas was getting air, but not enough for speaking and certainly not enough for comfort.

13

Damian

Thomas's rapid breathing made Damian's heart sink.

Not again. Not another one.

His friend.

James ran out into the hall and called on his guards who stood in front of his chambers at the end.

"Have they finished the renovations on my bathing chambers yet?" He heard James ask Fitzherk, a guard who never seemed to be far from the king.

"Yes, Your Majesty. They finished the last of the repairs on some broken pipes this morning. Everything is running perfectly now."

"Good. Come and help us get Lord Hellion. Put him in, quickly!"

Then those guards were hurrying to Thomas. Before he knew it, they carried him down the hall. He and Draes trotted behind them as James led them all into his massive bedroom.

It was astounding. So big that Damian wondered how it fit in this palace. There was a massive hearth on the left, and an entire lounging and eating area before it. Lush furs covered the dark marble floors in reds and blacks. Damian could barely see the bed in the back of the room, mostly because sheer black sheets hung from the ceiling, creating some privacy.

He didn't want to think about that. Flinched at the thought, actually.

They passed through the door on the right and came into the most magnificent bathing chamber he'd ever seen. Damian had been in more *natural* baths before, hot springs in the jungles beneath the mountains on the Isle. Had brought company of his own to those springs. But he'd never seen something like this.

The floors and walls were all a large, sand-colored tile, with beautiful gold symbols etched into each large square. But in the center of the room, the floor sank into itself. Into two levels. The deepest one having small holes in its center. Damian was bewildered.

"Lay him in the pool," James said to the guards. They did as he commanded. Thomas just lay there, struggling to gain his breath, but still making do.

James turned a blue lever on the wall to his right, and cold water cascaded down from the ceiling. Damian's face betrayed his surprise, with his eyes widening and his lips parting in disbelief.

"It's called a shower! Almost everyone has hot and cold running water in the capital. I intend to make that available to everyone in the kingdom!"

James yelled over the loud roar of water pouring down on Thomas. He wasn't moving, though. Draes moved into that cold water and pulled Thomas into his lap.

"Will he be alright? Will this help cool him off?" Damian asked.

"Yes, the cold water is constantly falling on him, and then draining through the floor. It will stay cold until it's over." James assured him.

There was nothing to do now but wait. Even though Damian couldn't stop noticing James check the time on the grand clock outside the door every so often. That dinner with the court would start in less than an hour.

"James, go. We've got this," Damian said, walking to him and placing a hand on his shoulder.

"He's my friend. I'll stay."

"Your *friend* would kick your ass if he knew what he was keeping you from, and you know it."

"Ha, I am still his king." James laughed and rolled his eyes.

"And he is still a *god*." Damian popped back and tilted his head with a close-lipped smile.

James gave him a nervous look and said, "I think I'll go get ready."

"That's what I thought." Damian mocked.

"Shut it or I'll *command* you to wear guard armor tonight," James said with a smile.

Damian lifted his hands in mocking surrender, and James trotted off to get ready. He tossed back a worried glance in Thomas's direction before he continued through the doorway.

14

Thomas

The cold water against his burning skin felt like being submerged in an ice bath. Only instead of drowning in the ice, he was being stabbed with small shards of it.

But then his chest released, and Thomas took a deep, gasping breath. Draes's arms were on him, and he was leaning against him… in the rain?

Thomas blinked to clear his vision. Draes's hand was pressed against his forehead. Like when he was a boy and Astriea had given him Tali fever. Draes never left his side.

"Tell me what's been happening to you." He said, more like ordered his little brother to spit out the truth. He couldn't lie, it should've made him angry to be spoken to like a child, but he'd missed being scolded by him. Missed the only father he ever really had. So he'd lie here in this freezing rain chamber and let Draes tell him how pissed he is that no one said anything.

"Nightmares. They trigger my powers." Thomas barely got the words out through his chattering teeth. But the water stopped flowing as Damian turned a lever on the wall.

Thank the gods. This felt more like a punishment than a relief. But he was grateful for the air flowing freely into his lungs.

Draes—drenched and furious—never moved his angry eyes away from him as Thomas sat up.

"It's really not that big of a deal." Shit, how was he going to get out of this?

"You nearly burned down your room. It's a problem." Damian cut in.

Damn you, Damian.

He came down into the empty pool and sat on the step in front of him and handed him a towel.

"You're right." Thomas took a deep breath. "I don't think it was just a dream. The other times, maybe. But tonight I *saw* her. Spoke to her. She thinks they're being held at the Northern palace…" He paused and looked at Draes.

Draes's eyes went wide. The mention of the unknown city washed away any confidence he had on his face.

"So, Sera is alive?" Damian asked.

"Astriea didn't say that she wasn't. Said that Vera had them moved from the dungeons to nicer chambers, but keeping her knocked out most of the time."

Damian nodded.

"We'll go over everything you saw later. What we need to know now is why these dreams are triggering your powers." Draes said as he stood and grabbed the clothes from a servant entering the chamber.

"I'm not sure…" Thomas said, drying himself and turning around to put on his pants. When he turned again for his tunic, Draes threw it at him.

"Well, I'm sure of one thing." Draes began. "You will go see Evangeline and have the coven assess you. And you will stop asking James to send me into the field in your own misguided way of *healing* me."

Thomas tried to cut in but Draes lifted a finger to silence him. This was not the type of scolding he thought he'd be happy to have again.

Draes took a step towards him, towering over him even now. "My first and most important role in this life is being your older brother. Keeping you safe. I will not let *my* baggage keep me from achieving that goal. Do you understand?"

Thomas swallowed and nodded. What else could he say? God or not, Draes would make his life a living hell until he went to the coven. Thomas threw his tunic over his head and then looked down at himself.

"What the hell am I wearing?" he asked as he looked at the black sleeveless tunic lined with slim gold trim. His pants were loose and matched the tunic in every way, flowing lightly down him and then cinching at the ankles. Making it less of a hassle to throw on his boots. It was then that James popped back into the room. Still dressed in his clothes from earlier.

"No worries, Damian, I have some for you too," James said as he handed Damian a set of clothes. His were deep navy blue and gold.

"No offense, James, but do we *have* to wear this?" Thomas said, fidgeting with his collar.

"Of course! Black, for The King's Chancellor." James's smile was bright as he walked over to Thomas and placed an armband on his tunic. It was a slim strip of gold with a diamond-shaped symbol of burning flames atop its middle. Large enough that anyone could tell what it was. He'd only heard stories of Shadonian court pieces. The Chancellor would receive an armband, and the crown prince or princess would wear a single golden band around their head. He didn't know about the others, the King's Chancellor and the Crown heir were the most popular. The most talked about.

But it was beautiful. Thomas was stunned into silence. Eyes wide and mouth gaped open.

Second in command to all of Shadon. A place he was not even born to.

A gift that did not belong to him, but to someone else.

Someone who never gave up on the people here. Who sacrificed their heart for it time and time again, but kept moving forward.

When he finally found words again he said, "James... Thank you, but I'm not sure I am the person this belongs to as if I... I've stolen it. And what about when I'm gone? Won't you have to find a new Chancellor? I'm not sure I know enough about politics to really be qualified..."

"In times of peace, the Chancellor's duties are less challenging, more open to free time. And when the person you speak of returns, I will pass it on to them. But you are my friend and I trust you, whether or not you or the court agrees tonight. However, you won't be handling political issues.

I need you to train my men to ride those dragons. You've done well at helping them bond, now I need you to keep doing it. Then teach them how to ride."

I *don't even know how to ride a gods' damned dragon.*

"It will be you who leads my armies, second in command, only to myself. And Mira, of course, once she is crowned."

"So, more like your general?"

"Yes, if my general were to become the ruler of Shadon if I die without an heir or my crown does not glow for one of my siblings."

Thomas' breath hitched and his eyes went wide.

Oh no, no, no. He thought. *I am not stable enough for that.*

That's when he realized the bastard did it on purpose. *I need you to get your shit together*, he'd said.

James then made his way back to Damian and placed a pin on top of the stack of clothes. Their design was similar, only the entire piece was covered in golden waves instead of flames. Thomas was utterly dumbfounded.

"I have also chosen an admiral for my navy."

Damian looked just as stunned as Thomas must have. Finally, he said, "You want to go with us, don't you? Not just to Telas, but Sirey as well."

"I do." James turned back to Thomas, who now had his own shock written on his features. "I am the king of all Shadonians. I will follow the path our patron has laid out before us."

"The court will likely not allow that," Draes said softly from the corner of the room. It spooked Thomas a bit. He'd been so eerily quiet, that even he had forgotten Draes was there.

"Speaking of that, how far out are they now?" James asked Draes.

"They'll be arriving any minute if they limited their stops today."

Thomas raised a brow and James laughed.

"Mira cannot be my spy now that I am going to make her queen. So yes, I've asked Draes to be my royal sleeper. No one knows much about him, and I'd like to keep it that way. So, if asked, he is simply Ravok, Knight of Bastan. Is that understood?"

James seemed more serious now. He gave Draes a look that signaled something Thomas didn't understand.

"Get dressed and meet Mira and I at the royal entry into the great hall. And please, be mindful of the way you speak tonight. Be mindful of your tempers." But then James winked at him. So Thomas asked, "What role should I be playing tonight?"

James made his way to the door but stopped and said over his shoulder, "Try out, *easily irritated God of flames.*"

Thomas, although exhausted, rolled his eyes and smiled as James strode back out the door.

15

Damian

D amian met with the others at the royal entry into the great hall, a secret door in the wall behind the royal table. From the other side of the thin wooden boards, they could all hear people piling in. Sometimes they heard laughter and cheering, other times things grew so quiet that whispers leaked through the cracks of the doors.

And then a trumpet sounded.

"Presenting His Royal Majesty," the herald began, and the doors opened before them. James and Mira stepped forward while Thomas and himself fell in line behind them. "King James Aurelius, The Golden King of Shadon."

The four of them stood behind their seats at the royal table and the room was so quiet it made Damian feel very uncomfortable. No one spoke… but they all bowed.

Still, James didn't take his eyes off the crowd of people.

He didn't let them think for a moment that he had any reservations.

But the silence grew heavier and now it seemed like the King was looking for someone. Seemed like he was considering sitting down at his seat until quick, faint taps sounded down the hall.

"Out of my way!" A female voice echoed from a distance and through the doors. Damian could've sworn he saw a smile almost break James's grim expression, but he steeled it. Those massive doors banged and then swung open with a mighty *SWOOSH*!

A lovely, golden-haired, middle-aged woman stood on the other side. Her breaths were heavy and a small swarm of people ran down the hall behind her. James quickly made his way around the table and stopped at the edge of the dais.

"Is he dead?" She asked. "Is that *bastard* dead?" If she sounded like anything in this world, she did not sound afraid of what might happen to her should Herold be alive. The type of fear lanced in her voice was only that felt by a parent for their child. Like her worst nightmare had come to pass and James had gained his crown through darkness and pain. She looked at him like she was afraid of him.

Afraid *for* him.

The crowd of people all leaned in and listened intently. A few angry-looking nobles made repugnant faces, as though they were not happy with the change in leadership.

Damian took this moment of quiet to observe the others scattered around. It was easy to spot the nobles and their children. Most of the young ones appeared normal enough, although the teenagers seemed to toe the line between dark and light. Like they wanted to appease their fathers, but desperately wished for something else. Damian thought the hope there resembled a kernel of corn. Buried deep but ready to break soil in a desperate reach for sunlight. You could tell a lot by the expressions on a teenager's face. Especially nobles who never really cared how much it gave their intentions away.

"He is dead." James said with his chin held high.

"By your hand?"

Damian knew at this point the woman was James's mother. "Did Scythe offer you the throne as well?"

Two young girls in shimmering dresses approached, being escorted by a young man—maybe fourteen—in brown riding leathers. A small sword sheathed at his side. They all had the same golden hair, except for the youngest girl. Her hair was the deepest black. Perhaps the only child of Herold Berelda who actually looked his heir, save for her bright green eyes that matched her mother's and siblings.

For a moment, James froze. And out of some instinct Damian couldn't explain, he stepped forward and spoke for the King.

"Just a few weeks ago, Herold Berelda faced defeat in these halls at the hands of Astriea, the Goddess of Life, Magic, and the Stars. He was later executed by the Shadon Witches after the Goddess herself banished this 'Scythe' from these lands." Damian smiled when he noticed the witches. "Some of you seem to have already made yourselves acquainted with *The Royal Coven*," He tried to hold back a chuckle by nodding at the witches. All nine of them stepped forward from their places in the crowd. They'd been chatting with people all evening and guests gasped as they lined up in front of the dais. Appalling some of the court that they had even been speaking with a witch.

Then Evangeline said, "We are the Daughters of Astriea. Created as the great goddess broke apart the earth, pulled strings of magic from its heart, and used it to shift our bodies into our immortal forms."

This caused a stir of whispers and frightened expressions. Mira made her way around the table and hooked her arm through James's.

Damian nearly felt ashamed at the fact he hadn't noticed how beautiful his sister was. Her dress was long, and deep red, with shimmering golden trim twisting and turning in lovely patterns up her arms and down the seams of the gown. Her hair, a tangle of long, bouncing curls, moved freely in every which way. Only two golden pins held the top half back and away from her face. And atop her head was a small ruby-studded tiara.

Something a crown princess would wear, Damian thought.

But that wasn't the thought that made a tear well in his eye. It was the fact that his sister was honoring their mother on this night—her debut to the people. James' house color had been changed to green but tonight… Tonight she donned the color that meant the most to her. She looked like their mother, reborn and shining in the god's light. *The Ruby of Aurelius* now outshone the King upon that dais.

A voice that Damian could only describe as *prickish* yelled over the now-silent crowd, "You expect us to accept your claim? That what you say is even true?" The man was a noble, of course, and he looked like he'd never really worked a day in his life. He had greasy black hair and his face had swallowed his chin and neck entirely.

Another man across the hall stood quickly and yelled with a pointed finger at the rude lord, "You will accept his claim because he is the eldest child of the previous King! Or has the House of Benning forgotten our laws of inheritance?"

"Piss on you, Matten! And your useless house!" Benning yelled back.

Verbal disputes erupted around the room.

"Aye! Matten is right! He became King the moment his father passed. There is no question to his claim, you bloody fool!" A woman yelled.

Benning's son sat next to him. A thinner, dark young man who honestly looked like he couldn't be more annoyed, but his father went on, his voice squealing over the crowd, "You offer us no proof of this. Why would we want this commoner filth," he shot his gaze at the coven, "to be granted noble rank? And if you think we're going to allow your servant whore to become Queen—"

He didn't get to finish.

The King raised his hand, and Damian pounced.

He jumped down from the dais and stretched his massive arms into the crowd, grabbing the now groveling lord by the throat and throwing him onto his knees in front of the King.

The room went silent.

"How do we even know you tell the truth? If the goddess has returned, then where is she?" The lord sputtered at the King's feet. The words earned a stunned tilt of Damian's head. Even on his knees, the entitled prick still had more to say. But James didn't answer him immediately. He looked back at Thomas and they exchanged a mirrored nod. Damian shuddered as Thomas stepped forward and squatted down closer to the man. Maybe two feet away.

"Astriea and our crew were taken captive during our journey to Telas. She risked everything to send some of us back. Now, we ready for war to ensure her safe return." His words were cool as ice, which was something Damian found a bit unsettling but didn't question. The words themselves started an uproar of disagreement. People were yelling and cursing, "BLASPHEMY!"

"MAGIC IS DEAD!"

"THE GODS ARE DEAD!"

Those words were the breaking point as Thomas gestured for James and Mira to step back.

Flame erupted from him in spirals of red, yellow, and blue. The crowd cowered on the floor, even James's family. But James and Mira and the rest of them stood firm.

When Thomas spoke again, his voice was not alone but intertwined with ethereal grace.

"I am Hellion, God of the Sun and all things that burn." Something different happened then. A golden staff shot from his hand and thundered against the ground. At first, Damian had to hold back a chuckle at Thomas's bravado but then wondered if it was safe for him to be using his power after the incident they'd just narrowly avoided. He figured, for now, he'd just trust his friend's better judgment.

"See the crown upon your King's head! Its golden dust will only glow for the rightful heir to this throne, and will never shine for any with a crooked heart! This is the gift Astriea and The Royal Coven have granted this land. So that it will never consider any evil as deserving of rule in it again." Thomas's flames went out, and this time he didn't burn off his clothes. Like he'd simply told the fire not to touch his new uniform. The crowd seemed to relax, if only for a moment.

He spoke again, that second voice more guttural; lethal as he said, "As for who should sit as your queen, you all should consider yourselves quite lucky to have a kingdom left after how you've all treated its people. Should consider yourselves favored that you have not been stripped of your titles, lands, and income for the atrocities committed on this soil." He turned to look at Mira.

"The Ruby of Aurelius shall be Queen, and while I commend King James for his restraint, and that he would likely have you killed quickly," Thomas turned back to Lord Benning, now groveling on his knees, and yanked him up by his collar. So close the man could most definitely feel the heat radiating from Thomas's eyes that were now filled with blue flame. "I will not be so humane."

"Guards, take Lord Benning to the dungeons for evaluation. Any who share his feelings are more than welcome to join him." The guards came and dragged Lord Benning out of the great hall while he cried and wailed for mercy. His son seemed to have nothing to say. He didn't try to stop it either.

When the doors shut, everyone in the room bent to one knee and bowed their heads. Damian wished it hadn't taken threats and violence to solve the ascension issue, but for now, things seemed to play out well.

Mira didn't speak, and Damian didn't expect her to. Not when she was not yet guaranteed her crown.

That thought almost rocked Damian to the floor. That his sister would be Queen. He wished his mother and father could see this. Wished that somewhere in the stars, as his parents journeyed to the next world, they would look back. Even if only for a brief glimpse. He wished more than anything that they were saving it for the moment a golden crown was placed upon Mira's head. Damian didn't know everything about his mysterious sister. However, he was aware that she carried the pain of losing her brother, shouldered the responsibility of caring for their parents, withstood the hardships of slavery, and bravely escaped it.

Mira locked eyes with James, and as they turned back to their table, a strange sensation tugged at him. Something deep in his chest whispered: *A great many wonders will come from those two.*

Yes, Damian thought, great wonders indeed.

After James led Mira back to her seat, he rounded the table once more and said to the entire royal court, "Though some of you are already aware, there will be great changes, starting with this..." He pulled a scroll from his coat's inside pocket and began reading from it.

"From this day, and all days that follow in my reign, I do so ban all markets in association with the slave trade."

The crowd gasped and their eyes went wide. Including Damian's.

"Any found in the sale and distribution of any persons upon Shadonian soil, or any attempts made to distribute from Shadonian soil, shall result in an immediate, personal trial and beheading by your King, James Aurelius of Shadon."

There was a beat of silence, so quiet it sent shivers down Damian's spine. His stomach turned and fluttered against hope and joy and gratitude. His mind raced to know what reaction the court would make, and that long, unending moment was threatening to make him scream. In that time he had a moment to think about how so many had ended up in the slave markets to begin with. Mira told him that twenty or so years ago, Herold turned his eye away from his soldiers collecting spoils of the sea. So much so, that he allowed his navy to arrest anyone on the ocean without royal traveling papers. Even fishermen and women off their own coasts weren't excluded from this. Mira said that the sea was never a safe place and that she hadn't stepped foot on a ship since they were brought here.

But Damian *loved* the sea. Longed for it.

The scream building from the silence wasn't voiced as a roar of applause erupted across the room.

Some cried, including Mira as she sat stunned in her seat.

The look in her eyes, as she and James shared a moment from across the table, was likely making everyone in the room envious of their love.

Only they knew what happened in that story.

At this moment, Damian paid no mind to the four angry lords who were seeing themselves out of the hall.

He only stood there, grateful that his sister would always have someone at her side.

16

Thomas

As the feast continued, Thomas did his best to make rounds and assure everyone that he wasn't a violent, uncontrollable god. He laughed with them, drank with them, and listened to their stories and theories about the gods.

He *assessed* them.

While he truly needed them to respect him, he didn't want them to be afraid. But every blessing has the potential to become a curse.

He wanted to know them, these people who were willing to follow a king and god into a war they had nothing to do with. No one seemed happy about it, but Thomas figured he had a few weeks to gain their trust. With limited time on his hands, he still opted to give it a go.

It was evident from Damian's furrowed brow that he was wrestling with the same thoughts. He made rounds of his own, talked, and laughed even.

A wave of realization washed over Thomas, causing his heart to sink. Damian had his sister returned to him but lost every other person he cared about. Sera and every member of his crew, whom he loved like brothers. Not to mention Tristan. Even Thomas would never forget what he saw that day.

Still, Damian was graceful and full of tact. Utterly charming to be around while Thomas was lighting his room on fire when he slept. He quickly made up his mind to speak with his friend before they departed for Telas.

When the two of them made their way back to their seats, the crowd quieted, and everyone sat down. Everyone except four young men and a young woman. They approached the dais and spread out before taking to one knee. They drew swords and pressed the tips of their blades into the stone floor. James moved from his seat and stood above them.

In Shadon, it was customary to wait until after the coronation feast to choose new knights for a new king. Having James crowned here, in Triscillia, might have even robbed some of their right to volunteer their names to him.

"What are your names?" He asked and lifted his chin at the man on the far left. He raised his head.

"I am Lorenzo, fifth son of Lord Titus Caarmanan, and I kindly ask to serve." Thomas noticed the man's features. His smooth black hair was long enough to reach his eyebrows before curling up in little wisps. And while his face adorned a beard kept close to the skin, it did not hide his youth. He was eighteen at best.

"Why?"

"I'm sorry, your grace?"

"Why do you wish to serve me? I do not know you."

"Because I know you. *Of* you. We all do." He gestured to the entire room of people. "My family wanted nothing more than to have a just ruler. And when we heard rumors that the crown prince was kind, generous, and forgiving, we found hope again. The previous King kept most of us on a stern leash and drowned our people in darkness and debt. My friends and I found each other through whatever path allowed our meeting." He gestured to the others kneeling next to him. And they all raised their heads. "Diego, third son of Randall Thorne." The second man rose from his knees and placed both his hands on the hilt of his sword. Diego bowed his head to the King. His shaggy brown hair was wild and unkempt, but his face was that of a mischievous young man. Someone who gave little weight to the opinions of others. Thomas felt as though he liked the man already, and suddenly became very excited to have another troublemaker around here.

Lorenzo skipped the woman standing next to Diego and went on to the next man. "Valtan, eldest son of Lord Emente Tridellious." Valtan stood and bowed. He differed greatly from the other men—even the woman standing in the center.

Valtan was ghostly pale with nearly glowing silver eyes and long, white hair. There was something about him that was not *of Shadon*. Something ethereal and shimmering.

He actually reminded him of Astriea a bit. The main issue Thomas had with the man was that he could've been mistaken for a giant. A warrior from old stories. He towered above everyone in the room. Even Draes, who was the tallest of all of them.

"And—"

"Alec, second son of Nostranas Leora." The King interrupted Lorenzo.

Alec stood and bowed before saying, "Forgive me, your grace, you know of me?" Alec asked. Confusion written all over his face that was even more boyish than Lorenzo's. Surely they weren't all so young? While Thomas was only getting towards twenty-six, Alec seemed almost a boy. Sixteen maybe?

"Of course, I know you. If my plans hadn't been rushed," James gave Thomas some side-eye. "I would have brought you in. You can really give a speech. I followed you once. Three years ago, I saw you sneak away from my mother's gala at the Capitol Theater. I followed you and saw you speak at an old tavern. You said things that would've had you killed for treason even as a child. I knew right then that eventually, you would be part of the rebellion. I planned on seeking you out when I returned to the capitol." Alec's cheeks flushed, and he forced himself to hold back a proud smile. "I actually know of all your fathers. Except Lord Tridellious. I've never heard that name." He said, pointing toward Valtan.

Only the woman still knelt. She had long black hair pulled back in a braid going halfway down her back. James made note of her and glanced at Lorenzo.

"Finally, Your Majesty, Lavene Havi. Only child of Bastian Havi and sole heir to Devil's Gate." The crowd gasped.

The King remained motionless, causing even Thomas to shift. Devil's Gate was infamous for its unparalleled wickedness. A dry dungeon hidden beneath the sand dunes of the southern desert.

Lavene stood and her face said it all. She placed both hands on the hilt of her sword and bowed. She was a lovely young woman. Close to Thomas's age, twenty-four maybe. That wasn't what yanked his heart, though. It was that her attitude reminded him of Astriea a bit. Before the merge. Before she turned pale and white. Lavene was thinner, a little taller maybe. Perhaps it gave him confirmation of what the merge was truly doing to Astriea. That it was draining her.

His only hope now was that it wouldn't kill her to complete her task.

James spoke up then, interrupting Thomas's racing thoughts.

"All of my life, there has only been one person my father let be, and that was your own. I don't know if it was out of respect or out of fear. Do you have an answer for me, Lady Havi?"

"Yes, Your Grace. While my father's territory has served as Shadon's prison all these years, no one has ever dared to look deeper into our desert. Indeed, Devil's Gate is filled with great terrors, but a kingdom of its own lies beyond those gates. An oasis. A palace and city of sandstone and cool pools. My father has kept this place hidden, along with our people. Now that you have taken the throne, now that the mountains guarding my home have fallen, I am here to ask Your Majesty for leniency. I beg you not to punish my father or incite war on our people. Herold Berelda was a terror and—"

James held up a hand to stop her.

"I have heard enough."

Lavene's head dropped, but James went on. "There is no leniency to be given, as you and your father have done nothing wrong." Lavene's eyes shot up to the King. "I know firsthand what it is like to protect whoever you can from my father." James looked at his mother and siblings, who now sat at their own table. Then he glanced back at Mira. "I hope you didn't travel all this way in fear of me. That's not the kind of king I wish to be."

"No, Your Grace. Not at all!" Diego interrupted. But it was Valtan who spoke this time, his voice deep and thundering. "We have come for a much more pressing matter."

All five of them stepped back from the dais, and Lavene stood alone in the center of the open area of the great hall.

Then the hairs on the back of Thomas's neck stood straight up.

Lavene's eyes glowed bright green, like rays of sunlight beaming through two emeralds.

The ground shook. The crowd of people cried out and latched onto whatever sturdy object they could find as sconces fell and broke. Suddenly, Lavene stomped her foot into the stone floor and a large piece of it shot into the air in front of her. She held it there with nothing but an outstretched hand. With the other, she pulled the air above her, down. The remaining sconces grew dark, as long green vines opened the windows and crawled inside. People gasped, but this time they didn't panic. The vines began to blossom flowers and fruits of all kinds. Bursting with color and life.

Some in the crowd picked strawberries and apples off them. The young, dark-haired princess gently took a vibrant yellow rose that matched her dress.

Lavene took a deep breath and as she exhaled, the vines, flowers, and fruits all receded outside. The large stone she held melded perfectly back into the floor she'd pulled it from.

The green glow in her eyes faded, and she said, "I have come to seek out Thomas Hellion. Keeper of the flame. For I house Tala, Goddess of The Earth and Nature."

Thomas stumbled. Everyone gasped and turned their gazes to him.
Shit.

That made him nervous, and he could feel the sweat forming on his forehead. Astriea would've already been moving. She would've already been introducing herself, her mind buzzing with ideas and possibilities for the next steps.

But for Thomas, this was all becoming much bigger than he'd let himself believe. It wouldn't just be Hellion and Zaniah, but now *Tala.* Another god they know very little about.

Who would be next? Before Thomas could respond, James stepped forward once more. Then there was a hand on his shoulder. Damian's.

Damian gave him a look that translated to: *You alright?*

Thomas nodded, but if he was being honest, he wasn't alright. He was already sick of playing politician. Was sick of this castle and how empty it was without Astriea in it. But most of all, he was sick of the never-ending search for a place to settle down, a place that would finally feel like home. Somewhere he could just... *Breathe.*

They'd always been taken from him.

All he wanted was a little bit of peace.

He glanced at Damian and whispered, "Yeah. I'm just tired."

James started speaking then. "We will continue this *particular* matter in private. However, I look forward to all of you serving on my personal guard so I can keep an eye on the lot of you."

Diego, Alec, Lorenzo, Valtan, and Lavene all dropped to one knee and bowed their heads. It was Alec who said, "It would be an honor to serve The Golden King."

"Lavene," James said. "You will serve on Mira's guard."

Lavene stood quickly and said, "Your Majesty, if I may, and I mean no disrespect, but it has always been my ambition to be a knight in the *King's* guard. Not a handmaiden. I humbly ask you to reconsider." She spoke the words quickly as if she worried she would be killed for speaking so boldly. Thomas nearly laughed at the insinuation that she would be a handmaiden. But no one got the chance.

A small dagger flew from Mira's hand, straight for Lavene's face, and quicker than lightning, she caught it by its handle. A breath from the tip of her nose.

Mira leaned back in her chair.

"Yes, my love, she will serve quite well." She said with an impressed smile.

"You misjudge the future Queen of Shadon, Lady Havi."

Lavene didn't argue but instead looked at Mira with newfound curiosity and respect. She bowed to her and stepped back.

Thomas and Damian found their way to their seats and ate, but honestly, tonight had been so eventful that he couldn't wait to go to sleep. Even if it meant sleeping in that bathing chamber they'd doused him in earlier.

17

Astriea

They had started the next morning with a fright. Astriea woke to see Vera and a guard chatting on the couch by the fireplace. It shocked her at first. She nearly flinched in the bed when she saw Vera's pretty face. But she forced herself to remain calm and listen.

"It doesn't matter what I do, Sera will hear nothing I have to say."

"Perhaps if she heard the entire story from *you*, instead of a certain meddling princess, she would listen." The guard mumbled.

Astriea noticed his face even through her nearly closed eyes. But her lashes could not blur away the beauty of him. He reminded her of Thomas. Looked like him in a way that made her wonder if all Telish men had a dark and rugged handsomeness about them. His hair was waves of black, the top layers of it braided into intricate Telish knots that ran smoothly down the back of his head. His jaw was broad and whenever the Duchess happened to make him smile, *that* proved even broader. She couldn't tell the color of his eyes from the distance, trying to appear as though still sleeping. But based on what she could see, he and Thomas could've been related. Cousins even.

That didn't matter, though, not when she felt Sera lightly tap her arm with a finger. Once, then twice.

Astriea slowly raised a finger and tapped it twice on Sera's leg.

Then, looking into the dark of her closed eyes, Astriea felt a wave of

THRONE OF ICE AND ASH

panic. Not intense enough to make her open them, but enough to make her feel a little nauseous. She took a deep, slow breath and peered up.

Vera was standing above her. The handsome guard leaned against the post at the foot of the bed, his arms crossed.

With... with completely silver eyes.

"You're awake. Good." Vera said with a smile.

"What do you want, Vera?" Sera growled.

Vera didn't look at Sera but at Astriea as she said, "Get up, have breakfast. There's much to discuss." Then she moved away from the bed towards the hearth.

That was when someone threw a pillow across the room. Hitting Vera in the back of the head.

"I don't take orders from you!" Sera screamed as she threw it.

Not a morning person, got it.

The guard stopped moving, and Vera did, too. But she did not lunge for her or order the guard to take her back to the dungeons. Vera simply walked over to the table by the door and took up a pitcher of water before making her way back to Sera.

Who was now standing on her bare feet in the bed.

Astriea took an irritated breath and rubbed her temples.

This would not be a good day.

"Don't you dare!" Sera yelled.

Though, there was no stopping it. Astriea felt the spray of ice-cold water and had to hold back a squeal. But Sera was soaked, as well as the bed, blankets, and pillows.

The rage-filled shriek that Sera let loose was almost enough to make her laugh. But she restrained herself.

Vera sat the pitcher down on the nightstand, adjusted her hair and tunic, and let out a triumphant humph before making to walk out the door.

"What did I say would happen if I saw your face again?" Sera spat.

Vera stared at her for a moment, titled her head, and then pulled a razor-sharp dagger from the sheath at her thigh and tossed it into the air, allowing Seraphina to catch it easily.

She moved on her. Faster than thought, Sera lunged for the Grand Duchess.

But the blade halted only a breath away from the skin of her porcelain neck. Seraphina stood frozen, struggling to make the blow.

The guard she brought with her didn't move, only sat at the foot of the bed, picking at his fingernails. But Astriea was frozen right there with Sera.

Vera didn't even flinch.

Only looked down at her and said, "Do it."

Seraphina's nostrils flared and she flinched a bit.

But that dagger dropped to the floor.

Their eyes told a thousand different stories, a thousand different words that Astriea could not translate for the life of her.

Vera released a near-silent *hm,* before turning on her heels and walking straight out of the room. The guard grabbed the knife and followed right behind her.

* * *

"I'm surprised you didn't kill her. But I'm also *not* surprised either." Astriea said as she ran her fingers through the long white waves of her hair. Trying her best to braid the small pieces on the side that the witch-hunters chopped up.

"What does that mean?" Sera squeaked as she tried to dry her hair with a towel.

"I mean, I know you loved her. And it's getting pretty obvious you still do."

"I do not—"

"Don't. I *know* you do. Even if you won't admit it to me, even if you won't admit it to yourself. But Sera, she betrayed us. Maybe if she'd told us the truth and helped us like James did, things could've been different. But she lied to us, drugged us, tortured, starved, and... She killed Tristan. Gods know what's happened to the rest of the crew. If they're even alive—"

"You think I don't know all these things? You think I don't wish and pray to all the gods to rid me of this?" Sera spat out. Like she couldn't stop the words. "I am enraged every time I see her face. Because that is the face that betrayed us. I want her to pay for everything she's done." She paused, and as she resumed speaking, her voice wavered. "But… while you were unconscious, the first time we were brought before the Tzar, when he had his guards beat me she tried to stop them. They pulled her off of me. And then…then I see those bruises. I see those bruises on her face and it takes all my might to hold back the wrath I want to vent out on the one who put them there." The words were quiet. Enough so to send a chill up Astriea's spine.

"Then, when the time comes, you need to be able to walk away. So I can put someone worthy on the Telish throne. Can you do that? I won't make you kill her. I can make that kill. But you cannot stand in the way." Astriea said the words as lightly as she could.

"If the time comes. I'll stand aside."

Astriea dipped her chin and Sera nodded back before they took to their table and ate breakfast in silence.

18

Seraphina

They'd nearly finished eating when Vera and the same guard from earlier came strutting back into the room. Sera threw her napkin onto her empty plate just as they entered.

"In a better mood now?" Vera asked, her head cocked to the side.

Seraphina leaned back in her chair and said to the Grand Duchess, "You look lovely, on your way to fuck someone for information?"

She heard Astriea choke on her juice.

The guard slammed the door so hard it startled them both, making Sera retreat a little deeper into her chair.

Vera sat down and didn't look at her.

Gods, she was still so stunning. Her face was completely healed and her eyes shone like glittering emeralds. She had her long, blood-red hair pulled back into a lovely braid with smaller ones twisting and weaving through the former. It showcased her sleek jaw and her fincly pointed chin.

The pale sunlight bounced against her skin, reminding Sera of a porcelain doll she envied for when she was a girl. It didn't have Vera's red hair, but its pale skin had the same kind of freckles that she did. Though, no matter how much she'd begged, the masters never allowed her to have a doll of her own.

She'd been trying to use that method of detachment to tear herself from these meddlesome thoughts of Vera. But it did nothing whenever she entered the room.

"The Tzar feels he would like to get to know you. But there are parameters we must first discuss." Vera replied.

"I want answers then. Now. We'll tell you nothing until our questions are answered." Astriea said with an edge of pride and a smirk—her legs crossed as she leaned back in her chair, twirling a fork between her fingers.

Astriea's ability to shift into another person when needed awed her mind. Not physically, but in every other aspect. As someone who'd gotten to know her, she'd understood that Astriea was constantly under extreme pressure. Constantly worried about everyone around her. Most of the time—in private—Astriea was in a state of anxious nail-biting and fidgeting. But she became something else entirely when threats arose. A cool and confident leader of rebellions; a spymasters' heir; a god's mighty champion.

Now, there was an understanding in this room that Telas had tried their hand at wrapping a noose around the neck of a god.

Sera turned her gaze to the guard who sat next to Vera instead of standing behind her. She raised a brow and Vera leaned forward before she said, "I'm guessing the first question is about him?" She nodded her head at the man.

"Why does he sit with us and not stand guard? You don't allow your other guards that respect. Who are you?" Sera asked him.

It was then that Sera noticed he wasn't paying attention. He was lost in thought with his gaze fixed on Astriea even beneath his helmet. Vera kicked him under the table, snapping him back to the conversation.

"Right!" He said with a forced cough. "Killian. Killian Blackspear." He removed his helmet as he said so.

Sera's gaze widened, and she gripped her fork hard. There was no way they could be related. *Tienna and her family made the name up?* She thought.

Was what the voice had whispered to her in that cell telling the truth?

"How?" Sera asked. "Where did your family name come from?"

Vera winced, and Killian released a sly smile while rolling his wholly silver eyes. An act that shouldn't have made sense or been noticeable, though it was.

"Is there something funny?" Astriea spat at him. It was hard for either of them not to look at him. Eyes full of pooling silver that almost felt hypnotizing.

"No! Well, I mean, a little." He laughed and a lovely, wide smile broke loose. Sera could've sworn Astriea softened a bit at it. "The name *Blackspear* is the Telish bastard surname."

"What?" Sera said, in shock. "I'm an orphan, not a bastard. Why would *The Lady of The Isles* name me that?"

"It's likely she didn't name you. Or that your father was a Telish bastard like me. My children will also be Blackspears. It's really not as much of an offense as it seems. There are loads of us, and some of our fathers are very involved in our lives. We also keep a record of all Blackspears, so no need to worry about any *intermingling*."

Sera's eyes widened a bit at the last fact. Keeping a census of all the Blackspears was smart, but could there really be so many of them it was necessary? How often had long-lost brothers and sisters or cousins found their way into each other's beds before such drastic action was taken?

"I see that look, as I've seen it a thousand times when having this conversation. The record has stood for four hundred years. It started with the first royal bastard to hold a seat at court. Tzar Tamich cared very much for his bastard son and did not want him thrown out into the street as his wife, the Queen, commanded. So, he created an honorable title for all bastard-born children of Telas. Established a living record of each family they came from, what house they resided under, and even created a fund to shelter and feed any Blackspears in the realm. In Telas, it is a great crime to abandon one's child, bastard or not. Whether born from desperation during war or an affair made of sound mind, mothers and fathers are bound to their children. Tzar Tamich believed this deeply before he was... Well before his dark years came for him."

Could Tienna have known her father? Could she have lied about how Sera had been found? Or did she simply find a note on her with her name? There were too many questions to ask now. Too many questions that couldn't be answered by anyone but Tienna. Sera's mind was racing.

Sera moved on from the topic and said, "Why does your Tzar want to get to know us? What does he want?"

Vera's expression dimmed, and she spoke more softly than before.

"The kingdom of Telas does not wish for magic to return."

"Obviously." Seraphina sneered. Vera ignored it and went on.

"Why?" Astriea asked.

"Because we have other methods of advancement. We have healers whose skills are unprecedented. Treatments for diseases of all kinds, weapons never thought of," Vera explained. It was Killian who cut in. "We don't *need* magic."

"That's how the Tzar, the Grand Duchess, and the prized guard feel, but what about the people? Do they not wish for fertile land? Soil instead of ice? Those are the things that come with magic's return. The land in Shadon flourished almost immediately. Why would you deprive your people of that?" Astriea sounded like she was really coming into her role as a goddess. Her voice was determined and proud. Like she'd finally begun to listen to her own mind.

"And what of the evil some of those people could cast with that magic?" Vera responded. "No matter how pretty of a picture you try to paint for this, there will always be some who are just human and some who would wipe us out like insects."

Astriea tried to argue, but Vera continued.

"Your quest is noble. We all know that. But this is not Shadon. Our entire empire is reliant on this ice."

"I don't understand why you think I care about your *empire*," Astriea growled.

"If you want this to go well, I suggest you better answer something else," Sera said, pointing at Killian. "Why are you so important?"

"I am the Tzar's bastard."

Astriea dropped her fork and Sera's eyes widened.

"So, he's your brother?"

Suddenly, the slamming of the door made a lot more sense.

74

"Yes. My older brother. Our father fell in love with his mother when he was the second-born prince. Our uncle died and our grandmother deemed Killian's mother unfit to rule, as she wasn't a noblewoman." Vera explained.

"She was pregnant with me when the Queen mother sent her away. She died when I was seven, so my father had me brought to the southern palace to meet him and my siblings. I may never rule, but I am *High Protector.*" Killian added.

"Where is my crew?" Sera asked. Leaving Killian's story behind her.

"I can't tell you that," Vera said.

"Are they alive?"

"Yes."

Sera made a face of mocking shock and said, "Wish I could say the same for Tristan."

Vera's head dropped a little.

"Sera…"

"Don't. Don't even start. He trusted you. We all did, and you betrayed us. Why? Why not come to us as James did?"

"Because it was not my orders to bring all of you back." Vera stood up and straightened the collar of her navy blue tunic. She made her way to the window and looked outside at the city below. Sera noticed her lay a bag on the desk by the bookshelf she stood next to. Noticed her take three books out of it and line the shelves with them.

It was Killian who spoke next. His voice was smooth and intriguing as he said, "Our Tzar is not like Herold Berelda, who is well known for the butchering of his own people."

"Your Tzar is known to be just as bloodthirsty." Astriea interrupted.

Killian dipped his head but went on.

"The darkness that plagued your previous king also plagues ours. But we have treatments for him."

"Treatments?" Sera said with a raised brow.

Vera spoke then, not taking her gaze off the bookshelf.

"Our healers produced injections to be given to the Tzar in order to

75

offset the effects of the darkness infecting him."

"But—" Killian started before Vera cut him off.

"Not another word, Killian." She turned her head just slightly. Her tone pained and her fingers gently rubbed against her neck.

The room was quiet for a moment.

"But the injections don't always work, do they?" Sera asked.

"He tries to control it, but Scythe is skilled at finding ways around the injections. We have to change the formulas constantly to have any lasting effects."

"Who is *Scythe*?" Astriea asked.

"*Scythe* is the monster in the darkness. The voice inside my father's head. The one you must defeat without killing the Tzar." She said, looking a tad nervous as she glanced around the room.

"I cannot do that," Astriea said, turning her eyes away from them.

"If my father could be saved, you wouldn't take the opportunity?" Vera turned toward her, her voice irritated.

"The Tzar's soul is already too far gone. Zaniah has seen it. But I will say she is not always right about *some* things."

Vera started stepping forward, her face shocked.

"So if she can be wrong, why not try to save him?" she asked, her hands pressed firmly against the table now. A brow raised.

"Because Zaniah also said that you, *Vera the Vicious*, could be redeemed." Astriea stood and Seraphina mirrored her as she went on. "So, which will it be? Can your father be saved? Or can you be redeemed?"

Vera let out a frustrated breath, and the door swung open as four ladies-maids walked in. Knocking out the tension between them all.

"I'll leave you with your new staff. This is Morra, your head ladies' maid, and her three daughters: Helena, Briar, and Belle." Vera said softly as she gestured to the servants who curtsied to them, holding empty trays in their arms.

Sera could only assume it was the youngest, Belle, who stood before her now, reaching to place her dirty plate on the tray. She was lovely, as well as her sisters and mother. Morra looked a little stern with her faint wrinkles. It told Sera she'd spent years with knitted brows. Her face still seemed kind, though. Her brown and gray hair was pulled back into a long messy braid and her daughters looked like younger versions of the woman throughout her life. Each was beautiful with their chocolate brown eyes and porcelain skin. Not a freckle or blemish to be found.

Something slithered through Sera's thoughts. A sense of unease and marvel at the same time. Then her mind shot forward. The first time in weeks that she'd seen a glimpse of the future.

The image of the three sisters standing before a dark throne, their eyes cloudy and white all over. Nearly leaking with white smoke. Before she could see more, her mind snapped back into their room. She didn't know how long she'd spaced out, but she earned a strange look from Astriea, Vera, and the ladies' maids.

Seraphina shook herself from her stupor and it struck her then that there was one thing she never told Vera. Her gift of prophecy.

The rest of the group were aware, but Vera stood there looking at her like she was trying to figure out what had just happened. Sera may not have weapons or a way out of this prison, but she has a gift. A gift that could help her escape.

A gift that she was now bound and determined to hone.

19

Astriea

illian still sat at the end of the table. Staring at her. Which was becoming uncomfortable. Astriea stood and walked over to the balcony, but something glimmered in Killian's eyes.

Silver.

Astriea whirled towards him.

"*You*, you were the masked guard that unbound my shackles."

"Correct," Killian said with a devilish smile. Bright and wide and beautiful. "How do you remember that?"

Astriea strutted to him and pulled a chair underneath her so she could look into his eyes more closely. He leaned forward.

"How are your eyes like this?" she said, peering deep into them. They seemed so easy to stare at. Pooling and swirling like silver magic while Killian just sat there, a foot or two from her, darting his eyes to different features of her face. His gaze landed on her lips again and again but always returned to her eyes. Never losing his smile.

"Do you see well?" She asked.

"Everything but colors." He replied.

Astriea watched his eyes move, without the faintest idea how he could see anything at all. And even though she didn't want to feel sorry for him. She did. Living in a world with no color didn't sound like anything to envy.

She didn't know how long she'd been staring at him, but Killian's voice was smooth as honey as he said, "If you find my eyes as mesmerizing as I do yours, then I am quite happy to see my awe matched."

"My eyes couldn't be anything special if you can't see their color." She shot back.

"They're blue. Like the North River. Almost a glow to them, like the night sky during the equinox."

She blinked and yanked herself from the stupor. Astriea leaned back away from him and rolled her eyes before standing.

This only made Killian's smile more wicked.

"I thought you couldn't see color?" She said with her chin tilted up.

"Nothing else, just your eyes, *Goddess*."

They were silent for a moment while she silently interrogated him. But he continued.

"There will be a luncheon in a few days' time. You two are expected to join."

Astriea's head shot to him, "What *luncheon?*"

"*Luncheon*, as in, lunch with the Tzar," he said with a smirk. "Who else?"

"*Why* are we having lunch with the Tzar?"

"All of us actually, he has questions and so do we. There are things that must be addressed."

Sera stepped forward then. Shoulders back and strong.

"Why didn't Vera say any of this?" She asked.

"Well she was going to, and then you ran her out of the room with some rather frustrating information." He said with a more bored tone towards Sera. As though he was irritated with her. He crossed an ankle over his knee and threw a blackberry into his mouth.

Astriea noticed how he even moved like Thomas.

Killian wasn't as large or defined as her fire god, but the way he stretched his body and his muscles pushed against his leathers, made Astriea wish Thomas would storm through that door and unleash all his fury and flame.

Some part of her even believed that Vera was toting her brother around in front of her just to prolong her torture. But for now, she'd have to deal with this bastard prince fawning over her.

For now, she'd have to hold the line until Thomas arrived.

He would come for her.

If there was anyone in this life she trusted most in the world, it was him.

He would always come for her.

20

Astriea

That night, lying in bed, something pulled on Astriea like a heavy weight. Tugging on her eyelids to close. She laid down on the bed to rest for a few minutes at most. As soon as her head hit the pillow, she was blissfully sleeping.

It was like dreaming before recognizing the garden she was standing in. And it was stunning. Like Zaniah had been restoring it for a thousand years.

The flowers were bright and full of color as roses, tulips, lilies, gardenias, and a million others flowed around a lovely red stone path. The green grass and leaves made this place look like a dream all its own. Astriea had never seen a place more beautiful. Round pillars of alabaster guarded the perimeter with nothing to hold them. Attached to the tops of the pillars were strings of floating sconces to illuminate the already sunny garden. But, regardless, the voice she listened for remained silent.

Then she ran.

Down the paths, around and around in circles, forming a tight spiral maze, until it led her to the greenhouse. Panting, she swung the door open and stepped inside.

"Z?" She looked around but did not see her. "Zaniah? Please. Please be here..." she begged whoever or whatever was listening. Right as panic crept in on her, there was a shimmer in the light only a few feet away.

That light grew bigger and bigger until the entire greenhouse shook by its might. As it disappeared, Astriea's golden mirror materialized, her radiant presence impossible to ignore.

"Z!" Astriea shouted, holding back tears. She wrapped Zaniah in a warm hug.

When they pulled back, Zaniah cupped her hands around Astriea's face and smiled brightly.

"That was a big stunt you pulled on the ship. How did you do that?"

Astriea shrugged. "I have no idea. Whatever power it was, it wasn't light. I know that for certain, but maybe it was—"

"Do not linger on these thoughts." She stopped her. Looking around like someone might be listening, even here. "They are dangerous. But I am grateful for whatever it was. They are all safe, I've seen them. It took a lot, but they're all with James and Mira."

"I know." Astriea interrupted her with a chuckle. "Somehow, Thomas was able to find me in my dreams. He told me everything. Are you okay? You've been gone for weeks. Have I ruined everything? Are we still set to merge on time?"

"Easy, easy!" Zaniah laughed. "You may feel like shit on the outside, Astriea, but I have been doing quite a lot in here." She gestured to the greenhouse. "Where do you think *this* is?"

Her mind. Her soul; her essence.

"I'm not just in your head, this garden, these flowers, all represent a vein in your being. Look how far it's come. Though, some are… resistant." She glanced at the branches of a bush, littered with flower buds still closed tight. Refusing to bloom.

"With every injection you get, an infection takes hold. It creates a wall that doesn't allow your power out. I cannot stress enough how dangerous this is. And the effect it's had on your body… Astriea it's killing you."

Beneath the stubborn flowers, at their base, lie black soil. Like a shadow, the coloring leeched up the stems.

"I need you to try your best to convince them to stop. Whatever you can. I'm not sure I can hold everything together in here and fight it off for much longer. And if you don't expel this power soon, I fear it might—"

"Don't. I can imagine it well enough." Astriea stopped her.

All that power just boiling under the surface. She didn't want to think for a moment about how it would feel to be ripped apart by it.

When Astriea turned to look at some new sprouting plants, she saw straight through them. Revealing golden, pulsing strings. Then, realization hit her that she was falling into those strings, and then into her power.

Astriea split into a million different pieces of herself. All flowing in and out of her own body.

And then she was down the hall. She couldn't see herself or feel herself. But she could see the hall outside their room. Before she could think any longer, she was in that dark throne room.

With only another thought, she found herself standing on one of the massive cliffs of ice that shaped the fjord. She could see the two mountains on either side of the bay. Like beacons of shimmering ice, or towers to guard the fjord.

She willed her power to halt and it obeyed. If she had eyes, she would've cried. But she wasn't sure that was possible right now. Before her was the North Sea. Her first unobstructed view of it in weeks. Six it had been now. Six weeks of nothing but being torn from her home. From Thomas.

No food was easy to eat without him inhaling it next to her. No bed felt comfortable without him in it. Nothing felt like home. Nothing felt safe.

The sun was setting over the horizon and Astriea turned to look at the shining silver city behind her.

It was glorious. Every building a glittering silver tower in hundreds of different sizes. Some were tall and thin, others short and wide. The castle was built directly into the cliffs at the fjord's end.

It was the most beautiful thing she'd ever laid her eyes on. A blanket of snow kissed the tops of the towers and the cliffs surrounding the city.

Gods. This place looked damn near impregnable.

A wave of fear washed over her. How the hell would Thomas get through? Without another thought, she jumped back to Zaniah in the garden.

Going back into her inner mind did not feel good. Honestly, it felt like having a dislocated shoulder shoved back into place. But it was her whole body. She let out a yelp and gripped Zaniah's shoulder tight.

"Gods!" Astriea panted. "What was that? How did I do that?"

"That was astral projection. It's actually something most people are capable of, though it takes an immense amount of study and focus. And it's harder for us because we're never really at rest."

"How long have I been gone? The Tzar wants us to attend a luncheon with him in a few days. I'm guessing as a new form of interrogation." Astriea said with an eye roll. Zaniah made a foul expression. "You are worrying Sera. I can feel her pacing around the bed. Hold on..." Zaniah squinted. "Oh, my..."

"What?"

"I see her. You better get back up there." Zaniah's smile made Astriea reflect it.

With the snap of Zaniah's fingers, a lovely woven hammock appeared hanging from the doorway. Astriea climbed inside and rested her head.

"Z?"

"Yes?"

"Do you still stand by what you said? About the heirs? About..."

"Vera?" Zaniah finished for her and knitted her brows slightly. "Yes. We are not seeing the entire picture with Vera. I know we have reasons to hate her. But... She's hiding something. Something shielded even from me. But I looked again and her soul burns bright in the light. Even more so than it did before. Whatever side she's on, it's not Scythe's."

"Do you remember Scythe?"

"Yes. Scythe was the priest who led my execution. But more than that, he is the maker of it all. The dark knight who imprisoned me."

Astriea swallowed. *Gods.*

"I don't have time to explain it all now, but every day you go without an injection, the more I remember. See what you can learn of this place, Astriea. Thomas will come for you with an army at his back. As romantic as that is, you cannot allow this. A war between the nations will only strengthen Scythe. Battle and blood-lust make minds easy to conquer, and easy to manipulate. You must broker peace however you can. So take your time, learn, and adapt to your new environment. I told you once to leave the mountain spy behind, but we require her services now."

Astriea only nodded. Then she closed her eyes once again.

21

Thomas

Thomas dragged the local saddlers and blacksmiths to the cliffs where the dragons nested. After three hours of coaxing, Night-cleaver let one saddler and blacksmith measure their back. When they'd finally finished, the two of them let him know it would be a few days before the armored saddle was complete, and kindly asked him to be patient with them. He obliged.

Days later, he found himself once again at the dragon's nest with the freshly stitched and forged saddle thrown over his shoulder. It was beautifully pieced together. The seat, made of luxurious, mahogany-colored leather, perfectly matched every strap. The outer pieces surrounding it were dark plates of metal. He'd thought it iron at first glance. His raised brows at the blacksmith.

"It is *Sharinian steel*, my lord. Mined from the cliffs your dragon emerged from. Strongest metal in the world. The kingdom exhausted its supply of it centuries ago, turning it into a mere legend. But now... Now there is enough to equip an entire legion."

He carried that piece of information with him all the way back to his dragon.

Thomas placed the saddle on the ground before Night-cleaver; allowing them to smell it, and get an understanding of what it was.

In no time, the straps were securely fastened around the dragon's immense neck and belly.

"Go on then, give it a test flight before I throw myself on there," Thomas sighed. Each word accompanied by a ton of dread. Night-cleaver huffed and stretched out its massive wings before darting straight into the sky with one great leap of its four mighty legs.

He gave the saddler and blacksmith their leave, and told them to expect to make at least fifty more armored saddles.

"Have you told the king yet? Of the *Sharinian steel*?" Thomas asked.

"My master did, yes my lord."

Ugh, *my lord*, he thought. The word felt like a scrape of rusted metal down his spine. But he steadied himself enough to say, "You are only an apprentice?"

"I am."

"You will advance quickly in your trade, I expect."

Thomas smiled at the young blacksmith.

"Thank you, my lord."

He bowed slightly before leaving him alone on the cliffs.

When Night-cleaver returned, the saddle remained in the same exact position as before they took off.

That was the moment he realized his hands were shaking. Terribly. Thomas was the only one who could communicate with the dragons. Not that he thought you could really call it *communicating*. The only one that even listened to him was Night-cleaver. He guessed it helped that all of them obeyed his dragon, though.

Even so, he had to learn how to fly them.

His stomach churned as he climbed up Night-cleaver's back. Palms sweating and slippery against the smooth black scales. His throat dried out entirely, and every time he tried to swallow, it was a fight.

He sat in the seat and adjusted the long, thick leather reins. Not that he'd need them for anything other than holding on. But he wrapped them around his hands and then clutched the lower handles on the saddle.

Then Night-cleaver started moving.

His skin felt like it was going to jump off his body as the dragon broke into a run toward the cliff's edge. Nearly galloping.

It's just like a horse... It's just like a horse...

But this was no horse.

This creature of flame and scale and fury.

His heart pounded hard against his chest with each barreling step Night-cleaver took. Something in his mind told him to *jump, jump, jump!*

He took in a sharp breath as he saw the waves crash against the rocky cliffs below, and then nothing. He'd shut his eyes.

But when he peeled them apart, there was nothing but the feeling of the open sky. Nothing but a song of sweet spring air dancing across his skin. He didn't look down, not yet, just ahead.

After about twenty minutes of deep ragged breaths and vomiting twice over the ocean, after the panic faded and he could release the heavy grip on his handles, Thomas leaned his weight to the right. Turning Night-cleaver until he could see the summer palace glittering under the sun. It looked so small from here. And so... *beautiful.*

Gods, what he would give to show this to Astriea. While she would have a hard time admitting it, she could be rather *patriotic* when the need arose. So, deep down, she would love to see how beautiful her homeland had become in her absence. Even *The Dead Forest* had come to life again, its unending shadow now waning to make way for gorgeous hues of green.

"It's lovely," Thomas said aloud to Night-cleaver. The dragon huffed and changed direction.

"Whoa! Where are we going?"

Like a bolt of lightning, they shot through the sky and headed north along the coast. Farther and farther until Thomas could see hundreds of stone columns, each of them only far enough apart for a single dragon to squeeze through. All of them were just rocky remains from years of the sea eroding the cliff's face. But looked sharp. Like they'd rip him to pieces.

Thomas swallowed hard, and if he'd had anything left in his stomach he would've hurled over again.

"Night-cleaver... I don't think I'm—"

He didn't get a chance to finish. Night-cleaver dove.

Down, down, down, until they were feet away from meeting their doom against a rough sea and rocky cliffs. The dragon's wings extended, and they glided along the water.

Thomas released a thankful groan as they evened out.

Then those columns of broken cliffs were upon them.

On instinct, Thomas wrapped the straps once around his hands and tightened his thighs around the saddle like he would on a horse.

He leaned left.

Then right.

Left again.

Then he dove underneath a huge natural stone arch.

Rose above another.

Then banked right again.

Thomas and Night-cleaver dipped and dove through the broken cliffs between the King's Wood and the North Wood over and over until their path cleared and they were met by the beaming rays of sunset.

High tide had just started, and the sky was colored in a brilliant mixture of pink and purple.

They hovered there for a while and watched as the sun fell over the horizon.

* * *

When Thomas returned to the dragon nest, he had a particular feeling someone was waiting for him.

It was *particular* because he could see him from a mile out.

Valtan Tridellious stood with his hands raised while Thomas dismounted and stretched.

He'd been flying for hours. Had overcome his fear of heights—for the most part, anyway. Now all he wanted to do was eat and go to bed.

"What can I do for you, Valtan?" Thomas asked while he unwrapped the bandages tied around his hands.

"I understand you are close to the *Lightbringer*?" he asked cautiously.

Thomas raised his eyebrows. *"Lightbringer?* That's a new one. But you're correct, I am close to her. Why do you ask?"

Valtan hesitated. Oddly enough, he began twisting and rubbing his fingers in his hands. A nervous habit Thomas was all too familiar with.

"I was sent here... From outside the dome."

The what? Thomas couldn't stop the look he let slip. And Valtan released a frustrated breath when he saw it.

"For a thousand years, the lands of Shadon, Telas, and Sirey have been cut off from the outside world. There are countries all around these. There are minor gods and goddesses outside of this place. But the most important, the most powerful, the primordial and elemental gods were trapped here."

Before his mind could spiral at the revelation of the world getting a whole lot bigger, training for the rebellion kicked in like instinct.

"And how do you know all this?"

"I come from a country on the western side of the dome. Every five to ten years, ambassadors from all over the world send a ship of volunteers to cross into the dome. It's always a suicide mission."

"Then why go? If everyone usually dies, why even try?" Thomas asked.

"Because the world needs magic again. While basic casts and conjures are possible, the lands have become barren and wasted. Our resources are draining away. Not even the minor gods can fight against it. Over a thousand years, their magic has all but left them entirely. The elemental gods are our last hope. Some people take the journey because they are devout. Some because redemption was offered to them if they succeeded. And some... some still believe there is a mighty destiny in store for them."

That last bit sounded a little distressed.

"What about you? Why did you come?" Thomas questioned.

"Well, if I'm being honest, I came because I hoped to find my sister."

And just like that, Thomas's heart ripped open for him.

"Why did *she* come?"

"The latter, I'm afraid. She told our parents that she felt something calling her from inside the dome. Sometimes it felt like a person. Sometimes a place. But she begged our parents to allow it. They refused, and she ran away. Took the next boat out to the dome."

"I'm sorry to hear that, Valtan. I know how it feels when a sibling disappears on you."

He patted Valtan on the shoulder, and they headed toward the castle together.

"We should bring this to James and Damian immediately. They should know what's out there. How did you manage to get in?" He asked carefully, doing his best not to startle him by keeping the questions going.

"We were standing on the deck of our ship when a flash of light—greens and blues and purples—broke out across the sky before us. We could see the shape of mountains through the dark mist, but the earth began to shake. Before we knew it, the mist cleared, and the mountains we saw before had broken; shattered. The impact against the sea capsized our ship. I was the only one out of twenty volunteers to survive. At least a hundred dragons shot into the air and headed east. So, I swam to shore and followed them. I'll admit I got a bit turned around and wound up at the edge of The Dead Forest and the South River. That's when I ran into Lavene and the others. We all sort of... fit."

Thomas smiled and nodded. They drew closer to the castle now, and his stomach growled ferociously at him when he smelled the scent of pork coming from the kitchens.

"I'd like you to meet my brother as well. His name is Draes. He'll be somewhere around here, I'm sure of it..." He paused for a moment too long because the silence had grown awkward. "So, if you don't mind my asking—"

"Why am I ghostly pale and huge?"

Thomas's eyes went wide, but Valtan just laughed.

"That's the *official* reason I'm here. It happened overnight. My parents worried about what it meant and sent me to the elders at our local temple to be evaluated. They told me it was the mark of *Astriea*—who you call Zaniah—that I was needed for her ascension."

"Gods, she couldn't have just given you a vision or something?" Thomas said as he pushed open one of the castle doors.

Valtan laughed again and said, "It's really not that big of a deal. Though when I find Atara she will probably tell me I look dead, and she'd be right."

Thomas laughed and then stopped dead in his tracks.

He looked at Valtan. At his features instead of the obvious changes made to him. Noted the shape of his eyes and the curve of his mouth.

"Valtan, how old are you?"

The man tilted his head and said, "Thirty-eight. I mean, I'm half fae, so my age halt happened ten years ago. Why?"

"How likely is it that your sister's ship would've been heading for Monolith?"

Valtan didn't answer at first. Just stared at him with wide eyes.

"What are you trying to say, Thomas?"

"I'll tell you this. I've only known one woman named Atara in all my life. She had silky hair, black as night. Tawny, golden brown skin that never faded, even in Monolith's coldest winters."

Tears welled in Valtan's eyes.

"A man named Aaron Blake found her on his journeys through the mountains. Healed and cared for her for a long time. She married him and bore him a daughter. Atara Blake helped found the Shadon Rebellion and raised Zaniah's heir." He paused for a moment, taking in the way everything had started to snap into place like a fated puzzle board. "The purpose behind Astriea's name is so clear now. Valtan, I don't think Atara knew how she fit into all this, but she was right to come here."

"She's gone, isn't she?"

Thomas nodded and rested a hand high up on Valtan's shoulder.

"Let's get you a drink, and I'll tell you about your sister and your niece."

22

Seraphina

The days that passed didn't come swiftly. Sera and Astriea went to great lengths not to be caught mapping and surveying the castle every time they were pulled from their rooms for check-ups with the healers or interrogations by the Tzar.

Today, they would attend a luncheon with the entire royal family.

Vera had been around more and more as well. Stopping in every few hours to see what they were up to. And Killian did everything in his power to be near Astriea. Yesterday, he'd sat in the chair across from where she sat on the couch and watched her file her nails like a little boy who'd seen a princess for the first time.

They had even come to have a secret language consisting of Killian spewing Telish poetry to her that she didn't understand and Astriea responding by rolling her eyes and changing her seat. Sometimes she added a vulgar gesture for dramatic effect.

Now and again, Vera would come in and just sit in a chair by the window. Like she was doing now as Sera glanced up at her from the food she'd barely touched at the table. Most of the time, she would read something. A different book just about every time she came in. But sometimes... Sometimes she just stared out that window at the city below. Or maybe she stared at the clouds. Sera couldn't be sure.

And there, in the rare beams of sunlight that fell in through the stained glass, Sera could see the other girl sitting in that chair. Like her vision had warped and taken new form only around Vera.

A young woman with long, red hair messily thrown into a braid. Loose, white tunic sleeves falling off her shoulders instead of the tight, dark blue one and black chain mail that nearly covered all of her. The vision was so intense, that she could nearly feel the breeze from the tide.

"Do you miss it?" Sera said without thinking. She hoped Vera didn't hear her, but the vision of Reyna faded away quickly as Vera's head snapped toward her. An expression of shock across her face. She steeled it, though.

"The Telish people are known far and wide for their skill on horseback. We are not a people meant for the sea..." Vera paused and started twisting her fingers in her lap, then looked back out that window. "But if there were no price to pay for that life, I would quickly return to it."

The grand duchess may have been skilled at hiding her pain, but her brother was not. Killian's fist was balled up and white. His face, the portrait of guilt and despair. His gaze now lost on the fire in the hearth.

The silence was only broken when Vera rose from her seat and made to leave.

"The luncheon is in four hours. It will be in the palace greenhouse, so it will be hot and humid. There is climate-appropriate attire in the armoire and I will see you both there. Killian will escort you."

For the first time, Sera had nothing to say. Neither did Astriea, so it seemed. So they both silently nodded, and Killian followed Vera out the door.

* * *

The clothes Vera mentioned were actually quite comfortable. The top's bodice only reached halfway down her stomach, and her skirt was raised high enough to reveal a single strip of skin above her belly button. Sera's were a dark gray and made from some of the lightest material she'd ever felt. It was smooth as silk and so breathable she worried about the integrity of it. How many hits could she take in a fight before she was naked? The sheer sleeves flowed loosely down her arms and cuffed around her wrists. The same with her pants around her ankles.

Just then, Astriea came out of the bathing chamber in her ensemble. It was similar to Sera's in its overall design, but white and lined with gold trim. Astriea's tunic also twisted between her breasts and then tightly fastened around her ribs.

"Damn, Sera," Astriea said with her brows raised at her. "You're going to give Vera a hard time." Her wicked smile had Sera blushing uncontrollably, and she couldn't help but curse herself for it.

Sera straightened herself and said to Astriea, "I was just about to tell you what a shame it is that Thomas can't see you right now." Sera picked at her tunic. "I bet he'd rip right through this flimsy stuff."

Astriea investigated her clothes and the sheerness of it. Then they looked at each other and took a step back from the mirror to see themselves in better light.

Before their eyes were every crease and crevice they had to offer. The shapes of their peaked nipples barely peered through the fabric.

"Oh, Thomas wouldn't stand a chance," Astriea said with a wide smile. Sera merely rolled her eyes and took two golden pins to pull back some of her hair that normally fell in her face.

Then Killian knocked on the door.

23

Astriea

The royal greenhouses were stunning.

Before her was a massive atrium that stretched on and on. The sun peered through the green glass above them. And the heat... Oh, the heat was the best part. Too warm with their cloaks on, but in the thin clothes they donned underneath? Perfect. It felt like a warm summer day by the lake. The air was a bit dense, but her nose was treated to a symphony of aromas from a myriad of plants. Eucalyptus, rose, lily, lavender.

Those were just the ones she could take in at that moment as they walked to the end, where a long metal table was stretched across a room surrounded by couches and small water fountains.

No, not water fountains, but tiny pools filled with colorful fish just swimming about.

Astriea noted the large metal vents above the walls and just below the domed glass ceiling. But she also noticed the sunflowers, gardenias, tulips, and a hundred others scattered about the area in neatly potted planters. Along the rounded walls of the tower hung vines and shelves and a small circling staircase. Their own tropical paradise, hidden in a cold silver tower and sheltered from the eternal winter.

She wished Zaniah was awake to see it.

As they approached, the table now laid out with an assortment of fruits and vegetables and slices of bread—a young, red-haired boy made his way toward them.

"Lady Astriea, Lady Seraphina, this is Prince Pilas Shataar. Fourth born son of the Tzar, and royal spymaster."

Astriea allowed the young boy to kiss her hand, and Seraphina did the same.

"Royal Spymaster? You're quite young for a job like that," she asked hesitantly.

"No younger than you were when you became heir to the Caltillion Mountains."

The shock of what he said made her tilt her head.

"I wasn't aware my story had been told." She said, giving Killian some angry glances now and then.

"I have eyes and ears in all sorts of places, my lady. Even where those mountains once stood." Pilas turned to walk away and made it all the way to his seat at the table before Astriea realized what he said. *Even where those mountains once stood.*

"What does that mean? *Where they once stood?* What do you mean by that?" She was walking towards him then. Suddenly desperate for answers. King Herold destroyed the town of Monolith, but the mountains? What happened to the mountains?

Pilas said from his seat, pouring a glass of wine, "You didn't hear? The day we captured you, something rocked the whole country. The entirety of the Caltillion Mountains crumbled." He traced a finger in the air. "All the way down your western coast." Astriea leaned against the table, intensely hanging on to every word. Pilas paused and took a sip of his wine. "Do you know what happened after that?" He said in an almost croon. He was teasing her. Baiting her.

And he'd done it.

Seraphina was at her side then, tugging her arm.

"Let it go for now." She cautioned. Then more people piled inside and made seats around the room on various couches and chairs.

A few more young men and the young princess, Thea, found their seats at the table as well.

"Hello, *Seraphina*," Thea said happily as she batted her sweet little eyelashes at Sera. Astriea noticed how hard her companion tried to keep her smile contained, but she nodded to the little princess.

As the two of them sat, Sera clutched onto Astriea's hand under the table.

"What's wrong?" Astriea whispered. She noticed the worry in her eyes.

"It's like I can sense her, Vera. She's almost here."

"Is it bad? What are you sensing? Is she coming to kill us or something?" Astriea quietly asked as she nervously looked around for the grand duchess.

"No... no, it's not like that. I... I—"

She didn't get to finish. Right then, Vera Shataar entered the room, and it seemed to Astriea that she had stolen all of Seraphina's breath.

24

Seraphina

Waves of panic and desperation washed over Seraphina the moment she saw her. Vera had pinned up all of her hair atop her head in an elegant, braided crown, with a small silver diadem peeking out from behind it. She wore the same fabric as they did, only there was no split in the middle. Vera walked toward her in a shimmering silver gown that flowed lightly away from her hips, her waist, her chest...

Her neck and shoulders were on full display under thin glittering straps. Her face healed of any bruises or cuts, and her eyes... Her eyes made Sera thankful she was sitting down. That her knees would not crack under her weight against the floor.

"Sera?" Astriea whispered to her as she squeezed her hand.

"I can't breathe," Sera whispered back. Her eyes still on Vera.

She stopped where she stood and those green eyes were piercing into hers. For a moment, the air she fought for became crisp and clear.

"Sera..." Astriea whispered.

She didn't answer. "Sera." She said again. "Sera, everyone is looking."

Like a candle blown out by a breeze, Seraphina blinked and her heart slammed against her stomach as it returned to her body.

"Seraphina," Astriea whispered again as she grabbed Sera's other hand and pulled it under the table.

The fork in that hand had been bent in half, and nearly everyone saw it. Vera claimed her seat at the table, Killian pulling out her chair for her.

Then the Tzar of Telas was being rolled out to the table in a wooden chair with wheels. Everyone stood, including Astriea and herself.

"Welcome, Lady Astriea, Lady Seraphina." The Tzar didn't sound the same as before. When he'd dragged them from their cell and had Sera beaten at his feet.

This time, he sounded lighter and happier. More at ease.

"I assume you've taken well to your new accommodations?" He asked.

"Anything is better than a cell." Astriea retorted. Sera leaned back in her chair to observe.

"Yes... I am sorry about that. I have a hard time keeping him at bay. Scythe. He is... as they say, *the monster under my bed.*"

"Who is he?" Astriea asked, this time a bit softer.

"We do not know who he is. Only that he is responsible for so much death and pain..."

The Tzar's eyes shot to Vera for only a split second. She didn't so much as look up from her food. But he went on, "I don't wish to speak about such things, doing so seems to draw him near. That's how it feels, anyway. And the new formula my brilliant daughter created has made my mind clearer than it has been in ages. I understand you have questions. I understand you are angry. But I implore you both to get to know the lot of us while the times are good. And know that we feel no pride in the image Scythe has made us paint of ourselves. The answers to *those* questions are forbidden to be spoken."

The look he gave them as he said that last bit made the hairs on her arms rise.

"So... It is not your wish to keep us hostage?" Astriea asked, slowly, carefully.

The Tzar's eyes darted back and forth across the domed ceiling as if he were looking for something.

But he looked back at Astriea and leaned forward before he shook his head in answer.

"Vera's elixirs will not keep him out forever. The next time we speak, may not be as pleasant as this, dear goddess." He reached a hand across the table and Seraphina went on alert. Her skin tingled a bit as she watched his hand wrap gently around Astriea's. And then he whispered, "Let us do whatever possible to see the good in each other while we still can."

Astriea looked at Sera and then they both nodded to him. He smiled so brightly that Sera saw it then, Vera's smile.

More accurately, Vera had her father's smile. And that was something both lovely and heartbreaking.

25

Astriea

The Tzar of Telas differed from before.

He was kind to everyone in the room, even the servants, as they ran back and forth refilling water and wine. The food was delicious; she had to admit. If Thomas had been here, he would've fit right in. The royals of the Telish court wasted no time eating with etiquette among their family. They laughed and even threw food at each other. The grand duchess threatened to gut her brother, Pilas, like a fish if he ruined her dress. Which was something Astriea never thought she'd hear *Vera the Vicious* say. But she caught Sera smirk at the threat.

Thea, the youngest princess, had the most infectious laugh she'd ever heard. Astriea saw the Tzar smile brightly at the sound of it. That's when some puzzle piece snapped into place and her heart sank a little.

She would have to kill this man.

This father that made his children's eyes shine. They had gone to extensive efforts to bring him back from Scythe. Astriea looked at Vera, trying to swallow her wine while Pilas poked her with a fork.

She developed the Science Guild. And while Astriea had her own grievances with the guild, it was impressive. The princess was doing everything she could to save him.

Her King, her hero.

And now, it seemed that today was one of those days where all Vera's hard work paid off. Even if it was just long enough for lunch and a peaceful interrogation.

Maybe this *is the woman who can be redeemed,* she thought. *And I'm going to rip away the only thing she cares for.*

The dread must have shown in her expression because the table grew quiet.

"So you've pieced it together?" the Tzar asked.

"How do you fight him? Other than the injections? There was nothing left of Herold Berelda's soul. How have you kept yours intact?"

"I see we're covering all the big questions, eh? Alright." The Tzar leaned back in his chair. "I met Herold Berelda in my youth. Before I was meant to be *Tzar.* And I will say this: he was always soulless. So much so that when Vera and his eldest *living* son, James, came of age to marry, I refused his offer to join our kingdoms. He offered more than any king would ever need. Enough to make you question where all that coin came from in the first place. And… that man came willingly to Scythe. I did not. But my soul is not, as you say, *intact.*"

"Father—" Vera started. The Tzar raised a gentle hand to her.

"How long did it take? Before he could take you completely?" Sera asked, and Vera's father would not look at her. Instead, he looked at Vera with so much sorrow in his eyes that Astriea thought they'd both burst into tears.

"I was ten," Vera whispered. He reached over and gently wrapped his hand around hers.

"We must banish Scythe. Surely you understand this," Sera said a bit sharply.

"Of course. While my daughter has done wondrous work with her Science Guild, when she ascends the throne, Scythe will come for her as well. I will not allow it."

"Then why not stand aside? Set us free! Let me restore magic here, banish Scythe from your lands," Astriea said a little louder than she intended. She didn't have time for this. She didn't have time to wait for the Tzar to change his mind. But if this could be done peacefully, she'd try it.

"Because we built our entire system on this ice." Vera interrupted. "These towers would fall. Our people would die under the rubble of the Silver City. Of half the cities in Telas."

"We could evacuate everyone. Get them all out before it happens." Sera added.

"And the other cities? Telas is the largest country in the world. We have six cities built into the ice. The caves house our greenhouses, and our water system, and there are many throughout the land whose homes are made entirely of ice. Your plan leaves them with nothing. Where will they go? There will be no palaces to shelter them."

"Are you telling me," Astriea asked, "that every home you have is built into the ice or made of it?"

Vera nodded.

"Well, there is one place at the southern border, but it's a small summer home in *Terrenia*. And *Dartellio*, on the western cliffs, but either would only hold roughly two hundred people, including the servants and guards already residing there." Killian interjected as he stood at the Tzar's back. "Though the cities would gladly take any refugees, Dartellio would be overrun."

"Look, as much as we'd love to just forgive everything that's happened and join in this twisted family meal with peace," Sera started, then she stood. Leaning with both palms pressed against the table. "My lady *will* unlock the magic here. The ice *will* fall, whether you wish it to or not."

Whatever Sera was doing was not a part of the plan. They were supposed to be getting to understand them so they could make a strategic plan for escape.

Astriea noticed Vera's brows knit with irritation. Killian then stepped closer to the Tzar and said, "Those are bold words for a captive."

"That doesn't matter," Astriea cut in. Irritation swelled under her skin. To hell with bowing and making peace with the people who'd killed their friend, and captured them and their crew. As well as everything after.

"Because Thomas is coming for you?" Vera interrupted. "The Dragon of Telas has been hunted generation after generation, for stealing power from our patron god, *Hellion*. I will be the next to snuff him out. Let him come here."

Astriea laughed. Loudly and boldly.

"You truly are a fool!" She could hardly get the words out, but she could nearly die from the irony.

Pilas spit out his wine, trying to contain his drunken laughter. "Don't let her ruin the fun. She's never approved of the hunting of Hellion house. You've just ticked her off."

"Quiet, Pilas," Vera said, smacking the back of the boy's head. He shut up instantly.

"Something I guess I never mentioned, Vera. The Dragon of Telas is the reincarnated spirit of Hellion himself." Seraphina said sharply. "Or, who knows, maybe I did in between rounds and you just chose not to believe it."

Vera rose from the table and strode off across the room. If Sera felt any regret from the sharp remark toward the princess, it didn't show on her face.

"Vera, we don't have much time left." Another boy, dark-haired and twin to the one sitting next to him, stated quickly as she hastened through the great doors.

"I'll be right back!"

Sera sat back down in her chair, and the family continued to eat dutifully while they all waited. Astriea watched the Tzar force himself to eat as though he were in pain.

26

Seraphina

No one said a word for the entire ten minutes Vera was gone. When she returned, she had an old dusty book in her hands. It was huge, and the pages looked ancient.

"Vera! That book is not intended to leave the cathedral!" The Tzar said sternly. Vera didn't even respond.

"What is it?" Astriea asked, peeking over her wine glass.

"This book," Vera started but glanced around the room and at her father. Then she opened it. "This book is the only unaltered record of Hellion we have. We have worked effortlessly to keep it safe. Away from *him*."

Scythe, she meant. Afraid to say his name.

"I've seen that book before. At the temple. The only place in the world untouched by the dark. I recognize the golden stitching on that cover, though the rest was once dark green."

Vera opened it and revealed a page with a drawing of Hellion in all his burning glory. Beneath the drawing were the words: *Hellion, Firey One. God of the sun and all things that burn. Guardian of wayward souls and patron of rebellion.*

Sera saw Astriea smirk. Could almost feel the pride coming off her.

Vera rolled her eyes and turned the pages towards the end.

"Here, *And Hellion fell from the heavens. In the ruble of the crater he lie in, a wanderer takes his power.*"

"That's it?" Astriea asked. "Generations of slaughter, of hunting families, over a single sentence in an old book?"

Now Sera could definitely feel the anger pouring out of Astriea.

"A sentence none of you ever had the good sense to actually understand?" Astriea stood with unnerving calm. Sera took up her position at Astriea's back. "This could get us killed." She whispered the warning. Taking a quick glance around the room. The courtiers now watched them from the corners of their eyes.

"Hellion fell and chose a mortal line to house his soul. *The wanderer took his power.* That doesn't mean it was stolen, and that doesn't mean those families deserved what yours did to them."

"May I see that book?" Sera said, trying to break some of the tension. She remembered something she read in that book once. Something that made no sense until now. But she had a hunch. She warily made her way to Vera's side and flipped through the pages until she found what she was looking for.

"Ah ha!" she shouted and tapped the page. "Here, read that aloud for us." Sera then turned and went back to Astriea's side. The pained understanding that flashed in Vera's beautiful eyes almost broke Sera's heart all over again. She hated seeing her hurt. Even if Vera might deserve it. But the thought of her in pain made her feel sick.

"While the golden one cherished mortals and his creatures, he knew no greater love than the keeper of the stars..."

"My Lords and Ladies of the Royal court of Shataar, may I present again, Astriea, Goddess of magic, life, and the *stars*," Sera said with a wicked grin and a mocking bow at her waist. "You've taken a great many things from Hellion. Chased him, hunted him. Killed him again and again. And now you have woken him fully. Stolen his only love. A *dragon's* greatest treasure."

They all winced at that.

"You are all fools if you think he won't come for her." Sera laughed.

"You've given us many things to consider," the Tzar began. "There has been enough talk of our differences, and I feel it is time for another

107

treatment and to retire myself before the evening festivities. I am no longer as lively as I once was." He chuckled a bit at that, and Vera stood to wheel him out. As they were leaving the table, the Tzar said, "I understand what you came here to do, even if my children do not. I only ask you to be patient with them. That you... *aid* them when the monster crawls out from under the bed."

Sera did not have the words, but Astriea spoke for both of them.

"We wish you a pleasant rest, your grace."

A smile tried to break free across the old man's face and he nodded before Vera handed him off to the guards and healers waiting for him in the hall.

* * *

The next four hours of eating turned into something else entirely when servants came lining up with ale, wine, and hard dark liquor. Something, no doubt, that had been immediately ordered to ease the tension in the room.

Sera and Astriea happily obliged in the wine.

Killian carted around the two of them for a while as he introduced them to all of his and Vera's siblings. Vera was *technically* the eldest of the royal line. Then there were the twins, Salrek and Dalron.

Salrek was second born with raven black hair like Killian's. As second in line for the throne, he served as commander of Telish Armies. He and his brother were two years younger than Vera, twenty-three.

Dalron—third born—was just like his brother in every way except his personality. They were very handsome, strong-jawed young men with the same rugged refinement as Killian. As Commander of the Telish Navy, Dalron was a bit more carefree, as he told them, *"There's not really a lot we care for on the sea, so my position is just a formality at this point."* He was funny and approachable against his twin's serious demeanor.

Later they'd met Caedyn, fifth-born son and coin keeper. He, like all the boys in their family except for Pilas, it seemed, had shaggy black hair as well. He was seventeen. Still a child, but smart enough to be named coin keeper. Killian mentioned later that Caedyn was the brightest of all the royal families, aside from Vera herself.

That was impressive.

With the court mingling around them, another dark-haired boy made his way towards them with the young princess, Thea, holding his arm.

His name was Nate. He was the sixth-born and too young for any titles and responsibilities. He mostly just enjoyed showing Thea around and talking to her. The two of them made it hard not to imagine Killian and Vera at that age.

Had there been anyone in this castle to shield them the way Nate and Thea have been?

Sera watched for hours as Astriea made conversation with courtiers and royals. Eventually, one by one, the Tzar's children retired as well. Salrek and Dalron escorted two giggling maidens with them.

Vera avoided Seraphina for the remainder of the night. Every time she tried to look at her, the princess had her eyes set in another direction. Or was laughing with nobles.

So, to deal with it, Sera let Pilas talk her into a few spiriters. Small doses of the dark liquor to be drunk quickly and washed down with something else.

"Alright, my ladies, had enough fun?" Killian slurred a bit. Sera and Astriea both nodded at him, and he led them back into the cold halls of the castle.

Even then, the heat in her blood from the wine and liquor kept her warm enough that she didn't even use her cloak.

She and Astriea just giggled again and again as they fell over on each other.

"You're going to get us in trouble," Astriea whispered too loudly.

"You fell on me!"

They toppled again and laughed uncontrollably on the floor. Killian didn't stop walking. He just kept going and going. Completely oblivious to his lack of prisoners. Which was hilarious.

The two of them didn't move. Mostly because they wanted to see if he noticed, or how long it would take him to. They'd never make it out of here this drunk, but it would still be funny to watch Killian lose his wasted mind.

When he finally realized and came back for them, he tilted his head as he said, "Look, I'm drunk too, and it's hard enough to navigate these halls like this. Stick together, so we find the right room." His smile and laugh made theirs start again, and it echoed across the hall.

They trotted along for a few more minutes before Seraphina stopped to look at a painting.

It was Vera. No older than fifteen and sitting for her portrait in a lovely pale-green, shimmering gown. Her red hair pulled back into a low regal ponytail and a beautiful silver and matching green kokoshnik—a traditional Telish tiara—sat atop her head. The real kicker here was her smile.

Bright and wide.

Genuine.

"That was a year before her mother, the queen, passed."

Sera didn't look at Killian but said to him, "She seems so different now."

"She isn't. She was good at keeping secrets even then." He took a deep breath. Filled with regret. Or maybe guilt. "My little sister is a wonder, a heavily fortified wonder who has known enough loss." She heard him turn up a bottle and take three heavy chugs.

She looked at him then. His silver eyes swirling more lazily than usual.

"Come on, let's head back." He breathed.

"You two go on, I'll catch up…"

"Are you sure?" Astriea asked. Sera glanced at her for a moment but nodded.

Killian gave her a mischievous look and slowly bowed his head to her. Then Astriea smiled a bit as they made their way back to the room.

"I'm trusting you not to kill anyone or try to escape, Sera… Don't let me down." Killian crooned from the other end of the hall.

She rolled her eyes before setting them back on the painting.

27

Astriea

K illian escorted her back to the room without a fuss but with great difficulty. Given that both of them were too drunk to find it. Eventually, Morra found the pair of them laughing in hushed voices as they tip-toed into the kitchens. Which, unfortunately, was on the opposite side of the castle.

Morra drug them all the way back and left them at Astriea's door.

They stood there at the entry, silently smiling at each other for a quiet moment.

"You know, you're not so insufferable when you stop flirting with me long enough to have a conversation." She said through her spinning vision.

He laughed and pulled a small bundle wrapped in cloth from his cloak pocket. In it was a small block of cheese and two slices of bread from dinner. He handed it to her. Somehow, he must've swiped it from the kitchen while Morra scolded them.

She snatched it from his hands and said, "Bringing me food definitely gains you points."

She could have moaned at how good the bread was. But she held back. Although she doubted Killian would've judged her for it. It was the middle of the night; she was drunk as hell and she was *starving*.

"Thank you." She said as she pressed into her room backward, pushing the door open behind her.

Before she could slide through the opening, Killian firmly wrapped his hand around its edge. Blocking her path.

He stepped closer.

"I don't mean to be insufferable when I praise you, my lady." He nearly whispered the words. Something sultry and starved laced his voice.

"I am spoken for, Killian," Astriea responded. A bit more breathlessly than she would have preferred. She knew for certain it was because of the wine and that everything in her had gone on high alert. Her skin tightened against her muscles and bones. Her throat quivered a bit, too.

"Can only one man speak for you?" He stepped closer. Nearly brushing his chest against hers. He leaned down a bit, a piece of his hair falling into his face.

"No man speaks for me."

"Then can he not share you? In Telas, you could have us both. Separate or together. I would never be so selfish that I would keep you all to myself."

Astriea swallowed hard. But steeled herself enough to say, "You don't even know me, Killian. Hell, I bet you're not even attracted to me. My power is what draws you to me." She rallied her steel, her twisted stomach, and said the words like a tease. "You are seduced by it day and night, it seems." She tipped her chin up.

"And you believe your Thomas is not?"

Astriea's eyes widened.

"No. Thomas loved me before I gained my power—"

"You've been without those abilities since before you landed on these shores, *my lady.* I do not speak of that power."

Astriea knitted her brows even as the tip of his nose was a breath away from hers.

"I am *constantly* seduced by the same power as your Thomas. Lured from my sleep to ache for your touch. Brought to my knees by the sound of your voice. Exhilarated by your fire." He brushed a crooked finger against her cheek. "The blue in your eyes the only color I've ever known."

But that one before was where he got it all wrong.

Because she was never the fire, the warmth and security. That was always

Thomas. He said she was the light. The guide.

And if Astriea knew anything in this world, if anything could guide her heart, it was that Thomas would always be the only choice.

The only hearth she called home.

There was no one else. Would never be anyone else.

If she wanted Killian, Thomas would go along with whatever she desired. He would let her take Killian to bed and he would forgive her if she did it right now.

But she didn't *want* Killian. And while he said alluring words and was honestly miles past attractive, there was no heat between them. No spark or world-halting emotion to be found.

She appreciated his feelings toward her, but the heart he asked for was already spent. Being kept safe and warm in godly hands across the sea.

So, Astriea pulled Killian's arm down from the door and stepped inside her room.

"Goodnight, Killian."

He nodded his acceptance and left as the door closed in front of him.

28

Seraphina

She went back to the greenhouse at some point, trying her best to find more wine.

Unfortunately, it had all been gathered up. So, she headed back to that painting again.

Seeing Vera so young and happy made Seraphina feel less angry with her in some way. Helped her sort through whatever she was feeling.

Morra stopped her on the way, ranting about catching Astriea and Killian sneaking into the kitchens and now finding another one roaming the halls. But all Sera could think about were the two full wine bottles Morra carried on her tray. Another servant said something to her and before Sera could give it a second thought, she snatched the bottles and ran.

"No wonder the grand duchess likes that one, ay, Morra?" The servant laughed as Sera bolted away.

She'd apologize to Morra later. Maybe help her with her work to make up for it. Right now, though, Sera wanted to drink and think about things she had no business thinking about.

* * *

The painting was harder to find this time. But she made her way back.

She got halfway through the first bottle of wine before she was ready to explore more of the castle.

Would she remember anything she found?

Probably not, but she set out anyway.

Because she didn't care. Not about her well-being, or her destiny, and certainly not about the fact that she should be trying to find them a way out of here. Right now, it felt good to just feel numb.

The first ten minutes of stumbling through the dark hallways seemed to be a bit of a bore. All the rooms were mostly empty. But what was worse was the fact that she had no idea where she was.

All the doors looked the same.

Killian wasn't lying when he said it was hard to navigate. They built this damn castle like a labyrinth.

But her drunken boredom vanished quickly as she rounded a corner into another hall, running straight into Vera.

They hit each other so hard, that both of them fell to the floor with a thud.

When Sera sat up, the world was spinning, and not just from the wine, but from the sight of an equally drunk Vera, who now brushed a fallen piece of Sera's hair out of her face and tucked it behind her ear.

The act sent shivers across her skin, down her spine. Made her heart ache even through the haze.

They struggled to stand together and lingered in a heavy silence for a moment.

Vera was a couple of inches taller than her, and Sera reached up and slipped the strap of Vera's dress back to its place on her bare shoulder.

Spinning, spinning, spinning.

They inched closer together. Sera's gaze darted between green eyes and red lips.

"What are you doing out here?" She asked quickly.

"It's my castle, I can wander how I like." She slurred a bit and leaned a hand against the wall.

Seraphina huffed and made to push past her. "I hate you," she said as she tried to leave. But Vera caught her arm.

"Do you?"

"I'm supposed to." She yanked her arm away.

The princess huffed and turned her head away from her. "Then be a good little soldier and hate me," she said as Seraphina started walking.

She heard the bottle swig behind her and turned back to glazed emerald eyes.

But there wasn't enough wine or liquor in the world to numb this feeling. "I can't."

The room spun again but Seraphina grabbed Vera by the waist of that thin dress and yanked their bodies together.

Vera's right hand cupped her face and her fingers laced into Sera's hair as she kissed her. Deeply, ferociously. The bottle dropped to the floor.

With a thud, Seraphina had Vera's back pressed against the wall. The strap of her dress ripped free as their hands roamed up and down each other once more. Their tongues danced lazily against the other, both of them savoring every taste they had the chance to get. Vera's breasts already prepared to break free from her torn gown.

Seraphina pulled her lips away, only to guide her teeth to the skin of her neck. Vera's breathy gasp ignited her senses. She wrapped her left arm around Vera's waist and slowly grazed her right hand up the duchess's chest to wrap thoroughly around the side of her neck. Sera's thumb brushing along her jaw.

Heat built with every shift of their bodies, every inch their hands moved across the other's skin. And with every kiss, some lost and weary part of Seraphina filled and filled and filled. So lost in the embrace of the other that all the world went mute.

Light blinded them both as the door directly across from them swung open.

In that light stood Astriea. Arms crossed and leaning against the doorpost. Eyebrows raised.

Seraphina broke away and followed Astriea into their room.

But Vera didn't take her eyes away even when she began to shut the door.

As it closed, Sera realized two things: That she found her way back to the room without meaning to. And that, maybe, Vera intended to stumble her own way to this door tonight.

29

Astriea

"What were you thinking?" Astriea asked after she dragged Sera into the room.

"I—" Sera started, but Astriea wasn't done yet.

"One minute you hate her, the next you're ready to fuck her in the hall. What is going on with you?"

Sera proceeded to fall onto a lounge chair before saying through lazy lips, "I want to hate her. I try *so, so* hard. And her having a hard time at home shouldn't excuse the things she's done, but I... I *want* to excuse them." She was silent for a moment. Her words sounded more sleepy than when she'd started speaking. "I wouldn't worry about it... too much. I doubt I'll feel this way when I'm sober."

Astriea made to speak but stopped herself at the sound of Sera peacefully sleeping. Her breaths slow and heavy.

Instead, she covered her under a soft, dark blue blanket, and watched her friend for a few moments.

"If I'm right, I don't think you'll ever stop feeling this way."

She knew she was right. Knew that for as short a time she'd known her small, deadly friend, there was nothing in the world that had such an effect on her.

Nothing like the influence of Vera Shataar.

Astriea gave one last stoke to the fire still bristling in the hearth and crawled into bed. Trying her best to let the events of the day fade so she could find sleep, and maybe Thomas, too.

* * *

The next morning, Sera slept until lunch, and neither Vera nor Killian came to their room. Whether cunning or embarrassment instigated their distance, Astriea couldn't be sure.

The tzar had asked them to give his family a chance. To get to know them. And had seemed to be honest with her about everything he shared. *Seemed to*.

Morra and her lovely daughters hauled in trays and trays of food all morning. Again and again until Astriea finally stopped Briar as she went to set down another platter of freshly roasted boar, still steaming from the kitchens.

"Please, Briar, we have plenty. You really don't have to keep bringing food." Astriea said with a smile. But honestly, part of her worried if the tzar was trying to fatten them up. She couldn't lie to herself. She'd grown rather thin in the past few weeks. Sera too. Neither of them cared for their new look and that was something they both realized made them furious.

"No ma'am. I may not. I was directed to bring in fresh food until I'm sure the Lady Seraphina has eaten." Briar said cheerfully.

"And does the *Grand Duchess* wish for you to report back on anything you might overhear?" Astriea asked without looking at her.

"My lady, I would not tell you if she did. I will tell you, however, that I was told that Lady Seraphina sometimes forgets to eat. So I'm tasked with making sure she's well fed."

The thought was sweet. Tender.

Astriea wished it hadn't come from Vera. Wished Sera had an easier love in her life.

Just then, Sera grunted and asked, "Vera sent all that?"

"Every half hour, my lady."

She let out a whimpered groan and threw the blanket over her head.

"What did I do? Gods, what did I do?" She whined.

"Got drunk and tangled tongues with the princess." Astriea crooned over her hot tea. Chamomile and honey wafted up her nose as she spoke.

Briar's eyes went wide as she set down the tray and did her best to contain her smile.

"How do you think this is funny, Astriea?"

"Because this entire thing is getting ridiculous. You can barely move when she's around."

Sera's eyes cut to Briar and back to Astriea.

"Briar, would you mind giving us the room?"

"Of course, my Lady Astriea." Quicker than a field mouse, the hand-maiden was gone.

"I have an idea, but I won't lie to you. It's pretty messed up."

Sera rubbed her temples but poured coffee into her cup and replied, "Go ahead."

"*You,*" Astriea said with a pointed finger.

"Me?"

"Yes. Go along with her. Get to know her, *bed* her, try to convince her to our side. Vera seems incredibly loyal to Telas. I want to see how loyal she can be to *you.*"

"You want me to play her?"

"Is it a game if the feelings are real on both sides? Who knows? Maybe she'll change her mind, but at this rate, we'll never know unless we can get her to talk."

"And if she won't talk? You want me to betray her?"

"She betrayed you first."

She didn't respond for a while. The silence looming over them lasted until Sera finished the last bit of food on her plate.

"I'll do it." She finally said. And it was the worry and pain in those obsidian eyes that made Astriea falter on the idea entirely and say, "We don't have to, Sera. It's not just a messed up thing to do to Vera, it's a messed up thing to do to you. If it's too much, we can find something else."

She didn't want to cause her pain, in any capacity. Something like regret congested in her chest.

"Just promise me something?"

"Anything."

"Don't kill her. I know we said—"

"I promise."

"Then I'll do it."

So the decision was made. Soon, Sera would seduce the princess of Telas and try her best to keep her heart well-armored.

30

Thomas

Four days after Valtan told Thomas of his lineage, and his relation to Astriea, the massive male had begun trying to approach the white, silver-eyed dragon. Thomas thought it very appropriate, as they seemed to match quite well.

But the creature was very hesitant. Less hesitant than it was with Thomas, but wary all the same.

Around the fifth day, though, two young women came tiptoeing up to the cliffs while Thomas tried to introduce more dragons to potential riders.

Evangeline, the High Witch of Shadon's Royal Coven, approached with Lavene by her side.

"The younger ones will take better to an average rider, Thomas," Evangeline said sweetly.

Thomas and Valtan approached the pair, and as they went to introduce each other, Valtan froze. His gaze dreamy and stuck on the witch.

Thomas coughed and brought Valtan out of his trance.

"Oh, yes… Thomas, this is Lavene. You formally met at the commencement dinner."

Thomas reached out and shook Lavene's hand. If he was being honest, he'd been avoiding her. He had enough on his plate with the dragons, his recent promotion and position as the king's chancellor, and worrying about Astriea every second of the day. He didn't need anything else on top of that.

"It's an honor to meet you, princess," Thomas said casually.

"I am not a princess." She replied.

"Does your father not rule an entire hidden kingdom?"

"Well, yes, but—"

"Have you not traveled far and wide to protect your country?"

"Yes, but—"

"Then you are a princess, in every way that counts. And besides, the king has clarified that we treat you like one."

Lavene had little to say to that. She just nodded her head.

Thomas then looked to Valtan, who was once again staring at sweet Evangeline.

"Valtan, this is Evangeline, High Witch of the Royal Coven. Evangeline, this is Valtan. His temple elders say he is marked by Astriea, *and* he just so happens to be her uncle." He nudged him forward a bit.

Thomas gently placed Evangeline's palms onto Valtan's. A beautiful pale blue light radiated from her hands.

"Oh... yes, he is marked by Astriea. Likely a call made to him when she first accepted her power. And her uncle? It seems she called for the closest remaining blood tie..."

She lifted her hand well above her head, nearly touching his chin, the tips of her fingers lit with blue magic.

"Do you mind?" She asked Valtan while gesturing to her hand. He nodded and leaned down closer to her, allowing her palm to cup his cheek. They both closed their eyes and Thomas felt a pulse of power ripple from them. A small burst of a breeze and a tingle on his skin. Valtan fell to one knee at the impact. Kneeling on the ground before Evangeline.

They both opened their eyes, and she smiled.

Because Valtan's silver eyes were rings of gold now. Not glowing like Hellion's did, but nearly.

"Let's see if that dragon likes you better now that you're connected to the magic Astriea broke free here."

Valtan smiled and rose. Now towering over them all once again.

123

She turned to Thomas. "We found several books in the king's library about the dragons. Although we were not the first to ride them, they were selective about who they allowed on their backs even then. Sometimes, if a dragon cares enough for its rider, it forms a metal link with them and renders reins nearly useless."

"You found all this, and you didn't tell me?" Thomas said, mockingly pretending he'd been stabbed in the heart.

Evangeline smiled and said, "Just keep all that in mind while you try to get riders on these dragons. The smaller, younger ones will take riders more easily. The older ones require a bit more..."

"I hear you, I hear you," Thomas laughed. "So, is that all you came for?"

"Not quite," Lavene said. "The Sharinian Steel that was found, the king wants more of it. Wants to build an entire arsenal of it."

"Interesting. James mentioned he wanted to mine it. I didn't realize he wanted *that* much, but *he's* the king," Thomas said, throwing his hands up.

"Well, that's just it, he's already mined everything from the cliffs where your dragon—"

"Night-cleaver," Thomas corrected her.

She gave him a funny look but went on, "*Night-cleaver's* nest is now empty. He wants us to fly to Monolith and see if the other dragons left any behind. If so, we're to investigate the entire length of the Caltillion Mountains. I—" She stuttered. "I'd also be grateful to see my home, my father..."

Thomas was both happy to help and a little angry. Because he knew exactly what James was doing. Sending him off on a days, maybe weeks, long mission to keep him busy and out of the way. Did he deserve it? A bit, but it still stung.

"Wait, you want to ride with me? On dragon back?"

"No. No, I intend to ride my own." Lavene confirmed, looking out at the nest.

Thomas raised a brow and smiled before fully extending his arm to the open nest of dragons behind him.

"Take your pick, princess."

* * *

By sunset, Lavene had chosen and mounted *Sand-snake*. A light brown serpent-like dragon with razor-sharp wings that collapsed flawlessly into its reptilian body. Its scales were so tiny you wouldn't think they were scales at all, but sand made into skin. Its front and back legs were thin and pliable with three long talons on each foot and webs attached between them.

That night, Valtan escorted Evangeline back to the castle. The two of them peppered each other with questions as they left.

The connection to magic had worked wonders. Right after, the white dragon allowed Valtan to mount. It huffed and growled the entire time, but he made significant progress.

Now, Thomas strolled with Lavene to his saddle maker's workshop for her to choose a one of her own.

"You can pick any type of leather you like. Have an inscription engraved too. I think I'll bring mine in before we leave."

"You seemed upset before. When I told you of the king's command." Lavene said coolly.

"Ah, yes—well, I've been a rather unbearable ass lately. Haven't been the easiest to deal with… Or the best friend. I suppose now I understand why he's sending me off."

He didn't blame James, he wouldn't want to deal with him either.

Lavene gave him an empathetic smile.

After choosing her saddle, they went their separate ways. Thomas went back to his chambers and her to wherever spent her nights.

But tomorrow, tomorrow he would talk with James and ready for his first flight mission.

Sadly, Thomas doubted his ability to handle the sight of his home in ruins. He knew that never letting his eyes see the wreckage left behind would not make it so it never happened. It would not change anything. Everyone they knew was dead, the mountains had crumbled, and now… Now there was no need to find what lay beyond Monolith's Peak. Some small inkling in him had wished to see the mountains one more time before his passing.

He'd learned their feats well; grown attached to the mountain town, and nearly everyone in it.

31

Damian

It had been days since the commencement feast, and Damian spent all of his waking time either in the war room with James and a few naval officers inspecting ships, or sitting here on the rocky beaches beneath the cliffs.

Today, he felt like watching the water dragons again. They were beautiful creatures of the sea and sky. But as he sat there, a sheet of gray slowly took over the blue expanse, signaling an impending storm. Damian's thoughts drifted to Seraphina and how she might be coping. If she'd been eating enough, or if they'd hurt her…

With all he'd been doing lately to keep his mind off his oldest friend, he thought it completely appropriate to come down here and stew in some well-deserved misery.

He should have done more on the ship that day. Should have fought *harder*. Should've found a way to free Thomas and let him burn them all rather than let that Telish princess kill Tristan and make off with his goddess and his best friend.

That feeling of failure was another thing he'd worked endlessly to avoid facing. That his only mission had been to protect and die for the Heir of Zaniah.

And he'd *lost* her.

Let her slip right through his fingers.

Something that wouldn't be happening again.

The ships he'd been preparing for James these last few days came together more quickly than anything he'd ever witnessed before. Calling upon the royal navy was easy enough. They were nearly at port the day the three of them came through the portal. But half of the navy itself was released from duty. Bringing their numbers down substantially. But it had to be done. The half removed from service were known and suspected slave traders. Those that weren't immediately imprisoned, were banished outright.

Despite this, hope was not lost.

It was the citizens, venturing far and wide, traversing the entire country just to witness the age of a new, free king that shocked him most of all. Small, makeshift boats lined the harbor and filled the neighboring town's docks. At present, they had five thousand foot soldiers, one thousand horse riders, two hundred ships and, if Thomas's numbers are right, one hundred dragons now nested on the northern cliff's edge, all ready for riders.

They have the numbers, plenty even without the fifteen hundred sailors James removed. Now they just need to prepare. Well, all *he* had to do was prepare. He didn't want to think about how much work was cut out for James. Especially since he planned to come with them. To lead his army like a good king should.

It should only take three weeks more. The ships aren't ready for icy Telish conditions, and the dragons need at least a year's worth of training just to adjust to their riders. Time they didn't have to give them. All he could do for now was wait. Wait and hope.

Wait and prepare to launch a war against Telas.

* * *

An hour later, he considered going back up to town to get a pint, even stood to his feet and readied himself to leave. But the moment he turned around, a small figure stood right behind him.

Damian nearly leaped from his skin. Nearly slid off the rock he stood on into the sea a few feet below.

The figure pulled back their hood.

"Ula?" Damian said with knitted brows.

The lovely maiden was small enough that she barely made a sound as she moved. But Damian noted her face under the shining sun.

"Hello, Damian." Her smile threatened to burn holes through his chest.

Ula's golden skin had become nourished in the light of day. She'd been so pale in the dungeons he probably wouldn't have recognized her at first glance. She had rounded cheeks, a delicate point in her chin and jaw, and her eyes…

They were as blue as the sea behind him now.

The night she'd picked the lock of the dungeons for them, her eyes had been gold. Almost like his but more ethereal.

"You… you look different—GOOD! Good different, I mean." Damian blushed. He couldn't see it, but he could definitely feel all that warmth in his cheeks.

"It's good to see you again. Though now I suppose I should refer to you as *Admiral*?"

"Gods, no, *Damian* is fine." He chuckled. They stood there for a moment in a lovely silence.

"Were you heading to town, Damian?"

"I was, yes."

"Would you like some company?"

A glimmer of magic fluttered before him, and Ula's eyes changed back to gold. Shining and elegant like his own.

"How did you do that?" He said with no small amount of astonishment. But he shook his head and looped Ula's arm with his before leading her away from the beach.

"You know what? Tell me over dinner."

Ula's bright smile and flushed cheeks made his stomach flutter. He'd had lovers and flings and all the things that one considered a part of love. But he'd never experienced butterflies in his stomach. A strange longing to be next to someone.

The two of them happily walked into a charming restaurant. It had a large painted sign out front that read: *GRAND OPENING OF THE BATARIAN.*

Damian and Ula sat at their table and had a wonderful night full of laughter and interesting conversation.

"What were you doing out there on the rocks?" He asked her.

"Just making sure you don't drown yourself is all." She joked.

"I have been wondering about you lately and could never find you. Have you been following me, Ula?" He teased.

"You've been wondering about me?"

"You've been following me." He challenged.

Her smile could've melted him.

"And I will continue to do so. There's something about you, Damian Aurelius. And I enjoy interesting people." She leaned back in her seat and took a drink.

All he could do was smile at her. Or look at her. He probably could've done that all evening.

Occasionally, throughout the night, their eyes met in fleeting glances that stirred his chest.

But he stilled mind enough to tear himself from her company. Regretting every footstep away from her and toward the castle.

32

Damian

"So! Just a few weeks in Shadon and you've already overthrown an evil king, found ya sister, become *Admiral of the Royal Navy*, and now you've found yourself a sweetheart. This place isn't so rotten after all, is it, mate?" Thomas taunted him as they circled each other in the sparring ring right outside the dragon nest.

Damian swung wide and fast, but Thomas was quick as a cobra as he dipped down at his waist and struck him in the ribs.

Damian grunted and grabbed his side. Normally, Thomas wouldn't give him such a run for his money. Normally, they were pretty well-matched. Though, he could admit lately that he'd been distracted.

Thomas, however, was very lively for someone set to take an earth goddess on a dragon ride around Shadon.

He was just lively in general. Like the old version of him had returned. Like he had some hope again.

"She's not my *sweetheart*," Damian said and smiled. "Not yet, anyway..."

By the time he turned to face Thomas again, the only thing he saw was the world turn upside down as Thomas's foot collided with his ankles. Bringing him crashing onto his face.

When Damian rolled onto his back, he took note of the warmth of the sun and the fact that he wanted to be doing anything other than training right now. He wanted to be listening to Ula talk about the many different locks she'd learned how to pick in her youth. Wanted to hear her explain why her eyes change color. She'd said she would tell him that day she found him by the sea, but the closer they became, the more reluctant she was to share.

Thomas towered over him, laughing.

"You better be on your game by the time I return. I should only be gone a few days. A week at the most." He extended a hand and helped Damian to his feet.

"I've got a lot on my mind. Ula has been helping me move through it all these last couple of weeks. Maybe I'll have everything sorted out by the time you return." Damian said, dusting himself off.

Thomas's hand patted on his shoulder and they headed for the flight deck. A patch of flat dusty earth near the cliffs.

The golden dragons lie sunbathing in the wheat fields near the river and King's Wood. The young princess, Lavene, was already saddling her dragon—loading supplies and tightening straps—on Sand-snake.

Thomas said that Devil's Gate was a desert land, so her choice of animal companion seemed appropriate.

Damian took an extra moment to observe the black armor she wore. It matched the pieces of metal gracing her saddle and Thomas'.

Her breastplate and pauldrons were dark as night.

"You ever seen armor like that?" He asked Thomas.

"Can't say I have. But I guess I'll have all week to find out where she got it. Looks like the Sharinian Steel that was used for our saddles."

Damian turned to his friend and slapped a hand on his shoulder. "All packed? When do you leave?"

"At dawn."

"Thank the gods you can bathe before you go," Damian started holding his nose and swatting the air between them. "You smell awful." He laughed.

Thomas jabbed him in the shoulder before wrapping his arm around Damian's head and shoving his face into his underarm.

They wrestled and fought for a minute. The two of them laughed harder than either had in gods knew how long.

"Maybe if you weren't so busy looking pretty for Ula, you'd have time to get in the muck with the rest of us," Thomas mocked as they rolled into a puddle of mud. Then he laughed and said, "Never mind! You're positively filthy now."

They got up and headed for the palace, only stopping at the door for Helena—the head ladies' maid—to demand they thoroughly be rinsed off before stepping foot on her floors.

"I'll not have this behavior here or when we arrive in Telas." She said to them both. "Just because they are enemies doesn't mean we should present ourselves without manners, so hose off in the gardens or I'll swat you both!"

Both their eyes went wide and Thomas said, "I didn't know you were coming with us, Helena. You should stay where it's safe."

"I have a sister in Telas. One that I haven't seen or heard from in thirty years. Whether I am to wrap my arms around her again or cry at her grave I will be on that ship, my lord."

This was all he needed to hear from the proud handmaiden. He bowed his head to her, and he and Damian made their way to the gardens.

* * *

Later that night, after bathing and dressing for dinner, Damian met with the *near* entirety of the group in the great hall. Thomas and Draes were already stuffing their faces.

The two of them ate like they didn't get full meals every day.

It was only when James's mother commented on them—as Damian took his seat next to Draes—that he realized why.

"Good gods, didn't your mother teach the two of you any manners?"

The table went quiet. Even a couple of servants paused and backed away. But the pair of them remained silent. Both of them expressed the same grim expression and stared blankly at the table, at their messy plates. Those exact words made his mind reminisce on a memory from long ago, a time when he was a young boy making a mess at the table of Lady Ashin. She'd almost asked him the same question, but stopped herself. Remembered where he'd come from. And it was the Lady Ashin who taught him and Seraphina their table manners. Done so well with them that the Masters asked her to teach lessons on it at the temple for all the disciples.

Those lingering thoughts made him say, "It is difficult to learn such things on the run, Queen Mother, much less to learn them without a mother or father to guide."

The golden-haired former queen tilted her head a bit, and her gaze softened.

"I am very sorry. To the both of you…"

Thomas and Draes nodded their heads. Accepting her apology. Damian caught Thomas's glance and silent thanks to him as well.

Then the queen muttered, "I—I don't know if it will bring you any ease to hear this, but… Telas and Shadon have always done well to broker peace between each other. At one time, Herold attended the dragon hunts when Kahshyr, the tzar's older brother, was heir to the throne and hosted them. That bastard went so far as to seek out a marriage proposal between James and Princess Vera after Kaeon became tzar, but the queen there… She refused. I had no intention of letting the marriage happen as well, but Queen Raedyn… Courtiers said she fought the tzar with her bare hands. Refused to uphold her duties and killed three guards that tried to detain her. Then there was the princess herself… She was only a young girl, perhaps nine or ten years old, but word was she had a fit that sent rumors flying across the world. That she bit a finger off one of the lords in her court that held her back as her mother was being taken away and fed it to her demon horse."

James's youngest sister, the dark-haired one whose feet dangled from her chair, did her best to choke down a snorted laugh.

The queen mother gave her a look that sent her eyes wide and she quickly returned to eating her food. Although, Damian couldn't help but grin a bit.

"Anyway… I always thought that maybe I wasn't the only queen trapped in a cold castle. And I thought you should both know that the dragon hunts halted years ago. There hasn't been one that our court has gotten wind of after Kahshyr died. His brother took the throne, and they never even found Kahshyr's body. The tzar only ever said that he would be renaming the western cliffs to *Kahshyr's Cliffs*. Although, there's never been a record of a renaming."

Draes got up from his seat and excused himself. "Thomas will have to fill me in on the rest, your grace, I—I feel the need to retire." He almost looked sick. The royals nodded to him and gave a sympathetic smile. Thomas furrowed his brows at his brother, only gaining a nod from him and a pat on the shoulder as he left.

* * *

Damian had nearly finished his food when he spotted Ula eating at one of the tables below the one for court. She grinned at him and he excused himself before making his way to her. She finished her food and stepped into pace with him as they walked out of the great hall together.

"I haven't seen you since yesterday, been avoiding me?" He teased her.

"I do have *other* friends, Damian. You can't expect me to spend all my time with just you." The flirtatious grin on her full lips made his own part in a wide smile.

He clutched his chest and said, "*Friend*? And here I thought you cared for me. What will the masters say when they're told I've been ruined?" Damian did his best to perform as well as the actors from the island theater did as he feigned to be heartbroken.

The laugh the act pulled from Ula's lips rang in his ears like a symphony. His chest warm and delighted to hear it. Just then, her eyes shifted color again. They turned orange, deep and bright like flame.

He tilted his head, admiring them.

Ula nervously blinked four or five times and her eyes shifted to a lovely hazel. Green and gold and brown twisting around each other.

"Tell me how you do it. You said you would." He teased again. Lightly tapping her chin with a hooked finger.

135

She only smiled and looped her arm through his as they walked through the halls.

"Take me with you to Telas, and I'll tell you when I see the mighty black cliffs on the horizon."

"Oh, I see, warming me up for a free ride? Then you'll high tail as far as you can, huh?"

She elbowed him in the ribs.

"Quite the opposite, actually. Take me with you to Telas, then to Sirey, then to your island..." She paused. "Take me with you on glorious adventures, and I'll tell you everything."

Damian thought about the proposal. He already knew his answer.

"You'll have to pull your own weight on a ship."

"Damian Aurelius! You dare insinuate that I've never sailed before?"

"You have, have you? Seems like something I would need to know about before tossing you in with my crew—" He stopped.

My crew. Tristan.

Tristan was dead. His crew was captured across the sea in Telas and yet Damian... Damian was flirting and having fine dinners.

Guilt threatened to suffocate him.

But a gentle hand wrapped cautiously around his forearm.

"Promise me a life of freedom, and I'll help you bring it to your crew."

His eyes shot to hers, and they turned golden—like his and Mira's.

What sounded like lightning struck nearby. The sky lit up, and he felt as though the ground shook, even as nothing around him looked disturbed.

But something else happened at that moment. A thought jumped around in his head again and again and again. The words he needed to say.

The lightning, the thunder, the shaking, none of it ceased until Damian said, "It's a bargain."

33

Seraphina

"How do I even convince her to see me? She hasn't been by in two weeks." Sera said, leaning back in her chair, head cocked back and gaze set on the ceiling.

"Neither has Killian," Astriea replied.

Seraphina sat up and gritted her teeth, her lips pulled back slightly.

"It would embarrass *me* to come back here after that." She said.

Astriea told her everything that had happened with Killian when he escorted her back to their room. And that rejection had to sting.

Still, two weeks was the longest they'd gone without a visit from Vera or Killian. Most of the time they were together.

"I hope we don't have this problem in Sirey," Astriea said.

"I doubt we will. The merchants that got turned around at the Isle docks always said the same things: *Shadon is a gray slab on a map with the most crime in the world.*"

"That checks out." Astriea agreed.

"*Sirenians rarely leave their island and don't care for outsiders.* Mostly, because of all the raiding they have to fend off their gold mines."

"Makes sense. What do they say about the Telish?" Astriea asked, picking at her fingernails.

Sera plopped her head back again and stared at the ceiling before saying with slight irritation, "*The Telish are passionate in blood, battle, and love.*"

"Of course," Astriea replied sarcastically.

Seraphina almost asked her why she didn't already know all that. She risked a glance at Astriea and saw the simmering anger she was trying hard to bury in her expression. In her eyes.

It clicked then. Why she asked so many questions and didn't have many answers of her own.

Why she'd torn herself apart for what she did to Thomas.

Astriea had done to him what Herold Berelda did to an entire nation.

Kept them deep in the dark.

So much so that she had no idea what to expect of Telas or Sirey. Thomas knew some, but really only tales of skilled warriors around the world. He knew a bit about the current seat of power in Telas, too.

But Astriea had been yanked from leading rebellions and thrown into toppling empires, with barely any knowledge of them to guide her. Sera thought of how hard that had to be on a spy.

So she got up and opened their door before saying to the guard outside the hall, "Please tell the grand duchess I'd like to see her."

The guard tilted his head at her curiously but nodded to the other guard stationed on the opposite wall and left.

* * *

Two hours later, at lunch, their door swung open and Briar strode in with her sisters in tow behind her. Each of them carrying platters of sandwiches, fruits, vegetables, breads, and cheeses. Morra tailed at the end with two clear glass pitchers. One of water, one of wine.

Before they could question the assortment, Vera slowly stepped into the room.

It made sense then.

Her hair was in a loose braid down her back, and strays were fallen out of it in messy little pieces. Sera figured out where she'd been in a split second. Her riding leathers being her biggest tell. A chestnut-brown wool tunic covered her upper body, even stretching up her neck. Sera was thankful to be sitting, yet again, as she was held for ransom by the shape of Vera in her boots and pants. Her tunic tucked neatly into matching trousers that gracefully curved around her hips and snugged securely around the top of her waist. Her dark brown riding boots came up to her mid-thigh.

And she was panting a bit. A smile on her face and a glimmer in her eyes Sera had never seen before. One that almost made her seem to glow. *Radiate.*

Killian stepped in behind her. He looked the same as usual. Wearing his dark blue embroidered tunic and black pants. Although, this time, he didn't don his pauldron and breastplate. His hair was tied back, away from his face, and his silver eyes swirled as they always did. If Sera was being honest, sometimes they really creeped her out.

Without a word, the four of them sat down at the table. Sera noticed Vera fidget with the collar of her wool tunic as she sat across from her.

"My guard said you wished to speak with me?" Vera asked before taking a drink of water.

Sera contained herself enough to ask, "I was wondering if you might be willing to let us see more of the castle? If not, then the library would be comforting."

Vera looked at her for a long moment. Killian did, too. Astriea only strategically kept her gaze on the both of them. Assessing each for any tells, codes, or signs they might be communicating with each other.

Sera kept her eyes on Vera alone. Kept her expression soft and a little wary. Doing her best to present herself as someone who was... *questioning* things.

Which wasn't untrue.

She *was* questioning things. Everything. She wasn't ready to give Vera gentleness and doe-eyed gazes, but she did anyway. Using them as weapons.

"I suppose the library wouldn't hurt anyone," Vera said, picking at her food with her fork. "We'll have to escort you..."

Seraphina sat back in her chair before looking away from her shyly. She tilted her head just a bit and said, "I suppose that would be alright."

Vera took a bite of her food and played with the remainder on her plate again. This time she said, "And do you think the two of you can behave?"

"Don't we always?" Sera grinned.

Vera's fork went still, but she smiled and leaned back in her chair.

"When would you like to leave?" She asked.

"Now."

34

Astriea

The library was one floor above the dungeons and there were a hundred rows of books lying before her. She'd hoped it would've been more grand. More ethereal.

But the shelves were all made of metal planks. Each was stacked in rows crammed so tightly together you could barely fit two people down the aisles at a time. The lights above them were dim and cold. The air in the room felt the same.

Cold, cold, cold.

It didn't feel like a library at all, but a vault.

Sera had done a magnificent job so far, wooing the princess. She cautiously asked questions at Vera's side the entire time.

"And who is that?" She asked, pointing at a painting of an ugly old man in dark purple clothes and a golden imperial crown atop his head.

"That is Moisov Shataar. Seventh Tzar of Telas, known to be especially cruel towards the common people…"

"And her?" Sera said, now pointing to the next painting hanging on the cool metal wall. A young woman, her clothes nearly the same as the tzar's, and a mighty kokoshnik studded with diamond and pearl gently wrapped around the bun of orange-red hair resting atop her head.

"That is his daughter, Rhaksa Shataar. She did her best to rectify what her father did but died the day her son came of age to rule. In Telas, it's twenty-six."

That had caught both of their attention.

"Twenty-six seems oddly *specific*," Sera mentioned.

"Heirs of Telas have a habit of not making it to twenty-five," Killian stated plainly.

"Many of them choose not to." Vera's words were breathless, a whisper to herself perhaps. That all of them just barely heard.

Perhaps that was the reason Telish monarchs had so many children.

The realization dawned on her, that Vera herself was one year shy of her rule. Maybe less, depending on when her birthday was.

Would this be the year Vera herself would choose to join that specific line of Telish royalty that came before her?

The pain was evident in Seraphina's eyes.

Astriea watched her inch closer to the princess as they pushed in between the shelves.

"Here we are," Vera said, changing the topic and leading them to an alcove where all the shelves met and opened in a circle, allowing space for a few small tables and chairs. Vera sat her hand on a stack of books left out and said, "Feel free to look about and find something you like. I've already used up my allotted ten I'm allowed to borrow at a time, and these particular books can only be read here. So I'll be waiting for you all when you get back."

They nodded and left Vera to her books.

After a few minutes, Astriea found two different books on Telish history and the reoccurring wars with Sirey. Sera beat her back to the tables and had already taken a seat across from the princess. She looked up at her from the newer book she'd found about the installation of the *Science Guild*, and Astriea took her seat.

Killian hadn't spoken to her all day. Which irritated her. Because the least he could do was stop hitting on his captive and hold a genuine conversation. And she'd also grown fond of picking on him.

"Are you so badly wounded from the luncheon that you've just refused to speak to me now? I mean it's been two weeks." She whispered over the edge of her open book.

"I am not *wounded*. The luncheon was... awkward. I'm a little embarrassed about it. Fight me."

Astriea's jaw dropped for a moment, but she shut it and returned to her book before muttering, "*Hostile* is more like it."

She saw him scowl at her from the corner of her eye. But that was better than nothing.

* * *

The first book on Telish history described its first ruler. The first Tzar of Telas was Zhaphet Shataar. He was a short man with dark hair and dark eyes. There was little about his reign, only that he held parties for executions and, at one point, hung the bodies in town squares as a warning to any who defied him. He lived to be an old, evil man with five heirs. Succeeded by his son, Zhaphellion Shataar, who turned thirty-two on his coronation day. The oldest heir to ever take the throne.

Astriea fiddled through that book again and again, but the same error kept true. Kept popping back up in her head. The first sentence in the book said:

THE IMPERIAL KINGDOM OF TELAS WAS ESTABLISHED IN 4 B.F.

Before the fall of Zaniah.

She flipped over to the first page and stopped her finger on the date before her.

Zhaphet Shataar: First Tzar of Telas
Reign- 01-A.F. — 41-A.F.

Why would they go four years without a ruler? She asked herself.

What kingdom would ever do that? Even a small, up-and-coming country would need a leader, a king or queen. It made no sense to found

143

itself and not crown a ruler for four years. People would've doubted the entire structure of the realm. Would have packed up at the first sight of weakness.

Because young countries don't have the luxury of being fickle. The moment you claim your independence, everyone wants a piece of you. The entire world wants to test your metal.

Astriea spent two more hours scouring that pitiful excuse for a library. She looked everywhere for every book about the first ruler of Telas. Each led her to the same thing, *Zhaphet*.

After releasing a muffled scream of frustration, she slammed a book down on the table and stormed out.

Honestly, she didn't know why it mattered so much to her. But it did.

It felt like there was something she had to know. It couldn't have been just a piece of history gotten wrong, or some silly explanation of settlement years, like one fairly fictional book said on the matter.

No.

She stopped in the cold hallway. It was empty, eerie.

She took a breath, then another.

Show me.

Something in her chest hummed. Purred against her heart, then tugged on it.

Z?

No. Not Zaniah. Just *her*.

Just Astriea's power. Not enough to use, but maybe enough to guide.

She started putting one foot in front of the other and before she knew it, she'd made it to the other end of the hall. The tugging stopped, but the only thing in front of her was a wall with a painting of a horse racing tournament. She looked closer at the champion in the center holding a golden trophy shaped like a star.

The face wasn't easy to make out, but the general shape and the blood-red hair told her enough. It was Vera.

Why would her magic lead her to a painting of Vera?

Before she could question further, Seraphina, Killian, and Vera came into the hall.

"Glad you didn't try to escape. Father would've had you thrown back in the dungeons with the mood he's in." Killian said with raised brows.

Astriea rolled her eyes but followed behind the group as he and Vera escorted Seraphina and herself back to their room.

Throughout the entire trip back, she was preoccupied with the belief that there was something else at play. Something she couldn't put together yet. But she would. Astriea's magic wanted her to discover the truth of the missing years.

What for? She didn't know.

But if she knew anything else, she knew it was important, if not *vital*.

35

Seraphina

Sera was quite proud of herself for how well she'd done at asking Vera small, quaint, questions during their trip to the library.

And Vera seemed overjoyed to answer them.

Now, back in the privacy of her and Astriea's room, she had plenty of time to feel the guilt barreling in behind the pride.

Vera had been happy to show them the library, and based on how many books she showed up with every week, it must have been important to her. Sera thought about how many smiles her questions had pulled from Vera's lips today.

She rolled over on the couch and reminded herself of all the reasons what she was doing was justified.

I am a soldier, and she is the mission. She thought. Again and again. She was a soldier, Vera called her as much. She was Astriea's soldier, the temple's soldier. It was her first and most honored duty to serve the Goddess of Life. To aid her, kill for her, die for her.

Vera had lied to them. Betrayed them. Captured them and killed their friend. She could not allow herself to forgive her.

Sera tossed and turned for a solid hour. As the sun set, Astriea remained engrossed in a Telish history book, leaving her with nothing to do but ponder about what she was doing to Vera.

She deserves this; she thought. *She deserves it.*

Finally, Seraphina told Astriea she'd be back and went to change clothes. She wrapped herself in a thin black cloak and slipped out the door at exactly eight o'clock—when the guards changed shifts at the end of the hall.

With suspicion and doubt clouding her mind, Sera navigated through the castle, her only certainty being the distant location of the royal quarters. She turned right and slipped into the shadows.

* * *

She'd always been quite good at disappearing. Even as a child.

When she was young, she had this notion that the shadows were her friends. That they hid her when she wanted to win hiding games, or when she was being chased down by bullies.

The shadows had always offered her shelter.

Gracefully. Lovingly. A quiet friend by her side.

Turn left now. A dark, sickening voice loomed in her mind.

Seraphina stopped in the middle of the hallway. She looked around and saw no one. Heard no one.

Don't be afraid of me, dark and lovely flower. It cooed to her. And something like a cold, dead finger gently scraped its way down Sera's neck.

She felt frozen. Her blood pumping harder with every struggling breath she took.

Fear.

Terror.

Rage.

All of these things twisted around inside her and made her knees buckle.

That dead finger roamed down her. Down her chest and stomach. It stopped just below the lining of her pants. That's when she felt an invisible palm wrap around her jaw. It clutched onto her, suffocating her, leaving her desperate for breath.

I know what you are, and I will have you, daughter of no one.

"No—" Her voice trembled. "You will have nothing."

She angered it. Felt its fury as the grip around her face grew tight enough to bruise. Maybe to break her jaw.

Just as she was about to scream, the pain intensified, overwhelming her senses.

* * *

Sera wasn't sure how long she'd been passed out. And she didn't recognize the face pulling her back into consciousness. A handmaiden. Older, with a head full of gray hair under her bonnet.

Before she knew it, the handmaiden drug her to a door.

Sera thought she remembered stairs at some point. She shook her head to clear the fog.

As soon as it did, the door swung open and Vera stood at its entry. Her hair was long and unbound completely. The only thing covering her was a floor-length silk nightgown. Silver.

The thin straps held up the bodice and left Vera's arms and shoulders completely exposed. She looked like she was getting ready for bed.

Sera got dizzy again and leaned further against the handmaiden.

"What happened?" Vera asked, her face pale, and her voice filled with concern and shock.

"I found her collapsed in the hall. She said your name when I first tried to wake her, so I brought her here." The handmaiden said.

"Thank you, Nan," Vera said, helping to carry Sera inside.

They laid her on the bed.

"Should I get the healers?" She asked.

"No. I have everything I should need here." Vera replied.

Seraphina heard the door shut and felt Vera sit next to her on the bed before she opened her eyes.

There she was. Emerald eyes glittering in the dim hearth light. She was everything and anything. Both burning fire and searing light.

"Sera, what happened?" Vera asked, opening a healer's pack and readying a salve.

"I…I don't remember." She lied. She remembered everything. "I—I was trying to find my way here and…and then nothing." Sera did her best to give a convincing performance. Hoped it would be enough to sway the *Grand Duchess of Lies and Deceit.*

She sat up and rested her back and head against the headboard. Vera looked at her a bit curiously.

"Your face and throat are bruised. Sera, someone attacked you." She flinched at Vera's touch against her jaw. It hurt like a bitch.

"It's fine. I should get back to my room." Sera said and tried to get up, but got dizzy and quickly plopped back down on the bed.

"You're in no condition to try and make your way down the tower right now. And besides, you came here for a reason, right? Tell me what it is." Her gentle smile was nearly Sera's undoing. The way it soothed and caressed her. Wrapped her all over and threatened to slit her throat.

Vera's smooth fingers gently placed the salve along Sera's jaw. The act made her feel as though she would melt into the princess's hand.

She steeled herself then. Remembered why she'd truly come here tonight. Sera touched her jaw and shifted a bit. Letting her cloak drift off her shoulder slightly. Revealing a set of underclothes that left little to the imagination but still covered enough that Sera remained comfortable. Also, if it had been too flamboyant a set, Vera would have sniffed out the ruse immediately.

But the act did exactly what she wanted. Vera's eyes darted. An unearthly fast movement few would have noticed. But she did.

Sera saw it and pulled a small history journal from her cloak's inside pocket. She handed it to Vera.

"I—I just came to return this…" she said, handing her the book.

Vera only smiled at it as she took it in her hands. Then sat it on the side table. Sera stretched her jaw, the pain already lessening from the salve.

She leaned forward. Putting a majority of her weight on one hand, placed dangerously close to touching Sera's thigh. She said in an almost purr, "You fumbled your way through the castle in basically nothing, just to return a book to me? One that, I might add, I have ten copies of."

Sera hated this. Hated the lying, hated the pretending. But most of all, hated how much she *really* wanted this.

"Why did you come, Sera?" Vera asked, running the inner edge of Sera's cloak through her thumb and forefinger.

She tried to make the gulp she forced down unnoticeable as she breathed out, "Because I can't sleep. Because I can't stay away. Because I don't want to."

Each the truth, all of it a lie.

She wanted Vera.

She wanted to rip through any doors or walls or thin pieces of fabric that kept them apart. So she gave up some fragment of truth like it was being ripped from her throat, falling off her lips in a whisper.

"I want to hate you. But I want to have you more."

Sera moved forward and kissed her. It was short and quick. Something that may have been a mistake, because now? Now she knew she hadn't had enough. Her lips begged to meet with Vera's. Her center ached and leapt for her.

Vera's hands were on her then. Pulling the string of her thin cloak as their lips crashed together once more.

The cloak fell away from her shoulders and the bare skin of Vera's palm made Seraphina melt.

Vera's fingers danced their way up her neck and avoided all her pain and bruises. Sera could've moaned at the feeling of her fingers lacing into her hair. Her grip tightened around the back of her neck and for a moment Vera could have had her right then and there.

But a knock at the door sucked the heat and passion from the room.

"Your Highness, one of the prisoners is unaccounted for." A guard, she guessed, said through the door.

But Sera flinched at the word *prisoners*. Like reality had come knocking and slapped her across the face.

"I know where she is. I'll handle it, back to your post." Vera said to him.

"Right away, Grand Duchess."

Seraphina took up her cloak and rose from the bed as soon as she heard the guard's footsteps vanish.

"I shouldn't have come."

"Seraphina—" Vera reached her hands out to her as she stepped toward the door.

"I am a prisoner here, Vera. Astriea and I only see your city from a *caged* balcony. Caged!"

"I'll have it torn down—"

"That doesn't change what we are! But you, *you* could change it. You have that power."

"No, I don't, Sera. I wish I did, but I can't—" She stopped mid-sentence with a hiss. Sucked in a breath and grazed her fingers along her throat. Sera reached out, but Vera only held up her hand to stop her and went on. "You and Astriea want to tear down the ice we've had for a thousand years. It's been a hard enough time trying to convince everyone who matters here to get on board with the two of you being treated as honored guests. We have quests, traditions, and celebrations, all surrounding the ice that has made our country the stronghold of the world."

"But think of all your country could be if it had the resources to become an empire, a *real* empire."

Vera halted at the words.

"I can't discuss this with you, Sera." She said, looking down at the floor.

Seraphina huffed through her nose and said, "Right, I don't know why I thought you'd start being honest now. I'll be getting back to my cell then."

Anger sent her through that door and down those stairs without hesitation. No matter how many times Vera called out her name behind her.

36

Astriea

The next morning, Astriea had awoken to find Seraphina sleeping peacefully beside her and took a wild guess that her night with Vera might not have gone so smoothly.

Surely enough, though, Seraphina gave her all the gory details as they ate breakfast and dressed for the day.

"And she just said *I can't discuss this with you, Sera?*" Astriea asked, picking out a tunic from the armoire with a shocked look on her face. "After all that?"

"After all that," Sera replied.

"What the hell is her problem? I seriously don't understand how they can all be so dedicated to this ice. I grew up surrounded by ice and snow and the cold, too. Do you know what I would have given to have seen green grass more than twice a year? All my wages, that's what."

"She said they have all sorts of quests and traditions dedicated to it. Did you have such things in Monolith?"

Astriea's heart sank. She shouldn't have said anything about her home. The place now wiped from the maps.

"No. We didn't." She said, sitting down at the table for another helping of toast. "And if I think about it, we were a much more miserable people. Based on what I can see from the balcony, the cold doesn't seem to dampen their spirits here."

Seraphina nodded, but their conversation was cut short as Vera and Killian, along with four other masked guards, strode through the door of their room with heavy cloaks and outdoor boots in hand.

"Good news," Killian said, throwing the extra cloaks and boots onto the empty chaise. "You two have been cleared to visit the city."

"You're kidding!" Astriea said, clapping her hands together. "Does that mean we can send word to our loved ones that we're not being raped and tortured?" She said sarcastically.

Killian rolled his eyes and said, "Do you want to go or not?"

Astriea grazed her fingers over one of the cloaks before clutching it fully and snatching it away. "We'll get dressed." She said, tossing it to Sera before grabbing the other.

* * *

Killian led them out through the stables. The metalwork of the entire structure of the castle made Astriea pause to marvel at it.

It looked nothing like the interior. The inside seemed exactly what she would expect from a palace, stone walls, brick hearths, marble floors and pillars, even support beams in the rafters. But on the outside were only gleaming towers of silver metal. No abrasions save for that of the windows and balconies adorning them.

"It's... beautiful." Astriea breathed.

"Because of the castle, this place is called *The Silver City*. It has stood for a—"

Sera finished for him and said, "A thousand years. And it is said that only a dragon's breath could bring it down."

Vera and Killian both tensed.

"Hmm," was all Astriea said before she continued onward through the stables.

Seraphina halted, though. They all stopped and waited for her, but she seemed lost on something in the distance.

"Sera?" Astriea said, taking her hand.

She looked at her and blinked furiously.

"Sorry, I—I thought I heard something. Probably nothing but the effects of not being outside in so long." She said sharply toward Vera before walking ahead of the pack.

That was when she noticed Seraphina wasn't looking at the princess. Hadn't been this entire time.

Neither had Astriea. Because if either of them had, they would've noticed her busted bottom lip which looked like it was getting ready to bruise along the left side of her jaw.

It nearly matched the one Seraphina came back with last night, but hers was already fading thanks to the salve Vera had slipped into her cloak before she stormed out.

But the princess tailed after Seraphina.

Astriea grabbed Killian by the arm and whispered to him, "What happened to her?"

He jerked away and said, "She got you an excursion." Before following behind the others.

Guilt fell on her. Perhaps misplaced, but still earned.

She and Seraphina both had a hard time looking at her since she took them. And some empathetic part of Astriea's heart wanted to reach out a hand to the princess, who walked ahead with lost eyes.

Learn about us. The tzar had asked.

So far, Astriea had learned one thing for certain. That the princess was heading down a dangerous path.

As if she'd leapt into Vera's mind, Astriea saw two paths laid out before her. A quick and easy demise at the end of a blade, or an outright assault of the dark to be endured for all her life.

Death, or a life given wholly to the monster who'd chained her bloodline.

Her eyes moved to Killian, the brother who could not save her, who would gladly take Scythe on for himself instead of her.

Astriea decided she had earned this guilt a thousand times over.

* * *

Upon making it into the city, Astriea couldn't help but notice how happy the people surrounding her were. How children played in the streets and vendors sold hot foods and drinks. Killian even went so far as to bring them all *moonberry* tea. Still steaming and smelling of citrus and honey, topped with a little cream.

To Astriea, this blend of tea was scarce. But one of the sweetest brews you could get.

Although she'd never had actual moonberries, Seraphina said they tasted like a blend of blackberries with a mix of melon. The problem was, at the time, she'd never tried those either. But regardless, the tea was delicious.

It didn't take long for the citizens to realize the grand duchess walked before them, but it did take her by surprise how they doted on her. Astriea had expected them to cower and hide in their shops, but there was none of that. Only bright smiles and warmed baked goods they wanted her to try, or offered to her to take back to the castle.

As they walked away from countless vendors, Astriea heard many of them whisper the same thing again and again, *Tzarina sa macta.*

She tried over and over as they strolled, to piece together what those words might mean. Finally, as they found a restaurant for dinner, she decided she would continue it when she again had access to the library.

37

Seraphina

She'd tried. Seraphina had tried so hard not to look at her. She tried to hold on to the anger as long as she could, but the second an elderly woman came smiling toward them with a bundle of bread in her hands, she couldn't help but glance up to see Vera's expression. Her eyes lit up, but Sera's heart sank at the sight of a fresh bruise. At the gash in her perfect bottom lip.

She should've looked at her sooner. Because now, there was a different kind of hurt in her eyes that she did well to bury quickly.

Sera didn't ask questions as they found their way to the charming little restaurant and sat down for dinner. All of them starving from skipping lunch to see a collection of new ice sculptures on display in the arts quarter.

Astriea had even been so bold as to ask Killian for some coin to buy snacks and some clothes.

They all got split up at one point, and Killian made sure to grill them good for it.

She wasn't completely sure where Astriea had disappeared to in that short time, but she was smiling wide and bright when she returned with a new fur cloak and a cinnamon roll in her hands.

Now, sitting at their table, Sera couldn't decide whether to look at Vera or avoid it altogether. Killian left to get drinks and Astriea seemed to sense the tension and excused herself to the facilitates.

It was just the two of them.

"Vera—"

"Don't. You haven't spoken to me all day. You wouldn't look at me either. I know it doesn't seem like it, but I know the difference between right and wrong. I know that what we have done to you—what *I* have done to the both of you—is horrid and cruel. But you are mistaken in thinking that I can do more than *this*," she gestured to the restaurant bustling around them. "right now. That I can give you more than what I already am. I want to give you the answers, I do. But you have no idea what it will cost me."

"Your throne?" Sera challenged. But Vera just looked at her like she was a fool. The kind of look that spark some anger and maybe even insecurity in her chest.

"It will cost *everything*."

Her words made something like a warm hand reach out from Seraphina. Invisible and luring toward Vera. She didn't seem to notice, though, but something shimmered through what Sera felt was right in front of her. A vision but in real time. Like looking through a lens, she saw a black scar wrapped around Vera's neck. Some words written in another language, but scared like a burn. A brand.

Seraphina sucked in a sharp breath, making that lens and the scar disappear.

"Vera, what did he do to you?" She asked.

But she didn't get the chance to answer as Killian and Astriea returned to the table together, each carrying an assortment of drinks and bread.

They had a good time dining together. Better than what any of them expected. Killian and Vera told them tales of palace affairs and a few ghost stories about the castle. Astriea mostly discussed how lovely the city was and how she hoped to visit it again. And how she needed to borrow a few more books from the library.

Sera just sat there listening and clenching her hands under the table to keep herself from reaching out for Vera's.

She nearly got caught up looking for something again when they passed through the stables on the way back to the castle. But she pulled herself away well enough.

By the time they made it back to their room, it was nearly time for bed. Killian left and waited for Vera at the end of the hall.

With Astriea in the bathing chambers, Vera and Seraphina were alone again. Sera leaning against the doorpost with her arms crossed and Vera just outside it. Like she wasn't sure how welcome she was inside.

"I'll be going then," Vera said and made to turn.

Seraphina grabbed her by the waist and pulled her close, one hand gently raising up to caress her swollen lip.

"Let us kill him." Sera breathed.

"He is still my father. Fighting back in there. I know what it is Astriea has to do in order to cleanse the realm of Scythe completely. I know that one way or another, he has to die for the darkness to be released from our bloodline. It is... It is the real reason I do not want her magic. I could save him on my own, without costing him his life—"

"But what is it costing *you*?" Sera interrupted.

"I'm afraid that's one of those things I can't tell you."

"Are you close? To finishing the serum?"

Vera didn't answer, and she glanced down at the floor.

"You are running out of time, dangerously. You turn twenty-six in five weeks. Do you seriously think he won't take you then?"

"I just need you to trust me, even though that sounds impossible. There are a thousand different things to take care of, and I just need you to be patient."

"I don't want to see him take you, Vera." She admitted. Seraphina took a breath before she went on. "If I choose to trust you like that, promise me you'll do everything in your power to keep us alive. I need to know I can count on you to do that. That you won't betray me again." She didn't know if she believed those words, flowing so effortlessly out of her mouth. But she wanted to, desperately.

"I promise." She replied. Leaning a bit closer, their foreheads now pressed together.

"Now promise me you won't take your own blade. We can break the bloodline curse. Promise me you'll wait for us to do that."

But Astriea came out, and Vera quickly pulled away.

She didn't answer, only bid them both goodnight and left.

And now, laying in bed, eyes wide open in the room's darkness, Seraphina thought about all she was willing to do to Scythe for the pain he'd caused not only Vera but countless others as well.

If this quest had taught her one thing, it was that even though she had never been directly affected by Scythe or his influence on the world; it was very easy to hate him for all he'd done to her friends.

To the people she loved, and to everyone else.

38

Thomas

Thomas and Lavene were both mounted and ready for take-off.

He had to admit it was rather comical to see her reaction, as the sand-snake's massive body moved underneath hers. He'd paralleled the feeling to riding on an earthquake his first time.

The take-off was easy enough, though. Lavene soldiered through and rode without fuss as they dove in and out of clouds.

After a while, his eyes adjusted to the wind, and they dove back under the misty haze.

Just beneath them was the King's Wood. An entire forest dedicated to royal hunting. Although, James had said that his father never really cared for hunting and he didn't either. So it was more filled with beasts than game. The lands have since been opened up to allow citizens to hunt what remains in its woods. Thomas even considered taking his own time to hunt there if they ever got the chance. He even thought back on a time when he and Draes, sometimes Astriea too, would linger on the outskirts of the North Wood. Near the river.

When they would hunt for large game to sell in town. It would've ended with their heads on chopping blocks if they'd ever been caught, but even the townsfolk of Monolith were grateful for fresh meat when Herold Berelda and the last Lord of Monolith would let them go months with no food or supplies. On a normal day, there were those in town who would sell you out to the king for a single silver coin. But none of that mattered when everyone was starving.

The only thing he hated about this brilliant view was that Monolith's Peak was no longer on the horizon. It would take them about two to three hours to clear the King's Wood and then what? From their trajectory, it would put them right on sight for Monolith. But nothing would be there.

This was no triumphant return home, but the survey of a genocide.

* * *

They landed right outside the King's wood and over the lake. If Monolith's Peak still stood, you'd be able to see the monstrosity looming over the valley even from here. But the sun was setting and Thomas didn't particularly want to get a preview of what he was sure to investigate come dawn.

They'd taken over eight hours to get there. He'd hoped that Lavene would be a natural at flight, but alas, she was not.

Although Lavene made mistake after mistake, she did learn from them every time.

Every time the air pockets in the sky rocked her dragon, she reared back on the reins and flew much slower. Every time Sand-snake roared she would jump and slow down.

But by the end of the flight, she was coming along quite naturally. This trait made Thomas think she would continue to grow in the skill.

Now, curled in front of a fire on the edge of the river and the open plains that stretched on toward Monolith, Thomas lay gazing up at the stars while his stomach settled from dinner.

He didn't know if Lavene was awake on the other side of the fire or not, but he sat there daydreaming, anyway.

Those daydreams turned to real ones as he drifted to sleep, two dragons keeping them guarded.

The dream was not what he expected.

Heat and sweat.

Passionate cries and the taste of Astriea's lips. Almost like honeysuckle.

The feel of her skin touching his as she ground against him.

As she pressed him against the headboard.

Tugged his hair and screamed his name.

Then it shifted.

The two of them lay in bed, him reading a book to her while she ate some berries and cheese.

The third and final part of his dream shifted into a memory. One from a time when they were both just two orphans in a town not far from here. In a cabin with a small hearth and three tiny bedrooms.

Astriea sat on the couch building new arrows for a hunt she'd planned with Raja when Thomas stumbled in the door with a bruise already forming around his eye and blood steadily dripping from his busted lip.

It was like he was watching his own memories outside his body, only he couldn't hear anything now. He just watched Astriea annoyingly toss aside her arrows and strings, and drag Thomas to the couch to patch him up.

There was no need to hear what she said to him at that moment, though. He remembered it well. Remembered how she looked at him, like she took a blow every time she saw him injured. How her eyes made his world slow as they shimmered in the firelight.

I hate seeing you hurt.

I know.

Then why not stop? Just don't go back to the fighting pits.

I can't.

Why? She'd leaned closer to him. So close it took everything he had not to kiss her.

Because lately it's been the only time you'll look at me.

She made to argue, but he stopped her.

You have glances at me, what I'm wearing, and if I'm with someone. But right now you're looking at me with love in your eyes and I could drown in it.

Thomas then watched as Astriea broke that tension and guided him to lie in her lap. She handed him a book to read while she finished her arrows. But what he'd never told her, what he'd kept to himself all this time, was that there was only one thing that could drag Astriea out of her own head.

One thing that could open her eyes, to him, to the world: His own pain.

And that was where his mind lingered throughout the night.

His head resting on her legs and a fire keeping them both warm as she sighed, set down her arrows, and took a clean cloth to his lip.

39

Thomas

When Thomas woke the next morning, the rising sun was just illuminating the horizon that he foolishly hoped still housed his old home. But the land was barren. Flat and layered with the first buds of grass in spring.

As he and Lavene were saddling Night-cleaver and Sand-snake, she said to him, "You and the Lightbringer must be very close."

Thomas's brows rose a bit. "We are. And what do you mean, *Lightbringer*? She'll probably hate that." He laughed.

"That's what everyone is calling her now." She replied.

"Why do you ask?" Thomas questioned.

"You called out her name in your sleep last night. Twice, actually."

He blushed. Immediately.

"Ah… Well, you see—"

She laughed and stopped him. "Don't worry, I won't tell."

When they were mounted and ready to go again, Thomas said to her, "It should only take around twenty minutes to reach the Monolith restoration outpost, The king said a *General Barretta* would meet us there and escort us to the mountain remains."

She nodded, and they took off. Into the skies yet again. The feeling was the second thing in the world that made all his troubles drift off. And he only had twenty minutes of it until reality would come crashing down around him.

So, for the next twenty minutes, Thomas lingered in the sky atop his dragon. He ran his hands through clouds and took in the crisp, cool air. That fear he once had of heights now feeling decades behind him.

* * *

Monolith was gone. Wiped away like crumbs left out on a dining table.

In this wide spread of land once stood rows and rows of house-like shacks. On the other side of those was the city center. An old broken fountain used to stand in the middle.

Beyond that would've been the mountain entrance. Through the outer pass, his cabin once hid behind walls of ice and snow. Now only a set of black, broken cliffs remained there. And only a barren field where that town and all those people once resided.

General Barretta was as young as Thomas and generally handsome. His brown hair was slightly unkempt by a few stray curls that barely grazed the top of his ears and he seemed to have an inviting smile about him. Gray eyes met his.

"My Lord Hellion," He said with a bow at the waist. "It's an honor to have you home again, my apologies and grievances for the loss of your people."

"Educated in my history are you, General?" Thomas asked, falling in line behind the soldier escorting them to the large white army tent posted just outside where the city once stood. It took everything in him not to linger at each step on the soil. Not to look for a mountain nearby.

General Barretta nodded and said, "Yours, as well as the Princess Lavene."

Lavene's eyes shot up and went wide.

"Me?"

"Yes, I've heard you are heir to Devil's Gate. But... His Majesty did not mention your beauty." The General then proceeded to gently kiss Lavene's hand.

She looked a little shocked by it at first, but Thomas could see the pink flourishing her cheeks even as she tried to pretend she felt differently. It nearly pulled a mocking grin from his lips.

"Thank you… General Barretta."

Passing by the other tents, Thomas noticed something else. Something he'd never seen in previous Shadonian Army camps.

Little fires were placed here and there throughout the lawn and around each one, a set of five or six soldiers. All of them having dinner, all of them smiling—laughing even. Before, it was common knowledge to keep well away from anyone a part of, or dealing with, Shadon soldiers. Most of them were nasty pieces of work, but these men here were different. More innocent-seeming.

He didn't dare question where they came from until the general led them into the grand marquee. It wasn't much, mostly just a few desks and chairs, a fire pit in the center of the room to keep warm with a metal tube funneling the smoke out of the hole in the top of the tent, and a dining table with food laid out. Roasted boar stew from the smell of it, and some bread and ale.

He and Lavene went straight for the two empty bowls set out for them and sat down to eat.

The face Lavene made as she tried her hardest to eat the stew nearly made Thomas choke. But he held himself together as best he could and reminded himself it was rude to laugh at princesses who've never had *mess*. So he cut her a break and forced down another fat bite of stale bread and weeks-old stew.

General Barretta began to speak as he poured each of them a glass of ale—the only thing there that was fresh.

"So, we haven't gotten far in collecting the *Sharinite* the king requested. The wreckage left behind after the mountains crumbled… it's created something treacherous."

"Well, it was like that before," Thomas interjected between bites.

"No, this… This is something the men have begun to call *Caltillion's Curse*. I've sent three scouting parties in. Each one has come back either hysterical or on the brink of death. And… that was just the men who didn't

166

make it into the range itself."

This had both Thomas and Lavene setting down their spoons and turning to face him.

"How many lost?" Thomas asked.

"Seventeen." The general answered.

Thomas rubbed his jaw.

"We could fly in?" Lavene suggested.

"No. There would be nowhere for your dragons to land. The fallen rocks have made an impregnable field of sharp, jagged pikes."

"Show me," Lavene said with a furrowed brow.

Thomas followed behind them and tried to quail his stomach as they passed through his old city—now only an open field.

He tried to calm his nerves, but he could *feel* it.

The deaths, the pain. Some invisible force running across his spine akin to the tip of a blade.

A curse. This place was cursed. It had to be. He was about to think it was just him, that he'd gone crazy. Until Lavene stopped and said, "Does it always feel this way? This… *haunted*?"

Barretta gripped his stomach a touch. "Yes. It's an effort just to get through the field. That's why camp was set up outside the area."

"It's enough to make you sick." She replied.

Thomas took a step forward behind them and then hit his knees as his world shifted under his feet.

Like something cold and quiet reached up from the earth and yanked him down, down, down…

Before he opened his eyes, he felt warmth.

And when he saw why…

He saw it all. Monolith burning before his eyes.

He was on his knees before the fountain, air stolen from his lungs. And if he could've, he would've torn out his own eyes.

For a moment, there was no sound. He could only see the soldiers ripping women and children from their homes.

Thomas ran toward them, screamed as best he could, and reached out to grab one. Only for his hands to pass through them. Pass through the arm of an old man he tried to help, and a sword he tried to pick up.

He ran back and forth through the streets, forced to bear witness to it. To the horror of it all.

He saw women he knew being raped on Tellens Street.

Children butchered in front of their parents on Anders.

Then he saw the soldiers gather them all together. All that remained, and the bodies of the dead. Right in the city center. On top of the broken fountain.

That was when sound returned to him. When he heard all the screams and wails.

His face was swollen red, his eyes wet with tears that hadn't stopped falling since it all started. And he clawed at his own head in an effort to free himself from this place.

Lightning struck in the distance, and he stood to his feet. His eyes darting to the northeast. To where the mother oak tree once lingered on the edge of The North Wood.

He could see the battalion of soldiers gunning across the field through the cemetery.

The soldiers in the town square stopped to watch as well.

Thomas knew what would happen next. And he watched as the lightning struck once more, taking a pair of orphans with it.

He turned again to see them burning the survivors and the bodies.

This place… This place he'd once called home, this massacre he'd just narrowly escaped.

Friends he'd known since he was six years old.

It *was* a curse. This place was cursed and they never should have come here.

But something else happened. Something he never expected.

Soldiers from a different unit, with a different patch—a red serpent— stormed the square.

They beat and hammered at each other. Soldier fighting soldier.

He collapsed onto the ground, the surrounding anguish seeping into his

bones. That's what it felt like. Every ounce of pain and suffering felt here, flowing directly into him. Smothering him until he was nearly blacking out. And the screams… They overwhelmed him to the point that he reached for a blade on the grass. Reached and reached as his hands passed through it over and over. Reached for anything to *end* this.

But he saw someone through the haze. A woman with skin made of soft green leaves and hair of vines and flowers.

"Thomas…" She said.

"Thomas, you are not really here. You must remember where your body is, so you may return to it. Your power and love for this place is making you vulnerable. Remember where you *really* are. These spirits call out for your help. Help them in *your* time."

She looked like Lavene, but he knew it wasn't.

It was Tala, the Goddess of the Earth and Nature.

Thomas did his best to take a few deep breaths, and slowly, with each one, the screaming faded.

Then the heat.

And finally, when he opened his eyes, Thomas found himself staring at the night sky in a now open field. About fifty men surrounded him with water buckets. With others screaming to get more.

Because Thomas was burning so brightly, he lit up everything from here to the forests. Bright enough, he was sure that someone could see it from the capital.

He couldn't put it out. Was too numb to do it.

He nodded at General Barretta as best he could and passed out as buckets of freezing water doused him. Soothing him into a haunted, dreamless sleep.

40

Seraphina

The next day, Seraphina spent the majority of her time sitting on the caged balcony high above The Silver City. There was a solid roof above her that did well at keeping out the snow.

If she had to kick herself for one thing, though, it had to be that she had no more of that tea they'd had in town. The chamomile she was currently sipping while sitting by the small fire pit was good, but...

Briar came out with firewood in her arms and Seraphina jumped up to take them from her.

"No, my lady. My mother would have my hide if she caught me giving my duties off to our guests—"

"Then it's a good thing we're prisoners. Now hand them over." Sera said with a smile.

Briar tilted her head and looked at her for only a moment before she placed the wood on the fire and sat down on the couch. Avoiding Sera's empty hands.

"My lady, there are only three important people in this castle who consider you to be prisoners: *the demon*, and the two of you. The only hope we have, the only hope *she* has, is you." Her eyes were a little glazed as she spoke. Almost like looking into a hazel mist.

But Briar stood and made to leave, giving Sera a light pat on the top of her hand before doing so.

"Briar?" Sera called.

She stopped.

"Yes, Lady Seraphina?"

"There was this tea in town—"

"Moonberry with honey and cream?" She finished for her.

Sera looked at her curiously, "Yes, exactly that."

Briar smiled and said, "It is the grand duchess's favorite. One of the shopkeeper's sons serves here in the castle as the Royal Tea Maker."

"*Royal Tea Maker?*" Seraphina laughed. Briar mirrored it.

"I do find it a silly title, especially since he makes an assortment of other drinks and some rather tasty pastries, too."

"I didn't know such titles existed."

"They normally don't. However, the grand duchess loved the tea so much that she drew the title up and marked it with the royal seal. The shop owner's son and his entire family will now be cared for by the crown."

Sera said nothing. She only smiled. Her eyes lost on the fire and her mind wandering for a moment.

"Briar?"

"Yes, my lady?"

"If I asked you to go and get me a moonberry tea and something for yourself, and come back and sit with me a while, would you be obligated to do that?"

"I suppose I would."

Briar was only gone for about twenty minutes.

She brought the teas with her and two fur blankets.

Seraphina relished the taste and smiled a bit at the reason she loved it so.

"What can you tell me about the royal family? Can you tell me why Vera can't... *Fight back?*"

Something rumbled. The ground, the walls. It was barely a tremor, though. Not something most people would worry themselves over. But there was a bitter taste behind the feeling of it.

Briar even looked around before she spoke. Whispered, "It... It is like a curse—" The castle rumbled again, but she went on. "This place... this place is most heavily influenced by it. It is why you were brought here and not the capitol."

"The Silver City isn't the capitol? But the books in the library—"

"On paper and in ink, yes, but... not to the people."

The tremor started again and stopped. Briar got up and tucked her blanket around Seraphina's lap.

"I cannot say more of the subject, my lady. I must go and wash up for supper."

Sera smiled and nodded while Briar curtsied and took her leave.

Then she just let her head fall back against the couch, still clutching the warm tea in her hands.

What did Briar mean by a *curse*? She thought. Sera already knew Scythe had something on them. That much was clear to anyone with eyes. But what was it specifically? If she could just pry that bit of information from someone in this gods-forsaken castle, she might be able to find a way to free them from it. Free Vera from Scythe.

But I can't do that if I don't know where to start.

Sera did her best to enjoy the last bit of warmth in her drink, the sweetness of the cream before it inevitably melted away, as she watched snow fall on The Silver City and pondered what they were all hiding.

* * *

After dinner, Sera waited for Astriea to come back from the library. When she finally trotted through the door, she had Belle and Helena with her. Each of them carrying a stack of books behind her.

"Gods, Astriea, isn't this a bit *much*?"

"Well, as you know, I've been trying to find everything I can on the history of Telas and anything to do with magic and the *fae*."

"Yes, of course."

"Right, so this is all that the library has, and believe me, I rummaged through the lot. These here are the only ones that *might* be helpful."

Astriea set the stack in her own hands down on the table. Belle and

Helena deposited theirs beside it.

"Will that be all, my lady?" Belle asked.

"Yes, thank you so much for your help," Astriea replied, smiling brightly at them.

Once they had gone, Sera stepped over to Astriea at the table, where she was already flipping through pages once again.

"I take it you'll be researching all night again?" Sera asked.

"Most likely, any plans for you tonight?"

"I—I was thinking of going up to see Vera."

"Any plans on *that* battlefield?" She asked.

Sera hesitated but said, "Astriea…"

She looked up at her.

"I don't want to lie to her. Whatever ties she has to Scythe, they can't be of her own free will. No one will talk about it, but he has something on her, and if we can figure out what that is—"

"We can free her from it. Free them all. Perhaps even stop a war from breaking out. But that still leaves two things: Vera's commitment to the ice, and her father. The tzar must die for the bloodline to be free of Scythe's influence. Even if there is some goodness left in him, his daughter will suffer after he is gone."

Sera's heart sank, and she dipped her head.

Astriea spoke up once more as Sera walked away from the table. "Do you remember what they were calling her in the city? *Tzarina sa macta?*"

Sera nodded. "Did you figure out what it means?"

"Nothing, yet. If the topic comes up, you could see if she might translate it."

Seraphina tilted her head, brows knitting.

"Something to think about while you're gone." She said with a smile, tossing a piece of chocolate to her with a wink.

* * *

Seraphina climbed the steps of Vera's tower once again. This time, more conflicted than ever. She knew there was good in her.

These things wrapped around her mind as her hand knocked on the door.

It swung open and there she was, hair unbound again and this time an emerald green nightgown clung to her. Fabric so thin she could see the shape of her nipples peeking through the bodice. Her hips pushed the dress out wide and then shaped down her legs before spilling out onto the floor behind her. Only thin green straps holding up heavy breasts.

Then, the last time they'd been this exposed to one another came washing in like a hurricane. The air around them grew heavy. And this voice that she dared not give voice to whispered to the weary parts of her soul, *Together, together, never apart.*

"Sera—" The princess tried to say, but she didn't let her finish.

Their lips crashed together, tongues mingling and hands grabbing at whatever the other could find.

She remembered Vera's busted lip and pulled away.

"Oh, gods, I'm sorry..." she said, gently grazing her thumb across Vera's bottom lip.

Vera smiled and said, "I think you'll find I have more steel than that."

Fingers lifted Seraphina's chin and Vera kissed her again. This time pulling her to the bed and shutting the door behind her.

She sat against the headboard, Vera in front of her and peeling away Sera's tunic.

She grabbed Vera's legs, her ass, and pulled her onto her lap. Letting the beautiful princess straddle her.

Sera's hands reached and grabbed at every piece of Vera she could touch. Her fingers pressed tightly against magnificent thighs before traveling up her hips, then her back.

Their tongues clashed. Kneading together in strokes that made her crumble. She broke from her lips to bring her own down Vera's perfect neck. She reached her collarbone and quickly decided she was tired of barriers.

Seraphina grabbed the straps of that nightgown and pulled them apart so hard, the dress split right down the middle. All the way to Vera's waist.

Sera wrapped her arms and the two pieces of torn fabric around Vera's. Pinning her.

Vera's unbound, ample breasts moved up and down ever so slightly with her heavy breaths. She tilted her head back, her red hair falling behind her shoulders.

She moaned when Sera's tongue circled a peaked nipple. Ground her center against Sera's as her tongue slowly ran across it.

For a little while, that was all they did. For a little while, that burning, swelling heat between them built and built until neither of them could wait a moment more.

Sera's underclothes were now long gone. Vera's torn nightgown ended up on the floor.

She waited under the blankets for Vera to come back with a box in her hands. She opened it to reveal a few different pleasure toys in an assortment of sizes.

Sera's jaw dropped and her brows rose.

"Vera! These are very naughty." She laughed.

"Well… I'm not very entertained by men, and there aren't exactly a plethora of women at court that are *interested*." She said, blood running to her cheeks. "So… which one would you like to try?" She asked.

Sera pointed to the third largest one. Just because even the men she'd experimented with didn't have one that size, and the other two were far too intimidating. Even the one she chose would be a challenge.

"That one. Although, I'm not sure it will… fit."

"Well, let's find out together," Vera reassured her and plucked it from the box.

"You mean you've never used it?"

"No. I just got this set, so… this should be fun." She said with a wink.

Vera lowered herself into the sheets and their skin collided once more. Their breasts pressed together, legs intertwining and wrapping around each other.

Vera's hands wandered down until her fingers found Sera's middle. Her soaking, throbbing middle.

She thrust her fingers in and Sera moaned as they slid gently inside. Pulling in and out in torturous strokes, making her center coil.

She felt Vera's tongue then. Working down her until she was lightly stroking the bundle of nerves at the top. Teasing and looping around while her fingers thrust in tandem. Just before Sera was about to break, Vera pulled away.

Red lips moved to her breasts. Vera's tongue flicked the tips of her nipples until Sera was moaning against the touch. That was when she pressed that massive leather toy into her.

Gods.

Gods, gods, gods.

Sera sucked in a sharp breath and her back arched up, pressing her front against Vera's.

It was so big. So big it pushed and stretched her nearly to the point of pain.

"Do you want—" Vera started.

"Don't stop," Sera said through a moan.

So Vera pushed it deeper. Seraphina cried out, and the pain ceased. She couldn't stop the sounds of pleasure that poured out of her as Vera pressed it in and out. Over and over until the muscles inside her went taught. Gripped it tight as Vera continued to bury it again.

Again.

Again.

Again.

Vera moved her mouth back to the bundle of nerves and flicked her tongue across it. The act made Vera's name come off her lips in a moan. Because of that, she did not stop. She wrapped an arm around Sera's legs and pulled her knees together. Making the walls of her center squeeze harder against the leather pounding inside her right now. She fucked her until Sera's legs and body were shaking. Until her center coiled so tightly that release burst from her. Dripping down her legs and onto the bed.

While Seraphina caught her breath, Vera slid her tongue inside her.

Sera twitched and moaned again against the feel of that soft wetness slipping in and dragging across those nerves again.

Vera laid a hand on her stomach, pressing her down against the mattress, and lazily pushed her tongue in again.

"Vera—"

She flicked and Sera cried out.

"Vera, let me do this for *you*." She forced out.

She looked up at her, green eyes hungry and shimmering in the firelight. "This *is* for me."

Her tongue went back to work.

Stroking her until release poured out once more and Seraphina's legs were nearly locked around Vera's head.

After a few moments of breath, Sera took no chances and grabbed the toy. She dragged her other hand up Vera's center and felt her dripping down her own legs.

She leaned closer, her lips a breath away from Vera's. The peaks of their nipples barely grazed the other. Vera whimpered.

"I didn't know you'd missed me so terribly," Sera whispered on her lips.

"There hasn't been a moment I haven't." Vera breathed.

Then Sera pressed that soaking wet toy against Vera's entrance.

It stretched her like it had Sera. And the princess's moan was electrifying.

Vera sat back on her knees and then fell onto her back as Sera continued to press further into her.

When Sera saw, first-hand, what Vera looked like as her back arched against the final push, she could've come all over again. The sound she released again had Seraphina's teeth against her neck.

Her lips traveled across nearly every piece of Vera's body. Her skin tingled and hummed along with the princess's cries. Something nearly guttural escaped from her throat as she felt Vera cry out her name against her skin.

"*Lethal little beast.*" Vera moaned.

Seraphina reached her hand to the back of Vera's neck, fingers tangling in her hair, and claimed her mouth with her own.

Sera didn't stop until the air was thick with their heat and sweat and breath. Until Vera had come all over Sera and the bed.

Until Seraphina's tongue had tasted heaven dripping down Vera's legs. Only then did they fall into a dark, heavy sleep, wrapped in the other's arms.

41

Seraphina

The next morning, Sera's eyes peeked open to the first rays of sunlight beaming into Vera's long, stained glass windows. The rays refracting in colors of green, red, and blue.

She only took in the room for a few moments. There was a large hearth on her right, the flames from last night now only glowing embers, and small trinkets of knights and horses lined down the mantle. The bed itself was a massive behemoth made entirely of dark oak. The headboard stretched up and over, with a thick, spiraling post stationed at each of the four corners. There were sheer, pine-green canopy sheets hanging from the top and pinned back against the posts. And by the windows sat a desk with three chairs piled around it. Papers were scattered about and there was an ink spill on the top right corner of a map.

It was a warm, lovely, *lived-in* room.

She felt a flutter of movement and looked down to see the crown princess of Telas asleep next to her. The tousled mess of her hair decorated the pillows, with a few wisps gracefully draping down her body, barely veiling the bits of her that had consumed Sera's adoration last night.

She laid her head back on the pillow and watched her sleep for a few minutes. That was when she noticed how quiet it was. How blissfully and beautifully quiet the world had gone. There was nothing but herself, Vera, and lovely rays of light warming their skin. There was no worry or doubt.

No fears to cling to. And then, in the moment she felt as though this were a heaven, the mission set back in.

The guilt and shame.

Had this been what Vera felt all this time? Feels now? Would Sera ever know?

But the doors swung open before Sera could voice those questions, and a dark-haired man burst through. Four guards piling in behind him.

Vera lurched up from the bed, a sheet wrapped around her chest. She shoved Seraphina behind her. With one arm gripping the sheet and the other stretched out in front of Sera, she said, "Get out! Now!"

The guards took up defensive positions but looked at each other questioningly. The courtly man in the front stepped forward. "They don't take orders from you, *Duchess*. These are the guards of my house, not your palace rats."

His black hair was neatly combed back and away from his face. While he was generically handsome, he didn't really have any defining features that made him stand out. He was tall, taller than the two of them by at least a foot. Scrawnier than she would have expected from any man of Telas, but held his shoulders back with immense pride, carrying a heavily jeweled dagger on his belt. His perfectly straight nose tilted up at them.

"They are still *my* subjects, and they will obey the heir to the throne or they will be skinned alive and strung up by their ankles as a warning to all traitors." She said more to his guards than to him. The words were cold as ice. Nothing of the loving princess she was just admiring, but that of the next Queen of Telas, the next *Tzarina*.

Vera The Vicious.

The guards sheathed their weapons and left the room, all of them piling up in the hallway.

"Get out, *Yasarin*."

Yasarin was not a name she'd heard before.

"You'll only have so much sway for so long, so go ahead and bed your little *monster*." He said.

Vera nearly snarled at him as he moved closer to her, leaning one hand against a bedpost. Sera placed her own hand gently on Vera's lower back. Her other already clutching a cheese knife left on the bedside table as she felt Vera's repulsion echo across her skin.

"One day," he whispered, "Scythe is going to have you, and I will too, *my betrothed.*"

Yasarin pushed off the bed and left. The door slamming behind him.

Vera's breaths were heavy and uneven.

"*Betrothed*? Vera, you're betrothed to someone else?"

Her attention snapped to Sera.

Reality came crashing in again.

She knew nothing about her. It was all lies and secrets at every turn. She looked at Vera with the lingering thought that by the end, the princess wouldn't be able to tell the difference between truth and deceit.

"It's—it's not like that."

"Not like what? Who is he?" Sera questioned, getting out of bed and throwing on her clothes and cloak. Vera got up and followed, throwing on garments she pulled from the dresser as she spoke.

"He's a nobleman. His father is a good friend of the crown. Well, a good friend of—"

"Scythe." Sera interrupted.

Vera nodded and went on, "He's been trying for years, but last spring, as a punishment, Scythe betrothed me to him. Sera, I swear it has never been something I wanted. He's…he's vile and cruel. He loves it when Scythe is in control. His entire family is wicked and I have to send my personal guard to their estates and lands to ensure the people there aren't being mistreated."

They stood there, fully dressed, gazing at each other in silence for a moment. Vera almost looked like she'd said too much. Sera realized this was the most honest she'd ever been with her.

"I… I should get back to Astriea," Sera said quietly. Trying not to push.

"Of course," Vera replied, rubbing her arm. "Can I walk you?" She offered.

Sera nodded, trying to tuck away the ten thousand thoughts slamming around in her head before they walked down the many stairs and journeyed across the castle back to her room.

* * *

Before they got to the door, a squad of guards dressed completely in black armor she'd never seen stopped them in the corridor. Without a word, someone bound both of their hands behind their backs and forced them all the way to the throne room.

The Tzar sat on his throne, black shadows swirling in his eyes and flickering back to their original color of hazel now and then.

Yasarin stood at the bottom of the dais near the king's feet, a cruel grin on his face. That little bastard had acted quickly.

The dark guard shoved them onto the cold floor. Some feral part of her wanted to bite his fingers off for it.

Yasarin quickly approached Vera.

"You'll pay for this you rat." The princess said with her chin high.

He grabbed her by the collar of her tunic and said, "Your majesty, my betrothed defiles herself with this foreigner whore! I caught them in bed together not even an hour ago."

"And what do you want from me, Yasarin?"

This was not the Tzar. Was also not Scythe, but some horrid version in-between. Some part of the mortal man he once was, corrupted and twisted by the dark, and the serums trying to fight off the possession. This voice was almost hollow. Haunting.

"I wish to punish her for her misdeeds. I am to be king. She should remember that." He gave Vera a hateful smirk.

The Tzar said nothing. He just dipped his chin.

This was all the permission the young lord needed. He lifted his hand and backhanded Vera across the face. She didn't make a sound. And no one else did either.

But Sera...

Sera was seething and fighting against the guards that held her back.

The Tzar and Yasarin looked at her directly, but Vera's eyes never left the hand that just struck her.

Just as Yasarin let out a faint grin, the Grand Duchess of Telas quickly leapt up, swinging her bound wrists under her feet, and snatched the jewel-studded dagger from its sheath around his waist. Faster than Sera could suck in a breath, Vera's entire body twisted as she rose, and the blade of that dagger sliced right through Yasarin's wrist.

His hand fell to the floor with a light, wet thud.

The blood spewing from his open wrist and the screams he released made a twisted part of Sera's heart sing.

She looked at Vera and saw the same expression, the same look in her eyes. The same smile on her face only accented by a splatter of blood.

Yasarin cried out to the king, who now looked at him with disgust. Almost as if he was more upset about getting blood on the floor.

"You asked me to arrange this marriage. You asked me for a chance to become king and you want to be respected as such. But you will never be *Tzar*. That right is reserved for only *my* heirs. You make a fool of yourself and then beg me for aid? When she is mine, will you not be her loyal consort? You dare to lay your hand on her at the mere nod of my head. Because you are respectless. You find yourself to be above what you are. You are no one. No one against *me*."

Those words made her blood boil. There was nothing left of the Tzar now, in this moment. It was only Scythe.

"I will punish the princess for her indiscretions and the loss of your hand, only as a respect to your father as head of your house. But you will get out of my sight. You will leave this castle and return to the Easternlands. And you will tell your father that losing a hand was punishment for your lack of respect and your father's neglect on your rearing."

Yasarin said nothing and sobbed as his household guard dragged him out of the throne room.

Sera's eyes darted back and forth from Vera to the king.

"You." He said to Vera, an invisible force wrapping around her before launching her toward his feet.

But the guards were dragging Seraphina out.

"No!" she yelled, fighting back against them. "Let me go!" she screamed. The tzar stepped down off his throne. Even from here, Sera could see the whole of his eyes were solid black. No haze of the man who loved his daughter to be seen. Vera lifted her chin and closed her eyes.

"Vera!" Sera screamed again. Her breath now coming in short, ineffective bursts.

Vera didn't look at her. "VERA!"

The whole palace shook as Scythe fully woke once more.

The doors closed in Seraphina's face just as she saw the tzar's fist swing through the air.

Red.

The world went red, and it didn't matter who was good and who was bad. The only thing that mattered was getting through that door.

She couldn't let it happen again.

Couldn't be made powerless again.

She beat and clawed against the mighty wood. Pulled a sword from a guard's belt and ran it through two of them before something hard slammed against her head.

Everything went dark then. Everything went quiet.

42

Astriea

Killian came bursting through the door with a blood-covered Seraphina unconscious in his arms.

The book in her hands hit the floor and she ran to them even as the walls and floor rumbled around her.

"What happened?" She asked, more like screamed.

Without thinking, Astriea was clearing off the chaise lounge and Killian rested her atop it.

"I don't know. She was in a blind rage, killed two guards, injured four others, trying to get into the throne room, screaming for Vera. I had to fight her off and knock her over the head with the hilt of my sword to stop her."

His words were a worried pant. "I have to go find Vera, barricade the door, and let no one in but me."

Astriea couldn't take her eyes off Seraphina, bloody, but breathing. She didn't answer him until he took her face in his hands and made her look into his swirling silver eyes.

"Astriea, do you understand?" He asked.

"Barricade the door. Let no one in but you." She repeated back to him.

"Good girl." He smiled and left the room in a hurry.

Astriea did as he said and wedged a chair under the doorknob, and then pushed the dresser and couch in front of it for good measure.

She paced back and forth before the chaise Sera laid in. Paced and waited for her to wake. She'd nearly twisted her fingers raw before she gathered clean water and washed what blood she could off of her before it dried.

When she finished cleaning her skin and clothes, Astriea gently dipped Sera's hair into the bucket and washed it, too. She looked over at the mighty clock in the corner to see it had only been fifteen minutes. Her chest quivered and her eyes stung. It felt like hours. Days.

But Sera's eyes shot open, and she took a deep breath.

"Thank the gods." Astriea breathed. Her heart leaping forward after being clenched so tightly.

Sera rubbed her head and sat up. Her brows rose at the feel of damp hair.

"Killian brought you in—covered in blood. Said you killed two guards trying to—"

"Get in the throne room!" Her eyes went wide, and she tried to get up. Astriea jumped up and pushed her onto the chaise. She fell back easily.

"Absolutely not!" She commanded. "I'm not opening that door, and neither are you. Not unless it's Killian on the other side of it."

"Oh, suddenly you give a rat's ass about Killian? Scythe is going to hurt Vera. I need to *go*!"

"Sera, we cannot get involved! We have to remember what they've done to us and let them work out their own issues. We have no way to free her and if we're not careful, everything will fail." Astriea replied.

Seraphina curled her lip. Anger boiling from her.

"And Killian? You trust him enough to let only him through that door; he is worthy of some redemption, but Vera isn't?"

Everything went dark. Felt as if a mighty shadow had cast darkness over every room in the castle. Darker than the night. More terrifying. Too much so for nine in the morning.

For a moment, the air in the room seemed to shimmer as it got sucked out.

Sera noticed the change, too. Noticed the burning hearth, now only embers faintly glowing. They looked at each other, and then around the room. Every sconce was out. No light anywhere, save for the glow of those embers.

That was when the palace shook hard. As if a hand had reached out and rattled it in its grip. Strangled it until the furniture smashed against walls and paintings fell. Until every dish and mirror shattered and a loud growling sound erupted in their minds.

Astriea wasn't sure when she and Seraphina grabbed hold of one another. But now they clutched on to the other for dear life. The two of them smashed between the armoire and the wall by the window. Books she didn't know were there had fallen on top of them from the shelf.

Sera was pressed against her when that feeling of outright terror flooded through them. From the look on Sera's face, she felt it, too.

"This—this isn't like the last time." Sera forced out. Every word a struggle. Their arms locked in fear around each other.

"No." Astriea gasped out. "No, this is so much worse."

She couldn't breathe. Either of them.

The shaking of the castle stopped, but that dread remained. Barreling in on them in waves of nauseating terror.

She sucked in a breath as their door shook. They didn't make a sound. But instead, waited for whatever was on the other side to come in and peel them apart. Astriea felt Sera's grip tighten around her arms.

They both closed their eyes, heads down. Waiting for an inevitable end. A dishonorable one, laced with dread and fear, as they could do nothing under the weight of shelves and a table and the massive armoire.

Then it was gone. All of it.

The unending dread, the shadow that doused the castle, the rattling of the door. It all slipped away. Sunlight peered into the windows just enough to illuminate the damage done to their room. Everything was wrecked.

"Are you okay? Anything broken?" Astriea asked as she shoved the oversized dresser off of them and dragged themselves out from underneath the wreckage.

"I'm good, you?" Sera struggled to say.

"I think I'm alright..." Astriea paused as she looked at the door. "Let's go see if we can find her."

Seraphina's eyes lit up.

They marched through the remains of the dresser, couch, and chair Astriea used to block the door but stopped as it swung open before them.

Killian leaned panting against the door frame, a gash cut across his cheek.

"What happened?" Sera said, rushing toward him and wrapping his arm over her shoulder.

"I shouldn't..." He rasped.

Astriea ran to the second couch on the other side of the room that remained mostly undamaged and cleared it off before Sera helped Killian onto it.

"Be damned, you shouldn't. What happened?" Astriea spat. There was so much pain there, and... and anger. *Rage*.

Killian looked back and forth into both their eyes and said, "I got to the throne room but the new guard wouldn't let me through. And I *heard* her. I heard him beating her down in there and I could not get in..." His voice broke a bit.

Astriea saw the despair in Sera's eyes, but Killian went on.

"I disturbed him, so he opened the doors and while he had his guard fight me off," He gestured to the gash, "Vera was able to get a hold of the new serum from one of her guild officers. They caught wind of what was happening and raced to her, and were waiting for the right moment to hand it off..."

"So, she's alive? She's safe?" Sera asked, seeming to do everything in her power not to seem desperate for an answer.

"Yes, she's alive. But... None of us are safe." He got up, stumbling toward the door.

"Killian, sit down. Wait for aid to arrive—" Astriea said.

"I am the aid, Astriea." He swatted their hands away and barreled forward. "Stay here. When the palace is secure, either I will come and find you, or I'll send your ladies' maids." He slammed against the door frame yet again. Sera and Astriea were on him in a moment.

"The tzar?" Astriea asked.

"The tzar will be incapacitated for now. He is in a controlled sleep. Something new Vera added to the formula." He looked at Sera then. "Why was he punishing her?"

"She didn't tell you?" Sera asked, brows knitted.

"She's not awake." He mumbled. Eyes on the floor and not at either of them. *Gods, how bad was it?*

"I need to see her." Sera tried to push through the door but Killian stopped her.

"Move, Killian." She said, not losing eye contact.

"You can't see her right now, Sera."

"The hell I can't! I swear on the Light if you don't get out of my way I will move you myself—"

"She doesn't want to see you!" He cut her off.

Sera flinched, and Astriea reached a hand out and placed it on her shoulder. Killian sighed and went on, "She doesn't want you to see her... Like that, Seraphina. It's the one thing she asked of me before she collapsed, so no. You cannot see her."

"I came to her bed last night and when we woke this morning, some asshole named *Yasarin* caught us together, said they were engaged." Sera breathed out. Holding back tears.

"I hate that fucking prick."

"Yeah, well, that prick ran straight to the tzar and told him what we did."

Killian's brows furrowed in tight and he questioned, "But it's not a crime to love or bed the same sex in Telas? Everyone knows that. And I know for certain that Yasarin is always entertaining members of the opposite. What grounds did he even have to stand on?"

"He felt *disrespected*. Asked the tzar for permission to punish Vera himself."

Killian's eyes went wide, and Astriea then realized how intently she'd been listening as she caught herself leaning closer to Sera, clinging to every word.

"He backhanded her across the face."

"And then what happened?" Astriea asked.

189

"She stole his dagger from his own belt and cut it off."

"The belt?" Killian asked.

"The hand that struck her."

Astriea and Killian looked at each other and both sucked in a quiet breath.

"The tzar called Yasarin a disrespectful fool and threw him out, but promised he would punish Vera for both her indiscretion and losing his hand." She sighed and cradled her head in her hands. "This is all my fault."

"It's not. It's Scythe's fault. Try not to forget that." Killian said gently. "Thank you, Sera. I'll send for you when the healers have situated. Until then, the two of you stay put and be mindful of the ceiling and chandeliers. I'd hate for you to have come all this way just to die crushed under one of these ghastly things." He winked at Astriea and took off, disappearing into the darkness still lingering in the halls.

43

Astriea

In the time they waited for any sign of Killian or Morra and her daughters, Astriea tried to find ways to make herself feel useful. She started picking up the rubble and debris.

She found a broom in the hall closet and swept away the shattered glass, turned over and cleaned up the couches and dressers as best she could, and cleared the bed.

The last thing she did was try to salvage the books she'd borrowed from the library. Four or five of them were damaged beyond repair and scattered across the room.

However, in the corner by the window, where the desk and small bookshelf both lie on their sides, were about ten to fifteen books—mostly undamaged—littered about.

Astriea pushed the shelf back up and then turned the desk off its side before she gathered the books.

She didn't recognize any of them.

The Great Pool

World of The Fae

Bragus's Theories of Law

The Unending Dark

There were others there as well, but the former all bore the same mark upon the bindings: *PROHIBITED READING.*

Seraphina tossed in her sleep on the chaise, yanking Astriea from thought. She put the books down and went over to tend to her friend until she inevitably fell asleep beside her.

44

Seraphina

Seraphina didn't get any clearance to see Vera until the next day. She'd gone to her tower, but she hadn't been there, and every time she asked Briar or Helena, or Belle, they said she wasn't taking visitors.

So, Sera did what she could to track her down in the winding halls of the castle.

By lunch, she'd found her.

A distinct set of guards—six of them all donning silver armor and helmets that covered their entire face—escorted a cloaked figure through the corridors.

Even with her back turned and hood raised, Sera could tell who it was. She thought little about what she did, she just ran toward her.

Sera pushed through the guards flanking Vera and dropped a hand onto her shoulder.

Vera winced and yanked away. Two guards yanked her back and held her up off the floor.

The immediate regret made her mind lost on the pain she'd just caused Vera. Then stunned when her beautiful princess looked at her, hood still raised as though she could hide the pain in a thin shadow.

Her eyes were swollen and blackened. Her nose definitely broken. Both lips busted and scabbed. And her arm… Vera clutched her arm tightly.

All of this she saw with a cloak shielding her face and body. Something in her shattered at the thought of what Vera hid underneath.

"Put her down. Now!" she commanded, pointing with her good arm.

Sera didn't even register the ground making contact with her feet again. She only looked at her.

Vera didn't say anything. And wouldn't look Seraphina in the eye.

"Show me." Sera breathed. "Leave." She yelled at Vera's guards.

Vera nodded at them and they walked down the hall and stopped.

But she wouldn't pull back her hood.

Sera reached out and gently pulled it off herself.

And tears she absolutely could not stop streamed down Sera's face. She stepped closer and reached out to touch Vera's cheek, but hesitated.

Sera sucked in a breath and gently nudged her chin toward her. Guiding her eyes to her own.

"Tell me—" she begged her in the middle of that hall. "Tell me why he does this to you, my love—tell me and I'll fix it, I'll stop him I swear—"

Vera's tears would've hurt her less than the numb expression on her face. She pressed her forehead to Sera's and said in broken words, "I can't…" She forced down a breath, "I wish I could tell you. I wish you could save me from this, but you can't. No one can untangle my fate from his."

The guards returned before Sera could respond and Vera pulled up her hood.

"I'm going to the healer's guild just north of here for a few days. I'll be good as new in no time. Healers have more access to magic farther north, so I'll be better when I return." She paused, turning away to leave. "I'll be stronger, too."

Seraphina found her way back to her room and cried in Astriea's arms when she told her what happened. Then blankly stared at the ceiling until an unfulfilling sleep grabbed hold of her.

45

Thomas

Thomas slept in Barretta's war tent for two days. He didn't eat or drink or even piss in that time, so waking up to see Draes and Valtan asleep against his bedposts just piled on to the already pounding headache.

Great.

He tried to get up without stirring them but ultimately failed.

Draes was the first to jump up.

"Thank the gods."

Thomas just waved him off as he stumbled for the exit.

Draes and Valtan tailed after him, though.

"You've been fighting a fever for two days. You need to sit down." Draes said with that tone he hated. Like he was a child.

"I *need* to piss," Thomas replied, rolling his eyes even though they couldn't see him do it, before finding a private place outside his tent to relieve himself.

They were still waiting for him when he returned. He had to admit he felt clammy and a little nauseous but hoped he didn't look as sick as he felt.

The overwhelming urge to vomit was good for one thing, though, it kept his mind away from what he'd seen. The memories still clouded his mind, creeping up on him in the depths of his thoughts, but kept at bay by his tossing stomach.

He threw himself into a chair at the table and tried to force down some bread and water. Draes and Valtan took seats next to him.

"What happened?" Draes asked. This time less condescending.

The nausea stopped. So did the headache. It all cleared away for memories of flames and screams and pain.

He didn't realize how long he'd been silent until Valtan placed a hand on his shoulder and said, "Thomas?"

"I saw it. The bloodshed, the burning... All of it."

And that's all he would give them. All that he could.

"But why did it affect you so heavily?" Draes asked. "Why didn't anyone else see it?" Draes asked.

It was Lavene who said, stalking into the tent, "Because he is a god, and because he loved this place. It's people. Because their spirits called out for his help."

"How did you—"

She held up a hand to stop Thomas.

"When you fell, you caught fire. Bright white flames so hot no one could go near you. No one could wake you either, so... Tala reached out to Hellion. He let her into your mind and she coaxed you back. I..."

"You saw it?" Thomas breathed.

"I saw the end."

Thomas only nodded and dropped his head. The room went silent.

* * *

His headache and nausea faded by dinner that night. The only thing left now was the unending loop of pain running through Thomas's mind. The things he saw appearing and disappearing in a flash before his eyes.

Before the food was prepared, he and Lavene went back out to the dead mountains and stood at the barrier this time. Thomas was twitchy and nervous the entire walk. Part of him worried the dead might snatch his leg and drag him down again.

Lavene paced back and forth, her hands raised up toward the broken rock before them. Then, a beautiful green glow beamed from her palms. And when her eyes opened, they filled with that same light.

The real magic came next. Pieces of the broken mountain began to rattle and shift. The ground under their feet remaining solid. She gave a push, and the rocks parted, creating a path before them, leading straight through as far as he could see.

May the mountains move to clear your path.

She released the stones and panted, a bead of sweat running down her brow.

"Lavene, that was amazing!"

She smiled a bit.

"I think it will do for now, but I still have to open paths down the entirety of the range. Walking will take us weeks." She bent over, putting her hands on her knees. Thomas handed her the canteen from his belt.

"Well… What if you did it on dragon back?"

She looked up at him curiously.

"I mean it, we hover above the range—as low as you need—and open paths on our flight to Devil's Gate."

She seemed to consider it. Then she said, "Do you think Sand-snake will react badly? Using my power in flight like that?"

"I say, give them some small displays of power at a time so they aren't stunned. Maybe demonstrate your gifts to them before we take off, too."

Lavene nodded, and they headed back for camp.

* * *

At dinner, Draes and Valtan insisted on coming along. Draes not being delighted that Thomas was leaving at first light. And when he asked them not to follow, Draes became unbearably silent.

"Don't do that," Thomas said.

"I'm not doing anything," Draes replied, not looking up from his lamb and bread. "Not caring for you, not flying across the country on a half-broke dragon for you, and certainly not coming with you even though you look like you've been seasick for two weeks."

"Can we have the room, please?" Thomas asked gently.

Lavene, Valtan, and General Barretta all took their leave quickly and without fuss.

"What is your problem?" Draes asked with a bite. "I came all this way, on a beast that did *not* want us riding it—"

"You should not have come, Draes, I had everything under control—"

"Not according to your friend, Lavene, and the snow sparrow she sent. We just got here and you're already shoving me off. Why can't you just let us help—"

"Because I do not need your help!" Thomas's words burst out, refusing to be caged any longer. "If it isn't Astriea, then it's you. Or Damian, or James, for stars' sake. None of you think I can handle a single thing on my own, but I am not a child. You. Were. Gone." He took a breath. "You were gone and Astriea shut down right after. What did you think happened in the time since?"

Draes didn't answer, but he stood there, his mouth closed tight and eyes wide.

"Did you think I went to the Pearson's and had a warm dinner every night? I didn't. Instead, I went to the pits and fought for coin until I was the best. Until I was good enough to not only go toe to toe with Astriea, and Raja himself, but until I could keep her safe. Until I could look her in the eye and tell her I could give her something to live for. That I could fight for it and keep it safe for us. I even started contracting with Astriea and the Rebellion. I've kept myself, and Astriea, alive and stronger than anyone else. I keep reading and learning, I contain and nurture my power, I have done *everything* any of you have ever asked of me and yet all of you still doubt me. You still treat me like an ignorant child."

Draes opened his mouth to disagree, but there was no stopping Thomas now.

"But I can do this on my own. I don't need to be saved every time I pass out. I don't need my girl or my brother or the king dropping everything to go *make sure Thomas doesn't die.*" He mocked. "So I am begging you, Draes, take Valtan and go back and ready the army for the journey to Telas. Where you'll be helpful. Because I do not need you here."

By the time Thomas realized how harsh he'd been, Draes was walking out of the tent, not having spoken a word.

Regret wrapped its claws around his throat.

"Draes—" He stepped forward but slammed against the large support beam in the middle of the room as nausea and images of carnage swept over him.

He took a few deep breaths and pressed on.

Draes was already gathering his pack in the field where the white dragon rested. Valtan talking to Lavene a few yards away.

"You sure you're good, mate?" Valtan asked.

Thomas just cut his eyes at him.

"Alright, alright. *Silver* doesn't really like this place, anyway. Been real restless since we got here. Good to see you, Thomas." He said, holding out his hand to shake.

"Likewise," he replied, "Do me a favor and tell James I don't need a babysitter when you get back."

"Actually, Lavene sent the sparrow to me. I took it to James, and he specifically told us not to come. Said you could handle it yourself. Your brother, on the other hand… He made me saddle *Silver* and fly us out immediately."

That fact almost made Thomas smile. At that moment, he was happy to have a friend with faith in him and grateful for a brother willing to defy a king to keep him safe.

Regardless, Draes only gave Thomas a swift nod before *Silver* leapt into the sky, four sets of claws ripping up the earth as they took off.

46

Damian

The ship that was given to Damian had to be the most exquisite thing he had ever seen.

The hull was dark oak and stunning against the dark navy blue sheets contrasting it from above.

Inside the hull was enough room to station all of Damian's crew and a few more. Enough room for a nicer kitchen and lavatory. There were even three spacious officer's quarters and the Captain's cabin was so big and luxurious that he'd originally refused the gift from James.

James even made it known that he had another surprise up his sleeve, but it was already being rushed to finish before they left for Telas.

So, for now, Damian sat alone on his new ship. He leaned against the helm and looked up at the masts. Wrapping the sails tightly, he prepared to weather the oncoming storm rumbling in from the sea. He had maybe an hour before a downpour began.

That was when he heard light footsteps approaching. He looked over the rail of the quarterback and saw Ula walking along the edge of the ship, grazing her hand along the rail and looking at the clouds forming above.

He hurried down the steps to the lower deck. Even felt a sprinkle of rain on his way.

"This is your ship? Very impressive." She mocked. "Rather large, wouldn't you say?"

Damian bit down on the urge to say something repulsive.

She turned toward him then.

"You don't like it, then?" He asked. Trying not to be mesmerized by the auburn curls she tried to pin back. Or her hazel eyes, brightening the oncoming gloom. He tried not to crumble under the ache to touch her warm, golden skin.

She walked right up to him, stood a foot or so away, and said, "Do *you* like it?"

"I do." He said with a smile.

"Then I guess that's all that matters, isn't it?"

"I'll admit I'm not used to having things like this. We lived with masters of the mind, body, and soul. Deadly peacekeepers. However, they had a strong aversion to vanity and possessions. Yet, I now have a ship with gold doorknobs and enough coin to feed my entire island for a decade."

"I've heard the king's ship has a golden loo. Got one of those?" She asked.

All this did was yank a hearty laugh from Damian's chest. Hers ringing behind it like bells. A soft and soothing anthem he wished to hold close to him.

When their laughter faded, a cool shower drizzled them. The deck was now slick and wet. Ula lost her footing as Damian began to lead her off of the ship. She slipped right into his arms. Whether by fate or her own doing, his palms were gently pressed against her waist.

The look they both had at that moment was enough to melt him. Pull him into the sea like a siren calling to sailors.

Her eyes shifted. Shifted to gold just like his.

"Tell me why your eyes change." He breathed.

"Not yet." She whispered.

Then he kissed her. Her lips caressing his and softly moving in hypnotizing motions. His heart leaping, soaring.

She pulled away and smiled at him. Intertwined her fingers with his.

"Show me everything?" She asked.

"The whole world and all her secrets." He replied and led Ula on an official tour of *The Ophelia.*

47

Seraphina

One week.

It had been one week since Vera left for the healer's guild. And Sera had heard nothing.

Worst of all, tonight, Astriea and Seraphina would be presented to the nobles of Telas at a state dinner. As if that luncheon wasn't enough.

But she had to admit, things had changed. And so quickly she could barely keep up.

Servants came and went throughout the day. Delivering lunch, and later, clothes for dinner. Seraphina was appalled by the dresses hung out for Astriea and herself. Two of them were burdened with carrying massive, floppy, purple shoulder puffs. The sequins on another dress shimmered in at least ten thousand different colors.

Then there was another knock at the door, and Vera strutted in with four servants behind her, each of them carrying two black dress bags. She laughed when she saw their shocked expressions as both Sera and Astriea were holding the horrendous gowns.

"I told Killian not to bring you those," she tried her best to push her giggling down to a minimum. "Those are over forty years old. I'm nearly positive he left them for you just to make you both freak out—" She didn't get to finish her sentence. Not when Seraphina had thrown that ugly dress on the floor and collided against her. Sera wrapped her arms tightly around Vera's.

"Don't squeeze too hard. I'm still a little sore." She grunted, then laughed. Pausing for a moment to cherish the embrace.

Seraphina pulled back, observing her. Her black eyes were gone. Clear and sparkling green, as they always were. Her nose again was straight and delicately pointed up. The only thing left was a barely visible bruise along her jaw. Something you needed just the right light to catch.

"Gods. It's like it never happened." She breathed.

"It may look like that on the outside, but the inside is still deeply bruised."

Seraphina lifted her fingers to Vera's face and gently brushed the skin of her jaw. Got lost in her eyes for a moment, too.

The princess broke the connection then.

"I have clothes for you both—dresses." She said to the pair of them.

Helena, Briar, and Belle opened the bags and even for Sera, they were stunning.

She shook herself from the blatant stare she was emitting on the shimmering black gown, the last in the line of four. Studded all over with black obsidian. Although, sometimes—in the right light—you could see a shimmer of orange or red flash off it. She didn't know if it would fit, though, it looked a little small even for her. While she'd nearly withered away in the dungeons, that didn't make her generously wide hips shrink at all. And besides that, she had already been gaining weight again in the short weeks since they had been moved to this room.

There were barely any straps. Just two pieces of thin fabric studded in obsidian gems. They were honestly so small she didn't understand how someone could do it. Sew those tiny little stones to such a thin piece of fabric. But the straps were solid when Sera tugged on them. The last thing she needed was for them to snap in the middle of dinner and let everyone see *her* tits along with the chickens. Not that Vera would be too shocked.

That's when a thought flooded Sera's mind in a wave of delicious heat. The flashing image of Vera pinning her to the dining table knocking over food and wine. Sera's breasts exposed and pressed against Vera. And her hands, roaming and pushing against her waist as their lips danced around each other's, then her chest—

Sera shook her head to interrupt the thoughts and nodded to Vera as she left them to get ready. Her heart sank a bit as the door closed behind her.

I have to get her out of this castle.

48

Astriea

Astriea hadn't meant to sleep long. Or at all, for that matter. But she'd been so tired after Vera left. Felt nearly dragged into sleep. She hoped she'd see Zaniah in her dreams, but those hopes were fruitless.

She gained nothing but the rest she desperately needed during the hour she slept.

When she woke, Seraphina was already dressed and the look of her was captivating.

Suddenly she was being slapped in the face by what exactly drew in the Grand Duchess, *Vera the Viscous* herself.

That black dress shaped Sera flawlessly, with a slit up the side of each leg and stopping above her hips. The fabric on the front and back shimmered beautifully in the light, while the fabric around her waist was cinched in tightly by a studded corset. Her bodice left little to the imagination with the plunging neckline of glittering obsidian. The matching straps rested gently on her shoulders. Onyx jewels only meant to accentuate what she already offered.

"I wouldn't get too goo-eyed over the dress. Yours looks just like mine, but silver."

"What?"

Astriea ran over to the dress she'd chosen earlier and surely enough, it was the same one. Only it was made of shimmering silver satin and littered with white gemstones. Astriea laughed at the coincidence and made her way to the bathing chambers to change, but stopped. Her smile dying out.

She opened the door to the hall and peeked outside.

"Belle?" she called.

Sweet Belle popped her head from around the other side of the door.

"Yes, my lady?" She replied.

Astriea smiled and said, "Are there any dresses with…" She gestured to her neck. "Coverings?"

Belle led Astriea back inside the room and shut the door behind her.

Her lovely brown eyes held an abundance of empathy and kindness to them as she trotted over to the armoire.

"The tzar commanded that all your gowns worn before court were to match in every way but color. He did not say why. *But…* not a day later, he told us all to be sure the two of you were comfortable at all times." She pulled out a gown not unlike the first, but with a neckpiece and cape. More than enough to cover the scar she wasn't quite ready to bear. And gorgeous.

It paled only in comparison to the gown she'd crowned James in. The hem and cape barely brushed the ground, while the satin silver bodice sparkled with an array of white gems.

"When did you get this? I—I mean, how did you know?"

"That same day. The day the two of you were given this room, the grand duchess had this dress made for you."

Astriea was speechless. She took the dress in her hands and made for the lavatory to change. But she stopped.

"Why?" she asked.

Belle, already on her way back into the hall, replied with a smile, "She said that you would save us. That we would all owe you more than just a dress or an agreeable room. She said, '*Maybe this could be a good first step.*'"

Astriea's heart warmed with her smile. She nodded at the handmaiden and said, "Thank you, Belle."

She only dipped her chin, curtsied, and closed the door behind her.

49

Astriea

While Seraphina paced back and forth in front of the mirror, contemplating her existence, Astriea had somehow found her way back to the stack of books.

She opened *The Great Pool* and in it was the story of The Mystic, a magical pool of god's blood made when Zaniah cut down the other gods in the old wars.

And there, beneath the sky, where their golden ichor spilled, did the earth drink
wholly.
There, the pool of strength, of will and power, waits for the champions.
There does sit the great magistrate and her mighty scales.
Pray for her mercy or that of a clean death.

Astriea tried to piece that together, moving her cape out of her way to read better. But she looked at the time on the mighty clock ticking against the wall and pushed on to another book: *Bragus' Theories of Law*.

She pilfered through it, stopping only on a page that caught her attention the most.

The Fae were known to complete contracts and obligations by engaging in
'Bargains'. This act was a magically binding covenant, and when used

aggressively, could risk the lives of either party. Smaller contracts with less emotional attachment could cause the party to experience unease, and sometimes timid pain, if they did not uphold their end.

However, these bargains are not limited to only the fae, but mortals as well, given that at least one party is capable of magic. More serious bargains or bargains made under duress have the potential to strangle the very life of the opposing party. For this reason, the realms of Telas have banned all dealings in magical bargaining.

Astriea sucked in a breath and dropped the book onto the desk. She stumbled back and when she turned to tell Sera; a knock at the door cut her off.

In the brief moments she had as Sera made to open it, memories flashed through her mind.

Every time Vera came to this room, she left a book behind on the shelves. Left a clue with every visit. She couldn't tell them what was happening to her, so she found a way around it.

Vera was bound to Scythe through a bargain.

She didn't know what the exact wording of it was, or what either of them had promised, but the pieces fell together in her mind.

Every last one.

She has seven siblings, each of them unharmed and well cared for. Each of them loyal to her against all odds, even when drunk and bickering.

Young Thea's voice echoed in her mind, *"I know she loves you because she protects you, like she protects us."*

Vera Shataar bargained her compliance for the safety of her family.

50

Seraphina

Sera wouldn't have given much thought to how she looked if Morra and her daughters hadn't come in and helped her. If she was being honest, it felt nice to have them help her into her dress. It had felt even better when Morra pulled the top half of her hair into a stunning Telish braid. The pieces of her nearly black hair were just long enough to fit in the weaving now.

But Belle sat her down and painted her face with cosmetics. While she did so, Briar appeared at her other side. Comparing pieces of jewelry to match Sera's dress.

When James's servants did this, she'd felt so uneasy about it. But now, Morra and her daughters made her feel safe. Almost home. She almost didn't notice Briar attach stunning obsidian jewels to her ears and around her neck.

Astriea dismissed Morra and her daughters after they finished helping her get ready. They gave them a worried expression before turning away.

But Sera stood from her seat and held out her bare arm to Astriea.

"Come on. I expect they await the guest of honor."

Astriea took her arm with a smile and rose from her chair by the desk, though, through that smile, she looked uneasy. Like there were too many thoughts in her head to think clearly.

"Thomas would collapse if he could see you," Sera added.

A thick knock sounded at the door, and when it opened, Killian Blackspear stepped through.

He'd cleaned himself up nicely. His long black hair was braided into masculine Telish twists. He was clean-shaven and the tunic and trousers he wore were much finer than his daily ones. Light armor was strapped to him, solid black with small ridges dipping in and out of the chest piece. The hilt of his sword was shimmering in the light. It must have just been cleaned. Then those solid silver eyes stopped scanning the room and his jaw nearly dropped open.

It was clear to Sera that the look was not intended for her. She did her best to hide the teasing grin fighting to break across her face.

Killian tried to shake himself awake and approached Astriea and Sera both. He took Sera's hand and kissed it as he bowed his head.

"My sister will cut out her own heart when she sees you, beautiful shadow." Sera rarely cared what came out of a man's mouth, but damn him if that didn't make her blush.

Pooling silver eyes fell on Astriea then. Killian took to one knee and brought her hand to his mouth. He said nothing as he pressed her fingers against his lips.

"No sweet words for me today, Killian?" Astriea teased. Gods, Thomas was going to rip this guy apart, Sera thought.

Killian stood but didn't let go, and said, "If you think I do not know how your heart is spoken for, then you would be wrong, my goddess." Sera and Astriea knitted their brows and tilted their heads. He didn't let go of Astriea's hand.

"And while I can admit it is terrifying to think of challenging the *Dragon of Telas*," His smile was stupidly perfect.

Poor Astriea, Sera thought.

But Killian leaned into Astriea's ear. Sera backed away to give them some privacy as he whispered something to her. She couldn't make out what he said, but Astriea's eyes shot to Sera's like they would talk about it as soon as possible.

And they did.

Killian stepped away and waited for them at the door.

"What did he say?" Sera whispered.

"He said: *But I would swear my life to you if you'd only let me, have you command me as you wish.*"

Sera's eyes widened, and Astriea rolled hers.

Walking down the halls, Sera tried to count the turns even though she nearly knew her way around at this point. And they weren't even blindfolded, but it helped calm her nerves. They'd taken seven turns this time. Two lefts, a right, two more lefts, and then two rights. Before she knew it, they were standing before massive, black doors.

"Wait!" Astriea said before the guards opened them. Killian stopped and looked at them both curiously. Then Astriea took Sera's hands and looked into her eyes. Confusion moved through her like nausea. *What is it? What's happening? Who are we fighting?* All these questions started shooting through her. But Astriea's eyes softened on Sera's anxious expression.

"Forgive Vera. I know it doesn't make sense and I have my own problems with her, but... Zaniah was right about James. I think she's right about her, too. I believe that Zaniah cares about us, all of us. I hate what this does to you. We both do. I hate that I've asked it of you." Seraphina couldn't comprehend why she was being told this. But something like a hand seemed to grab hold of her soul and force her to listen closely.

"Because... Because no matter what those monks on that damn island told you or raised you to believe, I need you to know that dying for me is not an option. I need you to know that seeing you live a glorious life is a non-negotiable. If you are to serve me, in any way, then you will know love and passion and joy. If that is *her*, then you will have it because you deserve it, you always have."

"Astriea—" Sera tried to question.

"No—No, don't. I'm sorry I didn't tell you that before. You have always deserved to hear it. And Vera... she's worth saving, too."

Sera's heart sank only to burst forth with bounding happiness at those words, but the guard's patience grew too thin and they swung the doors open. Sera had no time to think, or move, or even breathe when that

211

stowaway stepped forward and extended an arm to her.

She looked to her right. Astriea had an arm linked with Killian and squeezed Sera's hand before he led her to the table.

Sera stood there frozen for a moment. Looking at Vera. She lost her breath and fought like hell for it back.

At least twenty different braids varying in sizes and shapes adorned the top half of Vera's blood-red hair. All of it ran flawlessly down her bare back.

Her pine green dress wrapped loosely off her shoulders. Letting sheer, split sleeves fall gracefully over her arms and spill onto the floor. Ribs and twists of darker green velvet across the bodice corseted her—pressing her breasts up and in tight, before loosening at the top of her waist and flowing gently out and down perfect legs in layers of lighter and darker greens. A simple slit ran up to her left hip.

She tried everything not to look at her face. Tried with all her might, but she had to. Sera looked up to see her eyes shining like emeralds in the candlelight. Freckles splattered her dainty little chin and up-tilted nose. Her lips, which tasted like moonberries, now matched the dark red coloring of them.

Gods, she was so fucked.

Sera took Vera's arm, feeling the warmth of her touch, and allowed her to lead her into the grand, illuminated great hall.

51

Thomas

T homas and Lavene made it down the range of broken mountains in four days. The princess had done a fine job of breaking apart the shattered stone and clearing paths for the king's men to pass through and mine. However, many of the men would have to be carted back to camp due to the sickness *Caltillion's Curse* brought on. A single man could only bear the nausea for a few hours at a time.

But Lavene's work became even more impressive when considering that she accomplished all of this while riding on a dragon.

They stopped and made camp north of The Bone River. Making certain to gain one more night's rest upon grass rather than sand. And enjoy the cool breezes of early spring before they become doused in the dry desert heat.

"How did you get so good at using your powers?" Thomas asked with a mouthful of dried boar and stale bread. "It's taken me ages to get a hold on mine. Any tips?"

Lavene's eyes shot up. She looked at him with a type of fury he'd only really ever seen in one other person. And he knew why.

Thomas hadn't spoken the entirety of the trip. If he was being honest with himself, he didn't care for the sound of his own voice lately.

In addition, he had not eaten until now, and he was completely covered in a thick layer of dirt and sweat, causing Lavene's reaction to possibly be due to his scent. Night terrors had plagued him since he arrived in Monolith, disrupting any sleep he managed to get. All in all, he was not good company.

He saw them every time he closed his eyes. Waking and not.

He heard their screams over the crickets and frogs who sang around Siren's Lake just east of here. Through the wind that barreled against him in the skies.

And as far as fire went, he'd used none of his.

So now, Lavene looked at him like she might hit him.

"So you can speak again? How lovely." She spat.

"Look—" He started.

"Don't. Don't try to explain it to me. I am capable of understanding your pain and being angry at you at the same time."

"I shouldn't have fallen into myself as I did. For that, I am sorry, Lavene."

And he was sorry. Lavene needed someone to guide her, and Thomas failed at that. He fell apart, and if he was being honest, he was not yet whole again. Was not free of the haunting. Part of him knew he might never be.

"I am sorry. For what happened to your home. Your people. It is not an easy thing to clear from my mind, either."

"So… the two of us are the only people in the world who saw what happened. There was no one left on that field."

"It seems we are." Lavene sat back down in front of the fire.

"If I start getting too quiet, too lost, would you… would you mind pulling me out? You seem to be the only person I know that doesn't treat me like—"

"Like a *princess*?"

This yanked a laugh from his chest. The first time he'd done so in days.

"I see now why you hate being called that." He said.

She smiled a bit while stirring the fire.

"I have always been obsessed with plants. Since I was quite small. My father says that the greenhouses become more vibrant when I am near and more dull when I am away. When he built our home, when he built

214

Hesperia, land of the setting sun, he said it was my presence that made our home an oasis."

Thomas's head tilted a bit.

"He was right. My power fully awoke on the night of a storm. Merely a drizzle in Hesperia. Nothing at Devil's Gate. But our towers are high and our telescopes are the grandest in all of Shadon. From the observatory, we, including myself, my father, and a fair portion of our court, watched as Monolith was ransacked. My father was discussing the possibility of sending aid with the court when the lightning struck."

Thomas felt his eyes go wide. Felt his mouth part a bit in the shock of it all.

"When the lightning struck again, I collapsed onto the floor. When I woke, I'd turned the Observatory into a new greenhouse. Flowers and fruits dangling from vines wrapped around everything in sight. No marble floors or stone pillars to be seen. All of it covered with greenery. Father even said I glowed. *An emerald in sunlight*, my father says."

"That was the night Astriea and I were taken by Zaniah. When she—"

"Claimed her power." She interrupted. "Yes. It seems that her resurgence awoke the rest of us."

"Zaniah had to unlock my power personally. Why not you?"

"I'm not entirely sure. But my power never felt like something to control. I allow the magic in my veins its freedom. I allow the earth to come forth and break or be whole once more. Never hide it away or cower before its power."

"I feel that is easier to achieve when said power is so *docile*."

Lavene smirked and said, "If I wanted, I could sink this entire continent into the sea. If I wanted, I could bring the entirety of the earth surrounding you, crashing down." The ground began to shake. Making Thomas clutch to the grass below him. "Dirt and debris suffocating you, stealing the very breath from your lungs. If Rala wished her world avenged, there would be no place to hide, no cave or mountain secluded or high enough to shelter you." The hairs rose on Thomas's arms, but the shaking stopped. Crickets and frogs were now silent. "The earth is perennial, unyielding. It was here long before us and will be here long after all of us depart. Perhaps if you did not so thoroughly doubt yourself, think yourself small and incapable of your power, you would not feel overwhelmed by it. Afraid of it."

"I saw what it did. The flames." He said, not meeting her eyes.

"When the earth quakes, does it not cause death or destruction? When tidal waves wash away coastal towns, does it not forsake the lives there? The same can be said of the air, of the wind funnels that tear through the country in early spring. And your love, do you think the power of life comes without its counter? What happened to Monolith was a crime against the gods, Thomas, and a crime against Hellion's gift of flame as well. A gift used for atrocity when meant to improve the quality of life. So, instead of being afraid of *your* gift, use it. Master it. And honor those lost by the abuse of it. But do not forget that you channel a force of nature. For now, it is all you can do."

Thomas appreciated the advice. He wished it hadn't been so terrifying, but Lavene had gotten the message across.

That night, when he slept, those dreams still haunted him. Only now, when he woke the following morning, he did not wish to fall mercifully off Night-cleaver's back when they took to the skies. That morning, before Lavene and the sun woke, Thomas curled up against his dragon, who still nested right next to him, and let out a bit of soft flame.

Night-cleaver only released a tired huff and closed their eyes, letting Thomas warm them as he rested his head against the dragon's front arm—neatly tucked under a massively scaled belly—and tried his best to catch another hour or so of sleep before they took flight to Hesperia.

52

Damian

In the week since Thomas left, a total of eight thousand soldiers arrived in Triscillia. All of them taking shelter at local inns down the eastern coast or in tents littered about The Dead Forest.

From here, all the way to Devil's Gate in the far south, soldiers readied for war. And the royal navy had no simple time preparing them for a two-week-long trip at sea.

Now, sitting at the mast of his ship, Damian tried his best to mind his business and not laugh at the sailors and soldiers arguing.

"No, ya landlubber, ya tie the knot like this!" a sailor shouted from the beach. Where a group of them were giving courses on ship survival and maintenance.

Damian chuckled a bit before seeing to his own knots and sails.

They would be leaving soon.

In three days, they would set sail for Thomas's homeland. For Telas. And now, for the first time since Astriea threw them all through that portal, he let himself break.

He was alone on the ship, as he was every time before, but now... Now the sight of fifty massive naval ships making ready for departure to rescue his oldest friend and his goddess made his heart shatter.

Falling to one knee, he grabbed the railing of the ship with one hand and clutched his chest with the other. Breathing became difficult and the world around him grew dark. His vision clouded. Then his ears popped and he couldn't hear the seagulls anymore. Couldn't hear the wind whisking by or the waves crashing against the ship's hull.

Damian couldn't tell if the drips of salt water on his lips were tears or sea spray in his struggle to find air.

But then a gentle hand gripped his shoulder.

He heard something, a whisper maybe.

Then that touch moved down his arm and slowly, lovingly stroked the skin along it.

"*Damian.*" He heard. "*Damian, it's alright.*"

The voice became clearer, familiar.

"*Damian, breathe in your nose and out of your mouth, alright?*"

Ula. It was Ula gently coaxing him back.

His vision began to clear, making way for the sight of a gorgeous woman with freckles and tight golden curls.

When his sight returned completely—lungs opening fully—he found his palms pressed flat against his chest. Ula was there, though. Taking deep breaths in her nose and exhaling through perfect, bountiful lips. Full and tempting.

When his breath slowed enough to speak, he asked, "Are you following me, Ula?"

Despite feeling like a rockslide had crushed his chest, he tried to grin and force a cheerful expression.

"I've not been following you. You are just always *here.*"

And, of course, she was right. He'd spent every waking moment on this empty ship. Imagining his crew delighted to see it, to work it.

"You torture yourself, Damian. We will have them back soon enough. In a mere fortnight, they will be freed."

"If they're alive." He replied in a much more haunted tone.

"They are. I can feel it." She said with a smile. Then went on to say, "Your sister says this ship will tail behind the fleet and guide the dragons. Are you excited for it?"

"When did you talk to Mira?"

"When she cornered me and said she wished to *get to know me.*"

He laughed then.

"She has got to be the nosiest person I know."

"Well, I am not going to deny the future queen, so we had lunch—and tea."

"Oh? How did it fare?"

"Quite well, actually, she said she'd heard of me when she was a spy for the king. That my services could be called upon at some point or another."

"Your services? Lock picking?"

"And some *light* burglary. Pickpocketing and vault cracking are both in my repertoire as well."

Damian's eyebrows rose, and he didn't realize how hard he'd been smiling at her until his cheeks strained against the act.

"*Royal Thief*, how scandalous." He said, winking at her.

The slight irritation in her expression, the way her hazel eyes squinted or her lips pursed just slightly, made a fire in him roar to life.

Her gaze softened, so before he could overthink it, he kissed her.

Pulled her against him by her waist and hip.

One of her hands tangled in the collar of his tunic, and the other grazed his face and jaw. Her thumb brushed softly against his cheek.

And her lips.

Her lips tasted like the first sip of water after training all day. Or the first cool swim in a humid summer heat.

Their tongues brushed together, soft strokes along the other that pulled and swayed them into maddening waves of serenity and passion.

Damian gently grazed his fingers up her back, along her spine. She shuttered at the touch but gripped him tighter and kissed him more intensely.

He brought his hands around her thighs and lifted her onto the railing. Pressing himself between her legs.

The kisses grew more aggressive, pulling soft pants from both their chests, until Damian broke the connection. Throwing any kind of leash he could onto the urge to keep going, keep touching her, kissing her...

"Wait—I'd like to wait a bit, before…" he said shyly.

"Damian Aurelius, did you think I'd just give it all up after a few stolen kisses?" She laughed. "You still have to show me the world, then maybe I'll have time to show *you* a thing or two."

Her laugh. Her laugh was a breathtaking melody to his ears. As was the sound of her voice when she teased him.

So, right then, Damian decided he would not be the careless fornicator he'd once been in his youth. He decided that the woman before him deserved everything he'd once been too childish to give anyone else before. He would wait, *and suffer*, until he was sure he'd get the chance to fall thoroughly, recklessly in love.

* * *

The following morning, Damian met with James and Mira at breakfast to discuss their strategy moving forward.

"My mother will act as regent until our return, but when we depart, Mira and I will be on the lead ship. You will tail behind the armada and lead Thomas and the other dragon riders." James said. Damian hesitated only to note the dark circles under the king's eyes as he picked at the fruit on his plate. His blonde hair was a bit disheveled, too.

"We will have to make stops at various islands on route. The dragons will need some place to rest after such a prolonged flight." He finally said.

"Yes, I've accounted for that as well. There are ten small islands between here and Telas. I've added six of them to the manifest so they can rest every few days."

"That is still quite extensive. These dragons have been buried for centuries. We don't know if they can fly for days at a time." Damian replied. "Let alone their riders."

James slouched in his chair and took a deep breath.

"All we can hope for right now is that being buried for such an extensive period only made them long for the sky even more. We will gain more insight into the dragons' endurance once Thomas returns from Devil's

Gate.

"Have you seen Draes since he returned? He's been rather touchy." Damian took a hefty swig of water and then went on, "What happened? I thought you'd told him not to go."

"That's exactly what I told him, and he went anyway. I knew Thomas was feeling rather useless waiting for our time to ship out. That's why I sent him with Lavene and no one else. When Draes showed up to save him from whatever happened, it did exactly what I thought it would, made Thomas feel inadequate. Like a failure."

"We don't think that of him, not for a second," Damian replied.

"But you fear him. His power." Mira spoke up. "The level of power Thomas possesses would naturally strike fear into anyone, but when someone as kind and beloved as Thomas is blessed with it, it opens up room for an entirely different kind of fear."

"And what kind is that, sister?"

"Fear of loss. All of you are afraid he is too good to handle his power. You are all afraid it will consume him. That is why he pushes you all away."

"I tried to tell Draes that and he hasn't spoken to anyone since," James added.

"Now that it's been said, I think I do worry for him often. I will do better to have more faith in my friend," Damian said, recounting all the times he may have been overbearing towards Thomas.

Mira smiled at him and said, "As morbid as it may sound, I believe all of us could use a little time on that island of yours. Seems to have instilled a great bit of peace in you, brother."

"Maybe when this is all over, I'll bring you there. Both of you." He replied.

Mira only smiled at him before placing one hand on James' shoulder—who was currently nodding off—to wake him.

"Oh, yes, one more thing," James started, trying to force his eyes open wide in an effort to wake himself up. "Make sure the two thousand new recruits are adapting well to the change in environment."

"Two thousand new recruits? Will we even have the room?" Mira asked, startled a bit.

"Yes," James was dozing off again. "Yes—and make sure they get their land deeds and citizenship papers. My scribe… Darceen, she has them all ready to go."

Damian cleaned himself off and rose from his seat.

"Get some rest, mate. We've got two days until departure, one day until Thomas returns and two thousand more bellies to feed. We'll need you at your best."

Two guards gently lifted James from his chair and half carried him to his chambers.

"Walk with me? I'm going to speak with the scribe."

Damian nodded and followed his sister out the doors.

* * *

The scribe's quarters were very well organized. Everything in the chamber was stacked in neat little piles and stored in perfect order. The papers, the books, the furniture, even the house plants and blue rugs lining the floors.

"My lady, Admiral, I was not expecting you."

"I'm sorry about the early hour, Darceen, but the king sent us to inquire about the two thousand new recruits."

Damian finally recognized the small woman. He'd seen her following James around many times with a hoard of other servants. He felt guilty in assuming. Onyx eyes gleamed beneath the tan hood of her cloak.

"Of course, my lady, I have the documents here." She gestured to the ten stacks of paper lined up in two rows on a desk by the door. "I've gone through each one and have their deeds attached to their citizenship licenses."

"Who exactly are they? If they need to be granted citizenship?" Mira asked.

Damian picked up one of the papers and said, "Citizens from Devil's Gate, perhaps?"

"No, my lord, my lady, not at all. These soldiers are the freed slaves."

"The what?" Mira demanded more than asked. Her eyes wide.

Darceen looked at them as if she were confused.

"The king, with the court hanging on such a thin thread, could not outright ban the keeping of slaves. King Herold had… underlings, you could say, followers, the golden king has been trying to strategically snuff out. So, since he couldn't ban it, he banned the sale of all slaves and peoples. Since then, the king has sent out riders, surveyors, to take a census. When they all finally returned, King James bought every single slave on record in Shadon and left scouts behind in certain towns and cities to *discourage* being caught keeping someone enslaved. Every single person freed received their choice of land and citizenship, or a substantial amount of coin and a ship out of the country, to nearly any destination."

Mira had to sit down, nearly collapsing into the chair by the window. Damian placed a hand on her shoulder, and she gripped it with her own.

"And the soldiers?"

"They all volunteered." Darceen gestured a hand to the window overlooking the vast field that now housed them all. *Two thousand.*

"We can't ask that of them." Mira breathed out.

"We didn't, my lady."

Damian and Mira moved to the window and opened it wide. In the distance, they saw pale blue lights glowing like fireflies.

"What is that?" Damian asked.

"That would be the Royal Coven, offering the removal of slave brands. I was under the impression the king would be taking the two of you out into the fields to meet them this morning. Is that no longer his plan?"

"It seems the king ruined his own surprise in his deliria," Mira said dryly. Though, Damian could feel her rolling her eyes.

"They've all chosen to stay? Even after all of it? It doesn't make any sense. They have no reason to fight for this place." Mira muttered.

"They do not fight for this place, my lady. They fight for their king. For their future queen, as well." Darceen slowly backed away from the window, "For the rulers who would not take no for an answer in the question of their freedom. They will not take no for an answer either." The scribe then bowed and left the room.

"I will not allow them to go to war. It isn't right."

"You cannot take that choice away from them, sister."

Mira released a deep sigh, and her head drooped slightly.

"The last time I felt this overwhelmed, it was by the way life was constantly unfolding around me. I'd been living in the tunnels under the capitol for days after I escaped. Then I ran as fast as I could. They almost got me, too. I hadn't expected to run face-first into the prince. Hadn't expected him to shield me from The Watch, either. It was a different kind of feeling then. I felt so relieved that they could not take me and so guilty for surviving it." She took a deep breath, and Damian hung on to every word. "Now I—I'm so overwhelmed by my joy that I cannot fathom allowing them to lose anything else, sacrifice anything else for this—" She gestured to her gown, her jewels dangling from her neck and ears.

Damian stopped her before she could go on. "Let us rejoice in this for now, and go to them later."

Mira nodded and made her way to the door.

Damian lingered at the window a moment longer, his eyes darting from one small blue light to another, and thought to himself that this was a good first step for the kingdom of Shadon. That as long as there were people like Mira, like James, on the throne, there would be hope.

Even thought of how desperately he'd love to see what the two of them make of this land once veiled in darkness, now that the light now shined upon it again.

53

Seraphina

Breathe. Breathe. Breathe.

Sera tried to settle herself.

Vera escorted her to a chair sitting next to Astriea's at one head of the table. At her right.

"If I could, I'd steal you away from here right now," Vera whispered to her. And when Seraphina looked up at her as she took her seat, she said, eyes lost on Sera's face, "Every time I think you couldn't be more beautiful, you prove me wrong."

Vera sucked in a breath and found her place behind her own seat at the right of the other head. *The Tzar's right hand, The Crown Princess, The Grand Duchess.*

Sera's surroundings became more clear. The walls of the room were made of smooth black onyx, which matched the entry door archway. Towering columns of dark stone held the great room up.

Curiosity made her look up at the chandelier above them, glittering white light. Something even more curious was the walls above the chandelier.

Sera touched Astriea's arm and glanced at her to look up. There was barely any silver left, but that wasn't what made them both pause. It was the way the black onyx leaked over it. Like pouring hot oil into clear water. Like an infection. The only thing making this room feel less like a tomb was the warm ambiance of the feast laid out before them. And the dancing nobles scattered about.

Seraphina was glad to notice them. Glad to latch her attention on the dresses and fluid movement of bodies before her. Instead of lingering on the princess.

She watched as a young couple—a golden-haired man and a dark-skinned woman—dipped and flowed through the crowd on the wave of a crescendo, desperate not to look at Vera and failing.

She'd tried to only look at her face, and now she could hold back her eyes no longer.

Sera would never forget the glow of sconces peering gently over the shape of her.

She would not give freedom to the image of Vera's hair that Seraphina was screaming at herself not to touch. Or part with the idea of dark red lips pressed against hers in front of royals and nobles alike.

Because *that* was what she wanted.

She wanted Vera. With no limitations or obligations, she wanted to wrap Vera in her arms and claim her before her entire court. Before the world.

Because they had done enough.

"Talk to me," Sera whispered.

"Well, the dinner is going well so far. I know we haven't eaten yet, but—" Vera began.

"No—No, talk to me like you used to."

Vera looked at her curiously, so Seraphina explained further.

"If we had met, in a more *stately* manner, what would you say to me?"

The look the grand duchess gave was nearly sinister. In all the ways that made Sera ache for her.

"If you were a noblewoman, if you'd come here tonight by invitation, I might tell you that Lady Bristoli over there is on her tenth glass of champagne in the hour since she arrived." She pointed to the dark-haired woman. Tan skin wrinkled behind pounds of powder and blush. Her nose tilted up as she swayed back and forth.

"Or Lord Caterson." Vera lightly pushed her chin in the nobleman's direction. Fat and bald, all but his ridiculous handlebar mustache. Blonde and curling up, as if desperate to escape his mouth. "He publicly shamed his son for taking another man to bed, only to find out Lord Caterson frequently enjoyed the pleasures of *ladies' attire.*"

Seraphina's mouth gaped open. "Hypocrite." She murmured.

"Yes, there are quite a few of those here tonight." Vera laughed.

"What else would you say to me?"

The grand duchess looked her over, then smiled brightly as she said, "I would tell you that you look ethereal tonight."

Sera laughed.

"The only *ethereal* beauty here tonight is busy making chatter with nobles." She pointed to Astriea, glowing like a star across the room.

Vera leaned close, her lips a breath away from Sera's ear.

"I see no goddess here tonight, aside from the one who loves me."

Seraphina's nose brushed Vera's as she snapped her head toward her.

The musicians in the corner began to play a lovely tune. The large timpani drums rattled the room as Vera led Seraphina onto the open floor.

Panic washed over her like a flood. Her eyes went wide, and she tried to focus on the music, the horns spilling out an intoxicating melody. But everyone was looking at them.

Everyone in that room, all the nobles, Killian, Astriea, and the other royal siblings as well.

All eyes were on the two of them in the center of the room, only accompanied by a few others brave enough to dance alongside them.

Vera led Seraphina into what she could only assume was a Telish waltz. However, Vera held her much closer than called for.

Her breaths became heavy.

"Eyes on me," Vera whispered.

Seraphina followed her voice. Took her gaze away from the crowd and onto the princess.

Emerald eyes shimmered.

"Come into the light, my *lethal little beast.*"

A challenge, a plea. Sera wasn't sure. But those words echoed something in her. Some creature, lingering deep in her chest, almost seemed to purr.

She'd been called a wild beast before, by enemies, but Seraphina wanted her to say it again, and again and *again*.

Then everything fell into place. Her steps synchronized with Vera's and the thought of being *seen* didn't make her retreat into herself. More people had already begun to dance around them, but to Sera, there was no one. Only Vera Shataar and herself. Only green eyes that made the island's flora pale in contrast, and the sounds of beautiful music, before the herald's staff banged against the floor two times. Revealing the Tzar of Telas standing in the entry.

"I thought he was unconscious?" Sera whispered.

"He *should* be."

The nervous expression on Vera's face made her heart beat hard, and all the dancing and music stopped immediately. Making everyone take their seats. Sera only made one move and took a single step in front of the princess.

* * *

Made of solid white oak, the long table stood as a sturdy centerpiece in the room. Its chairs a perfect match.

The food was something from dreams. It had to be. There was roasted boar and turkey. At least four different kinds of potatoes were displayed on the table alongside fruits and vegetables.

Apples, oranges, and strawberries. Stewed carrots and corn. So much food, Sera wondered how they would eat it all. How much of it would be wasted? But the rest of the tzar's children piled into the room and stood behind their chairs, waiting for him. Still, she wondered how they got those fruits and vegetables. She'd seen the greenhouses here in the castle, but what about the rest of the kingdom? Did they have access to such delicacies? The land here was a frozen, barren wasteland. The storms alone would kill any crops. Maybe their southern cities were more plentiful, more productive.

This time, there was no looming shroud of terror accompanying him.

Long black robes and a matching fur cloak adorned him. An antler crown upon his head.

"Sit, children! Sit!" the tzar said happily. Vera hurried to the entry and helped her father to his chair at the head of the table.

He smiled at her. Like Vera hung the moon and the stars before him. He rubbed his neck before pressing his brow to hers. The act was so soft it hit her in the chest. Vera never knew when this man was her father, someone who loved her, cared and supported her, or when he was a monster.

Astriea looked at Sera, both of them stunned. This man had beaten them, imprisoned them, experimented on them. Had beaten the daughter he now looked at so lovingly. And all his children just acted as if this were *normal.* More than that, they seemed happy to have him back. That *this* was the true tzar.

"Have you been doing as I asked, young goddess? Have you been getting to know us and our city?" He asked.

"I have. And we have questions." Astriea said sternly.

"That, I have no doubt of." He laughed. "Please, sit. Eat. We will break bread and speak of terms."

Astriea and Seraphina sat down at the table and began the dinner they would never forget.

54

Astriea

The tzar's entrance had stunned them all. Made everyone in the room fall silent and still. Vera and Seraphina even halted their beautiful dance at the sight of him.

Now, Astriea and Seraphina sat and dined with the royal family.

Only the royal family.

All the other nobles found seats at different tables around the room.

The young princes and princesses conversed and argued with each other over their dinner.

Caedyn and Nate threw food at each other while Vera had an intense debate with Pilas over the state of racing horses available this far north.

"I wouldn't know. My horse—" Vera started.

"Yeah, yeah, yeah! We know your horse is *the greatest horse to ever live.* No need to remind us." Pilas replied, spilling wine in his laughter.

"I've still yet to see this *immortal steed.* When do you think you could introduce me?" Sera asked with a tilt of her head.

All of Vera's siblings' eyes went wide. Astriea noticed the tzar's had as well.

"That horse is the most dangerous thing on this continent. Nearly killed me when I tried to saddle her in my youth. Disappeared entirely until Vera was choosing her first pony when she turned seven. Hypnia reappeared in a cloud of black smoke." The tzar laughed.

"She sounds delightful." Sera smiled.

Something brightened in Vera's eyes at that.

"So, the horse is truly immortal? How many lives has it lived?" Astriea asked.

"There are records of Hypnia being seen roaming the white hills, dating back to before Telas was founded. Not long before, but before, nonetheless. However, she first appeared in the northern wastes, in the war of the old gods, and has been legend ever since."

"Regardless, *delightful* isn't quite the word I'd use to describe her, Seraphina," Killian interjected.

"Oh? And what word would you use?" Vera asked, leaning forward with a raised brow.

Killian then retreated from his stance. Giving his sister a bright smile and raising his hands in surrender before him.

"I could start with *bloodthirsty*, but…" he murmured. Vera only responded to this by tossing an enormous chunk of bread at his face. Astriea almost shot wine out of her nose at the sight of Killian's entire left cheek covered in butter.

"Oh, very mature," he said with an eye roll.

Vera only smiled.

* * *

Dinner had gone surprisingly well. Given the late hour, most of the nobles had returned home, leaving only the royal family and their two prisoners remaining.

Astriea spoke again as everyone started to wind down. "I was hoping to learn the Telish language during our stay. Are there any books I may borrow to get started?" She asked the table.

It was the tzar who replied, "Of course. Vera will have some books sent to you and the royal tutor as well. We'll have you speaking fluently in no time."

Astriea smiled and dipped her chin.

"Were there any phrases you heard that piqued your interest? I know we can sound rather zealous when excited." He laughed.

Astriea thought about it for a moment and asked Vera this time, "What does *Tzarina sa macta* mean?"

The lovely smile on the princess's face died and Astriea swore she felt the entire room shutter.

Those words had done something. Snagged the attention of someone she hadn't intended.

Something tingled beneath her skin. Nausea caused her chest to tremble. *Gods. What have I done?*

55

Seraphina

The tzar twitched and took a deep breath. All of his children's eyes darted to him. He looked like he was in pain while he rubbed his neck.

"Papa?" Thea said shyly. She reached out her hand for him to hold across the table, but he froze. A nauseating chill ran up Seraphina's spine then.

"Thea, it's time for bed. Off you go." Vera said quickly as she snapped her fingers at the servants at the doors. They came to the table immediately and led Thea out of the dining hall. Quick as a whip, the tzar snatched Vera's wrist in his hand. Everyone at the table jumped to their feet.

Vera hardly moved, still as death.

"Everyone out.." she breathed.

Her siblings didn't move.

"Now!"

Still, they stood there. Hands on weapons strapped to their sides. All of her brothers, even the tzar's sole protector, even Killian.

"Please…" she said, more quietly this time, her voice cracking. "Go."

Pilas led the twins, Salrek and Dalron, away from the table. Caedyn and Nate followed begrudgingly behind them. Never turning their backs to their sister.

Sera and Astriea, though, stood their ground.

He wants us here. To witness it.

Her stomach threatened to turn over all the food they'd just been enjoying.

Killian stepped forward, trying to diffuse the situation. But a black shadow filled the tzar's eyes and his grip tightened around Vera's wrist. Sera couldn't even finish taking a step before Astriea stopped her.

"We can't just let this happen." She whispered.

"We have no power to stop it. Look *around*. If I had my amulet then maybe, but Sera, I have *nothing*." Astriea was more panicked than Sera had anticipated for. Guilt splattered across her face.

The darkness clouding the room was thick and suffocating. The overwhelming feeling of fear now pressed down on them. Forced them to the floor.

Sera could've screamed. Could've knocked the table over and slit the tzar's throat herself. But she couldn't move.

He yanked Vera onto her knees, and the bone in her wrist cracked. The whimper of pain sent Sera into a frenzy. She attempted to leap forward, but Astriea's arms enveloped her. Holding her back as they coiled together on the floor.

"You do not command this court yet, *girl*," Scythe growled through the tzar's mouth. The once kindly-looking man's face was now twisted and terrifying.

"My Lord, the grand duchess meant no offense to your rule—" Killian began, reaching up from the ground, but he cut him off as he said, "*Blackspear*, you will leave this chamber."

"Your grace, it is my first duty to oversee the safety of the crown—"

"Do not burden me with your excuses. Be gone!"

Killian's eyes locked with Vera's for only a moment, before a wave of shadow slammed into him and threw his body into the hall. Scythe twitched as though an invisible force turned something sharp into his neck. But he pushed through the pain as though it was nothing.

When the doors slammed behind him, Scythe backhanded Vera across the face.

"Stop!" Sera screamed, fury boiling her blood. Astriea strained to contain her and Scythe noticed. He raised an open hand and levitated them into the air.

"Let me teach you all a lesson." His voice screeched in their ears like grinding shards of glass. Sera and Astriea fell to their knees as black smoke solidified into dark, slick vines. They wrapped all around them and gripped them tight.

Fear and anger coated her vision in red. Was she breathing too hard? Was she breathing at all? She tried to scream, but a vine wrapped around her mouth before she could. Astriea, too.

"You, *princess,*" He said, grabbing Vera by her hair and dragging her in front of them. The grand duchess didn't even flinch, though. She fought against him but did not cower against the dread beating down on the rest of them.

"You were told to disband the science guild and cease your experiments. How long did you think you could keep this going? You will suffer dearly for this *disrespect.*"

The tzar had kept that from him. That the guild was still going. How he'd done it, she had no idea but... But they'd used Vera's serum on him multiple times. And if Scythe was just now punishing her for it, just now remembering how she'd escaped his grasp these last few times... No. She stopped the thought altogether.

He looked at Seraphina then, a glance to make sure she was paying attention.

It happened so fast, that Sera's breath caught in her chest. He balled his fist and hit her cheek. Then her eye. Then her nose. Vera grunted at each impact but raised her head for the next hit every time. Irritation washed over him because of it. Like it was something she wouldn't let him have.

Her fear.

She would not scream, she would not cry.

Oh, my resilient girl.

Then he kicked her in the stomach and knocked her onto her back. Sera fought against the vines, but they wouldn't budge. Her entire body howling, begging to break free. Astriea screamed through the vine around her mouth. Sera did too.

"Maybe if I beat your little *pet* again, you'll give me a tear or two."

Yes, please yes. Take me, *beat* me, *kill* me.

Scythe moved towards Sera, but Vera shot her hand out and wrapped it tight around his wrist. He looked at her, shocked, but smiling.

"Hit me harder." She breathed, blood dripping down her mouth.

"What did you say?" That smile died and pure rage filled his features.

Vera looked up at him and said in a broken cry, "I said, hit me *harder,* you weak, hateful bastard!"

He struck.

And he didn't stop.

He continued to hit her again and again.

Sera couldn't breathe. Couldn't break through those gods' damned vines, and couldn't save her.

So she begged.

Begged the gods and whoever else would listen to her suffocated pleas.

Please...

Please, I'll do whatever it takes. I'll do whatever it takes...

Vera lay on the floor, beaten and bloody and barely moving. He was going to kill her. If she didn't get to a healer soon, she'd die anyway.

Vera would die before she could touch her again. Before she could hear her laugh. *Really* laugh, not the one she gave to people as *The Grand Duchess.* The real one that sometimes developed into the most adorable snort she'd ever heard.

She would be dead before they got a chance to come clean to each other. Before they got to be honest.

Sera's breaths became quick and heavy, tears running down her cheeks. The shock and worry in Astriea's eyes didn't help. Sera needed hope, and it seemed Astriea had none to give her. Something in her eyes sent Sera a clear message: *I'm so sorry.*

No. No, that can't happen. Vera can't die.

She wouldn't let it happen. The red clouding her vision turned to black until there was nothing and no one. Sera drifted away but found no place of meaning. Just the empty darkness. She sat on her knees in the middle of it. Reached out a hand as swirls of shadow wrapped softly around her arms and fingers. *"What the—"*

She lifted the other hand and shadows appeared there, too. She looked down at the floor, except it wasn't solid. It was like floating atop a dark lake. The water stilled beneath her, and she stared at her reflection.

It was her, but it wasn't? She was so confused. But then the reflection broke like glass into three pieces.

Something familiar brushed against her heart, calming and easing her. Not extinguishing the rage, but channeling it.

The broken reflection still gazed at her until Sera nodded and launched her mind back to the great hall.

Scythe held Vera's limp body up by the front of her dress and readied to hit her one more time.

Slowly, the vines around Seraphina released her. Peeled back and slithered away.

As if bowing.

She rose to her feet and said under her breath, "Whatever it takes."

Seraphina Blackspear's eyes turned blood red as she launched an explosion of shadow directly at Scythe.

56

Astriea

Astriea hit the floor with a thud and couldn't believe what she was seeing. What she was understanding.

Sera stood and attacked Scythe with his own shadows. Those nearly black eyes now glowed red as rubies. Dark power barreled out of her, striking vipers of shadow, snapping at the monster possessing the tzar.

Astriea pulled herself out of it enough to run to Vera.

Picking her up as gently as she could, she kept glancing at Sera; still bombarding that terrifying power at Scythe. Every gust he throws sliding past her and joining her own power.

She tried to carry Vera to the doors, but Scythe lashed out and knocked them both to the ground. A familiar face came running in—ten guards behind him. He glanced at Astriea, his breath caught at the sight of his sister, and his pained expression was heartbreaking. He took a vial out of his pocket and ran for Scythe, whose focus was now devoted to Seraphina.

"There you are," He seethed.

Darkness against darkness. Shadow against shadow.

"Here I am," she retorted, a snarl close to leaving her lips.

"If Vera knew how to watch her mouth, she would've survived my trap to lure you out, *Heir of Alyea.*"

The name did nothing to Sera. Did nothing against her resolve as she said to him, "I am *no one* to you."

She had him so distracted he never saw Killian coming.

Never expected the needle.

But she was grateful for his timing because Scythe's words rattled her reality. *Heir of Alyea.* Who was Alyea?

Killian jabbed the serum into the tzar's neck, hard, and Scythe screamed. "You mangy little bastard! I'll kill you next!"

The rage was short-lived. His power halted, and he squealed.

The Tzar of Telas collapsed onto the stone floor.

Seraphina rushed to Vera in an instant and pulled her into her lap. Eyes still glowing red, and her body wreathed in shadows.

Cradling her head, she went to lay a hand on her, but couldn't. Whether she was ashamed to touch her or couldn't find a place that wasn't bleeding, swollen, or broken, Astriea wasn't sure.

"Vera…Vera, he's gone." Sera cried above her. "It's over now." She sucked in a sob.

Gods. No, this can't be happening.

"I—I'm sorry. I didn't think asking that would set him off. What does it even mean?" Astriea spit the words out, tripping over each one as she went along. "I'm sorry… Vera—I'm sorry." Then a quiet essence fell on the hall… A lonely eerie leaked into the air.

Killian was at Astriea's side. He fell to his knees in front of his sister, who was not breathing.

"Killian…" Astriea cried, a hand covering her mouth.

She pulled her hair behind her ear, listening as closely as she could. Trying everything in her power to find Vera's heartbeat.

But there was nothing.

She could pinpoint all the surrounding hearts. Even Vera's six younger siblings now piled into the room in tears.

"Vera, your family is here. You need to wake up." Sera whispered. Killian looked up at her, tears flowing from his silver eyes.

"Vera, please… I need you to come back. I need you to hear me. I need you to hear that I love you. That you are everything I ever wanted to be.

You are brave and loving. Cunning and fearless. I need you to know that I forgive you. For—for all of it. Just come back, come back and we can figure the rest out later."

"Sera..." Astriea reached out for her, but Sera just held out her hand to stop her.

"*No... no, no, no, no.*" Her cries grew louder and louder still. "No!" The red in Sera's eyes flashed, and she threw one hand above her.

Everything shook, everything darkened.

Killian leapt over to his younger siblings and shielded them from the debris falling from the ceiling.

"Death cannot have you yet!" Sera cried, a thousand voices behind her own, and dark power erupted from her; poured into the world.

Astriea found herself stammering back against the wooden door. The hairs on her arms rose, accompanied by nausea.

No, she can't—

Guards and servants screamed as shadows rattled the walls, the chandeliers, and paintings.

Only a small amount of light remained, enough to see everyone close by. The royal family gasped through their tears. But Astriea watched in astonishment as a cloud of gray figures swirled in a circle above them. Whirling with dim silver light. A small bit of green flashed in the center and Sera grabbed it. Snatched it right before the glow of it went out.

Her fingers turned wholly black, leaking down her hands and arms in sharp turns and curves. Before her eyes, Seraphina touched death.

She took her raised hand and brought that light to Vera's chest.

Now she'd stolen from death.

Or had she commanded it?

As the light fell into Vera's chest, Seraphina pulled the darkness back into herself, snatched it quickly, like a prisoner set free for only one blissful moment.

Everyone was silent and stunned. But Sera's eyes did not leave the princess.

They waited for what seemed like an eternity before Vera gasped and shot up.

Sera's eyes turned back to dark onyx, and she sobbed. Astriea didn't care how Sera had done it. She would've tried it herself if she could've. She would've tried anything to ease Sera's pain.

Vera fell back into Sera's arms. Killian, Pilas, Salrek, Dalron, Caedyn, Nate, and little Thea all piled into a huddle around her. Crying and smiling.

Salrek, next in line to the throne, and his twin, Dalron, had been clutching to each other so tightly, Astriea could still see the white tension on the skin of their knuckles.

Now their heads hung heavy with relief as each knelt on either side of their sister.

"Thank you, Sera…" Each of them wrapped their arms around her and cried against her as they gave their thanks again and again.

Pilas was at her feet. Lip quivering and a hand outreached but afraid to touch Vera's foot which was obviously twisted in the wrong direction.

As were most of her fingers, her right arm. Her left leg had to be shattered completely. And by the way she breathed… Astriea didn't want to think about the damage done to her ribs.

Vera strained to move. And when her cries inevitably came, Astriea realized something at the same moment Seraphina did.

Vera's body was too broken to house her.

And death does not heal.

"Don't. Don't move. We'll get you to the infirmary." Killian said, leaning forward.

"No. No, take me to my chambers." Vera croaked, then looked into Sera's eyes. "Did you mean it? What you said?"

Sera looked shocked, but she smiled and said, "Every word."

Vera leaned into Sera's arms and kissed her. Her siblings giggled through their heartache, but Vera whimpered enough from the pain of moving that Sera pulled away and tried to stand. She would've carried Vera to the infirmary herself if she could have.

But something heavy swept over her. And Sera looked as though she'd just poured out everything she had. Her knees wobbled, and Killian was there, gently taking Vera into his arms and carrying her out. Astriea saw the fatigue growing heavier in Sera and caught her as she passed out. Before she could try to carry her, Prince Pilas took her into his own arms.

He bowed his head to Astriea.

"Someone get father to his chambers. The demon has gone. There's no need letting him lie on the floor all night," he said, trying to blink away the terror.

Two guards quickly gathered the tzar and carried him away. Before Astriea knew it, everyone had gone, and she was alone.

No guards or servants. Just her left to wander a dreadfully empty castle.

* * *

Astriea wandered the halls aimlessly for at least an hour, trying to find her way back to her room. Or maybe just find her way.

It's her, you know it's her. She thought but did everything in her power to shake it away.

She didn't have time to think about what had just happened. Didn't have time to even think about Sera—unconscious in the infirmary.

Or the incredible, dangerous power she wields.

She only had enough time to find any bit of information she could about the gods—preferably something about the god of death—the prophecy, the fae, or a way to win over Telas. Maybe even save Vera from her father's fate. She had to at least find something to free her from the bargain. If she survived this beating, Astriea doubted she would survive another.

There was no telling how long it would take before the tzar woke and ordered they be imprisoned once again. Or killed before she was done readying for Telas's breaking. She started racing through the halls, unsure of what exactly she was looking for. What would Thomas do? She kept thinking, over and over.

Then it hit her. *The library. Books.*

Any books she could find that could help her understand the prophecy. If Vera had that book about Hellion and all the others she left in their room, there had to be more. And since the servants collected the former almost immediately, there was little chance Astriea could get her hands on it.

Finally, Astriea came upon a massive entryway of carved black wood. Whatever lies on the other side, looking grim and dark. It was far away from the royal chambers and nowhere near the official library. But there was an inscription at the top of the archway: *Mkvech, Amest et tu Votem.* The words glowed a brilliant blue as she approached.

Suddenly, all the years of listening to Draes teach Thomas old Telish came rushing to her, translating the text to: *Behold, Scrolls of the Commanders.*

Good enough, she thought.

Astriea darted into the dark hall, doing her best to harness all the stillness from her past.

The room inside was so dark. She couldn't see a single thing. Something like terror gripped her heart for a moment.

She stood frozen for a split second and then took one step forward. The moment her foot touched the stone floor, a shimmering mosaic of glowing, pale-blue light snaked across the room in beautiful patterns.

A trail of light to guide her through this enormous wing of the castle.

Astriea's eyes widened at the sight of the towering shelves of books and scrolls that seemed to go on forever. Like this place was beyond their world and could not possibly exist there.

What became even more curious wasn't how all the objects glimmered with blue light, dancing like dust, but how Astriea could read every single word she saw.

Shadonian was a common tongue, easy to understand, so it wasn't hard to pick up her native language. But some texts were in Telish, Sirenian and even a few languages she'd never seen before, yet she understood exactly what they said.

Astriea followed the trail of light into the never-ending shelves.

She had to hurry. Someone would surely see the lights and find her soon, but it was too late to turn back and Sera was counting on her. The world was counting on her.

An enormous book on a pedestal stopped her in her tracks, reading:

Blackspear Records.

Something tugged her to open it and she did.

Astriea flew through the pages of that book like her life depended on it, not even knowing what she was looking for until—She gasped.

It can't be.

Marked by a red ribbon, the page that listed the names of famous Blackspears, held something she prayed wasn't true: *Raja Polonius Blackspear, Royal guard to Prince Kaeon Shataar. Relocated to Shadon at age twenty-seven.*

"No. It *can't* be," Astriea whispered to herself. How could Raja have been the tzar's royal guard? How could he have never told her that? But none of that could have prepared her for what was written beneath those words: *Children: Alyea Ophelia Blackspear, lost at sea.*

Memories flooded her.

"I was orphaned by the sea, found adrift by the Lady Ashin, and taken to the master's of the island." Seraphina had said.

There was only one difference. One factor keeping the truth from connecting. That Seraphina was found on the beach of the Isle of Zani. That she had been named by the temple.

But what if that wasn't entirely true? Astriea had never heard that second name before.

Ophelia.

She'd never heard that name before she met Sera.

Raja kept so many secrets, but he truly seemed to mourn the loss of his daughter. His daughter named *Alyea.*

He held the position of a master on the island where Sera was raised.

All the pieces connected, yet she still had no *proof.*

Gods, how would Sera react? She thought. Nausea swept through her with a sense of urgency to leave. She peeled herself away from the book of Blackspears and ran back to the black arch.

Back in the winding halls of the palace, Astriea was so stunned she could barely move.

She turned around to glance at the archway once more, but only the stone wall lay before her. The library disappeared within a single breath.

When her eyes opened, she was on the floor against the bare wall. As though she'd been sleeping.

But the memories of that hidden library did not linger like a dream. They held strong in her mind as she somehow stumbled her way back to her chambers and plopped onto the bed before letting the events of the night wash over her in a flood of dread.

57

Seraphina

Sera woke in Pilas's arms not a few minutes later. He'd already carried her halfway up Vera's tower.

"Thank you, Pilas, but I can walk from here."

He nodded and let her down, but she nearly collapsed as soon as her weight pressed against her muscles. He assisted her the rest of the way up.

Vera's healers had already gathered around her bed, readying her to reset her bones.

One healer, a petite woman in a pale blue cloak, was leaning over to Vera, talking her through the steps.

Seraphina didn't hesitate. She ran for the bed, for Vera.

The healer turned and stopped her.

"Get back!" She yelled.

Sera grabbed her by the collar of her cloak and shoved her to the side. She hit her knees against the wooden floor with a loud *thud*.

She crawled into the bed and leaned her back against the headboard, gently moving to cradle Vera's head and body in her lap.

Her eyes were nearly swollen shut, but that didn't stop the shimmer of green from breaking through. Or the stream of tears that ran down her blood-soaked face.

"Can't you give her something for the pain? On the island we have Tamila root—" she started asking.

"All we have in Telas is Matellin, but she cannot have that." The healer she shoved spat at her. Disdain in her expression.

"Why not?" Sera yelled.

"Because she is *allergic*. The last time we used it, she nearly died," the healer retorted.

"Then what needs to be done?"

"We have to reset the bones, as many as we can. And she'll have to be awake."

Vera whimpered and squeezed Seraphina's arm.

"Can't we get her to the northern healer's guild? They were able to—"

"No!" the healer was yelling at her now. And if Sera hadn't been in the middle of the worst night of her life, she would've liked to break a few of that woman's teeth.

"The grand duchess should not be alive as it is! We move her now and she *will* die. And I doubt you can pull off *what you did* a second time tonight. There will be no travel."

Seraphina bared her teeth.

"Stay with me?" Vera pleaded.

"I'll be right here the whole time." She replied. Tears streamed down her face already.

Bear witness to what you have woken, she'd thought, *bear witness to the suffering it brings.*

For what felt like hours, Seraphina held onto Vera's hand and forced herself to watch.

Crack, scream.

Crack, scream.

That voice she'd heard in her cell when she and Astriea first arrived crept back into her mind.

Look what you have done, dark and lovely flower.

I didn't mean for this...

Crack, scream.

Suddenly, every shred of animosity, of anger, of betrayal pooled out of her and dissipated. Released her from its grip like the first breath after

247

escaping the battering of death and the sea herself.

I take it back; I take it all back. She pleaded.

Oh, but you meant for this, didn't you? Your love for her would not allow her passing. Would not allow for her journey to continue without you. How selfish indeed.

I didn't know it wouldn't heal her...

Are you sure? She betrayed you. She killed your friend and would have killed more if not for the Lightbringer. It would make sense if you wished to see her punished. But it does not matter now. Now I have seen you. I know what you are, daughter of no one. When I am no longer burdened by royal resistance and childish bonds, I will have her. I will have her and her siblings, I will have Telas, this world, and I will have you.

Sera became nauseous, her blood boiling beneath her skin, but she sent a message back with so much fury that something shattered as she thought out each word. *You know nothing of me. I see you for what you are now, Scythe. And my mind will not so easily be warped. You will die, by the Lightbringer's blade. You will die and you will fail. But first, you will beg me to let her kill you. You will suffer for the pain you've caused us all, but you will suffer most greatly for the pain you've caused Vera. I swear this on the shadows that bind us.*

Suddenly, all the broken pieces of her rose into the air and snapped back together. Like she'd never been shattered at all. And in that moment, something else happened. Something foreign and exhilarating.

All the healers halted as a beautiful aura of glowing, golden dust burst from hers and Vera's chests and froze in midair.

But all she could do was gaze into tear-soaked, emerald eyes. And they gazed back.

Then Vera said words that echoed her mind, body, and soul. Words that sent images flashing through her mind of every encounter she'd ever had with her.

And then hundreds of memories that she didn't recognize, all pouring over her in waves of light and assurance and glory.

The silence in that room was unlike anything ever not heard. The sight the healers surrounding them now beheld was a spectacle so ancient it was both known and unknown.

"I choose you." Vera's voice sounded as though it'd been layered over a thousand times. Wrapping around her like a warm embrace and calling her home.

"I choose you." Seraphina replied. Her voice echoed in the same way as Vera's.

The dust shifted, swirling and forming into mighty gold chains before snapping together with a metallic *ting*. Connecting them and sending golden dust flying. It shimmered in Vera's eyes before her lids closed and she drifted into a deep, peaceful sleep. The swelling of her eyes lightly fading. The deep cuts on her face now stitching back together.

She watched the light whither away and everyone in the room, including Killian, was staring at her.

Stunned, all she could get out of her mouth was, "That should keep her asleep while you finish. Maybe…maybe even a few days." The healers simply nodded and went back to work.

Exhaustion swept over her, beating her down like she'd been drained of everything. But she held herself up against the headboard and forced herself to stay awake.

"I give you…" she panted. "I give you my strength."

She'd never felt more tired. Her insides ached, every muscle and joint, right down to her own bones. The throbbing threatened to make her sick.

Vera's chest rose and fell a bit more easily.

But she kept herself awake. She would not rest until Vera did. *Really* did.

This time, with every *crack* of bone, there was no screaming, no cries of pain, and no tears.

Save for Sera's.

58

Thomas

Thomas could see the city of Hesperia. The mountains that once shielded it from the world were gone, and now the city shimmered over the horizon.

Spires and towers of pale blue stone clung to the western beach, encircled by a wall and a sprawling city with fertile fields surrounding it. He could smell the freshly turned earth, now already packed down and waiting for the first bud of spring.

The city surrounding the castle looked lovely as well. From the sky, he could see people bustling around in the streets below.

It wasn't until they'd landed outside the city that his shock had been almost unbearable.

As he walked beside Lavene, through the fields, he noticed the greenery brighten. Beside him, a cornfield that had been no more than small seedlings when they'd landed, was now up to his waist and growing still.

"This is incredible." He murmured. Eyes lost on the fields surrounding them, now full of harvest-ready crops. Sunflowers and spider lilies broke through the soil and bloomed in the ditches on either side of them.

"This is what your father meant, wasn't it? How you made the flora more vibrant just by being near."

Lavene dipped her chin in response.

"I'm just happy to see it still standing. I am not so certain I will be forging paths in this section of the mountain's remains."

"Why?" Thomas asked as they approached the outer walls of the city. Red bricks towering far above them wove and circled the entirety of it.

"Devil's Gate is a horrible place. If the scoundrels there were allowed passage to Hesperia... I do not wish to think of it."

Thomas only nodded as Lavene led them into her brilliant city.

* * *

Hesperia was lovely. Flowers and plants on every corner, fruit trees planted in the medians of all the streets, and free for picking. The aroma of perfectly seasoned meats and noodle dishes filled his nose. His stomach twisted and ached at the delightful smell.

"Don't worry, we'll stop and eat before we make our way to the palace."

"You think they don't already know we're here? I mean, we *did* land two dragons right outside."

"I'm positive they know we are here. But I'd like to eat before I take my scolding."

Thomas twisted toward her so fast he shocked himself.

"Scolding? Whatever would you be scolded—wait."

He paused and thought it over. No one here realized who they were. People walked about and around them without a second thought. Not a soul seemed to know who they were or how they got here. They didn't even look at them twice.

"No one here seems the least bit upset or happy that their princess has returned. No one has greeted you or even looked twice your way. So, either you are not who you say you are—which is doubtful because your countenance is too refined. Or, you *ran*."

Lavene's eyes shot to his.

"Your father could never afford an uproar. If an entire secret kingdom mourns the lost princess, they could easily be found out." Thomas looked around at the crowd again. "Does this not hurt? To know they aren't looking for you?" He asked, hoping the words were gentle enough for such

251

a harsh truth.

"My father has searched for me far and wide. Has sent his best spies and mercenaries to return me. I am not sure whether he will be relieved to see me, proud that I bested his men, or furious that I endangered our title and stability of our land. My father sees himself as a lord and no more. He... holds tight to that title so that we can forever be grateful for it. My grandfather was a spy, he founded Hesperia and died just before I was born, so my father is quite determined not to let anyone take it from us. He is also determined to ensure that we are never found out. I ran because I felt called to. Because I was *needed* but... but I betrayed everything he worked for and I'm not sure how to make him understand. I'm not sure he will."

"It'll be easier on a full stomach. Let's go." Thomas replied.

* * *

They sat down at a small pub and ate some lunch before heading to the palace.

It was the only time he felt it appropriate to ask her about the armor she wore.

"Your armor? It is Sharinian steel?"

"It is." She responded, not looking up from her plate.

"I'd very much like some of my own. Can your armorer accompany us back to Triscillia?"

"No need. The armorer is already coming with us."

"Oh, good—" She looked up at him then. "Wait... *You* made that armor?"

"I did."

"Well, I have to say, it's impressive. Damian is dying for me to get my hands on some. Could you teach me?" Thomas said with a mouthful of bread.

"You want to learn how to forge?" She questioned.

"Why not? I *am* the God of all things that burn. I should know how to forge weapons from my power."

252

Lavene was silent for a moment. A long moment. Making Thomas question whether or not he should have ever asked.

"I will teach you, but as long as you promise to tell everyone that you learned from the best. And you will mention *who* the best is."

Thomas laughed. The act felt almost wrong, but there, rattling his chest nonetheless.

"I promise." He chuckled.

The two of them finished their lunch quickly and made their way to the palace gates.

* * *

The giant arches before them were white, accented by flourishing designs of gold. Twisting and turning in sharp strokes.

"Who comes before the gate?" A guard in the tower above shouted.

"The Lady Lavene Havi, the only child of Bastian Havi, Lord of this city." Lavene's words were forceful and assertive.

The gates began opening immediately.

Inside, servants and courtiers filled the courtyard leading to the palace doors. All of them looked like Lavene, like Astriea. It made his heart ache that she could not be here. It was so rare for her to find another with her features, but when she did, Thomas could always see her eyes light up.

That day in the street, when she'd set her eyes upon Amir, the man who'd been taken as a slave and beaten outside the steps of a shop, he knew there would be nothing that kept her from doing something, anything. He was the first person they'd seen who looked like her in years, in Shadon anyway. He could not speak on the diversity of Telas, having not been there in so long.

But here, here, everyone looked like her. Except for the eyes. Most of them had brown eyes, all in different shades. One's like the mahogany trees in the King's Wood, others soft like amber or so bright they were golden like Damian and Mira's. Each pair was unique. Thomas then remembered what made Astriea's different. Her father. She'd once told him that Atara's eyes were golden, but Aaron's eyes were the same silver blue as hers. Said she was grateful to have at least one thing of his when she looked her mother's spitting image. Grateful to look at her eyes and feel as though there is a piece of him with her.

Interrupting his thoughts, a swarm of handmaidens ran out to them as the palace doors swung open halfway through the courtyard.

The eldest one among them, the head maid, as far as he could tell, was the first to speak.

"Where have you been?" She shrieked, waving a handkerchief in the air as she approached.

"Madam Heli, I can assure you I am alright—" Lavene's words were interrupted as that woman threw her body against her and wrapped her in a hug. The other handmaidens followed until there was a large group of women surrounding Lavene.

Thomas couldn't help but smile.

Madam Heli pulled away and wiped her eyes with her handkerchief. "You must come inside. Your father is already on his way to the throne room. Let's get you washed up—"

"No. I'm going now. My father does not care if I am clean. Only if I have ruined his kingdom or not."

"Your father cares whether you are *alive* or not, my lady."

This gained a wide-eyed gaze from Lavene, but she shook her head, and Thomas followed her inside. Where Bastian Havi, Lord of Devil's Gate and Hesperia, waited for them.

59

Thomas

Bastian Havi was a tall, dark-complected man. His black hair was peppered with gray, his beard the same and neatly trimmed close to his face.

He was standing in front of a throne. Well, a nice chair, at least. It wasn't quite regal enough to count as a throne, in his opinion, but Lord Havi wasn't in it.

When the doors opened up, and Lavene's father saw his daughter, covered in dirt and cuts and stinking of dragon, Thomas expected him to scowl. Expected him to start yelling or something. But something else happened instead.

Lord Bastian Havi took off in a dead sprint toward his daughter and scooped her into a tight embrace. Lifting her off her feet and twirling her around.

Through that commotion, Thomas heard a breath of relief come from the Lord.

"Do not *ever* leave like that again, Lavene." He said, now standing still and holding her face against his chest. His cheek smashed against the top of her head.

"I'm sorry, Papa. I shouldn't have gone the way I did."

"If going meant that much to you, *tulip*, why not come to me?"

"Would you have honestly let me go?"

The lord thought for a moment and answered, "No… I supposed I wouldn't have."

She gave him a gentle smile, and he returned it.

"So, tell me of your journey, and why you brought a Telishman with you." He said with a raised brow at Thomas.

"It is an honor to meet you, Lord Havi."

"Papa, this is Thomas Hellion, Heir of Hellion, God of the sun and all things that burn, and Chancellor to King James Aurelius of Shadon."

Lord Havi's eyes went wide, and he retreated two steps. His hand slowly moved toward his sword.

Thomas threw his hand up to show himself unarmed.

"What have you done, Lavene? The crown can never know of us and you've brought the king's second hand to the heart of our city!"

"Papa, please listen—"

Thomas spoke up then, his voice cool and relaxed as he said, "The *former* King of Shadon is dead. His son now rules and has heard your daughter's testimony. There will be no punishment for your creation of an independent region on Shadon's shores as long as you agree to some terms."

"Do you hear this, Lavene? There are always *terms*. You should have never left the city."

"Sir, the terms are simple. You are to do two things: Supply an appropriate amount of soldiers from Devil's Gate to the war effort—"

"War? What war?" Lord Havi interrupts.

"The war against darkness, my Lord, the war against a dark sorcerer. Astriea, Goddess of life, magic, and the stars has banished him from the shores of Shadon. She fights in Telas now, trying to do the same thing for them. Trying to save us all. Shadon will be the first nation to ally with her. King James asks for your support in the form of soldiers from Devil's Gate, and healers from here. From Hesperia."

"Why would we want to do that? What would we have to gain? And if we say no, does the new king intend to destroy us if we reject him?"

"The only thing you could do to deserve King James's wrath, my lord, would be to ally yourself with the darkness. Only then would you become the enemy. We offer you trade with Shadon. Hesperia will keep her borders and lands, you keep your control over them and its citizens, you even keep the taxes you collect from them if you choose to do so. You answer only to the king or queen, but you come when they call. You honor your oath to serve him when he is in need of you and make yourself a helpful ally. And because… if *he* wins, if he defeats Astriea, that darkness will spread to every corner of our known world. The mountains that once shielded you from it have fallen, and I think you already know what that means. *The Golden King* only asks that you contribute to the cause."

"Why would he offer us this? Why does he care?" Lord Havi asked.

"Because, even though I know it is incredibly hard to believe, James is a good man and an even better king."

Lord Havi was silent for a few moments. Pacing back and forth and rubbing his chin.

"God of the sun you are?"

Thomas only answered by allowing warm flames to break loose from his head. His hair turned from black to gold.

Lord Havi stepped back, locked in awe.

"Tell the king I accept his terms."

Lavene let out a breath of relief and Thomas smiled as he reached inside his tunic pockets, removed a scrolled stack of five papers, and handed them to Lord Havi.

"What is this?" He asked as he began opening them.

Thomas made himself ready to leave. He would, no doubt, be going to find a bath and a hot meal sooner rather than later. But he answered. "Those are the official documents solidifying Hesperia's independence as a free state and its friendship with Shadon. Also included are your new official titles. Congratulations, Your Highnesses."

In Bastian Havi's hands were two other documents, new titles for them both. Officially promoting Lord Havi and his daughter to Prince Bastian and his heir, Princess Lavene.

"Grandfather would be proud, Papa."

"Of you, my girl. I kept you shielded from the world, but the moment you got out there, you freed us all from generations more of secrecy. Your grandfather would be so proud of *you*."

Lavene hugged her father, and while she did so, Thomas made his exit. He asked the handmaid out in the hall to escort him to his guest chamber and followed her.

After a bath and much-needed food, Thomas crawled into bed.

Someone knocked on the door and entered after he gave the command.

A young man, a servant no older than twenty, with dark hair and onyx eyes, came inside.

"Is there anything else you might need before you retire, Lord Hellion?" he asked.

He'd almost said nothing, but he *did* want something. Anything, really, that would help him sleep a bit more peacefully.

"Do you have any good books?"

"Of course, my lord. Do you have any favorites?"

"Something with a happy ending, if you wouldn't mind."

"Right away, Lord Hellion."

The servant left and returned quickly. And by the time he'd finished that beautiful novel, the sun was on the verge of rising. He'd stayed awake all night for that happy ending. Desperately clung to the hope of it as he closed his eyes and tried to get at least an hour of rest.

60

Damian

The scouts immediately alerted the palace when they spotted Thomas and Lavene on the southwestern horizon. Flying low above the creaking trees of The Dead Forest and startling the soldiers camping throughout.

Something was off about Thomas, though. He looked like he'd had a hard time, but only in the dark circles under his eyes. The real kicker was the fact he'd been so *silent*.

Now, with only a single day left before departure, breakfast in the great hall seemed full of nerves. Damian sat across from Mira with James on his left at the head of the table. Thomas beside him and across from Draes— who ate his food a little angrily while Thomas nervously darted his eyes back and forth between his meal and his brother.

James did his best to break the tension and said, "Damian, the carpenters have finished your ship's figurehead. I actually enjoyed the design concept so much that I ordered one for mine as well. Slightly different, but gets our message across."

"I cannot wait to see it unveiled, Your Majesty," Damian replied.

And he was very excited to see it. He'd wanted to replace his old ship's figurehead since they'd left the island, so the idea of getting a new one lit a spark in him.

"Ugh, please stop. I get enough, *your majesties* every day," James said with an eye roll. He looked much better than before. Two days ago, he looked like a man on the brink of collapse. While the circles under his eyes still lingered there, his skin and expression were much more cheerful. His hair was well-kept, too.

"We *are* in front of court, my love." Mira attested.

James nodded gently to her and then kissed the top of her hand.

"I have still yet to hear of your story, sister. The full story, that is."

Mira smiled brightly. "What is so intriguing about my story, little brother?"

"I have missed too much of your life. Would it be a crime to know you better?"

"I'm not sure if we have the time for such a tale, but rest assured, I will tell it." She said.

"Perhaps if I can steal you away to assist me in leading the dragons, we might find the time."

"I think I would enjoy that."

Damian smiled in reply.

When he looked again at Thomas, the conversation shifted.

"So, tell me how the trip went, then. Valtan says Lavene cleared away the rocks on dragon back." He said, clasping his hand on Thomas' shoulder.

"I'd rather not. Though, we could speak of the fact you freed all the Shadon slaves while we were all busy. Two thousand of them volunteered?"

"It was supposed to be a surprise. Though, two thousand men and women showing up overnight was a surprise for me at least," James replied. "I was going to make the official announcement at the farewell feast tonight, in front of all the lords at court. But now, they're already whispering about it."

"Well, I don't care how you did it, or how soon the news of it was leaked, you did a good thing, James." Thomas dipped his head and got up from his seat, making to leave the hall. It was the only time Draes looked up from his plate. Concerned lanced about his features.

Damian looked around the table to see everyone else was just as worried.

So Damian excused himself and followed right behind him.

With a swift swing of his arm, he wrapped it around Thomas' shoulder. "To the beach then. I want to learn how to ride the water dragons and you are going to teach me before we leave." Thomas tried to interject, but Damian cut him off. "No, no. I won't be the only one not riding a dragon at some point. It would be shameful. You wouldn't let everyone be pickin' me apart, would you?"

Thomas' mouth snapped shut, and he rolled his eyes but smiled. The two of them left the palace grounds and made way for the beaches along the cliffs where the dragons nested.

* * *

Damian's heart leapt at the sight of the water dragons up close.

The expressions on their smoothly scaled faces were very curious looking. Like they were trying to understand something about him. They sniffed and splashed him with a bit of mist.

Thomas stared at the dragon for a moment before he bowed his head and then climbed onto its turquoise back. He held out a hand to Damian.

"Come on, then!" Thomas yelled.

Damian jumped onto the dragon's back and, to his astonishment, he felt as if every problem he had just drifted away for a while. Back on the island, Damian was the one out doing adventurous things that could've and *should've* gotten him killed. Seraphina had always been there to coax him back from going too far. But *here*, Damian didn't have Sera.

It was necessary for him to be well put together.

Had to be ready at all times.

The water was warm in the bay, and the winds brushing against him made him feel at home. At peace.

The beautiful blue dragon twisted its long slithering body side to side for a moment before it stopped and changed its pattern. They began moving up and down, dipping in and out of the water.

"Hold your breath and hold on tight!" Thomas yelled as he wrapped his arms around the dragon's neck. Damian grabbed hold of Thomas' waist and took a deep breath just before the dragon took a deep dive into the water.

When the pressure receded, Damian opened his eyes to see a school of shimmering green fish darting by him.

Something about the sea... it was so clear, so beautiful. When his eyes had first opened, they felt dry and his sight was a blur, but in one blink, the treasures of the ocean were more clear than the light of day to him. Coral, in at least a hundred different colors, spilled across the reef as the dragon turned to go back up. A school of blue and white damselfish fluttered by his face. Almost tickling him. He laughed a bit and then realized how easy it was to hold his breath. Maybe it was because he was so distracted by the beauty before him. By the glittering blue and gold scales beneath him, by the lovely shape of the sea floor. Or maybe even the peace and tranquility in the silence of this place.

That heavenly sight was short-lived as the dragon shot through the water like an arrow let loose. Nothing could've prepared Damian for the blast of cool air that slammed into him as the sea-serpent broke into the sky.

The dragon went higher and higher until they halted and sat motionless for only a split-second. Then, those sheer wings extended in a quiet *whish* and caught on the breeze.

Damian was stunned. He finally sucked in a deep breath as they passed through a cloud. It felt like sailing through a heavy mist.

Then he saw the view.

It was beautiful.

The coast of Triscillia was so small from this distance, but the navy ocean turned to turquoise beaches against nearly white sand. The summer palace glittered under the sun. Damian looked beyond the palace to the open plains he couldn't make out and beyond to a dark line that bordered the horizon. Thomas's eyes were also focused on that area.

"Do you see that spot there? The upper northwest." Thomas asked him as the dragon hovered in the air, beating its wings. He nodded.

"That was Monolith. It wasn't an *easy* home. But we thought that was it. I grew up with the people there and now Astriea, Draes, and I are the only ones left. We don't talk much about home or the people we knew and cared about. It's just too much and not enough time to mourn. And..." He paused. "And it is cursed now. There are only two people in this world who have witnessed the sins committed there."

"Are you one of those people, Thomas?" Damian asked.

Thomas only turned his head to look at him and that was all the answer he needed.

There was only one person he would talk to about this. One person half a world away.

"I am not the only one avoiding things. Meditation cannot spare you completely from grief or fear for the ones you love, Damian."

"I know." He replied, albeit a bit guiltily.

Damian hadn't really spoken of Sera or Tristan. Sera was different, though. He had a strange feeling that she was going to be alright. She might struggle, but Sera has more grit than any warrior the temple had seen in years. *That* was something he legitimately overheard the masters saying as he once passed by the viewing pavilion they'd sat in. Although, he wasn't going to tell Sera that. She loved to mess with him too much.

Tristan, on the other hand, he hadn't sought the time to mourn him for one reason. He simply did not want to accept what his own eyes had seen. He couldn't.

"Maybe when we aren't drowning in worry, we will have more room to grieve."

Thomas looked back at him at that. He gave Damian a half smile and nodded.

Damian returned the gesture, and the blue-scaled beauty dove towards the sea. It halted just above the water's surface before gliding over it and heading back to the beach.

They'd been gone all day, and now, their stomachs begging for dinner, they returned to the palace for one last feast before the dawn.

Before the war.

II

Ties that bind.

61

Seraphina

Seraphina slept for three days.

She spent another three waiting for Vera to wake. On the first of those days, she was surprised to find that someone had returned her to her and Astriea's chambers. And even more surprised that the tzar hadn't sent them both back to the dungeons.

On the first of those days she'd been awake, Astriea told her of the magic library she'd found and how she'd been unable to find it again. She seemed uneasy, though. Like she was holding something back.

"What is it? You're not telling me everything. I've learned that look. It's a good poker face, but it's specific. Your others aren't the same."

Astriea stared at her for a moment with a raised brow.

"It's you. The Goddess of Darkness, of Death. It's you."

Sera's head drooped.

"I know. *Now*, anyway... How long did you know?" Sera didn't know why, but her cracking voice came off as a plea. Begging for answers. But it appeared Astriea had none.

"I think some part of me has known since I drew that power out of you on the ship. Maybe I even suspected it as you leapt in and out of shadows when you rescued me from the witch-hunter's camp."

"And you said nothing?"

"I was hoping it wasn't true. That you would not have to be an *Heir*. I have only ever wanted you to know happiness and peace. This life does not offer you that." She took a breath. "But it offers you a sister." Astriea sat down next to her and took Sera's hands into her own. "The light and the dark do not have to battle. We can find a way to stay together, to fight together. That's why I'm hoping to sneak out and hunt down the library entry tonight. He won't take anything else from us. Can you play injured and stay here to keep up cover?" She asked.

Sera nodded her head but looked at Astriea's face curiously.

"What else?" Sera asked.

Astriea's expression relaxed, and she said softly, "Nothing. Just tired. Have you gone to see if Vera is awake yet?"

Sera felt the blood rush to her cheeks at the mention of Vera's name.

"No. But honestly, I want to know why we haven't been sent back down *there* yet. If Scythe is in control of the tzar as often as it seems, he should've been furious. We probably shouldn't even be alive right now. But I haven't seen a single royal today. None of them."

Astriea's eyes wandered like that realization had just dawned on her. They hadn't even seen Killian today.

"I'll try to cover for you as best I can, but I might leave the room tonight as well. I think while you look for the library, I should find out what's keeping us from our punishments."

Astriea didn't say anything, but she nodded. Later that night, after Astriea had gone, Sera raised her hood and slipped quietly out the door.

They spent the following days in vain, as neither of them found what they were looking for.

But on the third day, Seraphina walked through the halls of the grand duchess's tower once more. Hoping the sleeping princess would soon wake. Maybe then she could beg Vera's forgiveness like she'd begged Tristan's spirit every day. Begged him in her prayers to forgive her for loving the hand responsible for his death. And now Sera could not stop thinking about how she had plucked Vera's soul from her journey through the stars and forced it back into her broken body. Had taken a choice from her she would've killed anyone else for.

Part of her was so happy to hear Vera's voice radiate down the cold, black halls. But another part of her, another part of her heart, crumbled under the weight of hearing the beauty she had not earned. She approached Vera's door and stopped.

"Ah! Ouch Nan!" Vera said.

"Hush girl! The hotter the water, the cleaner you'll be!" An older handmaiden was helping Vera into the bath. An elderly woman she only knew as *Nan*. She was almost sure it was the same woman who brought her to Vera's room the night Scythe attacked her in the corridor. But based on the little information she knew of Telas, someone's *Nan* was considered their primary caregiver. Such as a nanny—hence the nickname. Nan had been by Vera's bedside every day. Tending her wounds and checking for fevers.

The door was cracked, allowing Sera to hear well enough even though she couldn't see them. She heard Vera splash into the water and make a hissing sound against the heat.

"Honestly, I don't understand how those healers missed this old blood. I know they didn't want to move you too much in your sleep, but they ought to know better than an old maid."

"Ah!" Vera yelped. "They have other duties that don't involve making me look pretty, Nan."

Sera heard the water splash lightly.

"I know dearest, I just hate seeing you like this. I hate when they bring you back to me bruised and brokenhearted." There was no splashing then. Only clear and unrelenting silence.

"I… I have to—"

"I know, little queen." Nan's voice became a whisper that Sera would've never heard if she hadn't been eavesdropping so intently.

"But sometimes I ask the gods to take you far away from here. I know what deal you made when you were a child. I know why you did it. But sometimes, even now, I wish that someone—even that small, terrifying woman who's been visiting you every day—would take you away and let you live a life surrounded by soft hearts and gentle hands. I would give

269

the air I breathe for you to have it. You deserve to have that."

"Don't say that, Nan. You… I've already lost one mother and I don't enjoy lingering on thoughts of losing another. I don't know what I'd do without you. So don't speak of us parting. I'm not ready for that. I'm not sure I ever will be."

There was silence and a sniffle, but Sera heard Vera laugh through it. "She's visited me every day, you said?"

Nan huffed out a laugh and Sera heard her pop Vera with a wet cloth. "Every day."

"I don't understand why…" Vera whispered. "She couldn't have meant what she said. How could she truly forgive me?"

The water sloshed again and Nan said, "I think, if you were to be honest with her, as honest as you can be, at least, that she would love you even more fiercely. You do not have to bear the cold alone, not anymore."

"Unfortunately, Nan, it is my duty and my curse to bear this cold alone."

The silence became deafening, so Seraphina stood and knocked on the beautiful oak doors.

62

Seraphina

eraphina's heart pounded against her chest like a hammer as she entered the room, causing a wave of unease to wash over her.

The swelling had gone down, thanks to Vera's hoard of healers and whatever she and Sera did the other night. Despite her bruises and limping, she exuded a newfound vitality and appeared less burdened by pain.

Sera would never forget what she'd witnessed just six nights before when Killian brought Vera here and the healers had begun their work setting her broken bones. She'd never forget Vera's cries. Her screams.

Now, looking at her, standing—albeit with some aid—and walking out of her closet in a green silken robe, all Sera could feel was that chain of gold dust, the beautiful magic that bound her to a beautifully battered princess.

"What is this? This *bond* between us? It's so much stronger than before..." Vera grasped her chest. Her heart.

Sera sucked in a sharp breath and stepped closer to her.

"You... You feel it too?" She breathed.

Vera limped closer to her, Nan helping her along and sitting her on the edge of the bed before leaving the room and shutting the door behind her.

"Of course I feel it, but what *is* it?"

"How are you healing?" Sera asked, lost on the bruises running across her collarbone.

"Seraphina, don't change the subject." Vera pressed. But she remained silent. And tears burned in the back of her eyes but she refused to cry right now. She could hold it together for Vera. She could do that.

The princess sighed and said, "I'll need more extensive healing. Now tell me what you did."

"I'm not sure. But I am sure of one thing, of many things, actually."

"Yeah... What's that?"

Sera took to her knees before Vera and brought her hands into her own.

"That I'm sorry. I—I am so sorry, Vera. I took a choice from you that was not mine to make. Ripped you from your peace and threw you back into a broken body." She couldn't find air. Couldn't breathe no matter how many words spilled out of her. Part of her praying to the gods to release it all, and let it be clear enough to make sense past her rambling.

But Vera could hear her perfectly. She pulled Sera closer as she went on. Pressed their tangled hands against her chest and her forehead against her own.

"I am so sorry for the pain I caused you because *I love you*. Your presence always leaves me breathless, the air only to return when you are mine again. I know that I never want to lie to you because when I do, it feels like swallowing nails. I meant everything I said. There is nothing I won't do for you, nothing I wouldn't be for you. Be it a spy, an assassin, a concubine..."

"Stop," Vera whispered. "Stop, Sera, the fault is mine. It is all my fault. I never should've betrayed you. I'm sorry for what I did to Tristan. There's so much more I wish I could tell you, but I can't, and that feels like being torn to pieces. My lips beg to pour out every secret and truth to you, and yet I choke on them. But all I want is *you*. All I want is to feel your hand in mine. To hear you laugh. See your smile every day. Since our meeting, there has not been a day I haven't ached for you. I will love you in any form you take. Through any choice and mission, I will love you, Seraphina. If you will have me."

Sera's eyes watered and she lightly wrapped her arms around her, gently pulling her into a hug. Vera let out a deep breath and let her head rest on Sera's shoulder.

"You… You don't hate me for bringing you back?"

"I couldn't hate you even if I wanted to."

"No more lies?" Seraphina asked softly.

"No more lies," Vera responded. "There is so much I have to tell you, and so much that I can't."

"Just start with what you can."

63

Astriea

striea never thought much of her dreams. All her life, they had been wild and sporadic. Always blurred and out of order. Sometimes she had trouble even remembering them when she woke. So when she'd fallen asleep after hunting for the library until the dead of night, she didn't expect such a vivid display of events.

She was standing in an icy wasteland of snow. There were mountains in the distance that she didn't recognize, and a small stream no wider than a foot, snaking through the ground and leading farther north. The water in it shimmered with a golden hue, swirling and flowing. Rushing north.

Why isn't it frozen? She thought.

"Zaniah? Is this you?" She called out to the cold. But no one answered. The only sound was that of the wind. How could she be so cold in a dream? She brushed past the thought when the wind started pulling her forward. It wasn't long before another gust shoved against her back. Something wanted her to move, to follow the stream.

To go north.

So Astriea took step after step, every breath stinging like ice piercing her lungs. She walked for a while before hitting her knees. It felt like she'd been walking for years. Until, finally, something stunning erupted across the night sky.

Lights. Streaming banners of light rippled through the sky in greens, blues, pinks, and purples. Her eyes widened at the sight and Astriea let out a laugh. She lifted her hands to it, and the world twisted in on itself. The lights swirled together like a hurricane before crashing into her.

She blinked, and when her eyes opened, Astriea was kneeling before a massive frozen oasis. The pool was a perfect circle, surrounded by tall crystals of every color and shape. All of them were smaller at the river's point of entry and larger toward its back. The water a shining gold, splashing against the ice. At the farthest point of the pool, where the crystals stood their tallest, sat a solid black beam scale.

The princess... A cool voice whispered in the wind. Familiar and forgiving. *The princess shall lead you to The Mystic. Though weary, her crucible has not yet ended. Tell her of this, and let her lead you here.*

Before Astriea could move towards the golden water, the world around her collapsed in on itself. Her mind twisted and bent until her eyes flew open in her bed.

She rose with a start. Panting and clutching her chest. Like she hadn't been breathing all night. She shivered, the cold following her into the waking world.

Standing, she shook her hands before pacing back and forth in front of the warmth of the hearth.

What the hell is *The Mystic?* She thought. Why did that dream feel *so real?* Why did that voice want her to follow the princess to the golden pool? She needed answers, and she knew basically nothing. She would have to confront Vera when she woke. Would have to get her to guide her there. Her dreams had always been meaningless, but *this.* This was too big to ignore, to brush off as a wild interpretation of her mind. Just when Astriea was about to take her first step towards the door, Killian stormed into the room. His breath was heavy and full of something she'd never seen on him before.

Rage.

But behind that, covertly hidden behind snarled teeth, were the knitted brows of unbearable anguish. Crying out, he threw the entry table against the stone wall, shattering the wood to pieces and sending parchment and ink flying across the room. He wasn't even looking at her as he continued to destroy the furniture as though he'd never get the anger out.

Without thinking, Astriea moved and stepped directly in front of him. His attention snapped to her. Nearly his entire body moved with his rapid breaths. She placed her hand on his chest, his heart.

"Killian." She said softly.

He released a hot breath mixed with some kind of guttural sound that didn't belong to a human.

"Killian, do you know my name?"

He blinked.

"Killian? We're friends. Do you remember who I am?"

His breath slowed and this time he blinked furiously.

"Astriea. Your name is Astriea."

"That's right." She breathed and pulled her hand from his chest. He snatched it in his own and placed it back against him. Tugging her closer to him.

"I'm sorry." He whispered. "The healers gave me news I hadn't hoped for, and yours was the first room I stumbled into."

"I suppose it's alright, it's your family's money, not mine. Startle me like that again, though, and I'll skin you." She said with a grin.

He was looking at her then. Just looking, his solid silver eyes never revealing much. But his devilish grin said more than enough.

He backed her against the desk, and her whole body went on alert. Her muscles already preparing to strike him down until she was free of his grip.

"Please, give me a reason to say fuck all to helping any of you. Give me a reason for the rage that would crumble your stupid towers." She snarled at him, teeth gritting.

He released her wrist the moment the words fell out of her mouth. As she withdrew her hand, Killian delicately brushed his fingers against her jaw, sending a shiver down her spine. She didn't move as he snatched her jaw to look at him.

"Did you tell yourself you were helping us when you sent Seraphina to bed my sister?"

Her eyes went wide.

"By that time, you already knew what would happen to Vera."

"I didn't know he would punish her for being with Seraphina, Killian."

"Because you think little of the risks. It is easy for you to leap into a fight, to send your soldier to manipulate my sister, because you think you've already lost everything. You would die for your cause without question because you have no family left."

"I have Thomas—"

"Oh, please," He released her, letting her drop down further onto the desk. "I've heard that the new Dragon is young."

"No younger than I am. Not many years younger than yourself."

"How bright his light must burn to have you so ensnared by him."

Killian leaned closer to her and moved his hand to lie flat against the wall on the other side.

"And maybe he's forgotten Telish ways. If you were to share my bed—"

"Maybe if you ask nicely, I could convince Thomas to bed *you.* Give you a little taste of what makes me ache for him day and night."

Killian smiled and backed up as Astriea pushed him away from her. He raised his hands, as if in surrender.

"Are you done pursuing me? Seriously, Killian, I entertained it for a while, honestly out of survival, but my heart belongs to Thomas." She said sternly.

"If Thomas is the one you choose, then yes."

"Killian... There is no choice. It will always be Thomas. Until I am nothing and the void has consumed us all, we will hold the other's heart. What part of that aren't you understanding?"

"I understand. I'm sorry to have bothered you, Astriea." He bowed and made to leave. "You said you entertained it out of survival, I'm sorry I made you feel as though you needed to do that."

"Just try to remember it is the light that you love. Not me."

"I don't think—"

She stopped him. "You've lived in the dark a long time, Killian. It's why

I've let it go on this long."

He gave her a silent nod and was almost to the door when she said, "Wait... I'd like us to be friends. Sit. Tell me what the healers told you that turned you into a wild animal."

He flinched when she mentioned the healers, but sat down anyway.

"Vera's healers told me that she will never fully recover from this last beating. This isn't the first time her bones have been broken and with the damage history... She'll need assistance to walk anywhere she wants to go. And she can never ride again. The one escape from this hell she has and now that has been taken from her, too." He took a breath. "Her body just isn't healing like it should. Most of the progress she's made has been external, her larger bruises and cuts wiped away, but her bones— her organs—are failing. They think it's because she was dead. And her body was too broken to heal properly this time. It is known that magic is stronger the farther north you travel here. No one knows why, but I had hoped we were north *enough* for the healers to fix more than they did."

"Gods. Killian... Does she know? Have they told her?"

He dropped his head but nodded.

"The Healer's Guild and Science Guild go hand in hand. They belong to her. They have direct orders to give all information directly to her before alerting anyone else. So, yeah. She knows."

Astriea sat there in silence with Killian, letting the dread of what happened wash over them. She thought about the story Thomas told them about Vera. How she rode on the back of a solid black immortal horse called Hypnia. That she'd cleaved souls into the darkness trailing behind them. How Hypnia hadn't chosen a rider in centuries and never a princess until Vera. Astriea's heart broke for her.

Then a thought occurred to her and before she could think, she said, "Killian, what do you know about The Mystic?"

* * *

Killian's reaction to her question ended up answering one: *Is it dangerous?*

Based on his expression, deadly.

"Why would you mention such a thing here? What do you know of it?" He asked quietly, like the walls might be listening. Astriea raised her hands by her chest and said, "Quite literally nothing. Other than two random outcries of *By the Mystic!* from town. But it's important, Killian. Please tell me what it is." He looked at her curiously. Like he needed to think very carefully about how he presented each word.

"Some believe it is The Well of the Gods, where they would gather and replenish their power—"

"That's amazing! Where can we find it?"

"Slow down, that's not all. That is what parents tell their children to not terrify them. The texts in the royal keep, however…"

Texts in the royal keep? She held on to that bit of information for later.

"Gods… what is it?"

"They speak of the Goddess of Life, of her… fall. And how she tore the Gods to pieces. Their golden blood fell from the heavens and created The Mystic, a pool of power and judgment. No one has ever found it. People have gone mad searching for it out in the eastern tundra—"

She was just thinking over the lines she'd read in *The Great Pool*, when the last of his words disrupted her.

"I'm sorry, did you say *Eastern?*"

"Yes, why?"

"Did it never occur to anyone to search north?"

Killian laughed, a bellowing chuckle that actually brought a slight grin to Astriea's lips.

"They imposed a ban on traveling north of this stronghold ages ago. Only the northern healer's guild in the mountain can be accessed. No one who has ever journeyed north returns. Ever. Eventually, the tzar tired of losing tax-paying citizens to the *Northern Wastes*—as it's called—so it's forbidden."

Astriea stood up then and paced back and forth, careful to avoid the broken pieces of furniture still littered about the place.

"Killian, I have an idea, but I need you to trust me. I need all of you to trust me. Can you do that?"

He gave her a worried look but stood and followed her out the door. Up to Vera's tower.

* * *

Bursting in on Seraphina and Vera as they held each other on a sofa in front of a warm, roaring fire was not what Astriea intended to do. She realized the moment she stepped through the door that she'd been quite rude.

"Oh, gods. I'm sorry, I should've knocked." Astriea said regrettably. She made to go back into the hall and try again, but Vera stopped her.

"It's alright, Astriea, truly." She said as she struggled to sit up. "What is it?"

Killian checked the hall three times before quietly closing the doors behind him. Both Vera and Seraphina were curious now. Sera looked at her with an irritated expression. Some small message in her eyes that said: *We should discuss this first.*

Astriea pressed forward, though. If anyone would be on her side for this wild plan, it would be Sera.

"I want to talk to you about The Mystic."

Sera's eyes went wide, as well as Vera's. "Astriea... The Mystic—"

"I know what you're going to say, that you've searched all over the Eastern tundra. But what if we went north? I had a dream of The Mystic. I never have dreams, not any that matter or make sense, but *this...* It showed me the golden pool, and there was this voice—"

"Voice? What kind of voice?" Sera interrupted. She leaned forward, listening intently.

"Soft and riding on the wind. Now that I think about it, it could've been my mother's voice... but anyway, the voice told me: *The princess shall lead you to The Mystic.* I know it sounds insane, but your treatments have nearly destroyed my power, Vera. If I have any chance at defeating Scythe, I need to bathe in The Mystic. We *both* do."

280

"You mean to have Vera bathe in The Mystic? No one has ever dared to do that and you want to toss the heir to the Telish throne into a pool of god-blood? Are you mad?" Killian said through his teeth, trying his best to keep quiet.

But it was Sera who spoke next. "I agree with Killian." The words threatened to break Astriea's heart. It certainly broke her confidence. She looked at Sera. I thought we were a team? She thought.

"Vera can barely move, let alone travel. How is she supposed to survive the journey?"

"We could help her. Vera, your people know the ice and snow well. Could you have a carriage assembled for the climate?"

"That *is* possible, something I've actually been working on, but…" She trailed off in thought.

"But nothing, no one returns from the North. It doesn't happen, and it's not happening now. I've already failed my sister enough for a dozen lifetimes. I won't let her die on a fool's errand." Killian spat.

But Astriea stepped closer to Vera and knelt.

"Vera, if you bathe in The Mystic, you could be healed—*gifted,* even. You could ride again." She glanced at the look of worry Vera gave her. That gaze darted to Seraphina, then back to Astriea again. And then it dawned on her that Sera was unaware of the extent of Vera's injuries. That she would not live long in the shape she's in.

Shit.

"We could find a way to beat him together, but we are no use to anyone if we can't fight. The Mystic said '*Though weary, her crucible has not yet ended.*'" She went on.

"She has done enough fighting," Killian began, but he was quickly silenced.

"I will decide if the battle is over, Killian. It may seem impossible to the two of you, but I fear my fighting has only just begun and if I decide to fight until there is no air left in my lungs, or every bone in my body is broken then I will do so and you will both support me. While I can see the irony, I will make my own choices."

The room went silent.

"You do not speak for me, Killian," Vera said sternly. Even bent over against Seraphina, Vera was a queen through and through.

"But I'm afraid they are right. The North is too treacherous, and I would not survive the journey. I'm sorry, Astriea, my answer is no."

64

Astriea

Astriea felt like screaming into her pillow like a toddler, but instead, paced back and forth in front of her bed.

She had hoped that there would still be broken pieces of furniture lying around for her to kick, but unfortunately, the maids had already cleaned it up. Her mind swirled with a thousand different thoughts, but all of them led to the same outcome. Astriea would have to find The Mystic on her own. She'd have to move up her escape from the palace and find a way to survive the treacherous cold. But how would she do that? Astriea had no idea where to go, and the vision was explicit: *The princess shall lead you to The Mystic.*

Could it have meant the other princess? Thea?

No.

There's no way a small child could survive the journey. Then again, neither could Vera. But kidnapping a Telish princess was out of the question, anyway.

She headed for the desk by the window. To the shelves of books adorning it, left there by the princess herself.

She pulled out the copy of The Great Pool and rummaged through the pages.

She saw nothing but different interpretations of the poem read at the beginning.

But throughout the years, scholars had been sure of only one thing. You must first survive the journey and then be deemed worthy by the Magistrate. Weigh right by her scales and be granted new life, or gifts. Or die mercilessly.

Now that she looked over it again, she realized the severity of what she asked of Vera.

In an effort to ease her racing thoughts, Astriea let herself find sleep in the reading chair by the hearth.

* * *

The rest felt like nothing. Like she'd simply blinked and shot up at the uncomfortable feeling that she was being watched. The hairs on her arms stood straight up.

She raised a fist but halted when her gaze landed on the young red-haired prince. He was dressed completely in black. A large scarf wrapped around his neck and some of his freckled face.

"*You?*" she questioned.

The prince dropped his shoulders, showing offense that she had forgotten his name. But Vera had a lot of siblings. Honestly, it was hard to keep up with them without interacting with them every day.

"*Pilas.* Prince Pilas Shataar. If it makes it easier for you, I'm the only boy with red hair." The tone was proof enough of his relation to Vera. He even rolled his eyes for dramatic effect.

"Well, Prince Pilas, what are you doing here? At…" She squinted at the grand clock in the corner. "At four in the morning?"

He stood and held out a hand to her. "Come with me. The grand duchess requests your presence immediately."

Astriea's eyes widened, but she took his hand and let him lead her out the door and back toward Vera's tower.

As they made their ascent up the spiral staircase, Astriea took great caution to follow Pilas step by step. The entire journey through the palace,

Pilas kept them both hidden in shadow. At some points, guards and maids walked mere inches from them and saw nothing. The young prince was good. A little *too* good for comfort. It made her think how he might interact with Sera, or Mira even. Or if his orders would be to fight against them, in the event that Vera changes her mind again.

Who else would they lose to her? Would Sera be next? She shook the thought from her mind and followed Pilas through a hidden door one level below Vera's chambers. He pressed his palm against the cold stone and an entire door pressed in and slid away.

The entryway was dark. All of this was making her feel uneasy. Suddenly, the endless dark of the hall became eerily familiar to her. In the back of her mind, she could hear water dropping onto a stone floor. Could feel the ghostly sting of pain across her thigh. The smell of smoke and burned flesh.

Her breaths shortened, and her stomach cramped into itself.

Flashes of the night Raja died invaded her mind. Then her short time in the witch-hunter camp.

The blood she'd spilled in her escape and the soul she'd marked for all eternity. And for a moment of great terror, she saw herself through Seraphina's eyes as she peeled the witch-hunter apart.

It was no goddess of life and light. But of vengeance and fury.

But to her delight, the darkness broke and warm light washed over her. Her lungs leapt for breath.

Pilas led her into a small war room with a roaring fire in the corner and a large wooden table carved to resemble the entire country of Telas. Small ship figurines adorned the beaches of the table, and knights were scattered across the rest of the map. Vera sat at the head of the table nearest the fire.

Astriea did her best to keep her dinner down and tried like hell to clear those lingering thoughts away.

"I trust you weren't seen?" Vera said as she tried to rise to her feet. Pilas was at her arm in an instant, helping her stand.

"Am I ever?" He responded. He tried to hide the concern on his face, but it did little good.

Maybe it was because she never had siblings of her own, but she couldn't understand them. This family.

Vera had committed unspeakable deeds, and yet, they were fiercely loyal to her. Astriea knew there was no hope in swaying any of them from Vera's cause, but, if she could sway Vera, there might be a chance to destroy Scythe. Maybe even a chance to avoid war with Shadon.

But weren't they all on the same side? Were they not all fighting to be free of Scythe's influence? Was that not the ultimate goal for all of them?

"What's the meaning of this, Vera? Why have the prince sneak me in at this late hour? Where is Sera?" The questions shot out of her mouth before she had time to think about which one mattered more.

"Sera is in bed. And we don't have time to talk for long. We have to leave immediately."

Shock swept through her. Astriea blinked. And then again.

Vera shooed Pilas off her and took a tall wooden staff in her hand to help her walk.

"Let's go."

Before Astriea could argue, she was following the prince and the grand duchess down another set of stairs at the back of the room. After two flights, Vera became quite winded, and Pilas took her into his arms and carried her the rest of the way down.

"Quickly," Vera whispered to her and they took a left before opening a heavy metal door to the outside.

A bone-chilling cold burst into the room but subsided some when they made their way out into the open snow. Astriea turned and looked up to see the tower hovering above them. *Shit.*

She continued to follow Vera to the stables through a thick layer of fresh snow. There wasn't a light to be seen except for one candle lit in the stalls.

"We can't leave without Sera," Astriea called out in a shouted whisper.

Vera stopped and leaned against her brother. "If we tell her, she'll stop us. And we both know that she can."

"Don't you ever tire of this? Of lying to her?"

"Don't!" Vera pointed a finger at her. "I can't answer those questions yet, and I can't answer them here. And I damn sure shouldn't have to answer them to *you*."

Astriea looked down at the ground and then back at Vera's tower, where her dearest friend slept.

"If you truly believe that The Mystic lies north, that it can help us both, then I believe I can lead us there." She said in the falling snow.

Astriea nodded and followed her and Pilas onward.

When they rounded the corner, her breath caught in her chest.

The largest, most beautiful, jet-black horse stood before her. At least five to ten times larger than any horse she'd ever seen, including Lijah. Even in the dark, Astriea could see the black shadow that rolled out of the horse's eyes. She stomped at the ground and whinnied when her gaze caught with Astriea's.

"Hypnia..." Astriea started. Something warm grew in her chest, in her heart. Something familiar and safe. Hypnia started to buck and move towards her. The horse master and Vera both reached to stop Hypnia from running Astriea down. But she did not freeze in fear. Astriea leapt forward and placed and gentle palm upon Hypnia's massive snout. Her hand was so small in comparison, that even with her fingers spread wide open, she couldn't reach either edge of the horse's face.

Something in her begged her to never leave this horse's side.

Don't leave.

Stay. Please.

Vera and the horse master were both shocked. Pilas too. They stared for only a few moments before Pilas urged Vera to get into the warmth.

"She must trust you deeply," Vera said as she made her way to the odd-looking carriage waiting at the edge of the stables.

"What is *that*?"

"That, Astriea, is our only way to The Mystic. Did you follow my instructions specifically, Master Daron?" The Horse master stepped forward and bowed quickly before answering, "Yes, Your Highness. I even lined the carriage with the new material you suggested. I also built those funny wheels you asked for. They should get you through the snow with little issue."

"Thank you, Master Daron. I appreciate your timeliness as well. You truly are an artist of your craft." Vera nodded at Pilas, to which he answered by tossing the horse master a plump sack of coin.

"I trust you to keep this to yourself?" Vera asked with a raised brow.

"Aye, Your Highness. I'll not breathe a word of it. But I beg you, Your Grace, this is only a prototype, untested as well. I did the best I could to finish her up these last few hours, but I worry for your safety."

"Have you ever built me anything that caused me harm or that I did not design myself, Master Daron?"

"No, ma'am."

"Then I have much faith in your work."

Vera nodded him away and then proceeded to the carriage.

"What the hell is this thing?" Astriea asked. Her eyes went everywhere. The near monstrosity before her was black as night and made fully of metal. The wheels were long and short, stretching down the length of the carriage with small spikes to pierce the snow.

"This is an ice-crusher. That's what I like to call it, anyway. But regardless, this *should* get us to The Mystic."

"So you've changed your mind? Why?"

"A question for the ride. Which will be hard. We'll have to stop every few hours and pour these canteens of hot water on the snow buildup on the front plates," Vera struggled to lift the seat of the inside of the carriage to reveal at least thirty large, steaming metal bottles of water. Astriea could feel the warmth inside wash over her, feet away from the open door.

"We'll have to melt the ice buildup on the wheels as well. This journey is going to push us both to our brink. The Northern Wastes are treacherous. If we're not careful, *deadly*. Are you sure this is what you want to do? Do you understand that it is very likely you created The Mystic, and its judgment of you and myself could end *very* poorly?"

Astriea thought about that for a moment.

Questioned herself.

Could I have been responsible for tearing the gods apart?

But yet she answered, "If you're asking me if I think we will die, yes, I do. And if you don't want to risk it, then I beg you to send me on without you. But this *grand destiny* has had me place the ones I love on the line too many times. I won't do it again. I need my power back in order to keep them all safe. If there is even a splinter of a chance that I can save them, that I can destroy Scythe without risking them again, then I will gladly die for it."

Vera's chin raised slightly, a half-smile breaking from her lips.

"I have packed your supplies in the floor storage, Your Highness," said the horse master quickly. "There's a storm coming from the south. If you two are going, you best get ahead of it."

Vera's expression changed. Concern.

"The South?" She questioned, but Pilas was rushing them both towards the carriage. Tossing thick fur cloaks over both their shoulders.

"Don't worry about it, sister. You must get going. Stay out of the cold as much as possible. The North is not forgiving."

"We'll need a dozen horses to pull this thing," Astriea said.

"No. We only need one." Vera responded.

Astriea's eyes shot back to Hypnia. She could pull that carriage more easily than a normal horse could pull a toy wagon.

"She doesn't seem like the hauling type?" Astriea questioned.

"I'll just have to ask her," Vera said before limping over to Hypnia's massive head.

It might have been rude to listen in on what Vera said to the immortal horse. But Astriea's fae ears picked up quite a bit on their own.

"Hello, girl. I'm sorry I haven't been to visit you in a while. Much has happened." Hypnia gently nudged Vera's arm in response. This made her realize how much she missed Lijah.

"I need to ask you for a favor. I need you—ah!" Vera's hand slipped down her staff and she lost her balance for a moment before stabilizing herself. She lifted a hand to Pilas—who was about to jump for her—to stop.

"I need you to take us to The Mystic." Hypnia whinnied and looked at Vera. Then Astriea and the carriage. Then back to Vera again.

With no convincing, Hypnia backed herself between the two harness posts extending from the cart. Pilas and the horse master began attaching the straps, and before Astriea could really think about the level of intellect Hypnia possesses, they were ready to go.

Inside, the carriage was quite warm, so much so that Astriea had to remove the large fur cloak Pilas had given her. Vera struggled to get inside but, regardless, she spoke to Pilas one more time before taking her seat.

"You remember everything I told you to do?"

"Yes, sister," Pilas replied. A small tear rolled down his eye. Vera cupped his cheek in her hand and brushed it away.

"Tell no one. If questioned, you had no idea I planned any of this. Do you understand?"

"Yes, sister."

"I leave the realm in your hands, little brother. Keep them safe."

"Yes, sister." Pilas sucked in a small sob and began backing away, but Vera stopped him.

"Pilas... I love you. All of you."

"If this is what you need, Vera, then do it and come back. Whatever you do, just make sure you come back. Alright? Because we love you too."

Vera nodded with tears in her eyes. She sat back in her seat and the door closed. There was a moment of deafening silence before the carriage lurched forward and they began their journey to The Mystic.

65

Seraphina

The loud voices yelling across the great hall seemed all but muted to Seraphina as she stood in silence and shock.

Vera and Astriea were gone. Vanished in the dead of night.

No one in the castle had seen them, each of Vera's siblings accusing the other of aiding her. Killian called all of them liars.

They left me here.

Did you honestly think they loved you enough to stop this war? To end their thirst for power?

Seraphina shook her head. Trying to flush the monster from her mind.

"Seraphina!" Killian yelled, snapping her attention back to them.

"What?" she whispered.

"You must have known about this! I'll admit, taking my side about The Mystic was a smart play, but to endanger Vera's life by sending her into the north? And you claim to love her?"

The words hit her in the chest. Boiled something inside, tingling and burning through every nerve she had.

"Don't you dare presume to know how I feel about her! Or anything else, for that matter! If I'd known Vera had been so determined to go, then I would've gone with them! But instead, like all of *you*, she kept her secrets well. Instead, she left me here. They both left me here..." Those words said aloud, solidified it. Cracked her wide open and split her heart in two.

Everyone was silent as they watched Sera's hard expression die and give way to something more sorrowful. She went on. "I would have died for either of them, and they left me here without a word. You don't know how I feel. You don't know *me*."

"You're right Seraphina, we *don't* know you. That's the problem." Killian countered.

"We will solve nothing by screaming at each other," Pilas began, "They've gone. All we can do is try to keep the world spinning until they return."

The boy was quite calm, but his outstretched hand seemed to shake a bit. He'd done well at holding himself together and now he was trying to help everyone else do it, too.

If Telas had surprised her in one way, it was the royal family. They'd done a wonderful job convincing the world of their brutality, but they'd done even better at holding onto the good they had.

Killian spoke again. "And what if they don't return, Pilas? What do you suggest, then?"

"We give her a week. Seven days and if they haven't returned, we send out search parties."

"And what of your father's *other face*?" Seraphina asked. Every single one of their jaws dropped open and their gazes turned to her like the hottest beams of the sun. "What happens if he wakes up and they're both gone?"

"He never seems worried about finding Astriea. Honestly, he makes it seem like *she* would always find a way to him. As if it wasn't a problem. But Vera... He would want to slaughter us all just to hurt her. But..." Killian stopped and looked around the room before speaking again in a much more hushed tone, "When Vera was ten..."

And here it was. Answers. The seams of deceit dismembering before her at the truth now flooding the room.

"She made a bargain. A real one from old tales of magic and ancient peoples long before Telas was built."

Pilas stepped towards Sera and said to her with the saddest eyes she'd ever seen, "She kept fighting him. When father was crowned, Scythe attempted to manipulate his way into the heir's mind. He tried to bring

292

on her turning early. It was an experiment, really, to see how far he could push the bloodline curse. Vera wouldn't have it. She'd kick and scream and bite anyone who tried to touch her. Until he'd grown tired of it. He took Nate from his cradle and held him in the air with his shadows. Told her that if she didn't get in line, then she'd watch Nate die on the stone before he made her watch the rest of us follow him. She told him she would do whatever he asked, so long as all her siblings remained unharmed. They made a *real* bargain. I don't know how it works completely, but he can't hurt us. Not even Killian. Because of that..."

"Because of that, he takes it all out on Vera. Every time she disobeys, every time she speaks out of turn—" Sera said. Her soul felt even more crushed.

"Every time *any* of us do anything to displease him, Seraphina," Pilas said, his gaze lost somewhere else.

Salrek stepped forward, "So we take on roles that make Scythe happy."

Dalron placed a hand on his twin's shoulder.

"We try our best to keep each other out of trouble," Nate said as young Thea pushed past him and took Seraphina's hand in her own.

"We all do what we can to make him happy. But the one who wears father's face is never happy. I'm not sure he knows how to be anymore." She said, green eyes glimmering.

Gods.

Vera had been unable to tell her so much. Had cried out for help in the only ways she could. Had reached out again and again, only for Sera to swat her away.

"He made her kill Tristan, didn't he?" was all she could ask through her shaking voice. A sob begging to be set free.

"His exact words were to '*do away with the crew.*'"

Sera fell into her seat at a nearby table.

"Regardless, this may be her only chance to be free of him. To break the bargain." Young Nate said softly. All of them looked at Killian now. But he only looked at Pilas.

"Then we will have the Science Guild keep father asleep as best they can until Vera returns," Pilas said. Everyone nodded.

"Until then, we must prepare for the war to come," Killian added.

Sera's eyes shot to him.

"Yes, Sera, our scouts confirmed it this morning. Shadon's entire naval fleet sails for Telas. Along with an army of one hundred dragons and riders. The wind is with them and they will be here in five days, seven if we are lucky."

Shit.

66

Thomas

From the sky, Thomas could see miles and miles of open ocean. They'd been sailing and flying for a week and three days already. Stopping at small islands every two days for the dragons to rest.

He couldn't help but be thoroughly impressed by the battalion of riders that James had procured. Each of them well adjusted to their dragon and riding steadily. Although, there were a few *less gifted* in flight. Such as Matell Peron, who in fact, spent the majority of his time nearly falling out of his saddle. But the ruby dragon he mounted was fond of him, flying low and turning back to drag him out of the water each time he fell, and curling around him at camps like a hatchling.

The second issue at hand was keeping two particular dragons from mauling each other.

Another black-scaled dragon and a ruby one had grievances. The dark one growled heavily at the other whenever in passing, which would often spark some rage within the red one. Every time they landed on an outpost island, the two would go for the throat. Thomas was thankful they at least took the time to toss their riders off before the teeth and claws came out. But it only meant he had to climb on Night-cleavers back and throw himself in the middle of it. It started out taking about an hour to break the two apart. Now, in the twenty fights since, Night-cleaver needed only to raise their head and release a low growl at the pair, before they would huff and separate.

They made their halfway point and set up camp on another small island for the night.

Thomas even made three walk-throughs of the camps, checking in on everyone as they'd separated into groups and gathered around campfires.

Sea trout was on the menu, *again*. But he had to admit it was better than nothing. Damian also did well by them all by loading assortments of bread, cheeses, and ales in a longboat and rowing out to supply them for the night. James had offered that, but Thomas, in a more prideful moment that he honestly wasn't proud of, declined it. Thinking they would be fine on fish and stale bread for a couple of weeks.

But after two days, he realized he had been spoiled by palace food for too long and it was foolish of him to deprive one hundred soldiers of decent meals when he didn't have to.

He and Damian now drank with Valtan and Lavene around their own campfire.

"Full bellies under the night sky, surrounded by open ocean. This has the makings to be a wonderful place to summer. Too bad we're going off to war."

"Ha ha, you're hilarious, Valtan." Lavene retorted with an eye roll.

"Oh don't act like you don't love me." He teased back at her.

She rolled her eyes again.

They all grew silent for a moment.

"Does Ula not wish to join us?" Thomas asked Damian.

"Not tonight. She is spending the night in and researching our best routes to break into The Silver City with Evangeline."

Thomas gazed out at the ocean at those words: *The Silver City*. A location only made known to them by way of a messenger sparrow clutching a dirty letter that flew thousands of miles across the world to reach his hands mere moments before they were to leave Triscillia.

A letter that read:

Dearest husband,

We are well, as are the people here.
Nothing is as we thought.
Your return is the dream I never want to wake from.
I wish to see you at The silver pillar, only The silver pillar.
Leave all others untouched.
-All my love,
Triea Cartwright

He'd decoded it instantly: they were unharmed and everything was up in the air. She missed him. That tugged on his heart a bit. It took him a few moments to understand the silver pillar, though. But he remembered that Draes once spoke of the stronghold of Telas. How it was defended by towers upon towers of silver metal. That only a dragon's flame could breach it. He noticed the *T's* were capitalized where they shouldn't have been. Not unless it had been a titled place. A business or specific building named The Silver Pillar. But neither the S's nor P's were how they should be for that to be correct.

The silver pillar. The biggest pillar maybe? The largest tower in the stronghold would most likely belong to royalty.

Astriea constructed a way to tell him to attack the castle, but nothing else.

Leave all others untouched.

So he would.

Thomas relayed the message to Damian, James, and Draes before they left Triscillia.

And now, sitting around the fire, he could feel that letter sitting in his pocket. Cherished the feel of the paper she'd touched against his fingertips. Ached and longed to wrap her in his arms and stare at these stars together. It felt wrong not to have her here. Not to see Sera across the flames, teasing Damian for something. Not to hear Tristan singing to Koren on the ship, following his lover around like a puppy.

He missed Koren's tales, too. Late nights on the ship were always made better when Koren told of his travels. He had been captured at sea by

Shadonian slave traders, then he escaped six months later. After that, he sailed as a wanted man all around the world until he ended up on the Isle of Zani. The fights he described were unlike any other.

He was sad not to see Crenshaw or Bale. Nor Edgar or Starin. The Harper twins, who always tried to sneak extra rations between meals.

He shoved those thoughts away and said to Lavene, "Shall we?"

She nodded and stood. Thomas rose to follow.

"Where are the two of you off to?" Valtan asked, spilling his ale and then cursing himself after.

"Getting ready for battle, of course. I suggest you prepare what it is you will say to your niece when we arrive to rescue her, Valtan." Lavene snickered back with a smile.

"Oh yeah, you should get on that, mate." Damian laughed at him.

Thomas and Lavene strode off, laughing as well. Making their way to the makeshift forge she'd assembled at their dragon's nests. She took a few steps back, but Thomas had so many nerves to work out, that he didn't hesitate when he walked up to the large stone. Didn't stutter as he said to his dragon—now hovering directly above the large piece of black stone in front of him, "Night-cleaver, *burn*."

Dragon flame erupted from Night-cleaver's maw. Orange and red and magnificent.

Thomas soaked in that brilliant heat—similar to his own, but slightly different—before lifting a large hammer and slamming it down, again and again and again.

67

Astriea

The voyage hadn't been terrible so far. Astriea and Vera had been traveling for a few hours and the carriage was warm. The wheels hadn't frozen over yet and despite the horrible storm outside, Hypnia was trotting along like it was the best day of her life.

The only thing that bothered her was the overwhelming silence inside with the princess.

Finally, Astriea got up and started rummaging through things. She lifted the seat underneath her and was careful not to touch any of the piping-hot bottles. Vera quickly got annoyed and asked, "What are you doing?"

"I know you have it here somewhere…"

"Have what?" She asked again as Astriea kept looking, this time looking in the floor compartment.

"We may have an endless journey ahead of us and I'd rather not spend it watching you pillage through the supplies."

Astriea paused and looked at her for a split second. Vera just rolled her eyes before Astriea went back to rummaging.

"Ah ha!" she exclaimed as she pulled a tin container from the bottom of the seat and sat back down.

"I knew you'd have coco in here."

Vera smirked as Astriea opened the tin and the aroma of coffee filled the carriage.

"Wait—"

"Coffee," Vera answered.

Astriea made a foul face at it. "Damn, I've never really enjoyed coffee. And it makes me tired."

"You've never had *Telish* coffee. I can't imagine Shadon had much that tasted good. Fengrave surely didn't."

"How long were you there? How did you know where to find us?"

"Scythe sent me to Shadon about a month before I saw you and Thomas come into town. He didn't tell me how long I would be there. Or what you would look like. I saw you frequent a local pub. I had my suspicions but, it wasn't until I saw Thomas lose control of his flames in that alleyway that I knew the two of you were the ones I was looking for. Then I saw Sera and Damian. I don't know why, but I knew I was supposed to be on that ship." Vera reached into the insulated bag next to her and pulled a large thermos out.

"Did you ever feel like what you were doing was wrong? Was there ever a time you thought about switching sides?" Astriea asked.

"Did *you* ever think it was wrong to send Sera to my bed as a spy?" The princess countered. "To put her heart on the line while you forced her to toy with mine?"

Astriea's eyes went wide. "She told you?"

"She didn't have to. I knew the whole time. The only reason Sera would've come to my bed after I took the two of you is if she'd been ordered to. While I'm glad she's forgiven me and things worked out between us so far, that doesn't seem like the actions of someone *on the right side.*"

She took a breath, unscrewed the cap, and said calmly, "Scythe gave me specific orders: bring you, Sera, and Thomas back and do away with the rest. I am bound to follow his orders or… or things get much worse. For everyone. If you are asking me if I would have switched sides, no. I wouldn't. I will always go to extremes to protect them. But…" She poured the thick brown liquid into the cup and handed it to Astriea. "If you're asking me if I wish I could change it, yes. More than anything."

Astriea sniffed the steaming liquid and looked at Vera curiously.

"Sera told me chocolate was one of the most difficult things to get your hands on in Shadon. I don't have much with us, but I figured you would want some. Coffee isn't for everyone."

Astriea smiled at her and nodded before she took a sip of the sweetest, most delicious thing she'd ever tasted: *Telish hot chocolate.*

* * *

She tried hard to keep the conversation peaceful. Tried even harder not to ask Vera what she did with her crew or if there had been any updates on what Shadon's armies were doing. It'd been weeks since she shoved Thomas, Damian, and Draes through the portal and back to James. Since she'd last heard Thomas laugh or ran her fingers through his soft raven waves of hair. Her heart ached at the thought of never seeing his smile brighten the room again.

She *had* to survive this.

The Mystic *had* to work, or really, she had to be worthy of its power.

Even though Vera had committed atrocities far worse than she had, Astriea had more faith that The Mystic would heal *her* wounds than she did in herself.

If she was being honest, it was hard to feel anything but selfish right now. Like she didn't deserve the loved ones she had in her corner. And even with Sera and Damian being the most loyal friends, she could never stop herself from considering the fact that they were here for Zaniah. For the goddess that would save the world.

Not for her, not for Astriea. But for duty. Obligation and honor.

She didn't know why she should think she deserved friends like them, anyway. More often than not, Astriea found herself lingering on the anger she had for them being raised to die for her. Choices that were made for them so long ago that they saw it as a great honor.

It isn't fair to have the greatest guardians in the world as protectors only end up being people she would die for, kill for too, when they will just die for her. In the end, she will be all that stands and they will have moved on… And she left Sera behind. Left her locked in that castle. It was more than selfish; it was an outright betrayal. But she couldn't know for sure if Sera's love for her outweighed her love for Vera.

And the most honest thought she had of all was that she did not wish to make Sera choose. Not anymore. The only life she would ever put on the line again would be her own. No one else's.

Astriea pushed the thoughts from her mind as Vera reached a shaking hand into her bag and said, "It'll be a long ride. Care for a game?"

She pulled out a set of playing cards and showed them to her.

"What kind of game?"

"Any you like I'd guess. Have you tried *Maiden's Folly?*"

Astriea smiled a bit.

"I expected Telas to have different gambler's games than Shadon. But yes, I've played. Each card is face value, royalty cards are worth ten points each, first person to draw a Queen has to draw enough cards to add up to a King and Queen. If you draw a King and Queen or a Queen with enough numbered cards to equal Royalty, you win the round. If your opponent draws the King and you draw the queen, it's a draw. But if your opponent draws one of the four jacks placed in the deck *and* a king against your queen, you lose not only the round but the entire game."

Vera nodded her head and split the deck. She tried her best to shuffle, but her hands shook so much she nearly dropped them all.

Astriea reached out and gently placed her own hands on top of Vera's. She caught Astriea's eyes.

"You don't have to do it all. *Be* it all. I can shuffle." She took the cards from her and tossed them back and forth just the way Raja taught her all those years ago.

"Why are you being so… kind? We both know I don't deserve it." She asked.

Astriea paused, careful not to look into her eyes while she thought on the question.

"None of us deserves unconditional kindness, there is a time when you need to be held accountable. But I am kind to you for Sera's sake, I guess. I wish I *could* be a bit more cruel to you. I can admit that. There are things I hate you for. But… there are valid reasons behind the acts you committed against me and my loved ones. You hurt people I care about, and I have a hard time forgiving you for it."

Vera was silent for a moment, but she leaned forward and said, "How about this? For every round you win, I'll answer a question. If it doesn't *interfere*. I also expect the same in return. I have things I'd like to understand, too."

"You have a deal."

Vera shuttered, and in that moment Astriea could feel her blood rush through her.

"I'm sorry. That was a poor choice of words."

She nodded and Astriea dealt the cards.

The first three cards she dealt to herself were a Jack, a four, and a two. She drew another card from the deck, an eight.

Bust.

She laid down her hand and Vera revealed a queen, a five, a three, and a two.

Round one to Vera.

"What will happen to my lands once you break the frozen throne?"

"Well, you'll have many citizens wake to find they have magic. Some may even take Fae forms like my own." Astriea tapped the tip of her exposed ear. "As for the land itself, the ice will likely melt and the thousand-year winter will end."

"We don't know how to survive anything else," Vera added. "That would destroy our way of life."

"Then what if we agree to aid Telas in its survival? Help you learn new ways to live? With magic restored, your people could grow their own crops. You'd have an abundance of food that wouldn't need to be grown inside keeps and castles."

"I've worked all my life to ensure the Science Guild's necessity."

"With winter's end, your Science Guild would be free to find new and exciting discoveries. You have built something I've never seen before, Vera.

Medicines to treat diseases I've never even heard of. Imagine what it could be capable of if aimed at wonder instead of survival."

Vera was silent then. She took her shaking hands to the new stack of cards awaiting her and observed them.

Astriea made note of her hand. A queen and two fives. Perfect. She drew no more and waited for Vera.

She laid her cards on the table face down. A bust.

"You used Sera, and now you claim to love her. I want to know if it's real, *whatever* is between the two of you." Astriea asked.

Vera leaned back with no small amount of effort. Her entire body seemed to protest the movement.

"I never meant to fall in love with Sera. I never meant to care for any of you. But Sera especially. I tried to pull myself away from her. Tried to keep my distance, but… there was *something* there. Something strong and unspoken. I didn't realize what it was until the healers were mending my bones in my chambers. There had always been this force between us, binding us. But she cradled my head in her lap as I screamed. She leaned over me, pressed her head to mine, and I said, *I choose you.* She whispered the words back to me and the moment they came out, something changed. Like every force in the universe bowed to us in that room. Some golden dust formed into a chain and bound us together. Since then, the thought of ever parting from her brings me pain I can't bear. Even now, being away from her, sneaking off in the night. It hurts more than anything Scythe ever put me through."

If she wanted Astriea shocked, she succeeded. She could feel her widened eyes and raised brows.

Vera pulled an old leather book from her bag and set it on the table.

"Seraphina is my *Soul-bound.*"

Astriea opened the book and flipped through the pages until those words were in front of her. It was older than any others she'd riffled through. The leather binding of the book was falling apart, and Astriea couldn't understand the language in which each word was written until she found the pages that someone had translated into Shadonian, Telish, and Sirenian.

After the first birth of each soul, they are blessed with the ability to bind themselves to another.
To promise their hearts and souls for all their lifetimes.
So that they may find each other again when death has forced them apart.
This is the rarest and most pure act of devotion in the known universe.
This ensures that they will find the next world together.
If they wish it, the Soul-bound may walk the golden path to the Lightbringer's eternal city and live in peace at her side for all of time.
Leaving reincarnation behind them.
This great honor can only be accomplished by lifetimes of dedication to each other.

She took more notice of the book itself. And suddenly a memory flashed in her mind. The red and gold trim around the edges of the brown leather was hard to forget.

"You got this book from that library. Didn't you?"

"How do you—"

"I stumbled upon it the night you… died. I haven't been able to find it since."

Vera's expression turned curious, but her features relaxed quickly and she nearly smiled.

"I was the only person who knew about it. From what I can tell, it only appears when it wants to, and half the time I feel as though I've only found it in a dream. Though, this time, I managed to get this book out. What else did you find in there?"

"Maybe we should play another round. That's two questions we're each indebted now."

"I think we've moved past that at this point," Vera replied.

"Have you told her who she is?" Astriea asked with more tone than she'd intended. "Do you know?"

"That she is the daughter of my father's old guard captain? No. I haven't found a way to tell her yet. I honestly wanted to be sure it was true before I gave her any false hope."

"There is no false hope. She's Raja's daughter, the man who trained and cared for me all my life. His daughter, *Alyea*, was said to be lost at sea alongside her mother. But that wasn't true."

"How do you know that?"

"Because Raja was a master in the Grand Temple of Zaniah. He left the island only to keep an eye on me..."

"And that's why *you* haven't told her. You think he abandoned her for you, and that she'll hate you for it?"

Astriea only nodded and kept her eyes away from the princess.

"I don't think she'll hate you. I do think that the longer you keep it from her, the more angry she'll become, but I don't think Sera could ever hate you."

"Because I'm *the Lightbringer?*"

"Because you are her sister and her friend."

"I almost let her die to free Shadon from Herold Berelda. I don't know if I'm worth her friendship." A confession if she'd ever had one. Bare and raw and barreling out of her.

"Seraphina's commitment to the cause she was raised to fight for included a willingness to sacrifice her life. That same cause was thrust upon you, a mercenary with no idea what she was doing. I don't think you were ever willing to let Sera die. I think Zaniah was. Which is why I have a hard time accepting you. You carry a goddess of unbelievable power, power that is very capable of consuming you and all of us completely." It wasn't the words that made Astriea look into Vera's emerald eyes, but the concern in her voice. Like she cared for her, not the goddess, but Astriea, the person—the mortal.

"I think you felt so ravaged and empty that when the opportunity to avenge your family and save your people presented itself, you jumped for it with no regard for your own life. Because I don't believe you plan on surviving the final breaking. Do you?"

And there it was.

A truth that she'd kept to herself since she'd stood before Zaniah in that prison of alabaster and white and gold marble. Dug out of the dark by a princess who'd been paying much closer attention than she'd given her credit for.

Surviving the unleashing of magic had never been a thought on her mind. She knew she had to survive the first two breakings. Knew she had to survive the trip into this icy tundra. Zaniah said her body had to adjust to the power building inside her, but... even a full-blooded immortal Fae wouldn't survive that much. Zaniah had always been hopeful, but Astriea was, at heart, cynical about it. So much so that Zaniah never brought it up. And when the conversation would seem to drift in that direction, it was always a sorrowful expression on her features that made Astriea change the subject as quickly as possible.

"No. I don't think it's possible. I never have. Zaniah tries to raise my spirits, but..."

"Then we will do whatever we can to keep you alive. It isn't fair that you endured all that you did just to die for everyone else, leaving nothing for yourself."

"Life isn't fair."

"You are the *goddess* of life. Fair is whatever you say it is."

Astriea smiled at her, and Vera returned it.

"I think I'm starting to like you, Grand Duchess."

"And I you, my lady."

68

Astriea

Three days passed in the carriage with Vera and they'd stopped just as many times to melt ice and snow off the tracks. Now, with Hypnia slowing, the bitter cold started to take effect. They let her out of her bridle and gave the horse some time to run about. Let her get her blood pumping and warm herself a bit.

Vera helped as much as she could. She even brought out a massive wool covering for the magnificent horse, strapped together under her belly.

Hypnia nudged her giant face against Vera's in thanks before she darted into the frozen wasteland. A small trail of shadow in her wake.

The two of them hurried back into the carriage and began to warm themselves. Astriea helped Vera get comfortable under soft fur blankets before situating herself. They ate some hot duck stew—a few days old, but better than nothing—and then tried to rest their eyes until Hypnia would return.

Their hearts sank as a massive thud reverberated through the carriage, shattering the peaceful atmosphere. Rocking them hard enough for Vera to yelp and Astriea to curse.

"What the hell was that?" Astriea shouted.

Before Vera could answer, the carriage rocked again. This time accompanied by a loud scraping sound. Like claws grinding against the metal outside.

Then they heard something terrifying. A growl so loud and guttural it sent chills up Astriea's spine.

"Vera... what kind of beasts lurk in the Northern Wastes?" She asked in a frightened tone.

"The kind that doesn't leave people behind to tell tales."

She wished she felt more steady, more courageous. But nothing could stop her nerves from screaming at her.

Run. Get out.

Hide.

Run. Run. Run.

But there was nowhere to run.

Vera rose from her seat and pulled a short sword out from under it. She unsheathed it with great difficulty and went for the door.

"No! You are not going out there!"

"We don't have a choice! Whatever is out there will kill us both if we do nothing. You don't have your powers, and we can't risk losing you now. Not when you still have two more kingdoms to set free!"

The beast rammed against the carriage again, knocking Astriea back into her seat. Vera grabbed hold of a bar above her head and found her balance. "I'll distract it. You have to go on. Hypnia will take you to The Mystic, and you can heal what I broke. I'm sorry I ever did it in the first place."

She made for the door again, but Astriea launched herself in front of her before she could reach for the handle. She put her hands on Vera's shoulders and thought hard on the fact that the princess had finally chosen a side.

"And I'm sorry about this."

Before she could stop herself, Astriea reared back and slammed her head into Vera's. The act knocked her out immediately. She hoped it didn't make her condition worse, but she couldn't think about that now. She took the sword out of Vera's limp hand and laid her back on the seat. Shaking the dizziness away as best she could, she opened the door.

Astriea stepped outside into a cold, bitter storm.

* * *

It's just like Monolith. It's just like Monolith. It's just like Monolith.

The silence as she took step by step away from the carriage made her skin crawl. The only sounds were her panted breaths and the shrieking wind. Snow hitting her skin like shards of glass, she pulled her scarf over her nose and mouth.

Looking around, there was just enough light from the setting sun to see miles and miles of endless snow. Her feet were buried in it midway up her calves. That was when she saw them. A pair of viscous, glowing yellow eyes stared right at her. But when she saw the rest of the creature...

It was solid white and covered in fur, all except the black spiraling horns protruding off the top of its head. The beast was twice the size of the average Telish snow bear, and its razor-sharp claws glistened in the light of the fading sun.

But they weren't supposed to have menacing horns or razor-sharp claws that could tear a person in half, or teeth so sharp they could devour her in just two bites. Their legs were supposed to be short and fat while these were long and muscled under the fur. This was no snow bear. This was a monster made into reality.

With shaking hands, Astriea raised that small sword and waited for it to attack.

It didn't make her wait long and it pounced from the front of the carriage—on her in the time it took to suck in a sharp breath.

She didn't think, just moved. Rolling under its massive legs as it swung a mighty clawed paw at her head. Forcing snow into all the crevices of her clothes.

Before it could turn around, she sliced its back leg, right through what seemed like an important tendon. The beast screeched loudly as black blood sprayed against the snow, smelling of rot and decay. Before she could move, its other hind leg slammed into her chest, hitting her so hard that her body collided with the carriage.

She hit the snow on her knees and struggled for air against at least three

310

broken ribs. But there was *no time*, it was hurtling towards her again. Astriea rolled, away from the carriage. But it found her quickly, this time while swinging those terrifying claws, the beast made the slightest contact as she leapt away. Three slices ripped across her stomach. Her blood spilled out all over the snow. Not enough to expose her organs, but nearly. Not even the cold couldn't keep the burning pain at bay. The monstrosity prowled toward her, slowly this time.

Maybe the fear would make her taste better. But she'd gotten it away from the carriage and at the moment that was all that mattered.

She gripped the short sword in both her hands, letting her wrecked abdomen leak further as she waited for the snow beast's final advance. It's killing blow.

But the carriage door swung open.

The beast turned and made ready to pounce on Vera, who stood in the doorway, her brown leather satchel in hand.

Then it jumped for her.

Vera used all the force Astriea imagined she had to jump out as the demon crashed into the carriage—smashing it beyond repair.

It propped itself atop the broken pieces as it decided which of them it wanted. It chose Astriea. The prey it had already worked so hard for. The prey that had already angered it the most.

Vera got to her knees, her hands clutching that bag for dear life, and before the monster jumped on top of Astriea, Vera Shataar reached into that bag, called out Astriea's name, and threw her a shimmering silver necklace accented with a sapphire in the shape of a star.

Astriea's amulet.

The moment it left her hand, Vera screamed, bloodcurdling and pained, before collapsing into the snow.

Astriea barely caught it as the clawed terror was upon her. That amulet shifted in her hands, back into her brilliant silver staff.

Just as those teeth snapped to gobble her up, her staff blocked the bite. She held it there in the beast's mouth with both hands and used whatever power the conduit could pull from her.

The glowing yellow eyes went wide, as light—brighter than a star—erupted from the staff. From her. Pouring out in waves upon waves of iridescence. As cold as the snow she lay in yet warming her very soul.

When the smoke had cleared, the smell of burned hide encased her. She incinerated the monster, leaving its body headless and singeing in the remains of the last blizzard.

* * *

Astriea ran to Vera as quickly as she could, clutching her bleeding abdomen and putting most of her weight on the staff. Her eyes widened as Vera lay there, twitching and seizing—barely catching a breath. The veins in her hands, neck, and face were black and strained against her skin and muscles.

"Oh, gods... Vera." Astriea panted. "What's... what's happening to you?"

She couldn't answer.

Astriea dropped her staff in the snow and pulled Vera's body close to her own, her blood leaking onto Vera's fur cloak. The act stung like hell. Vera's eyes darted from Astriea's to the staff and back again. And tears threatened to break from her eyes.

"You can't disobey him. He told you not to give it back to me and you did it anyway. Gods, Vera..." Astriea ran a hand across her blood-red hair—wiping it away from her face. The tightness in her veins seemed to release her just a bit, and she wheezed in a fraction of freezing cold air.

"You... you have... to kill him." She rasped out. Her grip was tight on Astriea's arm. "Tell Sera... tell her I'm sorry... I'm sorry I left her there..." A strangled gasp. "Tell my family... tell them I'm sorry I failed them. Tell Seraphina I begged you... Tell her I begged you to beg *her* to protect my siblings. She is the only chance they have."

The tears broke through and froze on Astriea's cheeks. But she said through her teeth, "No. No, you are not dying. Sera would never recover. You are going to survive, and you are going to help me kill him."

"I broke the bargain. I disobeyed. This is the price."

312

"No, Vera. You are a *survivor*. And I am the goddess of life, so I make the rules, remember? I'll bend or break them however I like."

Vera's breath became more strained once again. Astriea looked over at the crumpled carriage and slowly laid Vera back into the snow.

First, she took the end of her tunic and ripped it free before wrapping it tightly around her filleted flesh. When she finished she took a deep breath and ran to the wreckage, and pried a curved piece of railing off the side. Then ran to Hypnia's bridle and tied the straps to the metal.

She tugged the makeshift sled over to Vera and gently laid her down on top of it, before attaching the loose ends of the straps to her waist and around her shoulders. It stung like hell against her wounds, but they didn't have time for that now. Astriea braced herself one last time and asked, "Which way is north? Look at the stars and tell me which way to go with your eyes."

Vera's eyes darted back and forth at the open night sky—the first snowstorm now passed before the next one was about to barrel onto them—and placed her gaze upward and slightly to the right. With that, Astriea marched forward, her staff as an anchor to the earth, as she carried Vera onward to The Mystic.

69

Seraphina

As Sera entered the grand hall—Vera's seven siblings all there, silently waiting for dinner to be served—her breath was stolen from her lungs. Her knees crashed into the cold marble beneath her feet and she clutched her hands against her chest. Killian was there in an instant. Hands cupping her face before her body went numb with pain. And then he was cradling her.

Every sound was clear as day, though as if she were being tortured on the inside, with a symphony blasting in her ears. Except instead of music, it was voices.

"What's happening? What's happening?" He shouted.

The others gathered in a circle around her. Concern and fear lanced in their expressions.

She could see them, too. Maybe she was dead. Maybe that was why everything hurt so badly, yet appeared clearly before her.

No... No, something wasn't right. *Something* was ripping her to shreds from the inside out.

She couldn't breathe, couldn't move. An image flashed in her mind. Astriea, limping and bloody—pulling Vera through the snow on a piece of metal. Black veins protruded against the skin of Vera's beautiful face.

"Vera..." Sera gasped.

"Pilas! Send the search party out now!" Killian commanded.

Sera could hear everything happening around her. But the pain... So. Much. *Pain.*

"Killian..." Pilas said softly, frozen at the grand door. Sera turned her eyes to him and before them stood the three handmaidens and their mother: Morra, Helena, Briar, and Belle. Morra dropped the decanter in her hands—the glass shattering as she beheld her daughters beside her. Each holding the other's hand. Their eyes white and glazed over. Morra gasped and covered her mouth as a cold breeze blew through the room and the sconce-light flickered.

Then they spoke, together and with eerie calm,

"Heir to the Throne of Ice and Ash has chosen,

Pain and suffering of a bargain broken.

The Lightbringer carries her upon thy back.

Rebirth in the ichor pool, re-solidifies a godly pact."

The three women blinked, and their eyes returned to their usual coloring. They released each other's hands and looked around curiously.

"What just happened?" Belle, the youngest of them, asked.

No one answered. Because no one knew.

Pilas turned back to Killian—still cradling Sera in his arms—and said, "Vera has broken the bargain. She's... she's dying."

Even strangled by pain, Sera could see the tears falling from Pilas's eyes. And she could feel Killian's breath shutter against her.

"No... No, she can't be dying. Why would she break the bargain *now?*" he said through a sob.

Sera felt as though she was dying, too. Maybe she was. Maybe their bond would take them both together. She wanted to cry but didn't know if she could as she seized against Killian's grip.

"How do we even know what they say is true? They don't even know what happened to them, or what they just said." Morra interrupted, trying her best to keep everyone calm. "Helena fetch the healers, now!" Her mother's voice snapped Helena from shock, and she ran out of the room, dutifully obeying her.

Killian rested his head against Sera's. "I'm the eldest. It should've been

315

me…Never her."

The others circled them on their knees.

"Killian, her veins are black…" Dalron murmured, his voice shaking as he and his twin, Salrek, aided Killian in lifting her twitching body from the ground.

"If the bargain is broken, then there is nothing stopping him from destroying us all. Salrek, take the others and get out of the city."

"Not without Vera," Salrek replied.

Dalron rested a hand on his twin's shoulder. "She has shielded us long enough. Let him come. Let him face us all."

"He will kill you… all of you." Sera coughed out. She could feel it. The shadow; a storm of it gathering somewhere in the distance. Now on the move.

"Morra, get word to the healers to have the tzar's next three treatments ready to go in his chambers. If Vera's bargain is broken, I assume he's already on his way." Killian said quickly.

Pilas was the one who spoke up then, "If he wakes, we will join our sister in the stars."

That was the last Seraphina heard before they left and the healers came toward her.

So she reached out for that chain, that steel connecting them. Reached until she found the source of the pain and said in broken breaths, "I gladly take your anguish."

Some of the pain meant for Vera must have heard that call and redirected itself accordingly.

All Sera could do now was scream.

70

Damian

D amian's ship sailed so smoothly that he almost thought it unreal. A dream, perhaps. And yet, his focus couldn't be held by the ship alone. Because ever since he'd ridden the sea-serpent, he felt a longing; a call.

His eyes would easily get lost on the great deep. On the waves crashing against the hull.

Or maybe it was the wind, singing the song of the sea as it rustled past.

He couldn't be certain, but the pull itself was frightening. There was even an overwhelming urge to step off the side rail while everyone was busy.

So, Damian had been doing his best to keep distracted from it. He worked with the crew during the day and let Ula distract him with stories and tender kisses at night.

She'd told him that she belonged to the Mountain People. And that she left her village in the Caltillion Mountains to explore the rest of Shadon. Or, at least, that's what she liked to tell herself.

The truth was that she was trained in those mountains to steal. From travelers passing through their territory. She'd become the best in the village, in all three villages. Until she'd stolen too much. Until a band of angry witch hunters came for the girl who'd robbed them blind. Their village fought them off, killed them, and buried them in the mountains before banishing Ula at thirteen years old and relocating deeper in. So that she may never find her way home again.

That had been her punishment.

He'd been lingering on that for the past few days. Thinking about how they'd raised her, made her a thief, only to cast her out when she did what she'd been trained to. No warnings, just desertion. But Ula defended this practice and told him that it didn't matter anymore. All three villages would be dead now with the mountains falling, and her family would've already burned her things. Wiped her from the village memory.

Still, with only two days left until they'd reach Telas and the mountains long gone, he didn't like the idea of her feeling as though she deserved to be treated that way.

"Come on then, to bed," Ula said from behind him. Startling him out of his stupor.

"Is it time already?" he asked, looking up at the night sky.

Ula lightly grabbed hold of his chin and lowered his gaze to meet hers.

"Yes, it is time. We have two days with no stops. We'll need you well rested."

Her smile was all the convincing he needed.

Damian walked Ula to her cabin and thoroughly kissed her in the doorway. Every time their lips touched, it became harder and harder to pull away again. But he managed it. Drug himself from her door and back to his own.

They all had a rough few days ahead of them. And even rougher ones after.

71

Astriea

She could see the storm coming from here, from the middle of this frozen waste. Snow was up to her knees now and her back screeched against the weight strapped to it.

Astriea could see the churning wind and barreling snow, racing across the plain as if they danced together. As if that's what they had done for all of existence.

She'd been dragging Vera behind her for a full night and day and, no matter what did not stop praying that Hypnia would find them. That Zaniah wouldn't abandon them for being stupid enough to leave the last place the immortal steed knew they were.

Vera had loudly chattered her teeth for a while until about an hour ago. When she became very still and *very* quiet. Though, she was glad the princess was still alive in the first place.

Astriea stopped and hit her knees as catastrophe narrowed on them. And the storm, gods, the storm would kill them both. Just the wind, howling across the wastes, was loud and cold enough that she was sure her ears were bleeding. Her jaw ached as though she'd broken it from her own chattering teeth.

No way around...

She turned to Vera and listened for her heart. It was there, slow—too slow. But steady enough. Strong even.

She started pulling off Vera's cloak, and then her own, before dragging her body into her lap. Then threw the cloaks back around the two of them and tucked them in snugly while she dug away some of the snow beneath their legs. Doing her best to create some sort of tent to help house what heat they had between them.

No way out...

Astriea couldn't bear this cold and Vera was so close to death she could taste it. That storm would kill them both before they had a chance to hear the Mystic's judgment. As it grew, circling them from all sides but the way they came, panic seeped into her.

Nowhere to go...

She held Vera against her, trying so hard to hand over some of her body heat. Vera's eyes fluttered open. Emeralds danced in sleet as the wind threatened to rip their cloaks away completely.

"Tell me about your mother," Astriea told her. "Tell me what happened to her. No one speaks of her. There are no portraits. I don't even know her name. Tell me about your mother, Vera." she said calmly, sweetly. Cradling her face as those black veins halted slightly.

"Queen Raedyn was the burning hearth of our kingdom," Vera whispered over the wind.

Good, Vera. Talk to me...

"She was the first to bear my father's wrath." Astriea's heart cracked. "The first to keep it at bay."

Vera rasped in the deepest breath she could. Her face held a film of ice frozen to her brows and her lashes. Her hair.

"She bore him seven strong children. Loved his bastard as her own. Their marriage was arranged, but with time, they grew to love each other—deeply. They grew to count on one another. So much so that when Scythe first took him, she began secretly installing political precautions and fail-safes to ensure her suffering would not linger onto the people. Kept Scythe's eyes on the horizon—on invaders, which we had no short supply of." Astriea sat there, stunned at the lengths a young queen, a mother not just of her children but of her people, went to ensure her kingdom was protected. From the outside and inside. Vera almost read that thought as she whimpered, "She funneled money from the crown to covertly supply aid for our realm. Had safe houses built all across the country." She paused for a moment. "My father knew. He knew… that she was doing all of it. And he managed to keep that knowledge from Scythe. For a while…"

Vera's eyes went to the night sky above them now. The last beams of the setting sun now vanished. The shining white lights breaking away the night. "My father was so happy when Thea was born… So happy to have another daughter. That I would no longer be alone." A tear fell down her cheek. "So happy that he let down his guard. And Scythe struck."

Vera's hand gripped around Astriea's forearm.

"I wanted to see her that night; see the baby. After everyone had gone. For it to be just us girls for one night before all the boys intervened." Another tear fell, and she choked out a laugh to cover her sob. "But Thea was with the healers, my mother was still resting in her birthing bed." She stopped. And her eyes fell to Astriea's other hand on her staff. "Can you… can you look into my memories? Do you… have enough magic for that?"

She didn't know if she did. She was so depleted, but there was still power in that staff. Not enough to channel into something that could save them after the altercation with the snow beast. No, not enough for that.

But this was something Vera would not give voice to.

On her deathbed, she offered Astriea a piece of her buried deep and kept silenced.

So she closed her eyes, letting the staff shift back into its amulet form, and placed it around her neck. Then leaned down and pressed her forehead to Vera's.

"I can try."

It didn't take much for the world around them to go silent. For Astriea's mind to drift into Vera's. It was blank. Dark and endless. But before her, a young woman appeared, a teenager. Blood-red waves of hair fell to her thighs. Unbound and messy. Glittering emerald eyes and a splash of freckles.

"Vera?"

The girl looked at her curiously.

"Can you take me to the last time you saw your mother, Vera?"

She only nodded and turned toward the darkness. So Astriea followed after her.

The lingering dark faded a bit. Shifted into something else. Somewhere else. The somber halls of the stronghold appeared before her. Illuminated by very few sconces and a single hearth at the end of the hall.

"Is this it?" Astriea asked. But her guide did not hear her. Was not listening.

She was tiptoeing through the halls. The healer's wing looked much older than it did since Vera started running it. They came to the room with the warm, burning fireplace. Astriea followed behind to see the girl looking around and frowning at the lack of a baby. She then went to the bedside of the beautiful woman sleeping in the corner.

"Hello, Mama." She whispered.

The woman blinked awake and smiled at Vera. "Hello my little star, did you miss me terribly?"

The Queen was stunning. Her beauty being nothing short of godly. And no one, save for her children, could have ever held a candle to her. Her long, unbound hair was full and bouncing with curls. A red as deep and dark as wine. And some sort of fire there, in the gleam of her green eyes. Vera's eyes. It was a crime that not one portrait could be found of her. That her face had not been carved into the cliffs surrounding the city. So that her beauty would smile over them forever.

The moment ended quickly. The ground quaked beneath their feet. Vera and Queen Raedyn's eyes went wide, and a commotion started down the hall.

"Under the bed." The queen commanded her daughter as she shoved her down by her shoulder.

"No—Mama, I'm not hiding! I can fight him off—" She tried to fight against her mother's grip. Astriea reached out, her hand passing right through Vera's arm. *A memory.*

"You will get under that bed and you will not make a sound!" That fire

322

lit in Vera's own eyes as she and her mother stared each other down. "He is coming for me. My love, I've bid my time for as long as I can. I know what you did for them, Vera. I know what you...*bargained*. If he catches you here, he will kill you and then your siblings. Hide, my little star. Do not make a sound, or the empire dies with all of us. You are *Tzarina sa macta*, do not ever forget that my brave girl. *Ever.*"

The fifteen-year-old Vera sucked in a sob as tears broke and cascaded down her face, and she slowly crawled under the bed. Her mother handed her an ivory throw pillow and Vera squeezed it against her silent cries as a cold and dark shadow fell over the room.

The tzar walked through a moment later. His eyes were wholly black and leaking with dark smoke. His face contorted into an expression of furious rage.

"The hour is late." The queen stated, unwavering, sitting up in her bed. Scythe didn't see Astriea stand right in front of him. His gaze never left the queen. Never relented. So Astriea stepped back. And watched with a twist in her gut as he lunged forward and grabbed the queen by her throat.

She could only watch what her own power pieced together in its *all-knowings*.

What Vera had only heard as she begged the gods to help them from under her mother's bed.

She thrashed and fought against him like a wild mountain cat. Scratching, clawing at his skin—drawing his blood. He beat her down. Again and again. Until that thrashing finally withered. Until the sounds of her gaping for breath faded. Her body slumped into the bed in such a definitive way, like all the sound had been sucked from the room. And this ringing in her ear... pulling her attention towards something. She heard it then, someone else's muffled breaths.

Vera lay on her back, under the bed as she'd been ordered, her face pressed harshly into that pillow with one hand gently pressed against the underside of the bed. As if she might reach out and feel her mother's presence one last time. And for a brief moment, Astriea could've sworn she saw a band of orange flame around the princess's wrist. First I was there then it vanished into nothing so quickly she questioned her sanity.

But that presence, the queen's presence, was gone. Slipped away and snatched from this plain.

The tzar lingered for a moment. Two.

Finally, he left. His shadows with him. *Finally,* Vera crawled from beneath the bed and sobbed against her mother's broken body. Her already bruised throat.

Vera's breathing turned ragged. Her cries uncontrollable. Astriea wished she hadn't heard it. Her heart quaked at the sound.

And she did not want to see the same mark of devastation that had once been on her own face. When she'd cradled *her* mother in her arms like that.

And just like Raja had, a woman ran into the room. The same handmaiden who'd been caring for Vera since they'd arrived. The sight of it stopped her at the door, a hand clutched to her heart.

She ran to Vera, who still clung to her mother's limp arm as she fell to her knees.

The room blurred and contorted a bit. But that handmaiden cried as if the queen was her greatest friend while she cradled the young princess—who now only cried out one phrase: *He killed her...I hid like a coward and he killed her.*

They were the only words she could say. And she said them again and again and again.

The room shifted a bit more this time. Reminded her how long she'd been here, in this world-shattering memory. A haunting tale that mirrored her own, in its own way.

The thought of her gentle, kind-hearted father doing something like that to her mother felt so wrong and heartbreaking.

The bristling wind woke her from Vera's memories. Launched her back into the oncoming storm.

"I let my mother die because when the time came to raise my voice, to fight back, I was afraid. Afraid for my mother, afraid for myself, for my brothers and sister. My people. I was so afraid I thought my skin was on fire. But I did as I was commanded—" a sob cut the last word short. "I was nearly a woman grown, and I hid under my mother's bed like a child—" But Astriea cut her off.

"You *were* a child." She said, tenderly. Then again, *"You. Were. A. Child.* Even then. You should've been falling in love or riding horses, not... not this."

Some sort of understanding shone in Vera's eyes. And it did something to Astriea.

Rage, hot and inviting, rushed through her core.

He would not have anything more. He would have no more kings or queens. No more princes or princesses. No nobles nor common folk. He would have no more spies, no more rebels. He would take no more from the mortals or immortals of this realm or any other.

And this girl, this woman not unlike herself, he would not have her either.

The vision, the memory most guarded by her enemy, that piece of vulnerability inspired her—woke her from the fog of impending doom. She didn't quite know how, but she rallied her strength and managed to gently position Vera's body onto her own back, taking the reins and straps from the sled to help secure her. Then another set over their cloaks. If this was going to work, they would both need the extra body heat.

She took a strained step, then another. With all the will she had, Astriea pushed forward. Into a storm of wrath and nightmares, with the Heir of Ice and Ash strapped to her back.

72

Astriea

The snow and ice bombarding her was enough to make Astriea wish she were dead. She hoped she'd succeeded in covering Vera's face as she lay unconscious and sprawled across her back. The storm was brutal and unyielding.

Astriea pushed and pushed through the rising snow and the howling wind. Pushed until her bones ached and threatened to crack beneath her. She pushed until she no longer could. Until she collapsed in a mound of snow. Mustering enough energy and might to pull Vera off her back before they huddled together.

"I...I'm...sorry I... brought you out here. I'm sorry I—got you killed." The words were like knives in her throat, but she said them. Vera just gently squeezed Astriea's hand with her own in response.

The mind became a little muted. Like someone had covered her ears. The wind and storm around them still ravaged, but the sound was hushed.

Something was poking her in the back. Something sharp under her cloak. For a moment, all Astriea could think of was that poking. That horrific prodding against her skin, like Thomas had been jabbing her hip with a quill for a week straight. Irritable rage swept over her and she shoved her free hand through the cloaks and grabbed the damned thing.

Only the *thing* was the blade of her short sword, twisted and its sheath lost. Wadded in some torn string of her cloak. She didn't even feel her skin slice open. But she looked at the red blood that leaked out of the cut, then ran down her arm. Studied it and all its mortal glory.

I did this. I dragged us out here to die.

She was supposed to be Sera's friend and yet; she had convinced the love of all her lifetimes to follow her into a death sentence with nothing but good intentions. Had abandoned her friend, her sister on a fool's hope.

She laid her blood-drenched hand into the snow. Thoughts of quietly becoming one with the ice now coiling around her senses.

The ground rumbled, and something like a mighty wall of wood or ice cracked wide open. Movement so rough it could've been felt across the realm. Could've been heard from the North Sea.

In the sky above them, the storm cleared like someone blew a world-trembling breath, and magic danced once more. The beautiful blues and greens and purple lights raced each other in slow, brilliant patterns. Twisting and turning together.

A warm, intense wind blew the lingering snow around them away. Until only a sheet of white ice lay beneath their feet.

The world cracked again and a small hole appeared in the ice. Thick golden water splashing around in it. A stream of it breaking free and shooting up the oncoming hill.

"Holy shit." Astriea breathed.

She got to her feet, hauling Vera in her arms, and climbed that icy hill. Fought against every screaming muscle and bone. Against every injury that begged for a reprieve. Until she reached the top.

Tears streamed down her face. This time, not freezing to her skin. As a matter of fact, all of her now seemed to *thaw*. Vera too, as her eyes beheld what now lay before them.

That eerie river turned into a thick, shimmering, gold pool of it. Bright as a star and warm like summer's day. Though the ice surrounding it did not melt, the pool was steaming and encircled by crystals and stones of every color and shape. Some large and intimidating, some small and heartwarming. Man-sized pillars of Citrine, of Tanzanite and Moonstone, nearly hummed to them in welcome.

She continued to drag Vera forward. Until the gold was lapping against the pool's edge. Reaching for her, for them.

Astriea was nearly lost in the sight of it. Vera, too, who might be choosing to spend her final moments gazing upon its glory.

The two of them were silent as a massive black steed took up a defensive position at the pool's entry.

Silent, as Hypnia returned to guard them and The Mystic.

73

Astriea

She didn't have time to balk and awe. Didn't have time to memorize every piece of The Mystic. Not when Vera was moments away from death. Not when those black veins were coming for her once more, making her twitch as it suffocated her one last time.

She dragged Vera to the pool's edge and was just about to dip her hands into it when a voice spoke in her mind.

Hello, Lightbringer. A sip will not save her, nor you.

That voice radiated with such ancient tenderness. A thousand voices all speaking together softly.

She gripped Vera a little tighter. Not knowing when, exactly, she'd started seeing her as someone she had to protect. Part of her always knew she'd kept her safe for Seraphina. But now, now that she understood Vera? Had seen her, *really* seen her?

Before she could think any more of it, she shook her head and said to Vera, "We'll go in together, alright?"

The princess gave her a small smile and nodded.

So Astriea brought her in tight and tipped them both over the edge.

* * *

Inside The Mystic, the fluid glowed in an almost amber hue. Rays of sunlight refracted from above them. They were floating for a moment. One long, warm, blissfully peaceful moment. Astriea didn't feel any of her pain. Like it was a foreign concept. Far away and unknown to her.

That lovely voice returned.

Hello, Lightbringer. Hello, Dark Rider. The day has finally come.

Astriea slowly turned her head to Vera, eyes wide and her skin cleared. Healed and breathing.

They were both *breathing* in the gods-blood. The thought made Astriea's stomach turn a bit, and that voice let out a reassuring wave of calm as it said, *Do not fear, the blood you spilled here millennia ago has become diluted in the pool. This water is the cleanest in the world. The magic thrives in it and spreads seeds of itself across all the seas, all the lands. It is one reason some places have a small amount of magic. You may speak as you normally do. You need not fear drowning in this place.*

"So... I did it? I killed the other gods?" If Astriea knew how to cry, she wanted to. But couldn't tell if it was happening or not.

Yes, Lightbringer. And no. If you wish to know how all of this began, I will show it to you. But you did not come here alone. The Dark Rider will also bear witness to what happened all those years ago. She will also hold the secrets of the universe in her mind. Is that something that she wishes?

Vera nodded frantically. Nearly begging to know.

Very good.

The water twisted and pulled Astriea and Vera to each other. She clutched Vera's arm as a chunk of the golden brown water turned to black. Then swirled into a memory.

People walked by on cobbled streets and horses chewed on hay in a small stable attached to a blacksmith's shop.

A handsome, dark-haired man in shining silver armor strode past, and the image changed.

One millennium ago, there was a knight. A grand champion to his kingdom.

The knight was standing on a battlefront, legions of soldiers rallying behind him. He raised a mighty oak staff, and green light burst from it. Destroying an enemy battalion ahead of them.

Blessed with magic, the voice said, and the picture changed again, this time to a golden-haired woman and a young boy. A babe on the verge of becoming a child. They were precious.

And a family whom he loved dearly. She went on.

The next image, an entire village of survivors, traveling down a broken path. Pulling wagons at their backs and hauling children on their shoulders.

But a great sickness fell upon the land. People died along with the animals, the crops, and the soil. The knight you know as Scythe traveled with his wife and son to the castle. To save them from the blight. But he would not arrive unscathed.

The next thing she saw made her flinch. Vera too. Saw it happening as *he* saw it.

They knew who he was, and they prepared. Chained him to pikes in the ground and made him watch his young son killed. Made him watch his wife raped and murdered.

Stay focused, she thought to herself. Thankfully, the image changed again. He was ripping the raiders' camp apart, splinter by splinter, tendon by tendon.

He broke free and slaughtered them all.

Something broke inside the knight. Hate, dark and vengeful, bloomed from his heart. He then turned his rage upon the gods. For allowing it. Doing nothing to stop it. The knight went to the temple and summoned the goddess, Astriea, *the Lightbringer, the one who ferried souls to the next world, and keeper of the Immortal City.*

That was when she saw that temple, saw Zaniah—or herself—floating before the knight. Shining like an ethereal star. Her white hair was perfect and her skin was glowing gold.

"I have known no one with the capacity to summon me in a very long time," Zaniah said to him.

Their voices muted then. As if that were the only account of words said that The Mystic had of the meeting.

He begged the goddess to return his family to him. Commanded her to. She

331

refused him, but not for the disrespect. She assured him that their deaths were not the end. That they had begun their journeys across the stars and would arrive in her realm, in the Immortal City, before his own life in this world would end. The same as all innocents whose lives ended in such ways.

The image went dark. But the voice continued anyway.

This did nothing for his broken heart. The goddess left the temple and when the knight emerged, his soul turned dark, twisted, and poisonous.

There, in the cloud of darkness, Astriea could see him clearly there. And understood what the voice meant. She could feel the essence of dark magic brewing from him. Seeping out of him. His once handsome face contorted and a near cannibalistic smile stretched wide on his lips.

That... *that* was Scythe's face. His true face. What he was behind all that smoke and shadow and possession.

Scythe studied the dark magic. Swore to end the gods and goddesses who allowed his family's demise for decades to come. But he did not possess the power to end Astriea's life. So instead, he sought out Alyea.

Both Astriea and Vera gasped at the name. Clutched each other's arms a little tighter.

Astriea's sister and her only equal.

Scythe did what none had ever dared to do, found a way into her realm. He took with him a dragon's claw, the only weapon that could pass with him into her world. He stabbed her in the heart while she slept. While it did not kill her, it weakened her enough for him to take her. Bring her back with him to his temple. A temple made of solid iron and warded by Alyea's own magic. Magic she herself deemed too dangerous for mortals to practice.

In the darkness, Astriea could make out the sound of one thing. Shuttering, panicked breaths. No sobs or cries. Just that.

He kept her there for four years. Tortured and mutilated her, until finally, he ripped her magic from her body and took it into his own. This act has made him more dangerous than anything any god or goddess has faced before. It is unknown to time, unknown to void, and the living memory, how he accomplished this.

The darkness cleared to reveal Sera's vacant face. Lying on gold, blood-spattered stone. Her open eyes were solid red and shining like glittering rubies. *Red* and sputtering out.

Her soft shadows abandoned her body and slipped into Scythe.

Then they were watching as it all just played out in front of them.

The transfer made him more powerful than any living creature in this world and many others. But a mortal could not bear it all. A piece of her slipped away. Hidden and quiet, like she was.

Scythe left his temple, and she escaped. Disguising herself as the magic he stole. She wasted no time after being freed and threw her essence into a mortal bloodline. Another knight who stood guard outside the temple.

Scythe only learned of it after he cast his dark curse upon the minor gods. He infected their heavenly bodies and turned all against the Lightbringer. Against mortals, too. Just so they would hate the gods. Even her greatest love, the sun-god.

Astriea was nearly defeated until a creature of the gods' creation intervened. A great white dragon with silver eyes sacrificed one of its claws to the beams of power that all the gods bombarded against Astriea. With it, and with no other option to save them and herself, she cut them open. Letting each of their souls, their power, slip free. To find a bloodline of their choosing and wait. Creating the pool you now bathe in. The act itself so unholy that her magic, her power, buried itself away. Leaving her nearly mortal, and very exposed. The goddess of life was captured, tortured, and executed by fire. In her own last effort to survive, the goddess split her soul, her power, her light, into two other pieces. Only one would escape him, the small bit that fell into a mortal bloodline.

Scythe, cunning and vicious, knew this and did his best to hide her away. As well as the bit that abandoned her. The waking mind of Astriea imprisoned in a beautiful, caged realm. The other, deep below the world's surface.

She heard Vera murmur, "That's horrible…"

Indeed. It was. But that is not all. The world you know, is small, quaint. But this is not all of your world. Scythe's magic would not be opposed. Armies gathered from across the world to defend the goddess. To seek vengeance in her name. So, a wall was created. A dome of dark magic to trap the kingdoms of Shadon, Telas, and Sirey here with him.

There is a reason that no one ever makes it beyond the Caltillion mountains, or thirty miles north of this pool, or east of Sirey. No one is allowed out, or in. You must go and find the Fate's vessels. They always look for Astriea and have been known to disrupt the stability of the dome, even from beyond it. With the gods gone, and the free-flowing magic stolen and locked away, the gods' creatures fell into the sea, into the earth and mountains. To slumber until the gods return. You have broken one of three great barriers when you unlocked magic in the throne room of King Herold's palace. When you split the world open and created your witches. You shook the earth, the skies, the sea. You must do so again, and once more, to break the dome. To free this part of the world and become one with it again. With all worlds. Because without the primordial goddess of life, all the realms suffer. You must free us all. This is your task, Astriea Blake.

She was stunned. Incoherent and blown away at the tale the lovely voice told. She brought all the knowledge she'd just acquired to the forefront of her mind before finally, she said, "If The Mystic judges my soul worthy, I accept my task."

Vera's head whipped towards her. And Astriea thought again of what she'd said to her in that carriage.

'I think you felt so ravaged and empty that when the opportunity to avenge your family and save your people presented itself; you leapt for it with no regard for your own life. Because I don't believe you plan on surviving the final breaking. Do you?'

And that moment of recognition clicked for both of them. That newly forged memory.

She would not live past the breaking. Not Astriea, the mountain spy.

No. Only Astriea, the goddess, would remain at the end of this.

That voice spoke again. *The moment you slipped into the pool, the two of you were judged. Your vision told you that the princess would lead you to The Mystic, not Hypnia because you needed to learn the story of your enemy. Needed to see her in yourself and become allies. Because without the Dark Rider, you will not succeed. And you, Vera Shataar, needed to find your faith. Someone heard you when you believed again and let that amulet fly. Your faith was heard.*

Its attention stayed on the princess now. *Now you, Dark Rider, Ancient Queen reborn. Would you like to know your story?*

334

Vera only nodded.

74

Seraphina

One minute, Sera could barely breathe. Could barely make out the figures surrounding her when she collapsed in the great hall. The next, she was lunging for breath as she threw herself up from the pillows on the bed.

The healers gasped. And Killian was on his feet a moment later. A hand gently outstretched to her. The invisible force that had threatened to choke the life from her was now gone. Released her from its mighty grip. Sera guessed that she collapsed. And was brought to the healer's wing.

"Pilas! Get in here, she's awake!"

The red-haired young man hurried into the room and sat on the edge of the bed.

"How are you feeling, Sera?" Pilas asked. But her mind was blank. She couldn't seem to get one thought to form into another. She looked at them both. Confused.

They tried again.

"Do you know if Vera is alive?" Killian asked softly. His eyes begging for answers.

Vera… *Vera. Yes, I know Vera. I love Vera.*

"She's alive," Sera said, barely a whisper. "I can't tell you how I know it, but… I do."

Killian and Pilas exchanged a wry look but nodded nonetheless. Killian spoke up, so much worry in his features it hurt her, and said, "Sera, it's been two days since you collapsed. And we've heard nothing from any of the search parties. None of them have returned. And the city... the city has been deserted. The castle is nearly the same. Everything in this kingdom is falling apart, and Shadon's navy is sailing far faster than what should be possible. Be it those dragons, or magic, or gods know what else. They will burn this castle to ash in another two days. I need to find Vera. And I need you to find a way to convince your armies not to destroy my sister's kingdom."

She could feel some shred of hope in what he said. Yes, they would definitely burn this place to rubble and ash.

But they were coming.

And not just for Astriea. But for her, too. She could see her friend, her brother, even now at the helm of a ship with Rala's waves propelling them forward. Damian would come. He would not abandon her.

And above all else, he would listen to her. If she begged him not to start a war, Damian would stand by her side.

But for now, all she wanted to do was find Vera and Astriea.

75

Astriea

The Mystic's full attention was on Vera.

The fates remember you, princess. You were the second child.

There were no images in the swirling dark this time. Nothing she needed to see. Only all the things she ever needed to hear.

"Yes, my brother Killian—"

The Mystic interrupted her. *No, Dark Rider, before the Fates found the child of prophecy, there were only two that could have been the heir. Astriea, and you.*

Astriea created the Fates in the Beginning. Handmaidens designed to help her hold a balance to all living things. When the dome went up, they searched for just shy of a millennium for a way to break through. Time was short, and there were only two women set to deliver a child who bore a trace of the mighty bloodline. Atara Blake, daughter of a great lord from outside the dome. The first and only person ever recorded to make it through the wall. Who was later found in the Caltillion mountains by a very handsome, golden-haired mercenary.

Astriea smiled. At the knowledge, at the thought of her mother and father's first meeting. How they'd fallen in love. How she'd made Shadon her home for them.

And Queen Raedyn Shataar. Centuries ago, Telas was led by a queen and a queen only. Centuries ago, the warrior Queen, Vaerah, went to battle in defense of the gods. Rode upon a large black steed to fight for Hellion, for Rala and Tala.

For Astriea. For the magic that was being sucked from her lands, her people. While she was away, her throne was usurped. She died in battle, her heirs hidden amongst loyal nobles. Until the day, young Raedyn married the newly appointed crown prince. This is the woman who brought forth The Queen Reborn. Who honored her own time as queen and protected her people.

To be certain the prophecy came to pass, the Fates bestowed upon each child a drop of the goddess's essence as they took their first breath. Astriea could not read your intentions when the two of you first met, because all she could see was her power. A light too similar to her own to get a good reading. This is the reason neither of you became consumed by the darkness. While you were plagued by horrid voices and tempted to let yourselves die, you were never consumed. Never taken. You cannot be but by the blood oath, your ancestors made many lifetimes ago. The Lightbringer must end the eternal winter. Or the house Shataar will never go free.

Scythe hates you, Dark Rider, because he needs you and yet is also repelled by you. So he punishes you. Because you are protected. Fates blessed by a drop of starlight.

"So... all this time, I've only been *decent* because of this blessing?" Vera asked.

All this time, you have been brave, resilient, and loyal to a fault. All the blessing did was keep Scythe from influencing your mind. With training, it is possible that you could channel the Lightbringer. Help her break this curse.

I thank you both for your company, but it is time for you to leave. It has been many days you have bathed in The Mystic. Your loved ones need you now more than ever. Go. And bring forth an era of peace, of growth. An era of new beginnings. Go so that all the others may be renewed.

Astriea, we have healed your body of the poison. The powers you would possess at this point of your transformation have been restored to you and even progressed.

Vera, your bargain with Scythe is broken. You are free of him, but it will not take long before he realizes this. And the longer you linger, the more danger your siblings are in. The Mystic has unlocked something to help you on your journey, both of you. Use it wisely.

In a heartbeat, Astriea felt as though she was being ripped from the water by a giant, invisible hand.

The pressure was enough to feel as though her bones would break against it.

Before she knew it, her body was colliding against cold, hard ice. Her lungs choking and fighting for air. Like she'd been holding her breath all that time.

After containing herself, she noticed Vera hadn't come up yet. She got to her feet and peered over the edge of the pool.

Come on... Come on!

Astriea sat there for half an hour before Vera came shooting out of the pool, hitting the ice with a thick smack.

She gasped for breath, gold leaking from her hair.

Astriea didn't know what Vera was about to tell her before her features changed and she started staring at her with awe. Astriea knit her brows in question of it.

She glanced down at her hands.

Her skin had begun to *glow*.

Then she felt it. Felt her power churn and race under her skin, in her veins. Heart pounding in her chest, heavy like the galloping beat of Hypnia's hooves.

And the world went still. Went quiet as Astriea leaned back on her knees.

Silenced, as her power came for her at all angles. Spearing into her like she would steal all the light from the world.

When all of it found its way home, the glowing under her skin flickered, and light burst out of her, the air surrounding them filled with tiny explosions of white, glittering dust.

Vera smiled at her. Lovely and grateful.

Then her hand grazed her own neck as if feeling for something, only to find nothing there.

"I never let myself think of what it would feel like to be free of him. It's like... like—"

"Like having an earworm removed?" Astriea cut her off. Vera smiled again but gave her a confused look.

"Close enough." Vera laughed. But when Astriea stood, Vera took to one knee. Golden ichor still spilling off her, dripping from her chin and hair.

"I've given you no reason to save me. You could've let me die and tried your hand at convincing one of my siblings to take your side, but you saved me instead."

"Saving the world isn't worth much if I'm willing to let the good in it die." Astriea sighed, looking down at the grand duchess. "You are a big part of that good, Vera. The world can't afford to lose you, and after all this, I'm not sure I can either."

Vera only smiled before rising to her feet.

A shuttering wave of fear washed over Astriea, then. Like a cry that she could hear across the world. Or maybe the rumble of an awakening beast.

"Something is happening. We need to go *right* now," Astriea said quickly, stumbling to her feet. Hypnia bolted to them and knelt so they could both climb on her back.

"Even with Hypnia's speed, it will take us days to get back," Vera said as Astriea settled into place behind her.

"I think I can fix that issue. Get her into the fastest stride you can and wait for my signal."

Vera didn't question it.

Only spurred her heels and let out a powerful, "RIDE, HYPNIA!" before the magnificent horse shot forward like a flying arrow. The speed at which they traveled was nearly a religious experience. The snowy terrain became a blur of pale white around them. Ice tearing at their skin once more.

Hypnia's powerful legs propelled them forward again and again until Astriea raised her hand, light glowing from it as the ground shook all around them. The horse flew faster and faster until a crooked white line, held a few feet from the ground, broke into a portal of shining light.

Hypnia carried them through without a moment to lose.

76

Astriea

Blasting through the light-gate only took them a breath. Astriea thought it best not to portal them directly to the throne room. Hypnia was so big, she didn't want to risk hurting her. Instead, they came in right where they'd left the stables.

They sat there for a moment. Listening to silence.

There were no guards. No people in the courtyard. All the stable hands were missing, too. And above them, dark thunderclouds spiraled over the castle. The rumble gradually intensifying.

"Something isn't right..." Astriea said, clutching her amulet. "Where is everyone?"

"They've gone," Vera replied. "You heard me telling my brother, Pilas, to carry out orders when we left, correct?"

Astriea nodded.

"I told Pilas to evacuate the castle and the city immediately and discreetly. Anyone who is still within fifty leagues of here has chosen so. Chosen to fight."

"And you knew the rest of your family would be so focused on finding you they wouldn't notice what? Two thousand citizens evacuating?" Astriea said more than asked.

They were at the door when Vera turned to her and nodded with a smile before saying, "I am putting my faith in *you*, Astriea Blake. If you need an army, then you have mine." She held out her arm.

Astriea paused for a heartbeat. Only to recall a time when they wanted to kill each other.

Now allies.

"The other ice-cities—"

"They've been evacuated, too."

And in that moment she even dared to think of Vera as, *friend*. She took her arm, and they shook.

"Vera... Your father—"

"I know what I have to do. Just keep his eyes off me and I'll do what has to be done."

"You're sure? We cannot afford for this to go sideways. If you don't kill him, we lose it all. He is waiting for us right now, and he probably has Sera and Killian and the rest of your siblings. In order to banish him, I have to funnel my power deep into the earth and break it free."

"Let's do that first, then."

"The breaking? He'll know the moment we start."

"Not if we can drug him right before. He can't possess me unless my father is already dead, and even then, I'm not twenty-six yet. He can't possess my siblings unless *I'm* dead. And *even then*, he has to wait until Salrek turns twenty-six, too. It's always been clear that the curse has to go down the line of succession, so even if I die, I'll have bought you all a couple more years. I'll get to Pilas and have him bring me the new vials I've been working on and inject Scythe, while you track down Killian, Sera, and *all fourteen* of my guard—"

"Fourteen? Why?"

"Because they can keep you safe, and they will. If you've ever noticed, my crest is a white dragon with a rider on its back. *Not* a sword through it. Find them all, tell them what you need of them and they will aid you, I promise. Now go! We don't have time to debate! Go!"

But before she left, Astriea reached into the bag that she hadn't been able to call upon since her first injection. Reached in and pulled out a wrapped bundle, before placing it in Vera's hands.

The grand duchess smiled, then shooed her through the door and Astriea took off through the darkness of the castle.

She halted in an alcove. And decided she would fare better if she looked the part.

Astriea pressed her hand against the amulet, and she shifted. Her hair braided itself down her head, her winter cloaks vanished and in their place, a sleek black tunic and tight trousers nearly fitted to her skin. A cloak and hood sprang from her shoulders and quickly masked her in shadows once more. Out of all her powers, this one was her favorite.

There, in the kind of darkness she was familiar with, Astriea the goddess rested her mind. While the mountain spy reappeared once more.

She looked above her head.

Nice set of railings.

Then she was climbing. Up the wall and onto the overlooking rails that crossed from wall to wall. A lovely attribute she'd noted when she was first dragged through these halls.

Step for step, leap for leap, Astriea Blake trailed for her charges.

* * *

Half an hour later, she'd found all the guards Vera had told her to. Now, she just needed Sera and Killian. And that didn't take long.

Astriea told the guards to meet her in the throne room. It was on the other side of the castle from the royal quarters where the tzar *should* be incapacitated, and she needed the space. But now, as she was about to open the door to Vera's chambers in her tower, it swung open as she reached for the handle.

Sera stopped dead. Killian mirroring the act. They were both shocked to see her.

She waited for Sera to scream. To hit her. She wished she'd just hit her. But knew she never would.

"I thought we were a team?" Sera said with a little bite while crossing her arms. Before she could answer, Sera cut her off again. "Where is she?"

"Readying to knock out the tzar, while I perform The Breaking."

Both of their eyes went wide.

"It worked? You have your power back?" Sera asked curiously. Astriea nodded and lifted her hand, allowing a small orb of beautiful white light to pulse out. They gazed at it for a moment and then moved on.

"And my sister?" Killian's face was a broken mess. Though he'd tried to hold it together enough to ask the question. What he really wanted to ask was, *does she live? Is she safe? How much more time will I have with her?*

Astriea took Killian's hands into her own. "Your sister is *free.*"

Killian yanked Astriea into his chest and hugged her tight. A shuddered breath escaping him.

"I'm sorry I didn't listen to you."

"Oh, don't be. I sound like I'm mad half the time." She laughed against him.

Astriea saw something in Seraphina soften at Killian's words. But she pulled away and said, "I need you both in the throne room to protect me should Scythe find another way to come knocking or burn through the serums."

They both nodded their heads, and Killian led the way back down the stairs. As Astriea turned back toward the hall, Sera gently grabbed her arm. She quickly looked into now obsidian eyes.

"I am unbelievably angry with you."

"You have every right." Astriea struggled to say under the weight of the guilt.

"But I love you, anyway." Her heart skipped. "I want details after The Breaking."

"I promise to tell you everything, Sera. There is so much you need to know."

"Well, let's get going then. And don't you ever leave me alone in a palace full of Telish royals ever *again.*"

The way Seraphina whispered it as they descended the stairs made a little snicker break from her.

Astriea knew there would be much more to hear later. But for now, Sera merely held her hand. They both let out a deep breath. Something like joy to be reunited. Even if it was only for a moment, they were happy to have each other back.

They held onto that feeling all the way to the Throne of Ice and Ash.

77

Thomas

There were no ships in the harbor.

No lights were shining in the distance, nor was there chatter along the shoreline.

For safe measure, Thomas took Valtan, Lavene, and Antony with him— Alec's brother and first-born son of Nostranas Leora—each on dragon-back to lead ahead for reconnaissance. To get a look at what might await them past the enormous silver gates that guarded a silver-towered city built into a crescent fjord.

There were no people.

Not a man, woman, or child to be seen on the cold, dark streets.

Now, returned to James' ship, discussions amongst them heated and tensions raised high.

"How could an entire city just empty out that quickly?" James asked. "With no one noticing?"

"If everyone has gone, maybe they took Astriea and Seraphina with them," Damian interjected.

"We don't know that! We won't know anything until *someone* goes in." The last one was Mira. Her words were filled with undeniable passion. Dedication. That she would leave no stone unturned, no building left unseen or mound of ice uninspected. Her lips voicing his raging thoughts he'd done well to keep bridled.

The future queen glanced at him and nodded when he gave her a grateful smile, an unspoken thanks.

"Sending someone in isn't as easy as that. We send one person past the gates, then we nearly condemn them to die. What if we sent a party? A group of us would have better odds," Draes said respectfully.

"Who?" James asked.

Thomas coughed, loud enough that he gained the gazes of them all.

"I did just bring a legion of dragons across the sea for the sole purpose of burning that city to cinders. You are all talking of the next advancements on an emptied kingdom but I don't understand why you don't just send *us*." Thomas spread his arms a bit, gesturing to his top ten dragon riders that lined the back wall behind him.

Antony was the first to look up. Normally he'd go on and on about how he's only here to make sure his little brother didn't get killed. But since he and his brother matched with their dragons, their demeanors had changed. Antony had the same overall image as his brother: dark brown hair and pale skin. Big brown eyes.

Alec stood right next to him, spinning a small throwing knife between his hands.

Lorenzo, Valtan, Diego, and Lavene also stood back against the wall. And he was sure Lavene and Valtan had already chosen at least four others. Based on the heartbeats he heard pounding on the other side of the door to the cabin.

James took a breath and said, "Because we will likely need you, *and* your dragons when we move on to Sirey. We can't start this war with our biggest weapon. It shows our hand too quickly. And Astriea's letter said to leave the city *untouched*."

"I know what she said in that letter, but do you honestly think word hasn't already spread? They know we have dragons, I guarantee *that*." Thomas said, his eyes rolling against his will.

"That doesn't matter, Thomas. We can't just send in our heaviest fighters first. It could be a trap."

"It *is* a trap! Of course, it's a trap! But I don't care, James. Astriea is in there, and I've stood here on the brink of having her back for long enough. She is so close I can taste it in the air. I can *feel* it under my skin. So I don't care what traps they have, I cannot spend another day like this. I'm going to get my girl. I'm going to get them both." He shot his eyes up to Damian, who nodded, strapped his sword belt around his waist, and went to follow him out the door of the captain's quarters.

"Thomas, wait—" James started. But he stopped, and Thomas could hear him frantically looking around the room. His head turning back and forth. Thomas could hear his heartbeat jump up.

"Where is Mira?" James whispered.

Surely enough, Mira was gone.

James was sprinting through the door in a desperate panic. Calling her name and hearing nothing back. Thomas and Damian scoured the ship and found it empty.

Draes returned shortly after having discovered a missing longboat, while James's guard reported seeing nothing out of place mere minutes before.

There were no signs of her on the water. Even with Thomas's enhanced sight, it was much too dark to make out any movements along the water's surface.

"Let's go," James commanded.

Thomas followed behind, along with Damian and Draes, and said, "Oh, so when it's your—"

"I know what I said."

James made to grab hold of a longboat and Thomas stopped him.

He let his thoughts wander off to a dragon, dark as the night with golden eyes.

Night-cleaver, he called.

And then, as if plucked from the void itself, the dragon descended upon them. Night-cleaver let down one of their wings and allowed all of them to climb on its back.

Thomas finally replied to James, now seated fully and readying to take off, "Don't worry, you can formally apologize to me later."

James's curse was cut short as Night-cleaver shot into the sky—golden

349

eyes set on The Silver City.

78

Seraphina

Sera paced back and forth along the throne room. Quietly waiting for Vera to arrive with Pilas and give them the go-ahead.

Astriea sat on the dais steps at the end of the room. Killian just leaned against an onyx column and bit his cuticles.

But then she heard light footsteps. Two pairs.

And then those giant doors swung open.

Two red-haired, emerald-eyed royals stood on the threshold. But only one made her knees wobble a bit.

Vera Shataar stood there, eyes glimmering in the moonlight, and smiling brightly.

They didn't speak, only ran into each other's arms. That bond deep inside her, reaching and propelling her forward.

"I felt you... dying... I felt it—"

"I am good as new now," Vera assured her. Placing a hand on her cheek and under her ear, she pulled Sera's lips to hers and kissed her. Passionate and without restraint.

All was right for that moment. All was good and fair and just.

They parted from the kiss and pressed their foreheads together.

"I—I can be yours now. I broke the bargain. Broke the curse." Vera shuttered.

But no, no, that wasn't right.

"No... You belong to only *you*."

Vera's smile was radiant and contagious.

"I'm sorry I left you here. I'll never do it again, I promise. Maybe I'll even tie us together with rope." They both choked on a laugh before pulling away from each other.

Killian came forward then.

"You could've told me... I am technically the eldest. It's my responsibility to keep you all safe. Especially you, Vera. Instead, you trusted all of this with Pilas..."

"I trusted all of this with Pilas, my dear brother because you feel all of our pain too deeply. Because I knew you would not allow the plan in the first place. You wouldn't risk us. *Me*."

"What she means is that I can't tell her no." Pilas laughed and rolled his eyes, before slapping a hand on each of their shoulders.

They all grinned.

"How are you?" Killian asked softly.

"Better than ever."

"Good. Because we need you all here when this is over, to convince Thomas Hellion and the King of Shadon not to burn down the city. They could be on our shores now. We don't know. Pilas sent all the guards and armies into the safe holds and villages for evacuation. To protect the citizens should things go badly tonight." He turned toward Astriea now, "The dragon of Telas rides on the backs of them now, and has a hundred more in tow."

Vera, more brazen than she'd known her to be with Astriea, asked her, "Still eager to '*watch him burn everything I love to ash?*'" But Vera had smiled when she said it, and curiously enough, it earned a soft chuckle from Astriea herself.

At that moment, Sera realized it might not be so hard to be in both their worlds.

That maybe they'd found a way to get along. And for now, that was enough.

79

Astriea

Once everyone had arrived and Vera confirmed the tzar would be incapacitated for a few hours, Astriea requested that they all encircle her in the room. Then she made her way to the middle and took three deep, long breaths.

Z? Are you there?

I'm here, Astriea. You went to The Mystic. You uncovered the truth. Redeemed the Dark Rider. I should think you will not need me for much longer. Why do you hesitate?

Because I'm nervous... Last time—last time I did this, I was fueled by anger and rage. Astriea thought back to her.

This time, focus on your will, on why you are doing this. Who you are doing this for.

Astriea nodded and pulled the amulet from her neck, letting it shift back into her staff. She slammed the bottom onto the marble and the world cracked open in a single, vicious quake.

Killian, Seraphina, Vera, and Pilas all anchored themselves to the walls and tried to steer clear of falling debris. The eight masked guards scattered around the room all took to one knee at the entrances. With the other six having gone to retrieve the youngest of the royal family and any others for the last evacuation. To get them all out of the castle and to safety before returning.

Then, Astriea's soul took a deep, unending dive.

Like before, she dove faster and faster into the heart of the world. As she descended, she couldn't shake the sensation of celestial gears, audibly clicking and harmoniously falling into their designated positions. Despite the trip feeling shorter than before, the heat was almost unbearable. When she arrived in that shimmering chamber of golden dust, she immediately went to work. This time, instead of using just her hands, Astriea spun her arms in half-circles. Beckoning the magic to follow her, pulling it closer in bigger quantities. With each pull and weave of the fine particles of gold, she could feel the weight of pressure quickly building, threatening to crush her like an ant under a boot.

Without a second glance at the last bit of magic she'd have to bring out in Sirey, she shot back up.

Zaniah spoke to her while she ascended. *You've taken too much, your body can't hold that amount. When we get to the top, you will only have a few moments to bind some of it to something or someone else. You got away with it last time because you bound each of the witches. I hope you have a plan for this go.*

I understand. Astriea thought back.

Her eyes shot open, and the ground beneath her feet had become nothing but a chasm of rock and hot magma. The ball of light in her hands was searing. She knew what Zaniah meant the moment her eyes opened. She could feel the blood running down her nose.

"I have too much." She grunted out. "I can bless two of you with magic... if I don't, it could kill me."

Her blood boiled in the heat of hot magic. But the doors slammed open, the tzar now stood upon the threshold. His eyes leaked shadows as he used his magic to toss the guards against the wall.

"You're... too late." Astriea struggled but said the words.

At that moment, Killian stepped into Astriea's light, and she bound the magic to him. It zipped through the air like lightning, right into his chest.

The floor snapped shut, but Astriea was still glowing dangerously bright. Another needed to be bound. Pilas took a step forward, but not soon enough.

Scythe's dark magic struck her. Hard and unforgiving. He covered her in shadow, then. Wrapped it around her while he suffocated her friends. Sera twisted her hands, trying to call on her own shadows to aid her. But she couldn't breathe.

That was the last thing she saw before the darkness covered her in a cocoon of screams and nightmares.

80

Astriea

The tzars' body barely seemed to be living. Struggled just to draw breath as Scythe sprawled out on the great frozen throne. His eyes wholly black and full of shadows.

He leaned against the arm, his head held up by his fist. And with his other hand, held an open palm. His fingers flexed and curved like Astriea's had been the day she tortured the King of Shadon. Because that's what he was doing. Holding all of her friends like that, drowning them in a state of terror and panic.

Fury flooded her.

And a voice spoke, Zaniah's voice, awake once again and screaming, *How he has defiled her magic! Defiled her spirit!* She had some of her memories back. They hadn't had time to talk about them yet.

For at every angle of the round throne room, one of her friends was bound by vines of darkness. Being suffocated by them.

"Bring them in here!" Scythe commanded. As the door swung open, Astriea was confused as to why the three young handmaidens were being dragged inside. A masked guard in solid black threw them to the ground before him. Their mother, Morra, cried and begged for them outside of the chamber. Pleaded with the guards and the tzar.

"Not my girls! Please, your grace, I beg you! Not my girls!"

The doors slammed in her face and Astriea heard her broken sob even then.

The sisters were silent.

"Confused, *Lightbringer?*"

"I don't know why you're dragging more innocents into this. You separate us because you know you can't beat us. You butcher innocents, torture children. All for me. The goddess who told you *no*."

He slammed his hand, and the room quaked, but Astriea did not.

And then quickly realized why her power was flickering in her chest. At every corner, behind her captive friends, were pillars of black stone she'd been drawn to stare at every time they came into this room. The same material used in the dagger Raja had found. The blade Astriea had given to Vera before she performed the breaking. Now those stones were humming. Pulsing out a dark power that would nullify her own.

Oh gods, The Breaking.

If she didn't bind the excess magic to someone, do *something* with it. She was going to burn from the inside out. Never in her life did she think she'd ever be grateful to be near cursed stones that made you so terrified your power just refused to work. And she could feel *that*. Her power fluttering in her chest. There and overwhelming in one moment, and gone completely in another. Scythe saw this in her expression as he said, "It seems you didn't do the spell properly this time, *Lightbringer*. The stones will not hold forever and when they fail, you will explode. Burned to ashes by your own foolishness. Though, I win either way, so what does it matter to me if you die early?" He laughed.

"The handmaidens have nothing to do with this *Scythe*. Let them go."

"Oh, they have *everything* to do with this, Astriea. I see you've found the elusive Mystic pool. Learned some things as well. But still no memories? Shame. The Fates that blessed you and Vera with a drop of starlight cannot cross fully into this realm—speaking of Vera. What have you done with her?" Astriea tried not to look around the room. Her Fae sight helped her figure it out enough, though. They did not capture Vera. She got away. Killian, Sera, Pilas, and some guards, were all here and struggling for breath under Scythe's grip. But she humored the monster before her.

"You know she broke your bargain, Scythe. I tried to get her into The Mystic in time. I didn't succeed." She hesitated for dramatic effect, even shuttered a bit. "She's dead."

"Ha! And you, like the selfish little god you are, left her in the Northern Wastes. No matter, there will be another heir now. But back to the matter at hand. The Fates cannot cross fully into this realm—"

"Because of your dome. Am I correct?" She cut him off.

He snarled at her but continued.

"They travel to every point of the dome. Seek weak spots and send their magic, visions, and prophecies through. They have done this since the walls went up." The expression he made was that of utter contempt. Irritation. Since the beginning, they've been relentless in their efforts to bother him in that way.

"They are *your* creations. And since being trapped here, they have been unabating to retrieve you. Now, they channel into these three young women. So it is not I who involved these innocents." He pointed at them. His magic released enough on her friends that they all seemed to take a breath.

Then Scythe roared, "FATES! SHOW YOURSELVES! PROVE YOUR POWER IS GREATER THAN THAT OF LISTENING THROUGH REALMS!"

The world seemed to shift under her feet. But not in the same way as before. This time it felt like her body shifted, too. Like something pulled and stretched her, before quickly snapping back into place. The sound had been the worst of it. The wave of power that surged into that room, into those women, was a roaring of the loudest thunder. All the glass in the room shattered against it. Letting in an unforgiving cold.

The women stood as one, their eyes dull-white, glazed, and just barely glowing. Like solid pearl, surrounded by soft white smoke.

"The Dark Knight's era comes to a close,
His destiny sealed as the Lightbringer rose.
Power unbridled bears an infinite cost,
Burned the soul until it was lost."

They all said in unison, facing Scythe.

"Enough riddles! You will see your prophecy die along with your precious *Lightbringer!*"

But he didn't attack her. No, he instead yanked Sera forward.

The world slowed. And all Astriea could think about was the dagger pressed by an invisible hand at Sera's throat. She didn't make note of the now fourteen masked guards that suddenly pivoted their spears. Not toward Astriea, or Sera for that matter. No, those blades turned toward Scythe himself.

The confusion on his face quickly burned away to rage.

"You *dare* betray me?" He snarled.

The guards and their spears took a step forward and halted in answer. She hadn't realized they were Vera's guard. The small white dragon patch with a rider on its back lie on all of their cloaks.

Scythe's gaze returned to Astriea, who still stared at that knife and Sera's throat.

"No matter. I don't think you'd let her die a second time. I think she means a great deal to you."

The knife nicked her skin. A single drop of blood slid down her neck.

Sera tried to murmur through the gag of smoke but to no avail.

"Now I'm going to tell you what's going to happen. You are going to let me kill you. Extinguish you. And things will go back to how they were. Or she is the first to die."

Astriea looked around the room. Killian and Pilas and someone else. Someone cloaked in black. Scythe saw her curiosity.

"Ah yes, I found this one sneaking about. I remember her... do you?"

A shadow vine yanked the hood off, and underneath it was Mira. The future Queen of Shadon.

The hair on Astriea's arms rose. Her stomach clenched.

"But—"

"Yes, they are here. Sent their little scout ahead on the back of a gold dragon." He ticked. "If you don't submit to me now, I will kill the Heir of Alyea. Then everyone in this room. And when your lover feels your death and is drowning in the agony of it, I will end his suffering, too."

Her blood heated. But the tzar croaked.

Gasped for breath as a dark blade, made of his own magic, pierced through his chest. A set of emerald eyes and blood-red hair peered from behind him. Tears running down her face, Vera Shataar stabbed the cursed blade Astriea had given her through her father's heart.

The small victory was short-lived. While blood pooled from the tzar's chest, Scythe only flinched and used his shadows to throw Vera before him, only inches away from Seraphina.

He released Sera's gag for a moment and she said, "I am Seraphina Ophelia Blackspear, and I give my life—"

"No!" Vera screamed.

But quicker than she could blink, that knife swiped across Seraphina's throat.

81

Astriea

Scythe released Sera to choke on her own blood. She hit the marble, sending the realm quaking. Rocking in defiance of it.

Regardless, Astriea was on her knees, panting and pulling Sera into her lap.

"No… no no no no," she rasped as blood smeared all over her hands. Shooting out of Sera's neck. The light in her chest was burning, hotter and hotter until she was sure that it rivaled Hellion.

Heal her.

There was no answer.

HEAL HER! I don't care what it takes, but help me heal her or I'll kill us all. I can't take it, I can't bear it. Please, please anyth—

The Lightbringer erupted. Her power beaming like an exploding star.

During her pleading, she didn't hear Vera command the room to cover their eyes. Didn't hear them all jump away to safety.

She didn't even see Scythe slam into the wall behind him. His body shattering the icy throne.

All she saw was that gushing cut across Sera's throat. Her grip on Astriea's shirt was so tight she worried her fingers might break.

And the heat… She took that heat, the molten agony beneath her skin that gave her a bright orange hue, and channeled it, funneled it into that stubborn bit that didn't think herself capable of inflicting anything but pain. This time, when Astriea commanded her magic to heal. *It did.*

The broken pieces of skin slowly weaved back together, sending sparks of hope, of joy to her. With the process nearly complete, the blinding light was fading away, until a great force of darkness hit her so hard she hit the wall on the other side of the room. The crunch she heard when her head collided against the stone was terribly unsettling.

She heard doors swing open. Heard the footsteps, but didn't see who it was. All she saw while her world faded in and out—her magic and body drained and dragging her into unconsciousness—was Scythe.

Bleeding and broken against the opposing wall, all she saw was that vile, slithering darkness, leak from the tzar fully and into what was left of the gash upon Sera's throat.

Before darkness took her, Astriea watched it take Sera, too.

82

Damian

Damian could barely believe what he was seeing. Mira risked her life by sneaking ahead with her plan. But that wasn't what shocked him.

No, the true horror was watching Sera's limp, blood-covered body rise from the ground and her once lovely dark eyes become perverted by Scythe's evil.

Turning wholly black and flooding the room with shadows.

He gained full control then. Cracked Sera's neck a bit and made a sickening expression. Vera was on the floor at Astriea's side, cradling her head in her lap. Her eyes filled with more fear than he'd ever thought her capable of.

Things have changed since last we met.

But then, Scythe's vile demeanor spoke through Sera's lips, through her voice, "I find the irony of this situation to be fitting. That I should torment you in a way that may finally break you. That I should take her from you and make her face the thing you hate."

"Why…" The grand duchess's voice broke. And tears streamed down her face. "Why do you hate me this much? Why do you never stop?" She sobbed.

"Because *you* never stop…. You never submit to me completely. You carry out my orders and bide your time. Then sneak and creep through shadows. *You*, this small insignificant human with no magical ability in your bloodline, fuels my rage more than the *Lightbringer* herself. A fly in my face I can never swat away. I should've killed you as a child, all of you. Though little Thea would've adjusted to me better than you did if she'd been all alone."

A small bit of shadow grew behind Sera. Something, it seemed, Scythe was now having trouble conjuring. Was working harder to do it.

The Breaking. She did it. He's being dragged out of Telas.

The thought was logical enough. They'd seen the flash of light on their way up to the castle. Felt the earth shake.

"I hate you because I have to beat you to death and despite that, you do the same thing again and again. *Get. Back. Up.*"

Scythe raised Sera's hand, an eerie smile on her face. Ready to kill them all.

"And now you will suffer for that resiliency." He paused for a moment, "You went to the Mystic... Tell me, girl, before you finally die, is it true? Are you *Tzarina sa macta?*"

Vera didn't answer. Only tended to Astriea as she began to rouse.

"It would be fitting, I suppose. I am the one who killed her the last time."

Vera's attention was caught then.

"Oh yes, the Fire Queen, *Vaerah.* What an annoyance she was. She tried to rescue her lover from me. I gutted her with a scythe in front of the death goddess she came for. The being she tracked me down to save. Abandoned her kingdom only for her to die inches away from her goal. Yes... Yes, I think it would be most fitting..." Scythe closed Seraphina's eyes and, out of smoke and shadow, a black scythe appeared in her hands. The blade rusted and now serrated from chipping.

Damian's rage took hold. Before he had another thought, he charged at Sera.

Those shadows hardened like a wall, and Damian collided with it. Only a few feet away.

"Ah, ah, ah." Sera's voice was so wrong like this while Scythe taunted him. Half hers, half his.

"She's still in here, you know. *Oh,* how she fights."

Damian beat on the shield.

"*Oh,* how she screams."

He beat again.

"I want you to know I've given her not a shred of gentleness."

Again.

"I want you to know that at this moment, Seraphina only wishes she were dead."

Again.

Scythe nearly moaned, "At this moment, she's begging me to stop."

Damian raised his axe and swung with all the force his body would allow. Swung hard enough to rip the castle apart. But it was not his anger that rattled the throne room tower.

Even Scythe looked up at the ceiling.

Behind him, Draes and James dragged Astriea and Mira out of the room along with the masked guards they'd passed in the city who were escorting four young boys and a girl away from the castle. All five of them dressed in finery and all bearing similar features to Vera.

Those guards had all returned now, fourteen of them standing in the massive open hallway outside this room. Vera and the large, dark-haired man limped out just in time.

Then the roof collapsed. Sera underneath it.

Damian paid close attention to the falling stone and metal. He moved as pieces fell toward him. Avoiding even a scratch as flame enveloped the space for a moment.

When the rubble and dust cleared, Night-cleaver descended onto the marble floor, cracking it under their weight. Thomas Hellion on its back.

For a moment, there was a great wave of grief. Of pain. As Damian realized his oldest and truest friend had just been crushed by stone. But he was smarter than that. It would take more to kill Scythe. Nothing short of dragon fire would rid the world of him fully. Not that Damian knew of, anyway.

While Thomas sat on dragon-back, his hair now golden and bathed in flame, he gave Damian a questioning look.

Where is she?

Damian just nodded his head toward the hall in answer.

Vera ran back in then. Her eyes darted around the room.

"She's still alive. I can feel it." She whispered, eyes wide. Perhaps from shock.

Then she started moving rocks. Pulling them back and tossing them aside.

Vera Shataar made no note of the destroyed throne or room. And paid no attention to the snarling black dragon or Thomas, who watched her every move. His face a portrait of anger and hate.

Weeks ago, he watched this woman betray them all. Now, he couldn't help but feel sorry for her. Thomas was about to attack, but Damian thought about what the Queen Mother of Shadon had said before they left. *'I always thought maybe I wasn't the only queen trapped in a cold castle.'* He held up a hand to stop him and Thomas listened.

One step toward the princess turned into two. Until he was just behind where she knelt in the rubble. And, as gently as he could, he placed a hand on her trembling shoulder.

A shadow appeared from nothing, just before them. Twisted and warped until a figure stepped out. Seraphina. *Scythe.*

Damian had been right. He felt Vera's shoulder tense, and she rose from the floor. Her hands bloody and shaking.

The laugh that came from Sera was a cackling shriek. A taunting reminder he was in there. In her. That he was torturing her from the inside.

"How sad," Scythe crooned. "looks like you all have a decision to make."

Those dark eyes glanced at the back of the room. Damian turned at the same time as Thomas, to see Astriea, an arm around Draes' neck in the doorway. Barely able to hold herself up, but awake and now pushing forward, ready to make a final advance. Night-cleaver growled and dug his claws into the floor, now looking at Sera again.

Though fear shone in Sera's eyes for a moment. It did not linger. She simply raised her hand and stepped toward Astriea.

83

Thomas

Thomas didn't give it much thought. He jumped from Night-cleaver's back and slid down the broken stone under the dragon's feet. A moment later, he'd thrown himself between Sera and Astriea.

His flames roared to life. His hair floated off his shoulders and shone like gold. Sera winced and retreated a few steps.

"Don't tell me you forgot about me, Scythe?" He teased. "You may have Seraphina, for now..." Thomas advanced, flaring his blaze. "But that one?" He pointed at Astriea, still on the floor behind him, clutching onto Draes's arm. Vera now lifting her from the other side.

"That one is *mine*. And you will never have her, Scythe. I will be there to spoil your fun at every turn."

Scythe backed away another step, black eyes searching for shelter from the light and heat. Sera smiled and raised her hand above her head. But before she snapped her fingers, Thomas laid one more blow.

"Before you run away again, take a good hard look at the faces around this room. Look into their eyes. Look into my own."

Surprisingly, Scythe dragged his stolen gaze across the room, then back to Thomas.

"You took our friend. You took one of *ours*." He inched forward, bit by bit. Doing everything he could to get his message across. "Now you will know what it's like to be hunted. Because I've figured you out, Scythe. I know it is my gift and my gift alone that brings you pain." Scythe stiffened, and Thomas smirked. "You took the gift of fire and abused it, but now you will know it. You will know it even when the clouds in the sky try to shelter you from it." The heat intensified. "You will know the dread of a million souls still trapped inside your dome as the night fades and the sun rises, and in the depths of that terror, you will pray to *me*. You will pray and beg that I am not behind the dawn as it chases you. I am coming for you and all your shadows."

Faster than a shooting star, Thomas wrenched his molten arm back and swung his fiery fist at Sera's face.

She dodged and jumped back a step. Thomas made to advance, but the moment he did, Vera Shataar was leaping in front of him. Crying out against the heat coming off him. He fell back from the shock of it. Astriea was on her knees behind the grand duchess.

Vera held Astriea's hand with her left and extended her right into the air before Seraphina.

It started as a small ball of white light. Just a glow from her palm. But within a blink, that small light shifted into strings of white *energy*.

He could feel the power radiating off her. Flowing from where Astriea crouched, through her body and into Vera's before spilling out of her from every pore on her hand.

Vera whipped those strings out at the exact moment Sera moved to shadow travel, and wrapped them around her throat.

Thomas's fire went out as he fell against Draes. He looked at him with wide eyes.

"I—I don't understand." He breathed.

Scythe seethed.

Through Sera's body, he twisted and screamed. Clawed at the light now gripped around his throat. But the bastard spoke as though it had only stung for a moment.

"Why don't you just give in? Let her go and die and all this ends. I've already ripped her to pieces, she'll be no use to you now." He'd almost laughed.

But Astriea... Her skin glowed a vibrant gold, her white hair floated off her shoulders as though she were underwater. Vera glowing in contrast with a brilliant silver.

Thomas moved.

He side-stepped around them both and watched as Seraphina continued to claw away at her throat. Moments away from blood spilling.

"No!" Astriea cried out. From her free hand, more strings of light appeared, and she whipped them around Sera's hands. Binding them together. "I have lived my entire life as a mortal. And there is nothing we won't do to survive. No matter how you hurt us. No matter how many of us you kill." Astriea rose from the floor and it took all of Thomas's restraint not to help her stay standing as she wobbled closer to Seraphina.

She moved forward, and closer still.

Leaning over Scythe she said inches from Sera's face, "We will fight tooth and nail for life, for air... for love." Her grip around Sera's wrists tightened. "You will run from here, but you will not be taking Seraphina with you. Every time, it seems like you forget one crucial thing..."

Scythe said nothing, but Astriea went on, "I pull the strings."

A blast of power flooded through the room and in a breath, she washed that power over Seraphina's body. Every ember of it pulsing through Vera first.

White smoke spread out all around Sera and her body fell to the floor, shadow erupting from her and shooting out into the night sky.

84

Astriea

They'd done it.

They'd cleansed Scythe of Sera's body, and now those tendrils of power rippled throughout her, throughout Vera.

Magic as strong as steel.

Wisps of it now moving through the air and twisting around a cloud of black smoke, holding it in place before them.

A screech—loud and blood-curdling—pulsed through the room, accompanied only by Scythe's voice.

You wasted too much time saving the girl; you cannot hold me here. Not when you've already performed The Breaking. So I'll leave you... with a gift.

The castle shook, but Astriea was the only one able to stand against Scythe's essence pressing hard into the room.

Let me go, or let them die. He said.

Thomas, Vera, Draes and Damian. All of them were down on the floor with their hands over their ears. Groaning against it.

Astriea decided the moment she saw a stone falling from the ceiling. The moment she saw Vera peeled over in its path.

She released the tethers, letting him vanish, and blasted the stone along the back wall.

The group of them took a breath as that unbearable weight lifted off them. Vera looked up at Astriea from the floor, a word of thanks in her eyes.

Damian was already carrying Sera out of the throne room and let Pilas lead him into the hall. More quiet and somber than she'd ever known him to be. But before she could fall into Thomas' arms, there was one thing left to do.

Don't look at him.

Don't look at him or you'll fall apart right here.

She told herself that again and again as they searched the rubble.

He looks very handsome. Zaniah said softly. *And dirty.*

A rasping cough rattled out from the back wall. Vera lunged forward, and there, she helped her move rocks until they found him. The Tzar of Telas, wheezing and dying under the stones and large pieces of burned silver metal.

Dragon fire.

"Father... I'll get a healer..."

"No..." He rasped. And quickly clutched Vera's hand in his own. "No, there is no.... no saving me, little star."

Vera sucked in a sob. So Astriea placed a hand on her shoulder.

"That girl—that girl you love is strong, my child." He coughed. "A soul as strong as your own. I felt it as he left me. That power was *meant* for her. He did not break her as he did not break you."

She sobbed again.

What do I do? She asked Zaniah.

You help her let him go. So the Fire Queen's age may begin again. He has already accepted this.

"You..." He breathed to Astriea. "You have freed my people—freed my children. Thank you."

Killian came to the tzar's side and caught his eye.

He's already saying goodbye. She nearly felt Zaniah nod her head.

It seems a kindness they were given the chance. She replied.

"My son... let your guilt die with me. You have stayed my hand enough for a thousand lifetimes. Be free of it now."

Killian cried, and then the tzar turned back to Vera, one last time.

"You are already a queen to be reckoned with. But it would give me no dishonor if you were to leave the throne behind should you wish it. Give it to one of your siblings and sail far away. Where your skin only knows the touch of warm breezes and cool waves on a hot summer day. Where you will never know pain and suffering—" His hand grazed her face. "Because I—I am so sorry." Vera leaned her face into her father's palm. "Because you have been so brave, my bold princess. You have been brave enough, *Tzarina sa macta...*"

The black dragon Thomas crashed in on, slowly climbed out of the hole it created before gently leaping into the air.

The Tzar of Telas spoke again, this time to someone long since passed.

"Ra—Raedyn. Raedyn, do you see that dragon?" He gasped and choked. "Black as night it is, Raedyn. Do you see it? Do you see it, my love?"

Those words were his last. He stared blankly at the dawning sky and watched the dark-winged beast vanish into the last remnants of night.

The room fell silent. And even with the tzar's blessing, it did not change the fact that when Vera rose from her knees. When she stood again, even in the rubble, she was Queen of Telas.

The masked guards piled inside and collected the tzar's body before leading Vera and her brother out into the hall. Their faces red and swollen and wet.

Their expressions hollow.

* * *

There was only one thing in the world that could've tried to mend her shredded heart right now. And he was staring at her across the ruined room. The flames in his hair had sputtered out. The gold died away to raven-black and covered in ash. Astriea didn't want to think about how she looked right now. Only about the pair of sea-storm eyes that drew closer and closer to her.

Her body was shutting down. Healing Sera and then exercising Scythe from her body had been enough to even her out. But it hurt. *Horribly.*

Like she'd seared her insides, or swallowed dragon flame. Which was *also* something she didn't expect to see today.

Thomas, bursting in on a dragon.

As far as moves went, he'd really outdone himself.

How he'd found them, trained them, flew them across the sea. She wanted to hear every bit of his story. But more than anything, she wanted what was about to happen.

Right... *Now.*

His arms were around her. They'd slammed into each other a little harder than either had intended. But it didn't matter. The world didn't matter for a moment. He was here. He'd come for her and brought an army behind him. Conquered dragons to hold her in his arms again. He was here, and she finally, *finally,* felt safe.

"Don't you *ever* throw me through a portal again." He said, breath shuttering.

She laughed into his chest, "I swear it by all the gods."

They were silent while they held onto one another.

Until James and one guilty-looking Mira came in, Damian behind them. The latter wasted no time and wrapped Astriea in a hug. She returned it. Needed it as much as he did. Damian wiped his eyes and James said, "I know this is a big moment, but what do you want me to tell the armada in the harbor?"

"There will be no war. Not here. But don't hurry home just yet. I have a feeling the worst is upon us. This isn't over." Astriea replied. She then pulled away from Thomas again and found Morra, the head ladies' maid, outside the hall. She was covering her daughters in blankets and handing them water. Her heart beamed when she'd seen them alive. Mostly unharmed.

They made to get up when she approached, but she held out her hands. "Don't. Please, rest. Drink."

Morra bowed anyway.

"You banished that monster. Saved my girls... Thank you, thank you so much. Whatever you need, it's yours."

"I just need to know if the rooms near mine and Sera's are vacant?"

"Yes, my lady. There are plenty in that hall alone for you and your guests. The queen has retired to her tower to ready for evacuation."

"Evacuation?" she questioned.

"Yes, my lady, the heat has already risen, and the towers will soon fall."

Something like grief settled over her at those words.

"Do not feel sad for us, now that her Majesty is queen, I can write to my sister in Shadon, and tell her she can come home now. To Dartellio. That is where the true capitol is."

Astriea held on to that information and thanked the handmaiden with a bow before she left.

* * *

Back in her and Sera's room, she told the group of them everything that had happened. It took a few hours, but she crammed in every detail. Except for Killian. She told Thomas about him in private after the others returned to their rooms.

"Well, darling, have you been torturing devoted courtiers this whole time?" He asked her with a wild grin as she stepped out of the bathing chamber in a towel.

"How else was I supposed to have any fun?" She challenged with a pouted lip.

"Well, I suppose that means I have competition..." he said as he climbed out of his chair. He was behind her then. Towering above, just a movement away from touching her skin.

While she sat at the vanity and dried her hair with another towel, Thomas gently caressed a dirty, calloused finger across her bare shoulder and scraped it up her neck. He pulled his hands away and retreated into the bathing chamber.

Before he closed the door, he crooned, "I dare not soil such a clean and beautiful maiden. Tell me all about your godly power to seduce Telish men when I'm clean enough to remind you why *I'm* your favorite." He smiled brightly, winked at her, and shut the door quickly as she launched her towel at his face.

Her smile almost hurt the muscles in her cheeks.

When she looked back in the mirror, it *did* hurt her heart.

Sera was unconscious, with no word yet on when she might wake.

She bottomed out her power and needed to rest to restore it. But... she couldn't stop thinking about what it felt like in there.

Sera was gone.

The only thing she sensed when she cleansed her, was void. She couldn't sense Sera anywhere, and even now, looking at her own reflection was sending her thoughts back into the unknown emptiness.

But she was alive, breathing. *Sleeping.* She would wake up stronger than ever because that's who Seraphina is. And when she woke, Astriea would tell her everything. Everything about her father, her lineage.

But for now, Sera needed rest.

And then there was Thomas.

Thomas, who for all measures, seemed to be perfectly fine. *Too* fine.

Flirting and smiling like nothing had happened over the last eight weeks. That wasn't like him, not when the night had ended, and the doors were closed. Not when the armor came off.

So Astriea didn't give it another thought. She stood from the vanity and walked inside the bathing chamber.

He was already in the water. The room was full of steam. Heated himself, she assumed. But he was leaning back in the tub. His hands covered his face.

Pulling a stool up to the head of the tub, she tilted his head back towards her and gently poured pitchers of warm water through his hair. She sorted through an assortment of soaps and lovingly scrubbed them in before rinsing again. She picked up the washcloth and leaned forward to place it on his chest when his clean hand wrapped around her arm.

"I already handled that part..." His voice was a whisper this time. And she dropped that cloth when he tugged her closer.

Astriea wrapped her arms around his neck and shoulders. Resting her chin lightly atop the groove between them.

"What happened, Thomas?" She breathed against his neck.

He took a deep breath.

"I went to Monolith. It's... It's gone. The mountains, the town, everything. And—" Another deep breath and a four-second pause before he spoke again. "And I got yanked into a vision of... of the night they wiped our home from the maps. The night Zaniah called on us. Herold's soldiers butchered them all, worse even."

She shuttered.

She couldn't imagine. But Thomas didn't have to.

"When you're ready, lay some of the weight of it on me. I can see your memories if you wish it. But only if *and* when you're ready."

He squeezed her and traced his palms up and down her arms. With that touch, Astriea let free a disheartened breath.

"We're almost finished, love. Just one more continent and we're going to make Scythe wish he'd ended his existence to be with his family." And there he was, even in unimaginable pain, that part of him that saw the world with hopeful eyes shined through. "When this is all over, we'll live out lives we once thought only dreams. Seraphina will travel the world with *Vera*." He mimicked the queen's name childishly. "Damian might actually work up the nerve to go for it with Ula..." He paused.

"And us?" She asked him.

"You and me? Pshhh. We'll spend a few more decades of our immortality defending the innocent. Maybe exploring the world outside the dome. But someday, you and I will live in a big, beautiful house on the coast of a glorious island. Built into the cliffs."

"Ohh? Very nice."

"Yeah?" He asked, turning toward her a bit. She only nodded.

"Yeah, I think so, too. We'll have a library,"

"Of course." She agreed.

"Rooms for all our friends..."

"Sera would be furious if she and Vera didn't have a room with a balcony." She teased.

"She'll have one then." His grin lit up her world.

They laughed for a moment.

Then he whispered, and the hurricanes that were his eyes darted back and forth from her eyes to her lips. "And our children will dance in fields of wildflowers. They'll sing lullabies our mothers taught us and see us into our old age. Fat and happy and... overwhelmed."

"With what, Thomas?" Astriea asked.

"Joy."

That was when she realized she couldn't go on with how she had been. She almost didn't get a chance to tell Sera...

Wouldn't wait until it was too late to be honest with Thomas.

"Thomas... The final Breaking..."

He turned towards her in the tub. "You don't have to say it. I know what might happen at the final Breaking. You *did* manage to dispel that extra magic before it blew you to bits, though. Maybe you can do it again—"

"I don't think so... Thomas. For the wall to shatter, I have to pull it all out. Use it all to burn through the curse. To expel Zaniah and the other gods from their heirs. I don't know if there will be anything left of... me when I'm through."

He pressed his head to hers. "Then when it is time to cross that bridge, I'll cross it with you."

She made to argue, but he stopped her. "Before Zaniah, you thought yourself unworthy of anything. You thought yourself soulless. But I saw it every day. I saw it in the way you were kind to the children of Monolith. I saw it when you gave up your apartment to the Pearsons after they lost everything in that ice storm. Bet you didn't think I knew about *that,* did you?" He laughed the last bit at her look of shock. "I saw it in your list of marks. The type of people you targeted. I think *that* soul is strong enough to make it out of all this."

"And if it's not? I'm supposed to let you die alongside me?"

"If it's not... I don't want to love a soul other than yours. I want to journey through the stars, together. If it doesn't work out on this world, we'll just try again in the next. And the next, and the next. Until the *Immortal City* stands before us. I don't want a peaceful life if it isn't with you, *Starlight*."

Astriea didn't know what to think or say. So she kissed him instead.

"I've missed you, my love." She breathed onto his lips.

85

Astriea

Around lunchtime, Astriea still didn't try to get any rest. Instead, she climbed the many stairs to Vera's tower. Thomas trailed behind her, refusing to be parted again.

But midway up those winding stairs, she stopped dead in her tracks. The hairs on her arms rose and her stomach coiled.

A familiar type of alarm started going off in her head.

Run. Run. Run.

The only thing that now kept her tethered to her body was the warmth of Thomas's chest pressing against her back.

She forced a breath in that horrid quiet.

"Do you hear that?" Thomas whispered.

Sure enough, from the bottom of the stairs, she heard it. A low growl, ferocious and terrifying.

"It's coming up," Thomas said. "Go."

The two of them took off up the stairwell, and whatever beast it was, heard them. That growl she'd barely heard turned to a monstrous cry and she could feel its massive feet trailing behind them.

Astriea, go now! As fast as you can! Zaniah cried out.

Astriea didn't even have time to be happy to hear her voice again. She only ran and ran until Vera's door was in sight.

It swung open and Pilas was in the entry, his eyes wide with disbelief.

Astriea heard Thomas cry out in pain, but before she could turn to him, he'd shoved her through the door.

Pilas shut it the moment she was inside.

"No! No! Open the door!" She crawled to Pilas, who now pressed all his weight against it.

Vera was grabbing her arms as she stood and tried to throw Pilas out of her way.

"Open the door! He'll die—"

A flash of yellow and orange interrupted Astriea's cries, shining through the cracks around the door. Sweet, beautiful heat followed.

The growls stopped and Thomas fell through, blazing as the sun.

In a shuttered breath, he returned to his Fae form. Flames vanishing.

She was holding him up in a moment as he fell to one knee.

"There are more. Too many, even for Hellion to burn away. We have to evacuate *now*."

Vera nodded and grabbed Pilas by his wrist before leading the four of them back down the tower, to the lower level, and then through the secret stairway they'd taken the night they slipped away to The Mystic.

Astriea placed a hand on Thomas's shoulder, and he winced. In the darkness of the hall, she noticed a large, jagged gash across his back.

"Thomas—"

"It's fine. Let's get out of here and we'll worry about it later."

And the familiar dread of limping through dark tunnels beneath her old home flashed through her mind. Thomas taking a gash to his calf, and arrows to the back for her.

The words hurt her heart. If she wasn't so burned out, she could open a gate. Get them all out safely.

But that wasn't on the table right now. So she rallied all the false confidence she had and pressed on.

"What of Sera and the others?" She asked Vera at the front.

Vera only spoke to the guard at the bottom of the stairs. "Go to the healer's wing, get Seraphina, get her to the stables, and ride outside the city. Everyone is to evacuate to the coast, do you understand?"

The guard nodded and took off.

"Not very chatty, are they?" Thomas asked.

"They aren't allowed to speak to you," Pilas answered.

"Lovely," Thomas replied with an eye roll.

"Let's go. Pilas and I are going to get Killian and the Fates. Do you remember how to get to the stables from here?" Vera asked.

Astriea nodded.

"Good. Go there, ready as many horses that are left. Take two and ride the hell out of here. Do not ask questions, do not look for anyone. Ride out and ride hard."

Astriea nodded again and Vera turned away to leave.

"Meet us at the Western coast. Where your army now camps." She said as she left.

Astriea gave it no other thought and ran like hell for the stables.

* * *

The growling intensified as they descended yet another set of stairs. The looming darkness was untouchable even by the sun rays peering through windows.

She turned back to see Thomas limping along. His left shoulder dipped lower than the other.

"Are you alright? Can you make it to a horse?" Astriea asked.

"Yes. I'll be fine. Just keep moving. They're getting closer… I can feel them lingering."

But they stopped. Didn't move a muscle as every sound in the room was sucked out. An eerie quiet that did only one thing, *consume.*

"Thomas…" she whispered.

His only answer was his arm wrapping around her shoulders from behind, the tight muscles along his forearm pressed across her chest and pulled her closer to him.

"Will your light be anything against them?" He breathed.

"It would repel them, but only enough to buy us a few moments."

382

"And my flame?" His words were the only thing masking the sound of steel gently being pulled from its sheath.

"Your flame seems to be the only thing that hurts him or any of them."

There was a scraping sound, and Astriea's head whipped toward it. The dark was now so intense, that she couldn't tell if Thomas had heard it as well.

Her arms began to shake and Thomas squeezed her tighter. A warm, loving gesture of assurance.

He then did something else.

Thomas placed his sword in her hands.

It was heavy. Heavier than the one he'd had before, but the way it felt in her palms…

Some sleeping thing in her chest hummed. Purred at the feel of steel as she blindly stroked the blunt side of the blade with her fingertips.

She felt the smooth etchings along it. Traced them out one by one as if she had all the time in the world.

"When I say, move forward. I'll hold off all I can."

Astriea nodded, invisible and lost in the dark, but Thomas felt it even still.

"Go."

Without another word, the corridor erupted in a blaze of flame and Astriea was running—Thomas trailing behind. This time, only his eyes resembled that of the sun god. Wholly gold and glowing, as he turned his arms in circles before him. Twisting the surrounding flames into a cyclone of fire along the walls.

The worst was the beasts that tried to penetrate the heat. Slick, dog-like creatures. Only tenfold the size. Each of them dark as night and foaming black goo from their mouths as they chased them down and down the stairs. As they came from below them, too.

The vicious growls and barks were so loud she worried her ears would bleed. The sounds reverberated off the stone walls.

She raised her sword as one pierced the flames and lunged up for them.

With all her strength, she swung up and across as hard as she could—

cleaving the beast in two pieces as they ran farther, towards the stables.

Another came for them. This time, as she rammed her sword through its head, she heard Thomas grunt.

She turned to look at him.

"Don't worry about me, go!"

She swung her sword again, decapitating a hound, and pressed on.

Mere steps away from the last door in the stairwell, another broke through the barrier of fire and tackled them both onto the floor.

Thomas's powers sputtered out for a moment when he hit the ground. She felt him move to restart, but it was too late for that. She heard him yell as they threw him against a wall. Then claws scraped her thigh, her back.

Teeth dug into her—deep. A giant maw now wrapped around her shoulder.

Astriea screamed so loud her throat burned, maybe split in two, she didn't know. The drool seeping into the bite felt like acid.

But with that scream, a wave of light. Radiating and pulsing out of her.

The light burned the one biting her to ashes and made the other beasts cower. Made them run.

And before she knew it, the teeth in her shoulder were gone. Thomas was limping and dragging her body through the doorway, and while she seemed to drown in agony, darkness subsided to a cloudy sky with the stables now before them.

86

Thomas

Thomas carried Astriea to the stable house where the queen and her court were waiting. Just long enough for them to get there, though.

"I thought the two of *you* were supposed to get the horses?" Killian asked. Running over to them and reaching out to take Astriea from his arms.

Thomas looked at him with disdain and pulled away from his reach.

"We were a little busy trying not to die in your gods' forsaken castle!" Thomas shouted.

He could see Vera roll her eyes from across the way.

"And what a fine job you did of that. She looks half dead!" Killian spat.

Thomas wasn't sure how to explain the fact that those words made him literally pop his top. He felt flames rise from his head and the light of it flickered off Killian's silver eyes.

Looking into those eyes, he noticed something. They *changed*.

Shifted into that of a cat's, or maybe a snake's. Then reverted to their original.

"Stop showing your cocks and get me on a horse." Astriea moaned, clutching at her shoulder.

That heat in his chest died out at the sight of her in the cloudy light. Air stolen from his flames.

She had a gash of three claw marks across her chest, her leg, and her back.

Along with a dentition of holes stretching from just under her collarbone to the middle of her arm and shoulder. Black ooze leaking from all the wounds.

Thomas's ears popped, and sound was lost to him.

The picture of the world went fuzzy, but he could see everyone fine enough.

Killian tried to take Astriea from his arms again, and he yanked back. Astriea's hand was grazing his shoulder in soothing strokes. He looked at her and she mouthed the words, *It's okay. It's alright.* And he begrudgingly let her go with Killian to the horses.

"I can't—" He said as best he could and gestured to his ears.

Vera approached with a healer by her side, and they both looked Thomas over. His focus was on who he was pretty sure was Seraphina, still unconscious and being carried on horseback by one of Vera's masked guards, and on Astriea, with another guard just beside them. He saw her reach out and touch Sera's hand.

Vera's face, on the other hand, was laced with much more worry.

Can you do it? He assumed she asked the healer. The woman looked up at the sky and nodded. The queen watched intently.

Then, before his eyes, she pulled six droplets of water from thin air. With both hands, she spun the drops around his head, again and again and again, until the small bits became a ring. Glowing just faintly.

Within moments, his ears popped once again. Allowing a small fraction of sound to make way. He could hear Killian arguing with Pilas from ten feet apart. The heavy weight on his blood even loosened its grip on him. His breath became clearer, too.

"That is all I have time to fix for now. You will need treatments." The healer said, her Shadonian clear even with a thick Telish accent. More northern than most.

"Let's get going then. The Fates and the rest of my guard are arriving now." Vera said.

Their eyes caught.

And for that moment, there was only pride. Only ego and rage and the need for justice.

But he would not break the connection. Let her look into eyes long since loyal to Telas and yet butchered time and time again.

Then he did what he wished of *her*. When he took the time to look into her own eyes, to see past his rage, he saw emeralds with a slash of silver.

Thomas shuttered and took a step away from her.

Vera's brows furrowed, but she turned away and commanded her guard, "Get Seraphina, Astriea, and the Fates out of the city. Pilas," she called to her brother. "Accompany the King and Queen of Shadon. Ride as fast as you can, and do *not* get in my way."

"Ay, my queen." All fourteen guards said in unison, along with Killian and Pilas, as they all bowed their heads before taking off. The sound of it was almost a song, one he knew deep in his chest but could not place.

Thomas jumped onto his horse and waited behind with Damian, Draes, and Killian.

Getting out of the city would take a while, even riding at full speed. His eyes kept darting back toward the direction Astriea and the others were heading. The sight of her lost among buildings.

Everything went silent again. So much so that Thomas began fidgeting with his ears to make sure he hadn't gone deaf once more.

But Draes, Damian, and Killian had the same look as him. And the horses became uneasy. Stirring as if something horrid approached.

Then, every door to the castle, every window and opening made available swung out wide. Thousands of venomous hounds burst from every point.

"Shit!" Draes yelled. And the horses nearly bucked them off.

"Go!" Vera screamed from the distance.

Killian was the first to turn his horse away and take off. The rest of them followed behind him.

"You'd just leave your queen to die?" Thomas yelled as their horses jumped and weaved through cramped streets and homes.

Killian's only answer was a smile as the earth rumbled. As darkness flooded the sky above them and thunder cracked loud enough to wake the gods.

All four of them turned their heads back. All four of them stopped. Dead in the middle of the main street of the city.

The hounds followed them all the way here and now... Now they knew why Vera told them to run. Why she told them all not to get in her way.

That's when he saw it, a dark cloud of smoke and oblivion being led by a horse the size of ten. He honestly couldn't tell from the distance.

Black as night and swift as shadow, with a rider of blood-red hair and a blade in each hand. A bow across her back.

Queen Vera Shataar and Hypnia collided into an army of volatile beasts and even from here, they could see her standing on the horse's back. Could see her slicing through hounds. Their bodies destroyed and vanishing into Hypnia's abyss.

"It's true..." Draes said. His voice full of astonishment. *"Tzarina sa macta."*

Thomas watched Killian's head snap towards Draes.

"We need to move, now!" He said.

The four of them took off, flying as fast as their horses would carry them.

And there, nearly a league away, Thomas could see over half the guard along with James, Mira, and Seraphina, standing on a cliff outside the city. But...

Astriea.

She wasn't up there. And they—the others were waving their arms at them, pointing down below.

"Where is Astriea?" He yelled over the wind.

Damian and Draes broke from the diamond formation on his left and right.

"She's not up there?" Draes replied, his eyes darting across the city as they sped through.

Thomas only shook his head.

"We don't leave this place without her. Split up and meet at the cliff. Don't get caught in Vera's path." Killian said, sending a tang of relief and even resentment through him.

87

Astriea

The guard that carried her through the city refused to speak when she asked where the people had evacuated to.

Every home and business was empty; barren. Tools were left upon workbenches, glasses and goblets were left behind at pubs, a child's toy snow bear was abandoned on the street.

The eerie of this once joyful place, now left to dust and wind, was nearly as unsettling as the poison in her blood.

And by the time she tried to ask him again, she was so dizzy the ride was about to make her sick.

Crashing into the stone street didn't help matters.

A set of six hounds appeared out of nowhere, one colliding with their horse and sending them spiraling.

Astriea dazedly ran to her guard, who now lay unconscious in a pile of broken wood.

She pulled his sword from its sheath and steadied herself. Her swimming mind, her tumbling stomach.

In your nose. Zaniah's voice whispered through the chaos, through the poison.

She inhaled.

Out of your mouth.

Exhale.

Now.

She turned, and like a viper—she struck.

Dull Telish steel ripped through black muscle and tendon as she swung up, up, up.

Black ooze, rot, and death given liquid form poured from the beast as its neck split open.

She pulled away and rammed that sword to the hilt into another hound's skull.

Her feet were now bare and bleeding as she kicked its body off her blade.

She heard the others growling from somewhere unseen.

Her gaze darted back and forth, breaths becoming uneven.

Turn now! Zaniah shouted through her misty mind.

Astriea turned without protest and saw two hounds attacking at once.

She planted her feet against the stone and called on whatever power she could.

It is yours. Use it.

She searched and searched in the moment of time she had. The instant before the metal would only meet one foe.

And, like lightning, that energy—*her* energy—answered the call in a powerful wave. All barreling down the blade of her sword.

The Telish steel sliced through the hounds, both of them falling to ash at its touch. The sound of the strike could've made her ears bleed.

Holy shit.

She turned to face the other two.

They growled and snarled side by side, readying to take her down.

But her attention left the beasts quickly as she saw two riders charging in behind them.

A sun god, and an honorable pirate.

Thomas and Damian raced toward her and trailing after them were at least a thousand sickening creatures.

And the dark cloud... the piece of oblivion ripping through the city...

She had no time to look. Astriea ran to her guard, waking him and helping him to the center of the street, as Thomas sent a blast of fire at the beasts blocking their path.

She tried to help him remove his helmet, only to have her hands pushed away.

Damian grabbed the guard's arm and slung him onto his horse as he rode by.

Then Thomas swept her onto his horse with one hand. Easy and swift. The feel of his back against her chest, the way her arms fit around him...

She decided quickly that only terrible things could happen when they were apart. This was the only peace she could find as they raced through the empty city. The only peace she could concentrate on through the poison.

But she turned her head back.

Astriea watched as the tales of Vera the Vicious were suddenly confirmed.

The Queen of Telas cut through an army of monsters and fed their bodies to Hypnia's abyss.

88

Thomas

They arrived to meet the others at the top of the cliff in a rush. Astriea was barely conscious and now they all awaited for Vera and Hypnia to finish the hounds off. If they could.

Thomas rushed Astriea over to the healer who had worked on him earlier.

She began pulling the droplets of water from the air immediately while lying Astriea next to Seraphina.

"This feels like shit." She groaned. He grazed his hand softly against her cheek and kissed her forehead.

"You'll start feeling better soon, *Starlight*."

He turned back to observe the wreckage of the city.

No matter how many Vera destroyed, more reappeared.

He was so lost on the onslaught; that he didn't hear Lavene come up from behind him.

"What do you need us to do?" she asked, giving him a start.

"When did you get here?"

"I literally just jumped off Sand-snake." She gestured behind her.

He looked over her shoulder to see the serpent-like dragon pacing back and forth in the fields behind them. The snow already nearly melted and making way for green grass. Part of him wondered if bringing Lavene to Telas might've even *progressed* winter's end.

"They keep coming up. No matter how many she puts away." He said. Lavene didn't answer, though. Her gaze had now become lost on Vera, tearing through everything in sight.

"Killian! Call Vera out of the city! I'm going to cast a ring of fire and hold them in until we can find a way to kill them all."

Killian didn't argue and rode down to the gates. That alone was enough to tell him it was a decent idea.

Draes and Damian approached, the four of them huddled in a circle as Damian asked, "*Can* you hold a ring around the city for that long?"

"I can try. It's all I've got right now. Until the healers get enough poison out of Astriea to at least ask Zaniah, we don't have any other option."

Draes, Damian, and Lavene all nodded and stepped back.

Thomas waited until Hypnia's cloud of doom vanished and Vera and Killian came through the gates before he ignited that power.

A part of him so happy to be let free.

Burn, burn, burn. It begged. The sound was small and whispering like a child.

A ring of orange fire engulfed around the border of the barren city. Towering flame so high, only a dragon would dare tempt its boundaries.

"Alright, little brother, hold it up for as long as you can. The queen is here." Draes said.

But deep down, it was only a fraction. A tendril of power that only wanted to grow.

Burn it all, burn it all. It pleaded. Making it harder to hold back than it was to cast the ring in the first place.

No. He thought. *Now is not the time to burn it all.*

He could see the beasts cowering and turning away from all sides of the city. All of them trying to find places to hide from the heat.

Hunted! Hunted, the dragon was! Burn it. Burn it all!

Hunted by men who no longer walk this world. Hunted no longer. He replied. And the voice in his mind went silent.

The need to release all his power disappeared, and holding the wall of flame became even easier than before.

"Lavene?" Vera questioned loudly, almost shouting.

Thomas's attention was snatched away. The flames stood steady, though, even without his full concentration. He grinned at that.

"Good to see you again, Your Majesty," Lavene said shyly, bowing at the waist. Averting her eyes, but drawn to look at her.

"What are you doing here?" This was the most shocked he'd ever seen her. Not that he'd known Vera a long time, but it seemed Lavene *did.*

"King James has recognized Hesperia as an independent region of Shadon. We are allies now and... I've come to fight."

Vera tilted her head.

"I—I'm also the Heir of Tala."

And then Vera's jaw dropped.

Thomas looked back at the city to see his border still intact before asking, "I'm sorry. I've been so busy lately training dragons and holding up giant rings of fire around cities. Please elaborate on what I'm missing here. You two *know* each other?"

"We have no time for that now, Thomas. What can be done about the city?" Vera replied.

"I'm sure a lot of things, but your healers are working on Astriea right now. Until she can see straight, all I can do is *this* or burn it all down. That or Lavene could probably destroy them all in a massive earthquake or something of that equivalent?" He looked at Lavene.

"I mean, yes, I could do it. But, Vera, *The Silver City?* Where your mother—"

"Do it." Vera cut Lavene off. "Burn it and bury it. All my people are safe, so wipe it clean." Her eyes cut to where Seraphina lay with the other healers and back again to her fallen home.

Even Thomas was shocked by the order, though.

Stunned, actually. But not as much as Lavene was. The most surprised he'd ever seen her. And yet, no one's broken expression could rival Killian's.

"Father's body is still in there, Vera. Your mother's too." He argued.

It was Astriea who stepped forward, limping and leaning against her staff.

"Your *queen* gave an order, Killian. My power can destroy them, but only in extremely high bursts. A burst I cannot pull off right now. Thomas has proved that fire can hurt and kill them time and time again. If Lavene— hello, sorry to meet you like this." She interrupted herself to say but then went on. "If Lavene and Thomas both use their power, we might stand a chance of ridding the area of the hounds for good." She said as she moved past Killian. "With Scythe banished, they must be trying to get out of Telas."

The smile on Thomas's face began to hurt. Just seeing her up, her eyes filled with starlight and tenacity.

That's my girl.

She placed a hand on Vera's shoulder and said, "And your parents are smiling today because, on this day, you are *free.* Free to build a thousand more cities, *Tzarina sa macta.*"

A tear lined the queen's eye, but she lifted her chin and said, "Do it."

Lavene took her place a few feet away from Thomas, and the work began.

89

Seraphina

Her body felt so foreign. Even with her eyelids breaking open to see cloudy skies, not feeling like her own.

Maybe her soul wasn't her own either.

Maybe nothing belonged to her.

Her eyes were immediately damp, but she didn't move. Didn't shutter or stir.

Flashes of what he did to her, what he made her see, were nearly burned into her sight. She could see the way he'd strangle her in the clouds. Relive how he tortured and tore into her mind. How he'd stick pins in her soul and cut, cut, cut. How he...

But she heard someone, a voice she knew better than her own.

Two simple words: *Do it.*

Seraphina sat up and a woman in a pale blue robe that she scarcely remembered was trying to say something to her. She didn't feel like listening.

Instead, Sera rose to her feet on wobbly knees and slowly stumbled over to a group of people. Faces she *knew*, but at the moment, could not place.

The white-haired woman... the white-haired woman she definitely knew. Despite that, from this distance, Sera was certain that it wasn't the same voice.

The city they all looked at erupted into flames. It caught Sera's attention.

She stopped and watched thousands of homes burn. The air was so hot she started sweating immediately.

The man on fire rose into the air, and... and someone else. Branches and vines of every kind lifted a woman made of flowers and wood and stone. Protruding from the ground and wrapping around her as she rose.

The earth shook. Sera's mind with it.

She stumbled around and tried not to fall, steadying herself on one knee and looking again for the voice she'd heard.

Could only think of that thing that made her feel grounded, and secure. Strong and unyielding.

And there, almost glowing, were waves of blood-red hair. Unbound and freely billowing in the wind.

She was the only one to notice the golden dust connecting them. Or how that dust shifted and formed itself into a chain only she could see. Adamant as steel, as it led her to the woman whose hand was shaking at her side while she stood alone.

Sera was an arm's length from her now, and when she turned around, the eyes that faced her...

Shock in her lines, yes, but...

She'd never known such divinity, such dreams.

The woman held out her hand, and she took it.

Memories collided into her like the silver towers now crumbling in the distance. The world tumbled out from under her and Vera was reaching out instantly. Looping an arm around her waist.

That was when she felt hands on her back, her shoulders and arms too. Sera never hit the ground.

Astriea, Damian, and Draes had all been standing there, waiting to catch her when she inevitably fell.

She moved her gaze back and forth between Vera and Astriea.

"You didn't let him take me." The words came out in more of a sob. But gods, she was so tired she couldn't even care if she wanted to.

"Never." Astriea gripped Sera's hand, her lip shaking.

"Never." Vera agreed.

"You could've killed yourself. *Both* of you. He was hoping you had."

"I don't care. You have followed me at every turn. Came for me in the camp. You've trusted and sacrificed for me to no end. You are my sister and he cannot have you. I—*We* will not allow it."

They'd lowered her down. Her legs rested on the ground while Vera cradled her in her arms.

She remembered it all. Everything he did to her. All that he poked and prodded.

Everything he touched.

"How do I forget?" she asked, choking on air as Vera's expression broke at the question.

Green eyes filled with tears, and she pressed her forehead to Sera's. Sobbing, "I'm sorry. I'm so sorry—"

Thomas appeared. The flames around his body now sizzled out. And the world around her grew dim. She blinked away tears as something smooth and cool pulled at her eyelids to close.

She turned her head to see the fire in the city only raged for a moment longer as the earth toiled and tossed itself into nothing. Smothering the flames.

Seraphina thought about the destruction of the Silver City. And how Vera kept her eyes on her the entire time. Weeping for Sera instead of her home.

Rest now. Your spirit requires healing. I will keep the dreams at bay until you wake. Sleep, child, this battle has ended.

A soft male voice echoed into her thoughts.

Who are you? Are you the real god of death? Of the darkness? She asked to that voice. Maybe this would mean it wasn't *her*. That this power belonged to someone else and she need only to give it back.

No, little one, I am Mataephas, God of Dreams. I live far from your realm, but the Lightbringer weakened the barrier just enough for me to send a fraction of my power through. As The Fates do. Alyea was my friend, and you are her heir. I will seek you out when I am able. For now, you must rest. You must be strong a while longer, even against the pain you feel now. Because there is no returning the power. There is only taking back what was stolen. Sleep.

There was no argument to be had.

Seraphina's eyes closed, her consciousness floating away on a peaceful wave of sleep.

90

Astriea

In the quiet aftermath of destruction, all of Vera's fourteen masked guards gathered around them atop the cliff. Damian, James, and Mira went on high alert—hands reaching for swords and daggers—as well as Thomas and Draes, who immediately took up positions at Astriea's left and right.

Vera never moved. She still sat on the ground, holding Seraphina's sleeping frame. Her sobs had long since died out, but the look in her eyes—natural rage. Something that makes men quiver and set down their blades. That makes the sea rip across the world in violent bursts, or the earth swallow cities whole. At this moment, Astriea could see worlds burning under the queen's rage. *Vera the Viscous.*

Or more accurately, *Vera, The Fire Queen of Telas.*

And as quick as she saw it, she stifled the thought. Suffocated it.

The entirety of Vera's expression changed to void and vacancy as she ordered the healers to take Sera away to sleep.

She stood then and looked around at the group assembled before her.

"James Aurelius, King of Shadon, state your intentions with my kingdom now that Scythe has been banished." She asked. At that moment, Astriea realized that Vera Shataar was holding court for the first time in her reign.

"If the Kingdom of Telas poses no greater threat to our patron goddess, then there is no need for further violence," James replied.

Patron goddess?

Astriea noted the new crest stitched onto his, Mira's, Damian's, Draes', and Thomas's cloaks. A white star, with a set of silver arms and hands coming out of it. Holding James's golden crown between the latter.

"Telas not only poses no threat to the gods and goddesses but will aid in the Lightbringer's attempts to free the realms of Scythe's influence."

"I am glad to hear it," James said casually before he bowed his head to her. Vera returned the gesture. "Though you still have Tristan's blood on your hands. And while I did not know him, he was beloved."

"As well as the rest of the crew." A young woman interrupted. While something about her seemed familiar, Astriea couldn't quite place her features. She pushed her tight auburn curls away from her face and said, "If they live, we wish them returned to us."

The woman stood next to Damian and wrapped a hand around his arm.

Vera took a few steps toward the middle of the circle.

"I betrayed you." Everyone knew who she was talking to. "I lied to you. Told you I was someone I wasn't. Took your crew, hurt you all..." The sting of what she did was still there. Still etched into all their expressions. Even Thomas was an open book. Though there had been little time to grieve.

"I made a bargain with Scythe when I was a child. To protect my siblings from him. And like all contracts, there are loopholes. Sometimes Scythe's direct orders were not utterly specific..." Vera's head guard stepped up beside her and removed his helmet.

The gasps of air they all sucked in were nothing compared to the shimmer in Damian's eyes.

Tristan stood there. A boyish grin across his face.

"I'm not gonna lie to ya, mate, she had me for a minute there, too, I'd say." He said by way of greeting before wrapping his arms around Damian's neck. "Stabbed me in a sweet spot, she did. Lost 'nough blood to knock me out and make it look good. Then I woke up in this private estate up in the mountains with the rest of the lads—" He pulled away from Damian only to extend his arms.

401

The thirteen other guards removed their helmets, and the circle exploded into smiles and happy tears. Even Vera was smiling a bit. She had meant every word of not wanting to do any of it. She had lied and maneuvered her way into keeping them all safe. Keeping them all alive.

Korin quickly found his way to Tristan and lazily wrapped an arm around his shoulder before pressing a kiss to his cheek.

"I am so sick of dry land. Are we getting our ship back now, Queen Vera?" Korin boldly asked. His pale skin glistened in sweat as he wiped his forehead, his hair now cut shorter and revealing his slave mark. A scar that was nearly a decade old.

"Your ship didn't get as far as the lot of you did. But, if you swear to learn a new instrument to play every waking minute, I'll guarantee your safe arrival to the new one your captain has acquired for you. I'm sick of that pipe." She managed a strangled laugh as Korin placed a mocking hand on his chest as if she'd wounded him.

Then, Astriea realized where Vera had been those first few weeks when they'd gone days without her checking in.

She'd been checking in on *them*.

"When did you get here? I imagined she'd had her guard's tongues cut out so they couldn't speak, and you're telling me you've all just been standing right in front of us the whole time, being *extra cautious* not to talk?" Astriea said as she crossed her arms at them all.

"Come on now, my Lady Astriea, you can't stay mad at us," Tristan crooned and approached her with open arms. She rolled her eyes and hugged him tightly. "I suppose I can forgive you all." She said with a smile, and the cliff full of people she loved cheered.

"If it makes you feel any better, I didn't risk them at the castle until my most recent trip back from the healers. Couldn't chance Sera accidentally killing one of them trying to get to me," Vera replied.

"How many guards did she kill?" Damian asked, eyes wide.

Vera and Killian spoke simultaneously. "Forty-two."

Astriea saw Damian fight the smile that brought to his lips and had to suppress her own.

402

When everyone had calmed for a moment, Vera looked at Thomas.

"I am sorry for what my family has done to yours, Thomas, Draes. I wish to mend that in any way I can. My uncle was the one who hunted your parents. I never wished to take part in the Rite. Until I met you, I foolishly hoped I would never have to. Those Rites end today. And it would honor House Shataar to have your blessing in restoring our crest and station of our patron god, Hellion."

Thomas shifted.

There was still some anger lingering there. It was then she noticed Draes standing deadly still behind a couple of crew mates and James. Vera saw that glance toward him and sighed.

In that silence, Astriea broke the tension by stepping across the circle, taking Draes by his hand, and leading him to where Thomas stood in the center.

The queen said then, "Both of you are sons of Telas. And Telas failed you. Please, allow me the chance to remedy that."

Thomas and Draes looked at each other. The former fidgeted with his fingers until Draes placed a steady hand on his shoulder.

"Swear it," Draes said coolly. "Swear that the crown will protect the Hellion bloodline. Write it in your books, etch it into your walls—" his voice caught a bit there and Thomas finished for him.

"Whatever you have to do to ensure a brother or a sister," He glanced at the queen, only taking his gaze away from Draes for a moment. "Never has to sacrifice themselves to save their sibling again."

When Draes spoke up, it took everything Astriea had not to sob. Not to cry. But his gaze softened on Vera. His eyes seeing her in a light Astriea couldn't place.

"Your uncle... Your uncle found us in a small village off the cliffs. I had left Thomas alone while our parents were speaking with a friend in town. They caught me, and on the way home, your uncle caught the three of us. We ran as fast as we could, ran to get Thomas, to grab him and run again. But they were too close. My parents told me to go find my brother and hide while they led him away from the house." He took a deep breath and took a step forward. "I *heard* him. I heard him chase them and laugh. Laugh until that horde with him drove my parents off the Western Cliffs. I heard them scream, and I heard it fade, all before I could make it back to the house."

Thomas's face was smeared with shock.

I'm not sure how they died. Just that they left one day and never came back.

But Draes had known. Had known and kept that horror to himself, shielded his brother from it. Kept the rage for his own heart.

Thomas had never known what specifically happened to his parents, and now he did. Some kernel of flame ignited behind his eyes.

"I think, if you give her the chance, you will find yourself and Queen Vera not so different, Draes," Astriea added. Someone needed to say something.

"I think you may be right." Draes softly countered.

And maybe it was because of all the things Vera had proved to her. How she'd sacrificed herself to save them in the wastelands. That she'd kept her entire crew alive. That she'd fought for them, died for them even, against her father. Against Scythe.

Or maybe it was just because Sera loved her.

That she was an intricate part of Seraphina that went beyond the love of one lifetime. Maybe it was because, in those moments right before Scythe slit her throat when he had Vera on her knees before him. Seraphina stopped fighting. Stopped pushing against her restraints the moment she saw her in danger. Had given her life the way she was raised to. It was so much clearer now how Sera had closed her eyes and lifted her chin. She sacrificed it all for Vera. And Astriea would not let it be in vain.

More than any of that, though, perhaps it was because she'd never met another being who felt so similar to herself.

But Thomas's expression dropped. And before he could say anything, Vera stepped forward.

"I swear it. By the Gods and the council who stand before you now."

Killian made a step forward, followed by Pilas, the twins—Salrek and Dalron, and Caedyn—the young Keeper of Coin she'd only seen a few times. The youngest of the bunch, Nate and Thea, hidden far away in a safe house.

"Then we accept." Draes said quickly. Thomas only dipped his chin.

Vera's nod was acceptance enough, though she turned to Killian and said, "Did you get the bag I asked for?"

Killian handed her a large leather tote bag and she sat it out on the ground before her.

One at a time, Vera pulled out weapons.

Seraphina's dual daggers, her sash, Damian's hammer, and his whip, too.

"Sorry I'm just now getting these back to you. It took a lot to find them after Scythe confiscated them."

Damian grinned and thanked the queen before he attached his whip to his side and his hammer across his back.

Then, he took Sera's blades and sash to the small wagon she now slept in.

91

Thomas

striea.

That was all he could think about as they rode on horseback towards a set of cliffs exactly three leagues from The Silver City— a place he'd dreamed of and heard stories about. A place he barely got to see before they brought it all crumbling down.

He was sure the sight of it would haunt his dreams. While he and Lavene finished burning and tumbling the city, he'd watched, with everyone else, as the shimmering metal towers lining the cliffs outside the city broke and slid down the sides of the mountains. Some even crashed into the waves of the ocean so hard, the horses stammered their feet.

Vera now led them west on Hypnia.

Hypnia, that beast, was terrifying. Beautiful, but the largest horse he'd ever seen. Large and muscled and ferocious. Vera looked so tiny atop her, and yet, he'd already seen what she was capable of. What *both* of them were capable of.

You could fit ten of her on that horse's back, he thought. A swift kick would send even Night-cleaver an obvious message.

But then there was Astriea. Trotting along on a lovely silver mare. Part of him wondered how excited she might be to see Lijah and Finnick back at the ship, waiting for her and Seraphina.

He was stunned by her this morning. Vera had given her a set of clothes, a silver tunic and gray pants. New black boots, and gray dagger sheaths and belts. She'd fastened them on tight, and he enjoyed watching every movement as she did.

It was Thomas who'd found a cloak for her. A beautiful white fur. A few scratches of gray and black accented it. He'd wrapped it around her shoulders and pulled her close to him for the brief moment they had before leaving the camp this morning.

And how it felt when he'd kissed her...

Thomas nearly groaned just thinking about it.

Astriea turned her horse from Vera at the front and rode down the line to the back. Where James and Mira were, where all the royals were except for Vera, who led the caravan with Seraphina still sleeping in the wagon everyone kept guard of. Lavene lingering toward the middle of the line of horses.

However, Astriea barely stopped anywhere near him for *three* hours. Would only smile at him now and then as she passed. So worried about Sera that she couldn't keep still. Thomas couldn't help but feel sorry for her poor horse. But eventually, he reached out and gently snagged her arm as she passed by him.

"Give your horse a rest, love." He said, and he couldn't tell if she was blushing at him when she smiled, or if her face had windburn. Either way, her cheeks were pink, and she inched her horse closer to his. He slid his hand down her arm and laced his fingers between hers. She dropped her reins for a moment to pull up her hood.

But she didn't speak. Didn't really look at him either. And then the moment came when he realized she was actively trying *not* to look at him.

Finally, Thomas tugged her hand to his mouth and kissed it.

"Why do you keep trying to get away from me?" He whispered.

She looked at him then, and this time it wasn't windburn that reddened her face.

"I..." she stuttered.

Oh, so it's serious? He thought.

"We can't talk about this *here*, Thomas." She whispered back as she tore

407

her eyes from his. She tugged her hand, but he pressed her palm onto his chest under his cloak.

Her breath hitched when he leaned over and dragged her hand up his neck.

"You are killing me." He whispered. Their horses had stopped, and everyone else kept going around them. Killian tried to divert his eyes but failed.

James snickered.

"You're all dressed up in Telish finery and all I can think about is tearing it off, so I can keep you warm all by myself." Not to mention every time she rode by him, her scent intoxicated him. A new one this time, the smell of jasmine and lavender filling his nose and nearly dragging him off his own horse.

The way she looked at him then. How she leaned closer and pulled her hand to the collar of his tunic and gripped it. He swallowed hard.

"With the way the heat is already rising, I might not need all the *finery*, anyway." She repeated his word back to him in a breathy tease. It *was* warming up, but at the moment, he couldn't tell where the heat was coming from.

"I don't think I can make it two more days. I don't even think I can make it to James's base on the beach." He said. And Astriea breathed on his lips, "Why do you think I've been trotting up and down this damned caravan all this time?"

Then she kissed him.

Thomas dropped his reins and grabbed her cloak, pulling her as close as he could while wrapping a hand around her waist beneath it. Her hands wandered up his neck and into his hair as her mouth parted for him. He swept his tongue across hers, and for a brief time, they just had *that*. That unyielding connection that never abandoned them.

Before things could escalate further, James shouted from the top of a hill just south of them, "Alright, you two! Get a move on before you get left behind!"

They broke apart. Chests heaving. But their eyes never left each other.

Thomas couldn't stop thinking about her eyes. Bright blue and streaked with silver. Couldn't stop thinking about the *want* in them.

The need.

He wanted to satisfy that. Wanted to watch her eyes roll back, hear the sounds she made, feel her nails cut into his skin—

The thought was cut short. Astriea finally pulled her eyes from his and took off.

She turned back and gave him a wicked smile as she rode up the hill.

So Thomas took up his reins and raced after her.

92

Thomas

Five long hours of riding later, they made camp in a clearing. He hadn't thought the distance too extensive when they rode into the city on dragon-back. But the fjord was enormous and while he rode across the cliffs surrounding it, he noted the difference in timing when traveling through the skies versus on land.

Now, the sun was readying to set when Thomas walked into Vera's tent.

"Thomas," she called out, her tone friendly and inquisitive, "what can I do to help you?" She asked, shocked to see him there.

He stood there awkwardly for a moment. Trying to figure out a way to ask the question he had without sounding foul.

Lavene burst into the tent without warning before he could further embarrass himself. She looked shocked to see him there, but her eyes were only that wide for Vera lately.

"Oh. Sorry, I didn't realize you two were speaking now. I'll come back later." Thomas and Vera both made to ask her to stay, but she was gone before either could.

"Okay, how do you two know each other?" he asked bluntly. Vera assessed him for a beat but said with no small amount of tension, "I've known about *Hesperia* for a while. Since I was fifteen, actually. Lav and I met at a banquet my mother brought me to on a southern island. It was all very hush-hush. No one was to speak of it because of Scythe."

"Alright…" He drug the last syllable of the word out.

Vera looked back at her map, awkwardly. Only breaking her gaze for one quick glance at Thomas to see if he bought it.

His jaw dropped slightly. "You were lovers!" He guessed. More excited than he honestly should be.

She sat forward and raised her hands up and down twice. "Shhhhh! Do you think either of us wants the entire camp to know our first loves just popped back into our lives? You think I want Sera dealing with that when she wakes? Keep it to yourself until I've told Seraphina, then do what you please."

"Fair, fair." He raised his hands in surrender.

Vera dusted some invisible dirt off her chest. "Now, what is it you came in here for?"

"I know, tensions are still… high, but I just wondered if—because you know the area—if there may be any private, *romantic* sites nearby?"

Vera knew what he meant immediately and seemed to bite back a laugh. But she composed herself and said with a smile that seemed genuine, "There isn't much near here. Not that you can get to on a horse—"

He stopped her.

"My dragon comes when I call."

She grinned.

"Sit down. I'll draw you a map."

93

Astriea

Thomas returned to their tent with a wide smile and pulled her into the fields outside. Where *Night-cleaver* was rustling their wings against the grass.

Astriea's breath hitched.

It was massive. Glittering under the starlight like obsidian in crystal clear water. Their giant head had two odd-shaped horns that eerily reminded her of the snow-beast in the Northern Wastes.

She wondered if there even was a Northern Waste anymore.

She took slow, shaky steps toward the magnificent creature and held out a hand.

Night-cleaver looked at her, its giant golden eyes dilating in and out, observing her. Then it laid its long neck and enormous head on the ground before letting out a contented huff. She opened her palm and held a small bit of starlight to guide her way.

Thomas was right next to her then, cradling her glowing hand in his, the light shining on both their faces.

The way he looked at her. His expression was so serene. She could've stared at him all night.

"You look as if you've seen the Immortal City." She joked.

"I have no need of Heaven, only you." His breath was a welcome embrace against her lips.

She became lost on them, only an inch or two away from her own and all she could think of was tasting him again.

"Climb on," Thomas said, pointing to Night-cleaver's saddle. On his back was an entire pack of supplies. Blankets, food, extra clothes, weapons too.

She gave him a worried look, but he held out his hand to her after he climbed on and suddenly, it was like the roles were reversed.

Once upon a time, she'd held out her hand to a boy who feared heights, to climb a mother oak tree with her. Now that same boy was all grown up and helping her climb onto the back of a dragon.

Gods, his eyes were perfect. The light in her hand illuminated him in a way that made her heart quake. Every line and dimple that appeared with his smile sent tender ripples across her skin.

He was bigger now. nine weeks had gone by and Thomas barely rested for a moment of it. That she could tell.

Not only was he taller—his transformation now seeming to be nearly complete—but his arms, his legs, gods, his *shoulders...* They were tight and, and... *thicker.*

His jaw and face now had the makings of a closely-trimmed beard. Like he hadn't decided if he liked it enough to keep it yet.

But Astriea liked it. Loved it.

All of it, of him.

She took his hand and gently walked along the dragon's back to the saddle strapped to it.

She sat down and Thomas settled in behind her. Her spine tightened as he pulled her closer to him. Against him.

"Hold on here," he placed her left hand on the left leather handle, "and here." He placed her right on the other. His chest pushed against her back as he leaned her over. He removed his hands and kissed her cheek as he shifted back. Grabbing onto his own handles near her waist.

Two sets, a pair for both of them.

Astriea looked back to see Thomas close his eyes. Not a moment later, Night-cleaver's mighty black wings rose into the crisp night air.

* * *

Take off was scary. She could admit that.

But once Night-cleaver's wings caught onto the cool breeze and they glided over the clouds, she felt as if it was all a dream.

The moon was full, bright, and beaming across the sky.

And *the stars...*

She sucked in a breath and fell back into Thomas's chest. He wrapped his arms around her.

Above them, the stars that were once hidden behind the clouds over Telas were the brightest she'd ever seen. Millions of them shining on them. Gods, she felt like... like she was *healing*.

Thomas took her right hand and showed it to her.

"Look, *Starlight*." He whispered into her ear.

Sure enough, Astriea was glowing. Silver and white. That burned place inside her seemed to cool in her chest until a friendly voice echoed in her mind, *What a lovely night to fly.*

Astriea gasped. *Z? Gods, Z, I was so worried. You did it, you healed Sera. Scythe took her body and—*

I know. Don't worry about that now. Bathe in the starlight. Breathe. Heal yourself and then we will speak. For in this moment, this new day, the world is not at risk of breaking.

Astriea nodded and smiled as she said to Thomas, "Zaniah is back. She's awake."

He smiled at her and said, "Would Zaniah mind giving us the night to ourselves?"

Before she could even think the thought, Zaniah said, *I am already going.* Astriea could feel her roll her eyes. *You know where to find me when you're... finished.*

"She's given us our privacy." Astriea laughed to him right before she swung her left leg over the saddle and slid herself closer into his lap. The wind died into nothing but a gentle breeze and Astriea could feel the warmth of his chest on her cheek. She looked up at him and put a hand behind his neck, in his soft black hair.

And kissed him.

Kissed him like she'd wanted to for all these weeks they'd spent apart. Like her life depended on it.

But... guilt made her pull away. He looked at her curiously and tilted his head.

"I broke your trust when I kept you from Draes."

"Astriea, don't. We already talked about this. It's forgiven, and I overreacted anyway—"

"No, no, you didn't overreact. I've spent my life feeling damaged. Worthless. Like it should've been me who died. Or... or that I was such a craven I couldn't even die with them. That when I said yes to Zaniah in her prison, it was an effort to avenge what I'd lost and prove to myself that... that I wasn't a coward."

"When you ended things between us, back then, it was because—"

"Because I didn't think I deserved you. I thought I would ruin you, hurt you over and over and you would keep letting me. And when Draes disappeared... I thought it was only a matter of time until you would too."

"Look at me, my love. There isn't a thing that could be ruined by you. Not to my eyes, not to my heart. My place is at your side."

"There is a difference between putting my heart on the line and putting someone else's. I was so consumed by my grief and need to avenge Raja's death, to avenge Monolith, that I was willing to let Draes die for this cause. Seraphina too. And then myself. I was willing to break your heart and my own. And... And if that is the cost to free the realm, I cannot pay it." She took a deep, shuttering breath. "I can't bear to lose them, to lose you. I can't bear to see you look at me the way you did that night in Triscillia—"

Thomas kissed her.

"There isn't a *thing* that could be ruined by you, *Starlight*." He repeated. "We aren't normal people with normal lives. So I get it if either does something insane or fucked up. We *are* pretty fucked up." He laughed, and she echoed it. "But at the end of the day, it's me and you."

The hateful part of her, the one that still whispered of love she didn't

415

deserve, eagerly seized the first opportunity to voice her fears after those words were spoken.

"I have laid every flaw and darkness and broken part of me out bare onto the table in front of you and instead of running... Instead, you build me armor out of it. I don't deserve you."

"Marry me," he said, placing a hand against her jaw, fingers tangling in her hair, and his thumb sweeping across her cheek.

"What?" she asked in a breathless gasp. Heart sputtering in her chest. Time felt the same. But his words brought her back.

"Marry me, and I'll never stop building that armor for you. Marry me and we'll explore every corner of this big new world together. I'll hold you every night and kiss you before leaving any room we're in. I'll bring you soup when you're sick and climb giant trees with you until we're old and hobbled." They both laughed.

Then, he said, his words beautiful and smooth, "Marry me, and I'll put a piano in our house. Marry me and I'll help you write out the music to all the lullabies your mother taught you. Marry me, and you can play them for our children someday."

"I may be a little too heartless for the piano and children these days. I don't know if I have room for it."

He laughed a bit before going on. "You try so hard to seem heartless. And you put up a good front, that's true, but someone with no heart wouldn't have sacrificed as much as you have for other people. A heartless woman wouldn't have stopped taking higher paying clients so they could focus on finding innocent girls being taken in the night. You sometimes forget that I have seen your triumphs, too. The ones that came before all of this. So, lay all your fear on me. I can take it. I want to take it. Marry me, *Starlight*."

"We kill Scythe," she said.

"We kill Scythe." Thomas confirmed.

"And then you're stuck with me forever, *Hellion*."

His smile put the stars above them to shame, and he kissed her with a soft laugh on his lips.

They only broke apart to grab hold of their restraints as Night-cleaver plunged down and landed on a set of tower-like cliffs. Four of them varying in height and each shaped like a hexagon. They landed on the tallest one and Astriea was stunned to see at least twenty steaming pools below them.

Hot springs.

94

Thomas

Thomas climbed off Night-cleaver, his thoughts screaming in excitement.

How that all just happened. How happy he was. The original plan was to ask her on the ship when they were all supposed to come to Telas together.

But things didn't work out that way.

He always knew he'd marry her.

Even if it took him a thousand years, he'd marry Astriea Blake.

He'd wanted to do it the moment she came limping into the tzar's throne room.

But... timing.

Then, when Vera said there was nowhere to go *by horse*, the idea sprang back to life. Now they were climbing the steps to the tallest cliff.

At the top were three massive springs—large holes in the ground, filled with hot water and surrounded by moss and grass.

The water bubbled lightly and warm steam wrapped around the entire top of the island cliffs. There was a large wooden canopy near a small spring. It had tables and chairs and couches for lounging. All the cloth and curtains were made from some kind of material to handle the wet conditions and flapping against the breeze.

He spent a little time unpacking their bag and laid out blankets and pillows. Even set out some food while Astriea walked all five edges of the towering cliff.

When he turned to look for her, she'd just shed her cloak. Breaking a sweat walking around and now her tunic and trousers clung to her skin. His chest tightened and his blood heated. He threw off his own cloak in an effort to relieve himself.

Thomas casually walked over to her. She looked up at him and he gently tugged her closer by her sheaths. Carefully unfastening each one.

All five of them.

Then, before she could reach down for the small, hidden blade tucked under her corset, he pressed her to his chest and gently pulled it out.

Like he'd ever forget where she hid her reserve dagger.

She backed away from him as he was about to lean over and kiss her, and walked to the farthest hot spring. He watched her kick off her shoes, watched her unbutton her pants, and toss them away. She turned away from him to pull her tunic over her head. He was already removing his boots, his weapons and sheaths.

She turned towards him then, letting the starlight shine a dull haze over her bare skin in the steam.

"You gonna help me in or what?" She mocked.

Then Thomas was moving. He pulled off his shirt on his way to her and tossed it aside.

He jumped into that spring, pants still on. The water was hot, but nothing for him, really. All he cared about was holding out his hand for the starlit woman to step into the pool with him. She took it and eased into the water.

He wasted no time after that. Thomas pulled Astriea into his chest and kissed her wildly. His hands were on her hips, and his tongue twisted with hers. He grabbed her ass and squeezed before wrapping her legs around his waist.

Then he pushed them, and Astriea's back, against the side of the pool— the smooth rock nearly polished. She reached for his pants and tried to unfasten them, but couldn't.

"Why didn't you take them off before you got in?" she asked, rolling her eyes and kissing him between words. Already almost breathless.

Thomas quickly pulled his belt open and peeled off the pants, before tossing them out of the pool, while saying, "Sometimes you make me stupid. It's fine, I brought spares."

Then his mouth was on hers again.

He roamed his hands all over. But there was this one position of his arms... When he'd wrapped one arm around her back and up her shoulders, and the other wrapped around the back of her hips. When held her like that, it *hurt*.

Hurt his soul itself, and he had no idea why. It felt like heartbreak when he held her like that. So he touched her everywhere else.

He cupped her breasts and flicked his thumb over her nipple while his tongue danced with hers.

She arched her back to the touch. Pushed against him. His length was hard and throbbing, begging him to have her.

Thomas lifted her out of the water and onto the edge of the pool. Running his fingers down the wet skin along her back and placing tender kisses down her chest. Then he gripped onto her hips and stroked his tongue across her nipple.

Astriea gasped, and the sound made Thomas go rigid. His grip tighter on her waist, he flicked again.

Again.

Again.

Her hands were in his hair as he softly laid her back on the moss. Kneeling in the pool, he took her thighs over his arms and kissed the inside of them in teasing little pecks.

The gasp that came from her when his tongue swiped across her sweet middle did nothing but make him want her more. So he flicked his tongue in and out again and again. Pulling out the tip for a few moments at a time, to brush against the bundle of nerves that made her twitch when he played with them.

With one hand, Thomas gripped her breast, flicking her nipple with his thumb. With the other, he held her right thigh as her legs threatened to close around his head.

Her fingers tightened in his hair, chest heaving in ragged breaths.

She cried out when she came. Her legs closed around him hard and released soon after *she* did.

Astriea pulled him out of the pool and he crawled up to her.

She pressed sinful kisses up his chest, his neck.

"I want to live in this. Like this, twisted in each other's arms." She whispered. "I want nothing else, just you."

He leaned over to kiss her again, but she pushed his chest up. He didn't even have a moment to think about the rock digging into his knees before Astriea's mouth was around him. Her tongue danced circles around his cock as she took him as far back as she could. His breaths grew faster, his toes curling as she approached the edge. Threatening to drain him of all he had.

Those circles... Those circles she made with her tongue had him at her mercy.

Thomas quickly laced his fingers into her hair and yanked her back.

She wiped her chin and their lips collided once again.

He laid her back on the ground. Rolling around in moss while they savored the taste of each other.

Then she placed her fingers around him and his own eyes rolled back a bit as she stroked. Before long, she was positioning him at her entrance and they both gasped a bit as he slid inside, inch by inch until he was buried deep.

She gasped as he stretched her.

"You feel like heaven," he breathed against her neck. "And sin." He thrust, seating himself more deeply inside. Her grip around his arm tightened.

Astriea moaned as he slid out and back in again.

He started slowly, his entire body begging him to unleash himself.

But he needed the time. Needed the moment to just be *present*.

To be aware of her skin pressed against his. Of how he pushed against her walls. How her beautiful lips parted to breathlessly moan his name.

He pulled himself from her and sat back on his knees before flipping her over and backing her onto him again. Astriea moaned as she seated herself and pressed her back to his chest. He pressed into her slowly now, savoring every bit of her he could touch as his right hand wrapped gently around her throat and his left worshiped her hip and thigh.

Her grip around his arm intensified with every brutally slow stroke.

"Are you going to come for me, *Starlight*?"

"Yes." She moaned. And gods if he couldn't feel it when she did. When her walls started gripping him so much tighter than before...

"That's my girl, just like that." He breathed against her ear.

After that, he just let go. Thomas turned her around and laid her back against the ground before he slammed himself back inside.

All he could think about was how her middle gripped him, how he stretched her open. Harder and harder.

Faster.

Until she was moaning his name again and her back arched once more. Until her nails were slicing into the skin of his shoulders just as he'd imagined. Her other hand holding a tight, tangled grip in his hair.

Until her breath was ragged and she was dripping down him. Flames whipped around them both. Raising higher with every breath he devoured.

Then he found release.

Tension flooding out of him like a broken dam.

95

Astriea

Thomas collapsed onto the pallet of blankets he'd set up for them. Even though they weren't being used how he seemed to think they would.

They'd quickly washed themselves in the springs and now lay naked under the stars. She sat there and admired him for a while. The way he slept with his fist balled under his chin. As if posing for a scandalous sculpture.

She watched him take in deep, peaceful breaths. Gods, he was so handsome.

And he'd asked her to *marry* him.

She couldn't stop smiling at that, no matter how hard she tried. She would be his *wife*. He would be her husband.

They never really needed the formality of it. He never really needed to ask. Astriea would follow him anywhere. Be with him all her life. And she knew he felt the same. Her heart thundered when another realization came to her. That she could have a thousand or more years with him before they pass. He'd asked her to marry him and she knew what that meant: to force their friends into watching them be horribly in love for the next two to three thousand years—if they managed not to get themselves killed.

She chuckled to herself and tossed a grape into her mouth.

Am I interrupting? Zaniah asked softly.

Astriea sat up a little straighter and answered, *Not at all. I'm just enjoying the view. Oh gods,*

She covered her eyes. *Can you see him through my eyes?*

No. Astriea.

She lowered her hand and opened her eyes while letting out a sigh of relief.

I can see him all the time.

Well, keep your eyes to yourself. Astriea thought back with some attitude.

I don't see how that's fair. It's not like either of you ever offer to check out for a bit and let Hellion and I have a go.

Astriea's jaw dropped open. Her eyes went wide.

Zaniah!

That's not my name. She sang that bit. *Just go to sleep so you can come to the garden and see what I've remembered since you completed the second breaking.*

Alright, I'll be there. Give me some time to wind down.

Didn't take Thomas long. Zaniah said a little playfully.

Well... Astriea searched for something to send back but came up short. She just let out a proud grin.

Zaniah laughed a bit and Astriea's mind became silent again.

She laid down atop Thomas's arm and stretched. Pulled and tugged at all the muscles she could under a cloudless night sky. It took an effort not to let her power slip a bit. She didn't want to start glowing again right as they fell asleep.

Thomas rolled toward her and pulled her closer to him.

There she drifted away, wrapped in a firm body and warmed from the cold by him and the steam.

* * *

The garden was twice the size it had been before. The homely path, now a cobblestone street imbued with shimmering stones. Leading up to a greenhouse that would've now towered over the one before. The statues were larger too and made of gold this time. She hurried along until the giant greenhouse doors were upon her and pushed one open with all the might she had, before stumbling inside.

Zaniah was waiting for her there.

Her skin glowed that lovely shade of gold. Her hair so white you almost couldn't see it at all. Like there was just a hole in the universe where her hair should be. Her gown was made of thin sheets of white silk. Her breasts pressed well against her by a golden corset frame, and small golden chains held the dress on her shoulders. The chain in the middle even bore an emblem; A simple sun charm. Gold like the chains, but an ordinary little sun dangled from her neck.

Zaniah saw this.

"Do you know why I fell in love with Hellion?"

"I'm guessing because he's so handsome?" Astriea said while cutting her eyes at Zaniah.

She dipped her chin and gave a *look.*

That *could you shut the hell up* look.

Astriea obliged.

"I remember who I am. However, much of my memories from my time in this world are still a haze. There are questions I should know the answers to, but don't." Her furrowed brow revealed her confusion toward the issue. But Astriea did understand that feeling. Missing pieces that you shouldn't.

"Zaniah, that's still amazing!" Astriea started. But Zaniah raised a hand, and she silenced herself.

"Alyea and I were here long before the universe sprang forth. We were like small children, clutching to each other so tightly, trying to find our mother or father. Trying to find anyone like us. But we never did. We are the only two of our kind. My sister and I traveled through the paths between stars before souls did. But slowly, over time, the lanes became flooded with them. All smashing into worlds with no regard for the damage it could inflict. My sister and I realized that she and I had no mother or father. No one to shelter us from the unknown. For I was the *Lightbringer,* she who would bear all life. And my sister... my sister, the *Harbinger of the*

Dark. She who all souls find eternal rest."

"Life burst forth quickly. I started to understand that I was unknowingly creating mortal souls. If life exists, it will persist. But all had strenuous lives before I started trying to perfect their forms. Aberrations that rarely even housed a soul. So about twenty-five thousand years ago I started creating mortals capable of housing souls."

"The universe is only twenty-five thousand years old?" Astriea asked.

Zaniah laughed at her a bit but said, "No, Alyea and I wandered for a long time before we even learned how to use our abilities. But still, ours is a young universe."

Then she touched the sun pendant and smiled.

"I met many sun gods. They were my charges as well. I'm not called *Keeper of the Stars* for nothing." Astriea smiled at that. "Before long, I started tinkering with gifting mortals with magical abilities in *this* world. Hellion and the other minor gods helped me. I'm not sure what, exactly, caused the elemental gods to wake. My sister believed that using my magic to create mortals must have woken them. But those gods would only emerge thousands of years later when I would already be on my way to the next. But I did return. That has always been something I pride myself on, that I always come back and help if I'm needed. Until I got here…"

"I asked Alyea to help me come up with ideas for the mortals here. Give some of them longer lives, give some of them magic, make their ears longer so they can hear better, their eyes slightly bigger so they could see a great many things… Alyea suggested the extended lifespan. She believed mortals lived such brief lives, that they never had enough time to sort through the damages on their souls. Didn't have enough time to heal. It would take at least two thousand rebirths to purify the soul if they only got to live a maximum of one hundred years."

"So… humans have to reincarnate *that* much to make it to the Immortal city?"

"Unfortunately, yes, it was something I was working on before my capture. In my realm above the stars, *The Immortal City*, souls live in paradise for eons. But… all souls must rest. Eventually, my sister comes for the eldest souls and they happily go with her."

"Where? To her realm?" Astriea asked as she sat down on a loveseat nearby. Zaniah nodded and went on.

"Alyea's realm is called *The Silent City*. You've been there before. It can be quite terrifying for a soul who is not yet ready."

Astriea shuttered at the memory. Of the dreams in the dark. Trapped under ice. Until… until Thomas pulled her out.

"*Hellion*, he wasn't like the other sun gods. The rest were very serious and hotheaded, as is their nature. But Hellion… He was more than just power and heat. He was… warmth. His core like a hearth. He cared deeply for the mortals of this world, and in the heaps of battle was the only time he ever seemed the warrior *type*. Other than that, he was funny and kind. He brought me little gifts when we first met. Never really stopped, actually. Glittering stones off the backs of comets, a crown of diamonds he formed in his hands with sunbeams and brute strength, and my favorite gift: *Dragons*." Zaniah was smiling. "He brought this lifeless little form to me, scaled and gray and unmoving. It had been earth shaped into clay by Tala, water to make the clay and for the blood from Rala, flame from Hellion to harden it, and *I* was the last step. He'd told me that this creature would roam all over the world as living monuments to our love. He said that one day when this world had ended, he would forfeit his soul to the Immortal City. That he would be there waiting for me."

Astriea was smiling at the lovely story. But something before shot to the forefront of her mind.

"How did Thomas find me there? In her realm. If Alyea is our sister, then I understand how I can wind up there, especially with the dark magic injections I was given. But how did Thomas access it?"

"Thomas found you through a bond I am sure you've only heard of," she hinted.

"You mean… Thomas and I… We're *Soul-bound*?"

"Not yet. Becoming *Soul-bound* is a rare and difficult accomplishment. It only comes to people who have loved each other with pure hearts in previous lives. Growing stronger and stronger as they find each other again and again. It requires each person to not only entrust everything they are to the other, but it requires a level of forgiveness and devotion that few are capable of. You cannot only accept the other as they are, each of you must accept yourselves as well. The day that you believe with all your heart that you deserve Thomas and he deserves you, that is the day your souls will bind. You have already chosen each other. There is only one step left."

"So... he found me through that bond?"

"Both of you entered the dream realm at the same time, and when you cried out for help in Alyea's realm, he heard you. Followed your presence and pulled you out. The *Soul-bound* connection is a powerful gift for a soul, but a strong disadvantage to the living. Vera and Seraphina will never have to reincarnate again. They will come to *The Immortal City* when their time in this world is finished. Live in peace forever, until their souls are ready to rest. But... *Here*, they will feel the other's pain. Vera is holding herself together considerably well, but Sera is in pain and I guarantee she feels every bit. They will live like that for the rest of their days. I have not seen a *Soul-bound* pair able to fight through each other's pain since before I came to this world. It is not a good thing that they have bound themselves so soon. When war and death and evil threaten us all so greatly. I would recommend you not pursue the binding until Scythe is defeated."

"I think we can wait until everything is over. We'll try, anyway." Astriea said a bit grimly. "But what I need to know is how we can get ahead of Scythe."

"I cannot tell you that. I gave most of my divination abilities to The Fates, a way to lighten my load a bit. But, my Fates channel Morra's daughters. I saw they traveled with you in the caravan?" Zaniah asked.

"Yes, they're at camp with Vera. And they all seem pretty... horrified. I'm not sure they'll want to help."

"Unfortunately, they won't have a choice. The Fates will guide their paths to where they need to be. If it is by your side, they will be there."

"Will they ever be free of them?"

"Yes, when the dome is destroyed. They fight for my freedom. They will not surrender or stop trying to bring the walls down."

"Am I going to survive this? Will I even get the chance to marry Thomas?" Astriea's voice shook a little when she asked. But the words were out. It had been an unspoken understanding they'd had all this time. That a mortal cannot hold a High God, cannot contain it. She knew it was why the transition had been so difficult. Thomas had been right those months ago. *What if that power drives you mad, too?*

"I wish I could say yes, Astriea." She dipped her chin.

It made sense.

"Did you know—"

"Why you said yes without hesitation when I offered you this path?"

Astriea nodded.

"I knew you did not wish to survive this. I knew it was part of your plan. To free the world and join your family in the stars."

"If you knew, why didn't you stop me?"

"Because my sister and I are the oldest living beings in existence, and I know how it feels to be *so* tired. To be ready for the end." Zaniah paused. "I never meant to split my soul in a *last-ditch* effort to save myself, Astriea."

"You thought that using your own power might..." Astriea muttered, then looked up at her.

"My sister was the kindest being to exist. She was gentle with every death, every soul. No matter their living offenses. She believed no one should ever be alone in the dark. So she ensured that none would be. And he... he tortured her, mutilated her. I thought—I even thought he'd—" She stopped. The goddess of all creation took in a deep breath before she moved past that part of the subject.

"But most importantly, Astriea, I did not stop you because I knew you needed this path. You needed Thomas, and Seraphina, and Damian. You needed to find James and Mira. Needed to free a slave named Amir, and a princess named Vera. I knew this path would make you *want* to live. Because your heart is mighty and vast, yet more heavily guarded than any castle or fort. You needed people to fill it."

"But now I will lose them all. I'll die in the end, Z. I'll die and it won't matter that I no longer feel pain or that I'm in the Immortal City, or that I might not even exist at all anymore. All there will be is the pain and grief I leave behind for them. I understand now that I am loved. I understand I deserve to have it. But how can I feel anything but selfish when I know what pain is coming for them?"

"You could tell them." She replied. "You said you didn't want to keep things from them anymore. Thomas and Vera already know. What is stopping you?"

"If I tell the others, they'll insist we find a way around it—which we don't have time for. Or they'll try to stop me from doing what I have to."

"And those are decisions you must let them make. Because those choices don't belong to you, Astriea."

The words halted her. Slammed into her like bricks.

She was right.

It's not up to her what her friends decide to do. They'll do everything to save her, they would never stop trying.

"I guess I can't stop trying to live, then."

96

Thomas

When dawn broke the next morning, Astriea was sleeping peacefully in Thomas's arms. Her bare skin shimmered under the steam, and small beams of light peered through the fog. Her white hair was a bit frizzy, and he chuckled under his breath at the realization that nothing could make her less breathtaking. Even when her hair didn't agree with the climate.

He laid his head back down and gazed at her for a while longer. Squeezed her closer with his left arm and used his right to caress his fingers up and down the skin along her waist and hip.

Last night she'd told him she didn't believe she deserved him.

Thought herself unworthy and a coward.

But he wished she could see herself the way he saw her.

Wished she could've seen the girl who had a million problems of her own, but showed up for everyone else before herself.

The woman who rescued children, who gave her services away for free to those in need. The woman he loved was someone who saved every bit of coin she had, to buy a gravestone for her parents, instead of a steady place to live.

He knew now what he always knew. That Astriea Blake was never cold or vain or hollow.

No, she was just a girl that needed to be loved, so afraid of it being taken from her, she hid who she really was from everyone.

She hid how kind and curious she was. How brave and resilient. Hid the parts of her that longed to travel the world, meet new people, and try new foods.

But what she never hid from Thomas was how deeply she cared for him. She'd *tried*, but he always saw through whatever front she'd thrown up.

That used to drive her crazy and was always a little funny. But he was glad that part of their relationship was over now. He was glad to hear her tell him how deeply she loved him. Over the moon, actually.

"I don't wanna go back," Astriea murmured into his chest.

He glanced down, and she pulled her head back to look at him.

"This is rather nice," he said, laying his head back down and squeezing her. She wrapped an arm around his waist and grazed her fingertips up and down his spine.

"Vera did say that they were packing up at first light. We're already running late." He begrudgingly stated. Honestly wishing he'd just gone back to sleep and found the lot of them later. But Astriea groaned and rolled onto her back before raising both hands above her head and stretching. He swallowed hard. The sight of her and the fact that it was morning had him hardening in an instant. Her breasts peaked as she arched her back through the stretch, legs crossed.

Thomas wanted to spread them open.

Wanted to dine on her like he had last night.

As she rolled onto her stomach, a sunbeam caught her face and she soaked in it for a few moments. Thomas ran a hand up her thigh and cupped her ass as he passed over it. Then he ran a single finger up her spine. She opened those beautiful eyes to the sunshine. To Thomas.

She was smiling at him when leaned down to kiss her. He whispered onto her lips, "I don't wanna go back either."

Astriea kissed him. Dragged him closer with soft lips.

They both sat up on their knees, still lost in the others' kiss, their touch. Breaths rapid and panting, she pushed Thomas onto his ass up against a beam holding up the cabana. There, she straddled him. Her mouth was on his again and as she pressed her tongue onto his. As it swept over, she ground her center against his cock.

The grip he had on her hip and thigh tightened. He pushed his other hand from the side of her neck, up into her hair. Gripped it hard enough to expose her neck to him as he planted small seductive kisses up her skin, before whispering in her ear, "Hungry this morning, my love?"

"Starving." She replied and wrapped her pretty fingers around his cock. Stroking him up and down... He released her hair and wrapped his arm around her waist. She gasped when his mouth met her nipple. When his tongue circled and flicked. He moved to the other, and before he finished, Astriea pressed him into her entrance. He sighed against her chest as he inched into her.

Warm and soaking, she eased down onto him.

When she was fully seated, he ran his hands up her back and squeezed while pushing her down just a bit more. Forcing a cry from her lips.

The sunlight lit some kind of fire in her eyes, something burning there that fueled her to ride him like she'd never get the chance again. And to relish in every moment of it.

She pushed him against the cabana, and moved up and down until his grip was so tight he worried it might hurt her thigh.

He moved his hands to her waist as they came together. Astriea cried out one last time as he pulled her deeper onto him. Neither of them released each other for a while.

In fact, it only took Thomas a few moments before he was gently pulling Astriea's head back by her hair. Peeling her skin from his just so he could lean down and run his tongue along her nipple.

He heard her whimper at the touch, and he felt her middle tense, too.

So he moved, grinding himself deeper inside her as he stood and pressed Astriea's back against the cabana log.

Tongues and teeth found whatever they could and she cried out his name again and again as he fucked her against that post.

Now, hours later, he could still feel the ache in his chest from their labored breathing. Even after bathing in the hot springs again, he could still feel her essence like a second skin. As if they were still pressed together.

James clarified that he and Damian packed up their tent for them. Since they were so late. Saddled their horses and hooked them to a wagon as well.

Thomas was sure to thank his friend, the pirate, and his friend, the king. He'd given them a big smile and hooked an arm around their necks. Playfully yanking them down.

"Alright! Alright!" James yelled as he and Damian broke free. "I had hoped our lovely Astriea might have tamed you a bit on your *excursion.*"

Thomas grinned and gave them a nod as he said, "She certainly did."

97

Astriea

Astriea's horse, *Titania,* trotted at an even pace up the road with the caravan. Most of the time, she stayed near Thomas, but whenever she could tear herself from him, she'd ride up to the front with Vera.

"How are you feeling?" She asked her quietly, looking up at her from where her very much shorter horse walked beside Hypnia.

Vera did not try to turn toward her. She simply shot her gaze at Astriea for a moment and replied, "I feel as if I only have one lung. Like I will never have enough air again. He tortured her. Even if it only seemed like a few minutes, he—"

"I know."

Astriea stared at her and remembered riding side by side with Sera on their way to Triscillia.

Sera had asked her how she knew Thomas was *it.* She remembered what she told her. It wasn't something that she would've told Vera, but it was something that made Astriea look back at Thomas. At his handsome smile and intoxicating laugh.

It was something that made her lean a little closer to Vera and place a hand on her arm.

"She will wake, and it will be hard. But she is the strongest of us. Scythe will not break her."

That seemed to give Vera some morsel of comfort as the horses made to climb a magnificent hill.

Twenty-one ships lined the coast just beyond them. Each of them was made of beautiful light wood with massive white sails flapping against the breeze. The largest at the front—James's ship—was lined with silver railings and posts. And the figurehead… A beautiful woman—carved to Astriea's exact liking—leading their way and lifting a staff in her left hand.

She could've cried at the honor. James left her no time to, though. His hand startled her as he patted her shoulder.

"My Lady Astriea, would you do the kingdom of Shadon the honor of becoming our patron?"

"James." She staggered for the words. "You hardly know me."

His brows furrowed, and he tilted his head before smiling at her.

"I may not have known you as long as Thomas has, or as well as Seraphina does. But you were granted the power to free us and wasted no time. Thomas and the others may have scolded you well for leaping forward headfirst, but every moment we waited to act, more died. More suffered. You understood that better than anyone. Zaniah herself probably let you have it as well, I'm sure." He looked at her, the statement being more of a question.

"She did." Admitting that was a little irritating.

"But Astriea Blake is *Shadonian*. Her family fought for the well-being of our country for generations. Died for it, even. She walks on silent feet and calls herself a spy, but she is so much more. She, gifted with the light of the goddess, set us free."

Mira appeared on her other side, then.

"She is a fighter." Her golden tiara glittered atop her stunning black curls, and then Damian circled the group.

"A giver, and loyal friend." He smiled at her. And in an instant, they were all around her. This crowd of people she'd never intended to love.

But here she was, being showered in and overwhelmed by it. Apprehension flooded through her in sickening waves. Suddenly, she was living through a nightmare. Like this was an intervention of affection.

"Defender. A hero's soul, through and through." Thomas nearly purred. Grazing her arm with a hooked finger as he passed by her. James and Mira rolled their eyes.

"Captivating," Killian said from his horse across from them. Thomas immediately turned toward him and summoned fire into his hand.

"What part of '*I will fucking roast you*' do you not understand?"

Killian waved his hands by his face and rolled his eyes in mocking surrender, making everyone laugh.

"Compassionate, even when she doesn't want to be," Draes called out, easing any residual tension.

"And sometimes when she shouldn't be!" Toni from the *Ruby* crew called out, making the whole of them laugh harder.

"Don't you laugh over there Korin, I'm talkin' about you! Ya really think she likes that thing you call flute playin'? Should've left it to Tristan!" Toni rattled again, and the laughter amplified.

The tone became grim, though, when Seraphina hobbled her way to their group of horses, still pained from her encounter, but more silent than ever. No one heard her approach. No one saw anything out of place. The horses didn't even stir. But there she was, below her. A hand now wrapped around Astriea's.

"My greatest secret keeper."

Astriea's heart locked up.

"You deserve to be celebrated. You could have held on to your power and let him take me. But that was not an option for you. You lent all you had to Vera and saved me instead." Sera's hollow eyes were heartbreaking, and her breath shuttered as she said, "You do not know the gravity of what you saved me from."

"Yeah, Astriea, let us admire you," Tristan called, arms wrapped around Korin's shoulders.

The rest of the crew laughed and spurred him on.

But she couldn't do that. She couldn't lie. Not now, not anymore. Of course, she saved Seraphina. In what world would she have let him take her? In what world would she have backed down?

But it wasn't the small victory of the day looming high in her mind. No, Astriea was confident she would succeed in the final breaking. Two out of three continents were already free. Now, all that's left is to free Sirey. To break the dome and release the primordial and elemental gods. Release them from their mortal hosts.

But she would not survive it. The blast of magic set free would rip through her. The only hope being that some sliver of her soul might survive it. Even if that hope was mere.

It was all but confirmed now. Zaniah didn't tell her to stop her friends from looking for a way out. A survival plan. But she didn't encourage it either.

And now, she was surrounded by people who loved her. Accept her for everything she is, aside from her role as Zaniah's Heir. *This* was the reason. The reason she pushed Thomas away and guarded her heart so tightly. Because if she gave it even an ounce of freedom, it would not be enough. It would never be enough to live a life giving a fraction of herself. If there were any doubt in how they all felt for her, it'd be easy to continue the lie and die without telling them. But there was no doubt. Astriea was sure that even Vera—whose eyes frowned at her with pity—cared for her enough to do everything to save her.

Through the laughter and rambling, Sera's eyes never left Astriea. Her brows knitted.

"I'm going to die."

Seraphina sucked in a sharp breath, and the surrounding laughter dissipated.

"What do you mean—" Damian started.

"I mean... the last Breaking will kill me. The dome around our realm will fall. I will free magic—Zaniah will be freed as well as the other gods from the heirs—but I... I will not survive it." With the words spoken aloud, a wave of anger boiled behind them. "The final blast of power will kill me."

"This has been confirmed? Zaniah has told you this?" Thomas said. Eyes she couldn't even look into.

"She has given me no reason to look for alternatives."

438

She heard him shutter. Then his hand found hers. Calloused fingers wrapping around her own and giving a loving squeeze.

"We will find another way. Anything—" Sera's face, her tone, everything about her was vacant.

"Try all you wish, but I will march to Sirey. I will free magic and the gods. I will bring down the dome. But then it is up to you to kill Scythe, while Zaniah rebuilds her immortal form."

"Seriously? The plan, right now?" The sudden hint of grief now on Sera's face was accompanied by irritation.

"She will be at her most vulnerable during the transformation. It should only take a few minutes, but Scythe will throw everything he has at you, or he will escape into a free world."

"So we protect Zaniah and when she's returned, she can resurrect you," Thomas said hopefully.

But that was somewhere Astriea couldn't go.

"When Zaniah is restoring her form, you kill Scythe. It will be your best chance. When there is the most light in our world."

She tugged on her reins, and Titania pushed forward. Leading Astriea away from them all.

She heard his exasperated sigh as she left and thought to herself, *No, Thomas. There will likely be nothing left to resurrect.*

* * *

Hours later, she sat at the beach, dragging a stick through the sand while Vera, James, and Mira all discussed further plans of action on the king's ship. The rest of their traveling party lingered on the edge of the bay, glancing at her now and then. Each of them struggled not to walk over and say something to her.

Doing their best to give her space, even if it was only twenty yards of it.

Seraphina was walking more steadily now. Pacing back and forth between Damian and Thomas. Draes watched her the whole time, as if waiting for her to collapse, though she didn't.

Thomas made his way over and sat next to her in the sand.

"I know you're upset, but there is someone here with us I think you should meet."

"Someone else I can let down? I think I'd rather not hurt any more people today." She took a breath. "I never wanted to get this close to them, Thomas."

His hand wrapped around hers as she still avoided his eyes.

"You can't do that."

"And why not?" She snapped her head towards him, eyes like a summer storm on this very ocean washing over her.

"Because even if we can't find a way out of this, you have to keep loving, keep living and caring. If you are bound to die... You deserve the family you've created for yourself, even if you didn't mean to do it. And I will be there every step of the way to make sure your heart is full when you go. I just need you to let me. Let me offer you the peace of knowing that you were cherished in this life when you journey on."

"You're not going to convince me to take the time to find a way out?"

Relief flooded her. And heartache.

"I will not risk our last days together being anything less than an epic tale the gods would write into scripture."

She had her plan, and now she had Thomas at her back.

"Then we need to get a move on. I expect Vera to return soon."

"You can try all you like to avoid them," He nudged his chin toward Sera, Damian, and Draes. "But they're going to try. We all will. You know that."

She did. Astriea only nodded.

"And they won't be letting me run headfirst into anything, either." She confirmed with him.

He nodded back.

"Unfortunately, we have other pressing matters here. I brought a hundred dragons with me. I just gave their riders orders to search the country for signs of any others. Hellion told me to return to my homeland and wake the dragons here. I can't leave until I do that."

"So we'll be sticking around a bit, then?"

"I'm afraid so. But, there are many things to show you, starting with—"
He stopped at the sound of mighty wings pounding overhead. White as
the brightest light of Zaniah's realm. A tear in the universe given the form
of a dragon. She squinted her eyes and noticed an iridescent shimmer
radiating around it. Coming from every scale and strip of tight muscle
layered beneath them. Ivory claws dug deep into the sand as it landed just
behind them. The weight of its body made the earth shutter, sending nasty
little waves crashing against the ships closest to the shore.

She didn't even realize she was standing so close when Thomas called
out, "Astriea, don't! They don't enjoy being startled!"

The dragon's head snapped toward her. Large white horns spiraled off
the top of its head, and its eyes...

They were silver.

Not silver like Killian's—now muted rings of silver instead of filling the
entirety of his eyes—but glowing silver like the streak through her own.

It narrowed its gaze on her before vigorously shaking its back, throwing
its rider straight to the ground.

She tried to pull herself from the trance so she could run to help the
white-haired man on the sand, but it was no use. It completely enthralled
her.

Another step and the dragon's nostrils flared.

"Astriea..." Thomas called nervously.

But she braved another step, and it rested its head on the ground.

She let out a breath of relief and stood before its snout.

The top of its nose was twice as tall as she was, but Astriea placed a single
palm upon the smooth, shimmering scales.

From the place of impact, a wave of energy pulsed. Rippling through
the water and blowing sand everywhere.

It felt like being connected to everything. For only that moment, Astriea
could *see*.

Could see the pathways between worlds.

And small orbs of light racing down each one. Some in groups, and some alone. Every one of them all reaching their destination.

Worlds upon worlds upon worlds.

And just past the paths, a realm of every color known and unknown. Towering castles of ivory and alabaster—marble and gold—resting atop clouds. All surrounding a mighty city.

She wanted to look closer, to see who was there. Get the chance to know where everyone else would end up.

But as quickly as it had launched her soul into the cosmos, she was yanked back down.

Back into her body, where her hand rested on a dragon's nose.

She gasped a deep breath and a smile burst from her. A tear even fell from her left eye.

"Astriea, are you alright?" Thomas said, helping the white-haired man up. As if no time has passed.

"Did you see that?"

"See what?" He replied.

She shook her head and rubbed her temples.

The overwhelm will fade soon.

A voice, feminine but *not*, said into her mind.

Zaniah? Is that you?

No, I am not Zaniah, but you needn't worry. I can only communicate with you and I am not very fond of talking. It is draining on the mind. Much easier for us to communicate with each other and our riders with an emotional link. It is strong enough on its own—once established—for us to push our thoughts out through emotions. They never know exactly what we say, but they feel us deeply enough that our thoughts become their own. It is especially useful in aerial combat. The emotional link can give dragon and rider an extra set of eyes, and faster response times.

Astriea couldn't help but wonder if it was disrespectful to a dragon to stare so hard her eyes hurt. Because that's what she was doing. There was no word for the type of stunned she was at that moment. Having a mental conversation with a dragon.

Why did that just happen? Who are you? Astriea asked, well-versed in this particular brand of social interaction. Her head tilted as she admired the massive silver eyes in front of her.

Mortals cannot understand our names, so we often are called by the meaning of that name. I am Light-Reaper. You named me upon my first breath, many lifetimes ago.

She felt a smile tug on her lips, one that felt as though it belonged to Zaniah, but it was welcome all the same.

So you're here for me? She asked. *You already have a rider.*

When the lightning struck, when Thomas and yourself were found by Zaniah, the first sign of the rising rippled across the world. When young Hellion fell into his grief at the eastern cliffs of Shadon, it sorrowed the worldly twins—Rala and Tala. They each heard his plea and responded. Rala, wherever she may be, sent mighty storms and hurricanes crashing against every coast. Tala—her sister—crumbled the mountains. Cracked open the earth and set us free. Night-cleaver was the only one of us on the eastern coast of Shadon when Tala took us one thousand years ago. She sheltered us all these centuries and the moment I was free; I set out searching for you. This one was all I found. But I made do with your uncle until he brought me to you.

Astriea's breath caught in her throat.

"Uncle?" She questioned Light-Reaper out loud. Pulling her hand away and stepping back.

Her eyes went directly to the white-haired man standing next to Thomas.

He approached her cautiously as if she might not be real.

His eyes were silver like the dragon's, his skin paler than hers, and he was massive. At least seven feet tall and beyond sculpted.

Honestly, she was frightened by him.

If he hadn't looked so nervous, she might've been terrified.

Yet his face... The shape of his eyes and how familiar they were. If the iris had been a golden color with specs of black, they would've been identical to her mother's. Astriea let her imagination take hold for a moment. Imagined this man before her with golden tawny skin and hair like the night.

Yes... The picture was becoming clearer now. Where his cheekbones sat on his face and the way his chin pointed.

He stood frozen before her, just as unsure as she was.

"You look just like her—" they both blurted out simultaneously.

Her heart dropped, but only a smile appeared on her face.

It was a call to your bloodline. Any that may have survived.

"A call strong enough to breach the dome?" She asked Light-reaper out loud.

Scythe has always been too proud for his own good. All of his spells were built on bloodline curses. While he built defenses against the use of magic, he only ever blocked out those specific curses enough that no one could interfere with his own, and so that he himself could continue to practice them.

"They said that Zaniah sent out a call to my bloodline, to aid me."

"No one knew what it meant at first, but… Atara—your mother—she felt the call long before you took your power. She knew she was needed and…" He sniffled a bit. "And I am happy to know she was loved and cared for here. I am happy to now have the chance to know *you.*"

For a split second, his soul reached out to hers.

Not anything visible, but a feeling of peace and joy and even a little grief reflected onto her. She didn't give it any more thought before stepping forward and hugging him. Her arms were barely wrapped around his waist, the top of her head level with the bottom of his rib cage.

When his giant arms wrapped around her, she released a disheartened huff.

"I thought there was no one left." She said against his tunic.

"I do not know of your father's family, but there are many in ours. Elders mostly, but you have cousins close to your age and grandparents—"

She pulled away and looked up at him, her head tilted all the way back to see him.

"*Your* grandparents, do they live?" She sucked in a breath. "Does your grandmother have a garden?" The words were almost too hard to voice. To ask.

Please let it be real, she pleaded to herself.

"Nana has the most beautiful garden in all of Masari."

Nothing could stop the tears, then. Or the sobs against his chest. And while some small part of her felt like a pathetic child clinging to an uncle she just met, he'd given her something she hadn't had in all these years.

Hope for the world her mother had always promised her.

98

Astriea

Hours later, Vera, Mira, and James came back to their horses on the beach and stated that the entire party would stay in *Dartellio*, which was technically the country's capital.

While Thomas searched for more dragons and trained more riders out in the Southern Plains, Astriea and Seraphina would work on their wielding, and the rest of the group would try to find the other god's heirs and a way to beat Scythe without Astriea losing her life.

It felt foolish to wait, but they all needed their rest, and they needed to be ready. Ready for anything Scythe might throw at them.

Vera made the argument that Sirey has been known to keep trespassers and never let them return home. Any who have ventured into Sirenian territory were never seen or heard from again. She recommended that they all tread very carefully when breaking the Sirenian throne. While the child emperor was young for his rule, rumors spread quickly of his strictness.

That he found it a great disrespect when his rules were broken. Merchants weren't even allowed to step foot on shore. The Sirenian fleet would meet them off the coast and make their trades out there.

So, Shadon's fleet followed down the coast while Vera led her family on horseback across the Western Cliffs and south toward Dartellio. Astriea and the others joined them with a trail of dragons flying overhead. All of

446

them dispersing in twos in different directions.

Four days later, they came upon the final stretch to the city, a massive hill, inclined so steeply, that Astriea nearly had to lean completely forward just to stay somewhat seated in her saddle.

It took them about half an hour to reach the top, but when they did, Vera cleared her throat and announced to them all, "Welcome to the western port and capitol, *Dartellio.*"

Astriea looked out at the sprawling city before her. Cobblestone streets ran in a hundred different directions. Children played, kicking a ball and laughing.

From this far out, she could see the newly assembled farms, budding fields of wheat, cattle, and blank pastures with nothing in them—though already turned and ready for planting.

All the snow in the city, on the farms, was nearly melted. Green grass peeked through the slush. Ice dripped off of beautiful, pink-leafed trees. Even Vera seemed a little stunned. So much so that she moved closer to her, and her eyes never left the sight.

"It was beautiful before, but…but this."

Astriea placed her hand on Vera's and gave it a squeeze.

"This is only the beginning."

A massive white palace at the top of a cliff overlooked the city. All of it sloped down the cliffs and opened up to the ocean. That was where she saw Shadon's naval fleet, anchored outside the harbor.

Thomas came up beside her.

"I've asked Night-cleaver to keep the other dragons away and safe. I'll call on them when they're needed. For now, they'll be searching for others."

She nodded and Vera led them forward, through the streets.

Though, Lavene rode forward—her horse trotting happily—and gently raised one hand into the air, a hue of green radiating from the tip of her index finger.

Roots rose from the ground quickly and within three blinks, a large tree stood along the path next to them. Its branches sprouting beautiful green leaves and bright red apples.

Lavene plucked one and handed it softly to the queen. A half-smile upon her face.

Astriea squinted and made a slightly disgusted expression but shook it away before anyone would notice.

Vera took it and dipped her chin as she moved her horse forward, taking a bite of the apple, and a deep breath.

Before they went into the city, Seraphina woke more fully and even rode the extra horse that waited for her. Staying just slightly behind her love as they went in.

Townspeople quickly stopped what they were doing and bowed as Vera led their way. Recognizing her immediately.

More gathered and lined the streets in moments. And it only took one street more before the air above them was filled with white flower petals. She looked down to see their source. Children lined the spaces beside their horses, carrying baskets of petals and tossing them into the air. And more lined the streets themselves, making sure to shower Vera before falling in line behind their friends.

Killian tugged on her arm and said quietly, "This is her redemption ride. It has only been done once before, but the histories are better kept here." Then Killian quoted, *"The true Queen of Telas will pass through the gates and ride up the spinning road. She and those who follow her will be bathed in light and washed clean."*

"Washed clean? What does that mean?" She asked.

But it was Zaniah who spoke to her then, *Of everything it took to get here. She is redeemed.*

"Never mind." She said lightly to Killian.

It had been a lovely ride through the city. Though, she could admit, her favorite part was riding through the food district. The aromas that drifted towards her were so seductive she'd nearly jumped off her horse.

Killian leaned back from Vera's side and said, "Don't worry, the best chefs in the city work in the palace when we're in town. And there will be *loads* of food to choose from since we'll be having the coronation here. Hasn't been done here in centuries—a thousand years, they say—so everyone will be celebrating."

Gods, another coronation. She didn't want to do that *again.* But she thought it would be a good idea to at least present the royal line with something. If word had already spread about James's crown, they'd probably expect it. The people of Shadon had been raised with the legends of the Child of Prophecy. Would accept nothing less than the goddess herself appointing the new king. But if she could sit this one out...

"Do... do they expect me to perform it? The coronation?" She leaned over and whispered to Killian.

His brows rose, and he laughed.

"No, of course not." His laughter grew. "We have a holy sept that handles those affairs. Traditions and such."

When his laughter died down, he noticed the look of relief on her face and said, "Damn... They made you do the coronation for *Goldie* back there?"

Her eyes cut to him and widened. She smiled when his jaw dropped.

"Brutal." He gaped.

Thomas appeared at Killian's side a moment later, so quick and quiet that Killian flinched as though he'd appeared out of thin air.

"Hello, Killian," Thomas said cheerfully. "What are you up to over here?"

Killian's eyes went wide for a moment, and Astriea tried to decipher what series of events might unfold as they trotted along. Now traveling along a stone street that curved and twisted up the cliff to the palace.

But the demeanor on Killian's face shifted into a mischievous grin. He made to ride back to Vera's side, but not before he looked back and said, "Just keeping my lady, Astriea, some company. *As always.*" And then he was gone before Thomas could respond.

She tried hard to hold back the laugh.

"That little—" Thomas started. Obviously pressing his tongue against his teeth.

"Don't even start," she interrupted. "You came over here and toyed with him. You're just mad he toyed with you back." She laughed.

He smiled at her before kicking her foot and riding off before she could smack him with her reins.

99

Seraphina

The ride up to the palace had been like something from a fairy tale. The white alabaster walls towered above the city that lay at the base of the black stone cliffs. Over one thousand years, the people had chipped and carved into the stones. Shaping cliffs into a spiraling road, up and up until they'd reach the gates. And at the top would be this place that she had never been.

This place that she somehow knew or *would* know. They passed along at least a hundred stores and cafes—carved deep into the surrounding walls along the spiraling road. Vera even stopped and bought her a piece of fresh honey bread, smeared with sweetened butter.

Seraphina took a moment while she enjoyed something so simple and delicious, to note the excitement on all the faces of the royal family. Salrek, Dalron, Pilas, Caedyn, Nate, and even young Thea all followed behind them and took up sweets from a vendor next to the bread shop.

As if the world had slowed for only her, she saw the light gleaming in their eyes. She saw the shells of grief and pain they had carried these many years fall from them. She put her eyes on Vera, whose own were closed. Her head tilted up as if to take it all in, to breathe in the goodness of this place.

Then there was a shift. Vera's skin was now slightly sun-kissed. The rest of them, too. Like the light had finally reached them, or they had it.

It did not matter.

The regular pace of things returned to her as the earth shook beneath them. Not violently, but as if releasing a mighty breath.

They all looked around, and the people in the shops surrounding them took to their knees before Vera's intimidatingly magnificent horse. It honestly took everything in her not to touch Hypnia, but something else made her stay her hand.

"Tzarina sa macta." They said, again and again as they passed by. *Our Queen reborn*, it meant. Astriea said they saw things; learned things about themselves in The Mystic.

She trotted up to Vera.

"Are you the queen reborn?" Sera asked in a whisper.

"Yes," she whispered back.

Sera's eyes shot up to meet hers.

"Tell me the story?" She asked although some part of her had already heard it. Already knew it before she took her first breath.

"The first ruler of Telas was Tzarina Vaerah, who fell in love with death."

Their hands found each other.

"The Silent Sister of the Goddess, Astriea, who could not speak. Before the dawn of Vaerah's fifth year of rule, Alyea was taken by Scythe. Hidden away and…. hurt. All of Telas's might was thrown at the Dark sorcerer. Vaerah herself rode into battle and fought him off long enough to see a small piece of her to escape him. And by the time she died on his blade, her throne had been usurped, but her greatest love had gotten away. To live on, again and again."

"You are Vaerah," Sera said. Confirming.

"Once."

"I am Alyea."

"Yes." She answered.

"This is where you were crowned the first time?"

Gates of spiraling silver vines, towering at least twenty feet above them, opened to reveal the loveliest courtyard. Perfectly trimmed patches of grass separated only by the white stone paths leading in multiple directions.

452

Beautiful marble sculptures of men and women in Telish history were displayed in a half circle.

At the center, a statue of what could only be described as Vera's exact liking. Though, her hair was fashioned into a long braid down her back, and wings with sharp points—unlike feathers at all—were attached to her back, towering over them.

It was definitely the first thing anyone else would notice, but Sera's favorite part was the sword she held in both hands at her chest. Though Vera's face carved into the marble twisted Seraphina's stomach. The thought of that stone one day being the only thing left of her. But as they moved closer, the inscription at the statue's feet read in Telish:

Vaerah Mossaris
First Tzarina of Telas
Life's Protector and Death's Hand

"*Life's Protector and Death's hand?* What does that mean?" Sera asked.

Vera only looked at her.

"I'm guessing you know more than just what happened in Vaerah's life, don't you?"

"I know that in every life, in every situation, we come back here. In every life, we scrape and claw our way back to each other. At the end of every one of them, I beg the gods, or whoever is listening, to send me back. Because I will not rest until it is you and I. Our happy ending. And I would do it again. Every time I would do it again, and now that neither of us has to, I'm going to do everything I can to ensure we get to enjoy this last life. That our friends enjoy it alongside us."

They had loved each other in *every* lifetime. Every death and rebirth.

And while Seraphina could not call on those memories, her darling Vera was looking at her with enough love in her eyes to fill a thousand of those lives.

Killian escorted everyone else to their rooms only moments after Vera and Seraphina had begun talking, and she was grateful for the privacy.

453

Thankfully, the unmasked guards surrounding the courtyard had even turned away from looking at them directly.

"This place—" Sera started. Something about it wrapped around her, soothed and assured her that Vera meant exactly what she said. That they would have that life, no matter what it took.

"This place is where Telas began. Where my mother's bloodline was hidden and *protected.*" The way she said that last word was confusing.

But Sera tugged her in by the collar of her tunic and kissed her. Gently grazing a thumb across her jaw.

"This place is home." She said, a breath from Vera's lips.

They stayed there for a while, after letting the guards take their horses. Leaning onto the other in the middle of the courtyard, then down the beautiful hallways of the palace.

* * *

Staff greeted Vera as though she were their favorite person in all the realms. They hugged her and followed behind the two of them with trays of bread and cheeses and even sweets.

They walked together to the new healer's wing and checked in on the ones that had traveled with them and from farther north. Where Sera saw the one who kept getting in her way again and again.

This time she only stood before a tray of instruments, organizing them in a tidy fashion, while Vera spoke to the rest of them. Asking them if they needed anything, how their accommodations were at the moment, and assuring them that there was enough room in this wing that all of them would soon have private quarters of their own within the next week.

Their next visit was to Thea's room in the royal sector. The sweet-faced young girl was ecstatic to see them both. She even insisted she trail behind the two of them and bear her their cups while they attended to royal matters.

Vera told her no, that cup bearing was a silly task for royalty too lazy to pour their own drinks.

Instead, Vera gave her only sister another task to do as she followed behind them to the Telish council chamber, to listen and write. She handed the princess a quill and ink and a notebook with a satchel to carry them in and told her to observe. To watch and write anything *she* might think was important.

Before they stepped inside, Vera said, "Your thoughts matter to me, little sister. Do not speak your council to *them* but write it down. Save it for me, or Sera. No one else. Can you do that, Thea? Can you be my secret keeper?"

"I will always be your secret keeper." She replied with a bright smile.

"Good, now let's go in."

* * *

The first hour of the council session was all talk of what's happened these last thousand years and why.

The ten councilmen and women at the table before them were all kind enough. Each had a different sort of apprehension about them, though. All of them seemed happy and sure about one thing: that Vera was the true Queen of Telas.

But by the end of the meeting, the council leader, *Lady Parrin* of the city's south district, asked Vera a question they did and *didn't* expect.

"My Queen, we know of and respect the love you carry for death's heir," she bowed to Sera. "Good graces to you, Goddess of The Dark—but the council and the Lords of Telas have agreed on two conditions to your ascending to *Tzarina*."

Vera leaned forward in her chair at the high table, her brows furrowed. "And what is that?" She asked.

"While you may take Lady Seraphina to wife if you wish it, you must also take a husband and sire an heir—"

Vera stood from her chair, fury pulsing from her like a roaring sun. Seraphina wrapped a gentle hand around her arm in an attempt to calm her.

"If you seek for the bloodline to continue, it will! I have six siblings of the same blood as my mother! The woman this council raised and sent to her death at the hands of the usurper's bloodline!"

"Your mother's death was a great tragedy, Your Grace. But your siblings are not *The Queen Reborn*." Lady Parrin responded graciously, though with a tremble in her voice. "We called the lords to a vote. In every district, they will have no Tzar or Tzarina lest it be you or your children."

"Prince Salrek could rule this kingdom with grace and mercy, as next in line he would be a great tzar—"

"We do not deny that, Your Grace," a heavyset man in dark red robes with gold trim said gently to her. Lord Hameel was his name. "Prince Salrek would make an excellent tzar, but the lords want their true queen, their true queen's bloodline, made new and blessed by the gods. And would also like to revert back to the old ways. Allowing only a *Princess* of Telas to ascend the throne. So any heir must be your daughter. They will have nothing else."

The rage she felt come off of Vera at those words… Sera thought that she'd be happy to hear at least that. But she wasn't happy at all. If anything, the queen seemed devastated.

"Have my siblings not done enough? Have I not given enough to be granted this—"

"Everyone is immensely grateful to Your Grace and the royal family for the sacrifices you have all made for us—"

This time, it was Seraphina who spoke, who cut Lord Hameel's words short as the room became immersed in shadow. She even shifted her voice into that otherworldly thing that terrified even herself. Not knowing how she was even commanding it in the first place.

She let the chill of death sprinkle in the surrounding air just enough to startle them all. "If it is gratitude you feel towards your queen, I suggest you shut your fucking mouth while she speaks. Or I will cut out your tongues."

Lord Hameel and Lady Parrin quickly sat down in their seats and their mouths snapped shut.

Seraphina twisted those shadows to form a small shield of it, only around herself and Vera. She blocked them out. Everyone in the room saw a ball of shadow and heard only silence while Sera said to her beautiful queen, "Vera, did you truly never wish to have children?"

"No, I would love my children deeply. But this is *my* throne. They have no right to keep it from me like this. I've completed all my trials. And my father... He told me I could give the crown to one of my siblings if I wanted. That I deserved a peaceful life. If I agree to this, I give that choice up. I cannot abdicate to my brother later on. I can only rule and... and *breed.*" Her voice broke on that last word.

"Then you pick him. I know you won't walk away and allow the kingdom to fall. I know you don't want to take a husband. But did you ever want children with...me?"

"Of course I do."

"Alright, well, how did you expect us to do that *on our own?*" She said pointedly, but soft enough that Vera wouldn't feel that she was picking at her.

"I understand the logic of it, Sera, but it was supposed to be something we figured out together and not something that was forced on us. Or with some man that was *forced* on us."

"You pick him, Vera, whoever you want. I know they'll put a rush on you since we're going into a war and they'll want an heir as soon as possible, but we can still figure it out together. But first, we get you coronated. Once you are Tzarina they answer to you."

"*We* pick him. Not just me. If we do this, it must be someone that will be good to and for the both of us."

The thought of adding another to their lives, to their bed, washed over her in the form of nausea, but she said through gritted teeth, "Deal." And pulled Vera into her body. Softly brushing the tip of her nose against Vera's. "You will be Tzarina, we will find you a king," Sera rolled her eyes at the latter. "And I will be your loyal consort or whatever." That brought a small laugh out of Vera, but her response took the breath from Seraphina's lungs.

"When I take you to wife, Seraphina Ophelia Blackspear, you will be my *queen*, nothing less."

Sera made a sour face and said, "Ooh, that's a big commitment." Before grinning back at her. Vera's smile was then accompanied by an eye roll.

Her skin tingled a bit and the realization of how long they'd been veiled in darkness set in on her.

"They're waiting." Sera breathed.

Vera nodded and she let down the shield. Ready to face the council once more.

100

Damian

Two days passed after they arrived at the royal palace in *Dartellio*. For two days Damian sat back and enjoyed absolutely everything about the city, but from the view of the palace. Mostly he'd lounged in his chambers or met with Mira to discuss political matters.

Since it was looking like they might be here a while, James needed envoys to sail home and report back to him. He'd meet them both later at the coronation, after sending off two ships, as well as Antony and Diego on dragon-back to escort them.

They would also discuss where to house the soldiers waiting in the bay, and how to pay for their wages and food.

James had assured them that there was plenty of money he'd pulled from the capitol before they left Triscillia. And he insisted that Damian take a few days to rest. So much so that he constantly sent Mira to make sure he wasn't working.

The coronation was today, though. Vera could soon assemble the Telish generals from all across the country, and then after that, they would discuss their plans to get into Sirey.

And then Sera...

Sera was keeping herself busy. Every time he tried to get her alone, to talk to her about what happened to her, she found some royal thing that Vera needed her for. But he knew what she was doing. And wished she wouldn't. Wouldn't shut herself down and bury it. Though he would keep trying. She could trick the whole world with that mask, but not him. Maybe not her Soul-bound either.

Until he could get her to open up, though, he needed out of this palace.

He took in a deep breath as he looked out the bay window he sat at. At least the city was lovely.

He noticed large puffs of steam shooting into the air in different parts of town. On their way in, he'd seen an unusual amount of workers running from home to home. Unusual even for a place like this. Many were covered in dirt, others traveling in pairs to carry large ladders as they ran through the streets.

Without another thought, Damian grabbed an average brown cloak and slipped out his window.

* * *

He honestly hadn't seen anything as lively since the island.

Damian smiled as he went along the food stands circling a park of green grass. A shining courtyard with benches and small bridges to walk over. There were even a couple of ducks waddling through a large koi pond in the center.

A young lady with flour smeared across her cheek smiled at him softly as she offered him a fresh roll. Still steaming from the oven.

"Take it." She said. Her Telish accent thick.

"I haven't any money with me. Thank you anyway."

He made to leave, but she nudged the bread closer to his hands. And looked at his clothes before she said, "You come from The Silver City?" She gestured to his clothes. "You do not have money to buy bread, you are a refugee. Take it." She placed the bread in his hands and walked back into her kitchen before he could argue further.

The young baker lingered on his mind as he walked up and down the streets. Tearing off pieces of the fluffy roll and tossing bits in his mouth as he did.

He thought about all the stories he'd heard about Telas. All the horror and violence. None of that was to be found in this place.

Damian was just about to turn down the street that led to the city temple—where the coronation would be held in less than an hour—when someone tugged on his arm and said sweetly, "What a wonderful city. Nothing like Shadon, I'd say."

He whipped his head to his right and the petite, golden-eyed, lock picker, Ula, stood there smiling up at him.

"What are you doing here? You were supposed to stay on my ship, Ula." Damian's core tensed up, and he backed her into a small alley out of view.

"I snuck away. You didn't think I'd just pass on the opportunity to see Telas, did you?" Her smile was electrifying. Her eyes glimmering in the sun. "Besides, your mind was wandering."

"A lot has happened… And you scared the lights out of me, showing up with Lavene in the middle of all that in The Silver City. Plus, I don't know anyone here very well, and if something happened to you—"

"Nothing is going to happen to me, Damian. You promised to show me everything. Show me Dartellio."

But something, for once in his life, made him afraid.

A golden-eyed thief who, at the end of the day, made him question if he was willing to die for his cause. A flirtatious young woman who made him want to live for something… Maybe for himself, maybe for her.

Ula turned him back onto the street and looped her arm through his.

"Let's just get to the coronation and you can scold me later. Besides, you owe me a romantic tour of the black cliffs." She said as she snatched a bundle of grapes off a fruit stand and kept walking.

Damian took a deep breath and escorted her to the temple in the center of town. Trying his best to hide his smile.

* * *

Snowdrop flowers adorned the square outside the temple, and gold sheets hung from four solitary pillars in the middle. Children danced around the perimeter, all of them wearing white—most of them muddy—but all smiling and cheering as they tossed rain-lily petals into the air. The wind swirled them beautifully around the crowd.

Damian and Ula moved through with their hoods raised and listened to the comments of the townspeople.

"My friend worked at the palace in The Silver City. She said that the queen fell in love with one of her prisoners..."

"I heard that one ate a guard's flesh and spit his blood at the tzar..."

"Oh please, that's preposterous, Renfa."

He snickered at the arguing pair but moved down the way a bit more and listened even closer.

"They say his name is Scythe... That he is the one behind the darkness, the eternal winter..."

"Tortured the queen's lover he did... If she's anything like her namesake, there'll be real hell to pay for that..."

Her namesake? He thought.

"Excuse me?" Damian said to the man who said it. Yelled over the crowd as best he could without causing a scene. "Is there a story behind the queen's namesake?"

The old man looked him over curiously but smiled. "You must be one of them Shadonian soldiers! Of course, there's a story behind the queen's namesake! Teach 'em nothin' about Telas over there, do they? Queen Vera was named after the first ruler of Telas, Tzarina Vaerah. She fought the darkness in the first wars. Fought for the gods, she did. When the dark sorcerer stole her lover, the Lady Death, and chopped her up good before tossing pieces of her body at the front gates of this here castle, Tzarina Vaerah hunted on the back of the great horse Hypnia, until all the Dark Sorcerer's generals were found." He chuckled a bit. "She told each of them that if they gave up the one who took her lover, she'd let them live. And those generals broke quickly. Once she found their leader she publicly executed them all before leaving this city, despite her promise. The tzarina quickly left for battle and died while she was away. And her throne was usurped. She was never to be seen again, but the story of their love has continued on for centuries."

Damian thanked the man and nodded before moving on to the square steps next to Astriea and Thomas. A new tale for him to stew on while he watched Seraphina's lover accept her crown. Sera standing behind her on the dais.

101

Astriea

The coronation began at midday. When the sun was highest in the clear blue skies.

And the queen... The queen was stunning.

While Vera had normally chosen some variation of green in her ensemble, this time, she floated down the steps—Killian, Salrek, Dalron, Pilas, Caedyn, Nate, and little Thea all leading her in—in a shimmering gown of deep admiral blue. Her long sleeves were split open at the top where the band of her dress wrapped around her shoulders to allow her bare arms to peek out as she held her hands together. A matching sheer cape was securely snapped onto the back, tinted with blue and studded with thousands of silver stones and gems. The bodice fitted her perfectly. Cinching her to show the subtle curve of her waist. The skirt flowed gently out just above the top of her hips, and a long, transcendent train of beautiful fabric trailed behind her in layers. In three different shades of blue. All topped by that shimmering cape falling and spilling out behind her.

Her siblings walked in front of her in a diamond formation. With Vera at its most southern point.

Seraphina held her arm below Vera's as she walked her to the dais. And Astriea's eyes stung a bit. Sera wore a dress of deepest black at the top of the bodice and sleeves, that faded into pure white at its tail. The stunning sleeves flowed loosely down her arms and cinched around her wrists. Atop her head, a small silver tiara was woven into her dark braids.

Vera though, regal and majestic as the dawn, stole the eyes of every single person in attendance.

Astriea was proud of her friend.

There was this unspoken reverence they held for each other since their trip to The Mystic.

As Vera made her way to the center, Astriea had a curious thought.

Z?

Yes, Astriea? Zaniah responded.

The Mystic said that if Vera were to train, she could channel me... Our power. And she did. *Do you think—*

Before she could finish the thought, Zaniah interrupted her, having predicted what she was going to ask.

I think that would be a lovely gift, Astriea.

She nodded and placed her eyes back upon the queen who—by Telish custom—would soon be named Tzarina of all Telas. Her formal title and station gave her complete power over her realm. A Queen of Telas would have to fight against councils and parliaments. A Tzar or Tzarina is their High King or Queen. Their sole ruler and protector from threats both inside and outside of the kingdom. Something Vera's mother had never been given but acted as such anyway. For the benefit of her people.

Though, Astriea thought about how out-of-place Seraphina seemed up there. As though she could feel her.

Her discomfort.

She looked back at the queen.

Z?

Yes, Astriea?

What did this cost her? What did it cost Vera?

Her choice.

Vera stood before the priests who approached her. Each of the three of them was adorned in sage green robes and matching fur-lined caps—clothes that would soon need to be replaced for the new spring weather—

465

embellished all over with swirls of golden symbols and twisting vines.

Draes approached from behind and quietly whispered the translation as the priests spoke, one on each side of Vera and one standing behind her.

"Do you, Vera Shataar, swear upon your soul and kingdom to protect Telas from all her enemies?" The one holding a silver sword asked.

"I swear it."

He handed the sword to her and backed away.

"Do you swear to honor the voices of the people in all your endeavors?" The other asked on her left side.

"I swear it."

He placed a large crystal sphere in her left hand. Vera didn't even flinch at the weight of it.

"And do you swear to rule by the Telish Code of Justice, Humility, and Mercy, all the days that you reign?"

"I swear it."

The sword really caught Astriea's attention. It was a double-edged blade that shimmered in the sun. Telish engravings graced its length, and they made the hilt of a swirling white pearl. It was *beautiful*.

Vera turned and knelt before the priest.

Then, he placed a stunning crown of antlers upon her head. The tan-colored pieces of bone twisted and shaped to a point in the center. And at its peak a large, near-glowing chunk of oval-shaped pearl. Just barely brighter than the hilt of the sword she held.

"Rise, Vera Estasia Shataar, Tzarina of Telas, The Resurrected Queen!"

Well, word about *that* had certainly gotten out. More quickly than she had anticipated.

But the crowd erupted into cheers and Astriea leaned over toward Thomas and Draes a bit, whispering, "I didn't even know she had a *second* name. Guess I should've asked."

Draes responded with a smile, "She doesn't. It's not common for any Telan to have one. A tzar or tzarina is only given a second name when all the temples unanimously decide they've completed a great trial before they came into the throne. *Estasia* was the second same given to Vaerah,

466

the first Queen of Telas, after her death. For fighting alongside the gods. The rumor, now legend, is that Vaerah died fighting for them. The story says that a slithering shadow wandered free from its master and took pity on her. Found a way to bring her back. No one knows for certain, what happened to the shadow, but the gods found Vaerah's body and were said to have buried her somewhere secret. *Estasia* means resurrection. They named her that because she always came back, even on the brink of death. And with her second naming, they hoped she'd return again." He paused. "I remember when the heir to the throne was born. People talked about Vera in every town we ran to. Said Queen Raedyn had witches tell her what kind of queen she would be..."

Vera slowly walked down the steps now. Moving past them all with her head held high. Seraphina, Killian, and the rest of the royal siblings fell into place behind her. Astriea and the others trailed after.

"I heard rumors when we were readying to leave Telas that Queen Raedyn was convinced her daughter was *The Queen reborn*, I didn't have a clue what it meant though," Thomas muttered. Late to the conversation.

Astriea's eyes widened, but she followed behind the procession and said quietly, "Based on what we learned at the Mystic, I'd say her mother was pretty spot on."

"It seems so," Thomas said.

"What about you, Draes? What kind of queen do you think she'll be?" Astriea asked.

She noted how his eyes never left her and tucked that little piece of information away for later while she waited for his response. As they passed through the crowd of people, Vera almost seemed to *glow*.

"I think she will be a tzarina, unlike any other. I think *Estasia* has finally come home."

Astriea smiled at that and followed the royals into the Holy Hall of the city.

102

Astriea

They had cleared the square for dancing and revelry within a few hours and as the full moon illuminated the city, Astriea made her way to the long table at which Vera sat at the center.

Seraphina sat to her right and all Vera's siblings lined down each side of her. At the ends were open seats for herself and all her companions.

Vera tilted her head a bit as Astriea stood before her. Then Killian tapped his glass with a fork and every gaze around them turned onto her.

"I am glad to see the throne of Telas in more than capable hands, *Tzarina*," Astriea said with a bow. When she rose again, her skin seemed to crawl. At least five hundred people were watching her, silent as a summer breeze.

"I'd like to present you with a gift."

Vera stood up and made her way around the table to face her properly. A wave of regal blue swaying toward her.

"It isn't our tradition to give gifts on coronation day?" Vera questioned.

"No, it isn't. But I like to honor my friends. I wish to honor you today, Tzarina." Astriea bowed her head and raised it again. She knew she'd said exactly the right thing to get Vera to accept the gifts.

Loudly. Publicly.

She couldn't refuse like she normally would have.

Vera squinted her eyes a bit but nodded.

First, she pointed her palm toward the very center of the square. At the open patch of grass there. And searched her mind for the image she needed. Focused on it while the air swirled around the empty piece of lawn. Whisps of silver magic whirled around and around until, finally, it was complete.

When the wind receded, a twenty-foot marble statue stood where the open lawn had been.

The spitting reflection of Raedyn Shataar. The last Queen of Telas.

A tear welled in the Tzarina's eye.

"A gift for your house, and…"

Astriea took a step back and removed the amulet from her neck.

She closed her eyes and commanded the cold silver chain to shift, and the staff elongated from her hand. Hitting the ground with a thunderous *bang*. People all around them gasped at the sound. At the ringing that followed for a few moments after.

Soft sparks of lightning pulsed out and then quickly disappeared. Leaving the staff glowing with a soft white light.

She took it in one hand and presented it to Vera. The light now glowing from Astriea as well.

"A gift for my friend." She said.

Vera hesitated for a second or two. Then took a step forward, and another. Astriea saw the conflict flicker off the light in Vera's eyes. But, she placed her hand upon the staff and the light erupted. Banishing the lingering clouds that threatened to cover the night sky. Funnels of gentle air blew past them all.

Small blue orbs of light cascaded from the clouds above, playfully bouncing and never losing their glow as they traversed the square. Children laughed as they chased and tried to catch them in their hands.

After the last traces of light vanished, Astriea released the staff, but its glow remained unwavering in Vera's hand. The tool accepting her fully.

The light that shone on Vera's face, though… It was beautiful and pure. Her expression full of wonder and awe.

Is she? She asked Zaniah.

She is.

Why didn't you say anything?

Not everything is your business. Or anyone's business. Most of the time, wrongs of a past life are righted in following ones. They figure it out along their journey. And it seems, I'll admit to my delight, that brave Vaerah has reclaimed her throne.

Astriea smiled.

Feels like the end of one of Thomas's stories. She laughed to herself a bit and to Zaniah.

Divination may not be available to me, but one thing is certainly clear, Astriea. This is not the end.

Milton Keynes UK
Ingram Content Group UK Ltd.
UKHW010741080324
438959UK00004B/286